Four Saints and an Angel

Four Saints and an Angel

by

Ronald A. Williams

DORRANCE PUBLISHING CO., INC.
PITTSBURGH, PENNSYLVANIA 15222

ISBN: 978-1-4349-0073-9
Library of Congress Control Number: 2008922799

Printed in the United States of America

First Printing

For more information or to order additional books, please contact:
Dorrance Publishing Co., Inc.
701 Smithfield Street
Pittsburgh, Pennsylvania 15222
U.S.A.
1-800-788-7654
www.dorrancebookstore.com

PROLOGUE

St. Auburn looked at the face of the guard who stood by the gate at Shady Lane Resort and experienced a moment of pure freedom. He hit the accelerator, and the thin piece of deal board that constituted the obstruction across the entrance splintered. St. Auburn heard the sound of paint being scratched off the car, and as if this was the means of returning him to sanity, he braked sharply, the abused tires sounding like the whine of a dog that had been unkindly struck. In approximate punctuation to his act, he heard the guard shout, "Jesus Christ!"

He waited for the guard to approach his window which, in the meantime, he had rolled down. The man outside the car had changed in the moments since asking him if he had business in Shady Lane. Then, he had been polite but officious, and St. Auburn had noticed the heavily starched shirt the color of the sky and the khaki pants that were seamed in colonial rigidity all the way to the brown shoes. The shoes had been a disappointment. The lack of polish and the scuffed toes were the unmistakable mark of a man who dragged his feet around with him. It was sufficient that the leather protected his feet. St. Auburn thought he looked like a schoolboy whose mother had dressed him in shirt and short pants and then, busy with something else, had left him to complete the task of shoeing himself.

Now, as he looked at the guard, St. Auburn realized the man's face had ballooned in anger, making him less human than even those impossibly starched clothes had made him seem only a few moments ago.

"Wha kinda idiot you is?" Balloon Face shouted, and St. Auburn, now anxious to comply, stuck his thumbs in his ears and wiggled his fingers at him.

"Uh rasshole idiot. Dat's wha you is."

Well, thought St. Auburn, *that mystery is cleared up.* The man had his hand on a nightstick and was staring at St. Auburn as if he believed him mad. Not an unreasonable assumption in the circumstances, but he seemed, in spite of the anger that had inflated his body, somehow smaller. St. Auburn looked at him again and noticed that the clothes had gone limp and that the once-muscular body that now had begun to develop a slight paunch also seemed slightly broken. The authority that lay in such a thin layer on the man was gone, and St. Auburn felt almost embarrassed, for, behind the anger, he sensed a fear of something he knew very well. The anger he saw was not directed at him only but at the exposure of the guard's impotence. He had had power up to only a minute ago, denying entrance to those who were not worthy of the hotel. He had even had the ultimate power: he could turn curious white people away. St. Auburn understood well what that authority, transient as it was, meant to this man. *He is probably from some mud-splattered village up behind God's back,* St. Auburn thought.

Now the authority had been stripped away and, worse, the proof of it lay like an accusatory finger across the entrance to the grand hotel. Another car had pulled in behind him and, ignored by the occupied guard and unable to pass, honked its horn angrily. The guard was torn. Then a remarkable thing happened. Balloon Face deflated, once again assuming the equanimity of polite subservience as he hurried back to the car behind, body bent almost double. St. Auburn could hear him explaining to the white face, and snatches of the conversation came to him.

"Can't drive...Musta buy he license... Brek the guard rail. No, sir, he can't move... Come round this way."

St. Auburn smiled to himself. Evidently, the guard had converted St. Auburn's act of rebellion into one of incompetence. He felt a certain admiration for that act of creativity and thought maybe he should move the car. More cars were backing up behind him, and since the entrance was just off the highway, the effects were being felt on the road itself. He could hear the impatient horns a short distance away. The guard, meanwhile, had raised the rail on the exit side of the guard post, and cars were streaming in that way, each driver casting his eyes in either disdain or anger at St. Auburn as he or she rushed past.

Things had actually begun to return to something approaching normal when a Rastafarian youth, seeing the commotion and having crossed the street, looked at St. Auburn with a gap-toothed grin and shouted, "Irie. Bring down Babylon, man."

St. Auburn laughed in relief, glad someone had recognized his act of rebellion for what it was, and he waved at the boy, who reciprocated with a black-power salute. In his enthusiasm, the youth had stepped off the sidewalk where he had been watching the whole thing, onto the entrance of the hotel. This was too much for the guard. He raised his nightstick and brought it down in a short, clubbing motion on the boy's neck. As he fell, St. Auburn could only think that the dreadlocks falling in slow motion after the boy looked like the tentacles of an octopus. It was only when he heard the sharp smack of the boy's head hitting the ground that he got out of the car.

CHAPTER ONE

"She got to go sooner or later."

The voice was authoritative but carried with it a hint of laughter, as if the speaker wanted to be taken seriously but could not help but acknowledge some absurdity in that very aspiration. The four women, of whom the speaker was one, sat on a broad, mosaically tiled balcony that hung over a sharp drop in the land, and before them lay the best of the glory of St. Euribius. The land fell away in waves of sugarcane sprouts, giving an impression of rich, brown chocolate that had been sprinkled with some green sugar. The flat plains of the northeast lay like a testament to the land's prosperity, and the four women, in spite of the confused mixing of the Chenelle's, Passions, Sexuals, and the multitude of mystical ointments with which they had doused, rubbed, and sprayed their bodies several hours ago, could also smell the deep sexuality of the land. The scent was not simply appreciated in their olfactory organs but lay in their memories like a genetic pattern. In the far distance, beyond the airport they could not see, though occasionally they could make out a descending plane, the hugeness of the sea lay in deceptive placidity. The deep blue, not the color of the sky but a deeper navy, gave visual testimony to the depths that the sunlight could not reach. It was vaguely frightening.

"Estelle ain't going to no prison, girl."

The respondent was rail thin, the lines of her chest showing clearly under the dark skin. As if in self-conscious celebration of her freedom from breasts, she wore a loose, low-cut dress with a garish floral pattern, and each time she leaned forward, which she frequently did, the little buds that lay like two lonely cherries on her chest were visible.

She looked like a thin man with two bulbs about to spring forth under her skin. From the way she constantly exposed those little nubs, it was evident she felt no discomfort with them. In fact, their very oddity gave her a distinction in this group.

"She's got to go sooner or later," the first speaker repeated, as if consciously wiping out both the rejection of her statement and the sight of those tiny breasts that stood in such contradistinction to hers. Her tone was, if anything, more authoritative, and she looked away to the east, where a wisp of dark cloud had formed on the horizon like a promise. Marjorie stared at it, ignoring the women, daring, in her very unperturbation, anyone to contradict her again.

For a while, no one said anything. Then Marjorie said, "Still, that is her husband. She got to go."

"Husband?" Anis, for such was the name of the woman of mammary inexcess, replied scornfully, her face turning into a moon-like sneer. "What kind of husband he is? You tell me dat."

The slip back into the dialect was the measure of her emotion, for language was a bridge that carried heavy traffic in this land, and nothing conveyed emotion for these women like the soft cadence of the dialect. They shifted language as they did lanes on a highway, using English to get from place to place, but shifting to the dialect when there was a need for acceleration. As Marjorie herself was fond of saying, "You can't get speaky-spokey wid personal stuff." English was the means by which their public world functioned, the vehicle to carry grand ideas, but the ideas of the heart, the passages of the spirit, were traversed by a different language, one that had sweat in it. As Marjorie would often say with a laugh, every woman lying on her back knew the difference between coming and arriving.

So the question, asked in the mellifluous rhythms of the dialect, signaled a shift in the content of their conversation. The question Anis had asked, therefore, was not for their response. Strictly speaking, it was not even rhetorical. It was a saber slicing through the air, leaving a bloodless wound in the relationship between these women.

"Estelle ain't going go because she too shame."

Marjorie's eyes strayed to the woman who was on the far side of this second-floor ballroom. She was in animated conversation with a tall man whose hair had just begun to turn gray but in the most attractive of places. Marjorie took in the slight lean of the woman's body that was encased in a beautiful gold lamé gown. *At least,* Marjorie thought, *it would have been beautiful if she wore it better.*

The woman who now occupied Marjorie's thoughts and eyesight was at that delicate stage when muscle starts to desert the owner, and the fat lumps seem to appear from nowhere. She had evidently not yet surrendered to gravity, and there was a tightness about her middle that suggested the use of some artificial restraint. *It must be a really good bodysuit because you can't see any lines,* Marjorie observed to herself. Nothing could disguise the impending collapse of the arms, however, and as the woman, Estelle, waved her hands in animated conversation with the distinguished-looking man, the deltoidal area of her arms swung in short, jiggling arcs in response. Marjorie, in spite of herself and asking God's forgiveness, felt a certain satisfaction at the sight of that jiggling.

The woman across the room, as if some internal radar had told her she was being watched, turned and, catching Marjorie's eye, waved. Marjorie blew her a kiss, and they both smiled.

"Yes. She going go," Marjorie said to the other women, something like laughter floating at the back of her voice.

Around them, the party flowed in circular lines, like a cloud of dust caught in sudden shifts in the direction of the wind. Evening had not yet come, but the softness of the late Caribbean afternoon was evident. In spite of the music which came from the floor below (Marjorie could hear Gabby singing "Gisela" and her body moved in unconscious sympathy to the grand calypsonian's infectious beat) and the buzz of conversation interposed with the occasional loud explosion of laughter, there was a quietness to the approaching evening, and on the large patio, the women could hear sounds from the village below. They looked at each other with a kind of guilty laughter as a disembodied, slightly angry voice yelled at some girl, "Get dem clothes off de line. You ain't see de rain set up?"

The slight guilt came from their recognition of that voice, for it lay in their memories like a footprint in plaster. They could see no one in the village, only the tops of the thirty or forty chattel houses that lay like half-hidden triangles between the trees and the half-grown canes. In a few months, the canes would be cut, and the village would emerge like a many-headed beast from myth. But for now, it only hinted at its larger, more powerful self. The four women listened to the silence that was brittle, easily broken.

"Why you think that he did it?"

Marjorie, irritated by the interruption of her reverie, looked with barely veiled malevolence at Maylene, who had asked the question.

"Don't ask foolish questions, Maylene. How would anybody know why he did it? People do things sometimes for no reason at all."

"That's true," Maylene replied. "But they say he was protecting de Rasta boy. That would be extenuating circumstances, right?"

Anis and Maylene looked at the fourth woman who simply smiled as she replied, "It depends."

"It depends on what?" Marjorie asked, a little bit of an edge in her voice.

"Well, it depends on a lot of things. What the Rasta boy was doing, for instance. Was he trespassing? Was he assaulting the guard? Was the guard assaulting him? We don't know the circumstances, so we can't say anything for sure."

"*The Clarion* said the boy was trespassing."

"I would suggest you don't get legal facts from journalists. They seem to report only what people tell them, anyway," Sandra responded.

"You think you might get the case, Sandra?"

Sandra, who was a judge, shrugged but did not respond.

"Well, all I can say is that two people are dead, and someone should get punished."

The other three looked at Anis, a little surprised at her voicing an opinion this strongly. Then, Marjorie said with a laugh, "You should forgive that man after all this time."

Anis' rail-like body stiffened, and her eyes narrowed to slits. Marjorie thought she looked like a black spear, except there was no point. This image made her laugh loudly, and Anis became even more rigid. The two other women looked from one to the other.

"Dat ain't got a thing to do wid it," Anis responded tersely, her jaw muscles showing the strain of her control.

Marjorie laughed, but, realizing what she had started in Anis, the tone was now more placatory.

"All right, all right," she said. "Keep your bloomers on. I didn't mean anything by it. But you need to understand that you ain't the only one, you know."

This comment brought a heavy silence on the group, and for a while each gathered herself in the friendly environment of her own thoughts. Around them, the party continued, and such was the magic of their circle that no one came out to the patio. Inside, the glasses could be heard clinking, and the butlers ran back and forth carrying trays of wine, champagne, and rum and coke. Marjorie found herself wondering who would order rum and coke in this woman's house, and she watched the butler as he approached the tall, distinguished-looking man and handed him the dark, smoldering liquid. Immediately, Marjorie's estimation of the drink changed, and it now seemed the epitome of sophistication. The hostess crossed her vision, approaching the balcony. Estelle looked at her four friends in the dusk and asked playfully, "Wunna want anything?"

"Nothing you can provide," Marjorie answered, the wave of the sugarcanes in her voice.

They all laughed. Then, Marjorie said, "Actually, you could send that tall one over here."

Estelle looked over her shoulder at the man. He was the only one at the party Marjorie did not know, so she asked, "Who is he, anyway?"

"His name is Bryan Edwards. He is here from Oxford."

"The university?"

"Yes. He is looking at some aspects of the sociology of St. Euribius."

"He is an egghead? What a shame. He is much too pretty to be an academic."

Estelle put her hands on her hips and stared at her friend, pretending to be insulted. She was a historian at the University of the West Indies in Barbados. Marjorie laughed, and Estelle could hear the sound of the sea surging in her voice when she said, "Well, for a man, anyway. So when you going tag him and bag him?"

Estelle shook her head slowly. "Take your mind out of the gutter. I just invited the man because he didn't know anyone here. It is a good opportunity for him to see St. Euribian sociology up close," she said with a laugh.

Marjorie and the others joined her.

"Yes," Marjorie said, her playful eyes taking in the guests on the second floor. "You cud write uh book on half dem people over there."

"Don't you start on my guests now," Estelle responded and, though she said it with a short bark of a laugh, something like hysteria lay at the back of her voice.

"No, darling. I ain't going put my mouth 'pon you guests tonight. Not unless you give me a chance at Mr. Long Dose of Salts over there."

Estelle did not have to turn to know to whom she referred. She soon left them and went back inside. The sunlight had practically disappeared now, and the quiet fire of the fireflies had begun to puncture the darkness around them. Each woman sat in the cloak of that darkness, together, yet alone. High above, the stars had come out, and Marjorie found herself doing something she had not done since she was a girl. She began counting the stars. She was also thinking about the man who sat somewhere on the west coast in a jail cell.

She looked inside, seeing Estelle greet a new guest who had arrived. He was one of the government ministers, and Marjorie felt her over-sized body cringe at the sight of him. She was not too fond of the party that controlled the government, and she marveled at Estelle's ability to accept whoever was in power. She always had the hoity-toity at her parties, and neither political affiliation nor race seemed to mean anything to her. Marjorie both envied and resented that social ease and often made biting, ostensibly playful remarks about it. Deep down, though, she felt there was something disturbing about Estelle's chameleon-like quality, her ability to be both visible and hidden in her social contexts. Marjorie watched her as the government minister bent over with laughter, and Estelle reached out and touched him on the shoulder, herself giggling. With the glass door closed, the party had a distant, almost unreal quality. Marjorie could hear the hum of activity, but it was indistinct, like bees buzzing. On the first floor, she could hear the pounding beat of a calypso. It sounded like Rupee, and she moved her fat body, lost in the rhythm.

"Well, it look like Estelle ain't taking it too hard."

Marjorie felt the resentment rise in her at Anis' interruption, but she responded with certainty.

"That is all show. She going to go see him."

Inside, they watched the woman who occupied their minds hug a short, dapper man who had come in with a tall, beautiful woman. He was as black as the night itself and constantly mopped at his brow with a white handkerchief. It must have been a nervous reaction because his face was as dry as a bone. Next to him, the statuesque woman stood quietly, a shy smile on her face. She was light enough to pass for white, and the four friends giggled in the darkness.

"It look like Left Foot find another one," Marjorie said, her voice soft but with brass balls in it.

"Yeah. I don't know where he does get them. I didn't think there were that many light to white women in the island," Maylene responded.

"Don't you know they does grow them on the south coast? I think dere is a factory somewhere 'bout down dere that does specialize in producing these women."

The sea breeze in Anis' voice barely disguised something else that was less accommodating. And though they laughed, they did so with a tense restraint that betokened a fear of the image before them. Inside, Estelle was pointing to the patio and saying something, and the little man started walking towards the darkness in which the four women sat.

"Oh, shit. The bitch betrayed us again."

When the man opened the door, the four women were all welcoming smiles.

"What the four of you doing out here in the dark?" he asked, peering down at them.

"We deeds evil, my boy. That's why we in de dark. We just watching the beautiful people go by."

"That's a shame, Marjorie, because we should be graced by your beauty, too," he responded gallantly.

Marjorie could not stop the surge of feeling at being called beautiful, though she knew Left Foot was simply being sociable. He soon headed back to get his drink and the tall, smiling statue that had accompanied him.

As soon as the door closed behind him, Marjorie said, "One of dese days, I going to see Left Foot wid a real black woman, and I going drop dead standing up."

Anis was almost able to control herself, but she gave in, saying, "He had a real black woman once."

Marjorie sucked her teeth, and Anis continued, "You left him because he couldn't dance."

They all laughed, and Anis added, "You remember how he used to hitch up he waist when he tried to do all of dem dances we used to do? That is when we started calling he Left Foot."

Anis got up and did an awkward two-step, first moving one foot clumsily forward, and then, with her arms embracing the air as if she had a partner, dragging the other hip forward with a painful-looking swivel. The other women leaned over, slapping their legs with laughter.

Sandra, the judge, was the first to recover, and she said with a mischievous lilt in her voice, "But after Marjorie left him, he joined the St. Euribius Dance Theatre and ended up being the principal dancer."

They all stopped laughing at this, and then Maylene said quietly, the hush of the evening in her words, "Life funny, eh?"

Marjorie could not help thinking that there was some criticism of her in the words. After a short silence, Anis asked of no one in particular, "We still hanging people 'bout here?"

No one answered for a while, and then Sandra responded, "Yes. Although there has been some talk about abolishing it."

"Dat is foolishness. De people 'bout here too wicked. Some of them want hanging. If dey know that somebody going pop deir necks, it might stop dem from doing some of de stupidness that dey doing."

"I don't agree, Marjorie. Look at dat case we had de other day. They kill dat man and den come to find out dat somebody else did the murder. Dat wasn't right, and you can't bring back a life once you take it."

"Dat is true, Maylene, but I say dat it better to miss and get a few innocent ones dan to let even one guilty one go free."

"Don't you think that undermines the system?"

This came from Sandra.

"How does it undermine the system, Sandra? I assume you would get mostly guilty people. Or am I to understand that you up there on the bench sentencing innocent people?"

"No. It is not that, Marjorie. But the relationship between the law and the people is actually rather a delicate one. Although there is some force the state can use, mostly the relationship is based on trust. People have to believe the judgments are fair and represent justice. If not, what's to stop them from moving outside the system to get their own justice? What you are suggesting is not as casual as you think. It is a recipe for disaster. It's chaos."

They were silent for a moment. Sandra was the least talkative of the group, so when she spoke, they generally listened. Marjorie was just about to retort when Anis, her body like a dark nail in the night, stood up and did her painful-looking dance again. They collapsed in laughter, and then, unbidden, their bodies uncoiled, and the four were dancing. Below, the sound of one of Ras Iley's old songs, "Spring Garden uh Coming" was playing. It was the sound of a calypsonian at the height of his craft, and the suggestiveness of 'Uh Coming,' the hook-line of the song, soon took the playfulness out of their dance steps, which had started out as a parody of Left Foot.

The music slid into them, moving like water between the cracks in a rock, taking them out of themselves, helping them to forget so much that burdened them. Ras Iley's voice caught them unaware, with its stretched out note on "Spring Garden uh Cominggg," like a lover who had lost himself in passion. Marjorie, the least agile of the group, had her head cocked to the left side and was looking slightly down at the floor, her hands in loose fists. She shuffled around the patio, fully aware of the bouncing of her huge breasts and the slow, rolling motion of her wide behind. *Venus Hottentot in motion,* she thought. She had long stopped being self-conscious of her body, and now she gloried in the sounds that pushed her hips into a slow-motion grind. She could see

Anis who, even at her age, still moved like a humming bird, her waist all fury and fight. There was an aggressiveness to her, and she seemed to have no bones. Her waist flew around as if her spine had gone on vacation, as if there was no connection between her torso and the tiny, rounded ass that turned so effortlessly. Marjorie remembered one friend who, several years ago, had said to her that Anis fucked like she had a bolt and swivel in her waist. The thought, the image of this, caused Marjorie to laugh out loud, and that snort broke the mood. They all stopped, moving to the balustrade and fanning furiously. The relief was in their faces but, more importantly, in their movements which, though they complained of being hot and tired, were more elaborate, somehow elongated and sensual. They leaned over the rail, looking into the darkness beyond the security light that blazed below them. That area of light seemed like safety, a circle of protection against the monsters beyond. A butler came out and took their orders for drinks, and when their hands were filled, Anis, leaning with her thin elbows on the balustrade, asked, "Sandra, what did you mean by 'chaos'?"

"I knew she couldn't leave well enough alone," Marjorie said with a note of triumph in her voice. Everyone knew she hated having anyone else in the group referred to for expert advice.

Sandra thought for a moment and then said, "You know, so many times when I am up there on that bench, I get the feeling I am the last thing standing between order and complete destruction. I look at these people, and you hear that they have killed somebody, and all the evidence points to it, but you can't see the evil in them. Particularly the young ones. They always look so innocent, and you can't help thinking that this is somebody's child or brother or something."

She paused, staring into the darkness, her soft breathing audible, as if her heart had raced as she spoke. With a loud sigh, she continued, "But then you see the faces of the victim's family, and it is always some combination of rage and sorrow, and you know they expect you to see their side. They are trusting you—not Sandra Mahoney herself, but this awesome thing called the law—to see their side and extract payment from their enemies. Sometimes, you see in their eyes that if you don't give them satisfaction, they will take it themselves. In their pain, they don't think about right or wrong, only about vengeance. It is the law that stands between us and that personal vengeance, Anis. Between us and chaos. All that we hold dear is protected by that thin layer of trust, that sacrifice of our personal right to vengeance in the embrace of civilized society. That is why it is so important to be right, why we can't be cavalier about executing a few innocents to make sure we get the guilty. That is why we must be just."

The silence of the night seeped into the women as Sandra spoke. It was, for her, a long speech. She had a reputation for sharp, biting comments from the bench, and people flocked to her court so as to be able to report her comments around the rum shops and domino tables the next day. The current one was that she had said to some lawyer in her court, "You must be non-compus mentis."

Though few knew what she meant, the rum shops were reverberating with the Latin phrase and the laughter that accompanied it. In this group of women, though, she often listened more than she talked. They were silent for a long time, sipping their drinks, and they thought of what she had said. Somewhere in their souls, her words lay like seeds in fertile ground, for instinctively they respected the order she had described, their ribaldry and irreverence notwithstanding. They stared into the darkness, seeing there the shadows and fears of their youth, the subtle shifts in the branches of trees and the awful creaking of one branch rubbing against the other, a mist that shaped itself into fire-hags and shadows that appeared as steel donkeys. The security light that created a circle around this grand house banished all of that, but out there, just beyond the faded edge of that light, the shadows called to them. There, disorder was always present.

Instinctively, as Sandra had talked, they had moved closer together, as if their concentrated warmth could fight back the disorder that Sandra saw in the eyes of the families of the victims. For disorder lay at the center of their lives. It came in many forms: broken marriages, failed and successful businesses, deceitful lovers, and the various betrayals of their flesh. But each clung to the idea of order through work, sex, or their social networks. So each heard Sandra in a different way, yet not so different that they could not empathize with her sentiment.

It was, therefore, with a sense of profound interruption that they heard Anis' voice slice into the silence.

"Oh, shit. John's here."

The effect on everyone was electric, though in different ways, for where Marjorie looked inside like a frightened deer, the other women turned to look at her, as she cried out, "Dat son of uh bitch. He tell me he wouldn't bring her here."

She looked with pathetic malevolence at the medium-height, chocolate-colored man who had come in. It was obvious that he was aware of himself, as he was constantly fixing something on his body. He pulled at his gold cufflinks one second, straightened his tie the next, and, from time to time, pulled at the waist of his pants as if to make sure they were still there on his perfectly flat stomach and slender hips.

The hips were the only thing slender about him, for, above them, his body flared out in the perfect V-shape of the body builder. The suit sat with suggestive intimacy on the huge pectorals, and there was just the barest hint of tightness in the sleeves.

Marjorie had only glanced at him. Her eyes were glued to the woman who stood quietly next to him. She was almost as tall as he, and most of it was legs. These seemed to start somewhere under her armpits and stretched all the way to hell. Unlike the other women in the room, most of whom had full-length ball gowns, she wore a skirt that stopped halfway down those impossibly long legs and showed the ripples in the muscles there.

She looks like a fucking fool, Marjorie thought, her stomach tightening. The young woman smiled, and behind the aggressive red of her lipstick, Marjorie saw perfect, white teeth. Her hair was cut short and seemed to be some shade of brown. Without thinking, Marjorie put her hand over her stomach, feeling the three separate rolls of fat there. Something inside her broke, and she walked quickly into the darkened entrance to the bedroom and turned right, going up a short flight of steps and heading outside. There, she sought the darkness. On the patio, the three friends craned their necks around the house to see her, but all they saw was her large, slanted shadow on the ground as she hurried to escape the light.

"Should one of us go to her?" Anis asked, concern evident in her voice.

No one answered for a while, and, not for the first time, they realized how much they depended on Marjorie to make decisions for the group. Finally, Sandra said, "Give her a little time."

John had found out they were on the balcony, and he came out, the antelope in tow.

"Hello, ladies," he said bluffly. "Let me introduce you to Annette."

The three reluctantly shook hands, feeling like traitors to their friend. John looked around and, not seeing Marjorie asked, "Where is the general?"

The three made noncommittal noises, and Annette, somewhat more attuned to the hostility in the group, pulled at John's arm, saying they should get a drink. He slung his arm possessively around her waist and walked inside.

Anis made a growling noise.

"Doesn't he just piss you off?"

The friends did not answer her but looked again towards the garden where Marjorie had disappeared. Downstairs, somebody had put on the old Draytons spouge song "Yuh Come Here to Drink Milk, or Yuh Come Here to Count Cows?" The broken rhythm of the spouge beat almost forced you to move your feet, but for the first time that night, the women heard a song from their youth and did not respond.

CHAPTER TWO

Outside in the darkness, Marjorie leaned against the prickly, uneven bark of the casuarina tree, her lips trembling as she told herself that she would not cry. High above, the sibilance of the moving pines played counterpoint to the heavy beating of her heart and the asynchronous exhalations of her sighs. Her mind was full of the image not so much of John as of the long-legged girl with him.

"I am as good," she said with a sob, thinking of herself twenty-five years ago. In her mind, she saw that girl, slender as a reed and light as the December breeze. Where had that girl gone? And how could John, who was her age, look the way he did?

"It ain't fair," a voice she did not recognize as hers said, surprising her as she leaned her head back onto the tree. She could feel the knit of her dress being pulled by the bark, and she knew it would also be in her hair, but she did not care. It had been almost five years since John had walked out and two years since the divorce, but she still fancied that she could smell him on her pillow at night. In fact, she had kept the pillow that he had used unwashed for months after he had left, burying her face in it each night as she cried herself to sleep. How had this happened to her? In high school, the girls had nicknamed her Marge the Man-killer. She had been pursued and almost never caught. Boys, now grown men, still hinted at what might have been and complained about how she had led them on. Their stories were still a source of pride for her. What had happened?

She knew what had happened. John had happened. He had relocated with his family from Trinidad when she had been in sixth form. She had been captivated by that Trinidadian accent and the social ease of the boy. He moved with grace and, even then, had those impossible muscles. He had been the first one to tell her that she moved like a reed, and when he held her with those nineteen-inch arms, she believed it, for she had felt like a feather.

She and Left Foot had just been getting a relationship started, but even before John had said "buh" to her, she knew she wanted to be free. So she had dumped Left Foot, telling the girls he could not dance, which he couldn't. Strangely enough, the thought of Left Foot brought some balance to her thinking about John. As is so often the case with women, she had unconsciously introduced a victory to negate the pain of a defeat. Still, as she thought of Left Foot and the fact that she had dumped him, the image of the two young women merged. John and Left Foot both had women who looked half her age. And they, too, looked younger. *Why did God do this to women,* she thought. Eyes closed, Marjorie listened to the soft music of the casuarinas and watched the gentle swaying high in the air. Mile trees, they were called, and sometimes, indeed, they seemed a mile away from the ground. Taking her forefingers, she slowly wiped at the streaks her tears had caused. *My mascara is probably ruined,* she thought, and, indeed, it was.

She was calmer now that the shock of seeing John with the girl had worn off, but she still did not want to go back to her friends, who would be solicitous and supportive and would destroy her instinct for self-pity. Marjorie wanted to pity herself. It was self-indulgent, she knew. *But why the hell not?* she thought. The night had embraced her like a lover, and there in the shadows, just out of reach of the security light, she felt as if she had escaped, as if she were invisible.

"And she don't even know how to dress. Somebody should tell she that you don't come to Estelle St. Auburn's home for her Christmas party in a damned mini-skirt. John coulda tell she dat at least. But he probably couldn't keep he mind out she crotch long enough to tell she nothing."

Marjorie could feel the anger coming, and she welcomed it, knowing it was the antidote to her pain.

"And dat stupid-ass red bag. Don't even match wid de dress color. John shoulda know bettuh dan dat. And she dere skinning she teeth wid Estelle like she is a dead dog. Like Estelle care 'bout she and she too red lipstick."

The girl's red lips came up in her mind, and she exaggerated them, making them, in her imagination, comically large, so that when the girl spoke, all that came out was a blubbery sound. So the girl said nothing, just stood there skinning her teeth like an idiot. Next, Marjorie destroyed her knees, making them knobby, like a horse that had raced too much and had developed inflammation. Having fun now, she took the girl's clothes off and discovered that one breast was smaller than the other. Not satisfied with the initial disfigurement, she made the breast even smaller, like Anis'. This caused her to laugh. Poor Anis. She had waited all through school for her breasts, but after the initial buds had come at about ten years old, they had gotten no bigger. That lack had been a terror for Anis all through school and had completely ruined her social life. She had been a good swimmer as a young girl, but after her twelfth birthday, she gave it up because her swimsuit had ridden down during a swim meet, and her flat chest had been exposed. Those assholes from the boy's school on the hill had teased her unmercifully, and, for a while, it had seemed that she would drop out of school to avoid the teasing. Now, they were all getting fat, and Anis was still skinny as a pole. No one seemed to mind her lack of breasts these days. *In fact,* Marjorie thought with a coarse laugh, *she getting more young dick than the rest of we combined.*

She pushed herself off the tree, becoming more aware of the music again. She could hear Alison Hinds singing one of her really fast songs, though she was not really sure what it was. Marjorie did not like the new calypsos. They were too fast and all sounded the same to her. Anis liked them, though, because it gave her the chance to show off her "wukkup-ability." That was Anis' word for the freewheeling, ass-twirling dancing she did. She loved it when some young boy would look at her dancing to calypso and say, "Cheese on bread, man. Ass' pon fire. Da woman kin wukk-up, boy."

Anis seem to grow taller when that happened, and more often than not, she would end up dancing with one of the young boys. Not infrequently, she would be cooking breakfast for him before sending him home to his mother the next day. Sometimes, but not often, if she got to scream, some boy might merit a second visit. Whenever Marjorie talked to her about AIDS, Anis would sing, "Uh doan give a damn, uh done dead already."

So she would go to the Anglican church and pray for her friend who seemed to be having fun for the first time in her life.

With this thought, she realized John and his long-legged mare were not bothering her quite so much, and, straightening up, she walked back inside the house.

CHAPTER THREE

Estelle watched as the shadow came through the doorway on the left, and she knew it was Marjorie. Worried since John had arrived with Annette almost an hour ago, she was happy to see her friend. Though it was dark on the balcony, she had sensed the absence, and, though playing hostess, she had been aware of a lack, and her eyes had constantly strayed away from her guests toward where her friends stood half-hidden in the darkness. She herself was not free of stress, for she sensed the subject that no one wanted to address standing like Banquo's ghost in the room, and she searched for it, imagining a thousand whispers. Whenever she walked over to a group and they turned to greet her, naturally changing the subject to tell her what a lovely party this was, she found herself wondering what they had been talking about before she had walked up. Still, the party was going well. She could tell by the animation in the air. She looked around, automatically checking to see if everyone had a drink (which they did) or if someone appeared lost or unconnected to some group (which no one did, except the two young girls who stood quietly beside John and Left Foot, patiently waiting for something. Estelle wondered what.)

The laughter—soft or loud, depending on the group—washed over her, soothing her soul. She needed this party to be successful. It could not have come at a better time since, on occasion, it had taken her mind off what she was sure everyone was talking about. More than most years, she had thrown herself into the preparations. There had been the Mount Gay and Campari to order. Noilly Prat and Cockspur. Someone had mentioned the prime minister had developed a taste for Puerto Rican rum, so she had made sure they had Ron Rico. She had ordered three cases of wines: two whites and one red. She had developed a taste for California wines, but most of her guests were still not sure enough of their taste to risk an American wine. French wines had pedigree, so she had ordered one case of Chablis and one Chardonnay. She smiled as she thought how just having the French name added the patina of civilization to things. St. Euribius was unapologetically English by instinct, down to carrying a faint distrust of the Irish and some inchoate disdain for the French. But on matters culinary, they, like their English tutors, had conceded the field, or the table rather, to the French. She knew the prime minister, who was quite the expert of the table, was known to say that, when in Europe, always eat in Luxembourg, because the Germans can't cook, but they imposed large portions on you; the French could make love to your palate, but their portions were dwarfed by your plate. Only in Luxembourg could you get the best of both worlds: German portions and French taste. Given the way he had blown up in the last ten years, Estelle figured he must have been spending lots of time in Luxembourg.

She unobtrusively signaled a butler to take an order from a group standing with empty glasses and walked over to the tall man from Oxford University.

"Are you having a good time, Dr. Edwards?"

"Quite," he replied with a smile. "Only, please call me Bryan. Not even my students call me Dr. Edwards."

"Only if you will call me Estelle."

He nodded gently, smiling as he said, "The lady of the stars. Well, I must say you do have a whole galaxy of stars here tonight. Isn't that the minister of foreign affairs over there? And isn't that the editor of *The Clarion*? And I am pretty sure I know the short gentleman over there."

"That's Guy Marcelle. He owns a number of stores in town."

"Yes. I think I met him at a reception. He is Jewish, isn't he?"

Estelle shrugged, indicating that she had no idea. She looked out to the patio, seeing in the darkness the shades of her friends, and suddenly she was tired of all this. She registered surprise as she recognized the emptiness of it all. The prime minister had not come yet, and no one would leave until he had come and gone, yet Estelle wanted the party to be over. Her spirit felt heavy, and she would not identify the cause. For a moment, everything around her felt like a still life, with her as the only living thing, walking along, examining and critiquing, but apart, not involved. There was Angus Hall, his big mouth open, as if he would swallow up his tiny mouse of a wife. And there on the wall, the large grandfather clock seemed to have stopped recording time, its long hand on seven and the short hand on eight. Twenty-five minutes to eight. All of a sudden, she felt like Cinderella. Only instead of the collapse of the dream at midnight, it would happen at eight. Estelle felt something like panic rise in her, and it was only when she heard Bryan Edwards chuckle that she came to herself. She looked at him quizzically.

"That was quite an interesting moment. The first honest thing I have seen since I came here."

"What are you talking about?" she asked a little too sharply.

"Your face. For one moment, it showed pure, unalloyed disgust. What were you thinking?"

Estelle looked away embarrassed, then replied, "Oh, nothing. Just an unpleasant task I have to take care of tomorrow."

"Something to do with your husband?" the tall man asked innocently.

Estelle looked at him sharply, overwhelmed by his breach of etiquette.

When she did not answer, he asked cautiously, "Did I say something wrong?"

She said nothing, and the tension soon was communicating itself in that strange osmosis-like way to the room. Estelle watched as eyes turned surreptitiously to observe her with the white man. She knew all she had to do was smile and say something innocent to him, but she could not.

The arrival of the prime minister saved the day. The door opened, and a plain-clothes officer stepped inside, his eyes sweeping the room in one swift, automatic look. Then, the corpulent figure of the prime minister walked in. He carried himself with the assurance that men with power do, no matter how they looked. Estelle walked gracefully to meet him, and she could feel his deep, smoldering eyes appraising her as she came down. She knew exactly what he was thinking, and she exaggerated her model's cross-step, emphasizing the sway in her hips. She felt sure that, from the second-floor ballroom where everyone was now moving to the edge to catch a glimpse of the great man, she probably looked like a harlot, but she did not care. Something in her soul craved the admiration, and she knew this man would give it.

He held her just a little too long, and his welcome was a little too bluff when they kissed cheeks, and she could see amusement in his wife's eyes when she reached out to give her a hug. Amstel St. Clair was a beauty in her own right, and her eyes said she was not at all threatened by some fifty-plus year old teacher of history, even if she did teach at a university. Estelle felt the coldness in her, a coldness that was reputed to extend to the prime minister's bed.

She escorted the couple upstairs and became a spectator as Anderson St. Clair claimed the room. She marveled at his deft touch. He had a comment for everyone, and his face was like an actor's, constantly shifting, plastic, as he matched the mood and attitude of his various well-wishers and interlocutors. The room which only moments ago had felt open, spacious, now felt full, as if the man's personality, like a protoplasmic, constantly expanding substance, had stretched to every corner. His wife walked with him, a starchy smile on her face, recording all this with an air that said she was not really there. She was more formal than he and shook hands with friendly reserve.

Looking at her, anyone would think she was shy, Estelle thought. She knew better. Amstel St.Clair was diamond tough, and they had disliked each other from childhood. Estelle moved easily around the room with the two, making introductions when necessary, although the prime minister did not need it. He pretended to have met everyone, and so convincing were his false recollections that women, knowing full well that they had never met him, walked away believing they had danced together at someone's party or they had been introduced at a play at Marlowe House, the national theatre in town. Estelle smiled at this, yet she admired the skill that it took. *No wonder Amstel always looks like she's got a pea-tree up her ass,* Estelle thought, smiling as the prime minister's wife turned to compliment her on the Christmas decorations.

As she accepted the compliment, Estelle thought she had outdone herself this year. Outside, the grounds were ablaze with the multi-colored flashing bulbs of the season, and the whites, reds, and blues flashed in incessant semaphore, confusing the fireflies which flew onto them and were often toasted. The tree was the largest she had ever gotten, stretching almost all the way to the ceiling. On it lay the scenes of the nativity in intricate, lighted patterns that, in sequence, showed the scenes from Joseph and Mary's arrival in Bethlehem to the birth, almost sacrilegiously graphic, and the arrival of the wise men. She noted with some satisfaction that all three wise men were dark-skinned, and the baby Jesus was olive-colored. As a historian, she felt accuracy was important.

"Very lovely," Amstel St.Clair was saying, standing before the tree.

"Yes. Altman's got it for me specially this year. Your brother is a love."

Amstel smiled, and Estelle thought she smelled the sourness of overnight fish left on the beach.

"Yes. He is, isn't he?" the woman replied, and Estelle found herself wondering if there was a suggestion in the comment. Meanwhile, the prime minister had turned back to her, saying in a stage whisper, "We got to talk, girl. We got to talk. This thing is a mess, you know."

Estelle's stomach tightened. She did not need to be told what he was talking about, and her eyes darted around the room like a deer's upon hearing the hunters approaching, searching desperately for an escape. She searched for a way to change the subject, but nothing came to mind. She was aware of Amstel's coy smile masquerading as sympathy. Estelle thought she looked like Satan in short pants. The old village expression made her laugh incongruously, and she saw Amstel's eyes change, becoming harder. *She is so blasted insecure,* Estelle thought, and this realization lightened the tension in her.

She and Amstel had always been rivals. Two plantation girls, they had been the center of attention at Princess Alice's Girl's Secondary School in Wilberton, the capital, attracting to them different groups of girls. Amstel had always been the queen, light-skinned with long black hair—good hair, as they had called it then. She had always had poise and charm, but also a streak of viciousness that could cut the heart out of any girl who crossed her. She was one year older than Estelle, but she worked out constantly and looked as if she was thirty. When they had met in secondary school, Amstel had at first tried to co-opt the younger girl, recognizing a rival in stature, but it only worked for the first year. By the time Estelle had gone into second form, she had started to attract her own group, and from then through sixth form, the two had fought for supremacy in the school. It was not clear who had won that battle, and when they had each married one of the three Saints, the draw had continued. Amstel had clearly become the winner after Anderson St.Clair had become prime minister, and Estelle's husband, Mark St. Auburn, had disappeared into the United States.

The thought darkened her face, and she looked away from Amstel's smiling, grayish eyes. Involuntarily, she glanced towards the balcony, but her friends were lost in the darkness. The conversation swirled around her like air over a desert, blown by a southern wind. She had been in Spain once when the harmattan had blown in. The hot, Saharan air had changed the northern Mediterranean, making it dusty and clinging, and she remembered standing still and dripping sweat. Yet, beneath the hot, muggy wind had been the threat of something else, an edge of coldness that felt like a presence carried in the wind. As she listened now to the voices around her, she had that same feeling of a presence that stalked the conversation and stole the ease of the night. A slow shiver coursed through her body, like a dog that had awoken and was slowly shaking itself.

Estelle looked at the objects in the room, among which the people counted, and that sense of still life returned. She was apart, though she laughed in the right places and always had the appropriate comment. Language had become her stairway to heaven, and it occurred to her how much was said without conveying anything. Yet, that was not quite true, for innuendo lay like a backboard against every comment, bouncing apparent inanities back and forth, carrying a subtext they all recognized. With the exception of Bryan Edwards, they all knew each other and attended the same parties, churches, and other entertainments, so nothing new was likely to be said tonight. And that was why the absence of any comment about the disaster at Shady Lane Resort's gate was so noticeable. It stood like a tear in the backside of a new dress; everybody sees it, but because of some social restraint, no one would comment on it. Still, Estelle knew she had not granted anyone permission to talk about it, and so, except for Bryan Edwards, the newcomer, they had stayed away from the subject. Now, the prime minister had introduced it, and she felt almost a relief in the guests, though no one would pick up the thread he had laid down until she said something.

She did not want to say anything because she was not sure what she felt. Mark St. Auburn had been gone from her life for a long time, and she had gotten used to that fact. She had, in fact, been glad when a formal break had come, because his periodic disappearances had hurt too much. He had never explained where he went, and she had been sure that he had some woman he went off with from time to time. And when he would come back, his eyes bearing a wild light that looked like fear coated in adrenaline, her body would seize up, tightening more and more around a core of anger that had gradually become calloused and which she mistook for hatred. Marjorie used to joke that she had become a virgin again since everything had closed back up tight from her tension. *Marjorie,* she thought, *was not too far wrong.*

The thought of her friend brought her mind to John, and she looked at him with an anger that was old and black in her soul. He was standing next to the silent girl, and she wondered how they did it and whether shame was part of the package God had given men. Yet, even as she thought this, Estelle could not help but notice the powerful, rounded shape of John's chest, and she snatched her eyes away, her glance colliding with that of Amstel St.Clair. The cool, gray eyes appraised her, the dislike evident, at least to Estelle's eyes.

"I love the dress," Amstel said, her eyes laughing.

Estelle tightened her stomach muscles, trying to flatten out the slight bulge she knew was there.

"Thank you." Her voice had a singsong quality like a wood dove on parade. "Anis designed it, and Marjorie had it made in one of her shops."

"Yes. I could tell it was one of Anis' designs. I really like the way she always incorporates some slight variation in the color. It's almost like a signature."

Estelle knew what she meant. Around the neckline of this particular dress, Anis had designed a series of slightly less golden triangles that set off the shimmering pattern of the gold beautifully. St. Euribian Cleopatra, Anis had laughed when she had first seen it on Estelle, the pride in her workmanship evident.

"Your gown is gorgeous, too."

"Yes. I picked it up in Paris. There is a little shop off the Champs de Lysee that absolutely works magic for you. You should try it."

The vinegar was back in Amstel's voice. At least, Estelle thought she heard it, and the bile rose in her stomach. She said, "Why don't you give me the address? I think I will be in Paris next summer, anyway."

"Oh?" Amstel replied, her face alight with a broad smile and her eyebrows arching upwards.

It was that backboard again. Estelle was sure that "Oh" was fully laden. Like a freight boat going down a river, it was heavy in the water, and, occasionally, it would stagger. That "Oh" bespoke knowledge of something Estelle did not know but of which she was now alerted. It really said "Paris, my ass." Yes, that "Oh" was fully loaded. Estelle felt a slight chill at her back, and she turned to see if the door to the balcony had opened, but it had not. Below, coming up the stairs and crawling across the ballroom floor like hell fire, was Edwin Yearwood's voice. It did not soothe her, for the calypsonian was singing one of his haunting songs about youth in prison, the guttural rasp evoking thoughts of another youth who was no longer young but sat in that same prison. Edwin (he was popular enough to be known only by his first name) sang from a place of pain, a revealed, if not a personal experience, and the pain was not just that of the boys in prison who got AIDS in defense of their lives but a whole line of boys who marched through time taking what the world gave and dying namelessly, flung in untidy heaps in unmarked graves. The voice pulled at something in Estelle's historical soul, but she found herself asking, *And what of the girls, Edwin? We have been taking it up the ass, too. What about us?* But Edwin did not hear her thoughts, and he continued to wail at the plight of the boys who had fallen out of heaven and could not find Jacob's ladder because the adults had pulled it up. Estelle felt a question lay like hot rubber in the back of her mind, but she could not phrase it. Around her, the symmetry of the room had broken down under the driving force of the prime minister's presence, and she watched as he became a magnet, drawing them all in. The party had lost its importance as he, like a whirlpool, pulled whatever was loose down into some unknown depth with which only he was familiar. Estelle felt lost in this place, her home having become unfamiliar, and, in desperation, she searched for reference points in the room. Things, objects were strange, and the clock, which struck nine when she was looking at it, seemed to be a voice tolling out some fate that she could not unravel. Slowly, the night slipped away, and the people too, leaving her alone again in a room that she remembered to be perfectly apportioned but which now showed the wear of occupancy. Her eyes were transfixed by a wine glass that sat on the floor, its bloody contents half drunken. No one seemed to be aware of it, and, as it was half-hidden by the chair, the butlers walked back and forth, ignorant of this defect in the landscape. The eddies continued about her, constantly breaking down the order she imposed on the room, so when her guests started to leave after the prime minister had hurried out claiming another engagement, she felt relief, not because she was tired but because directing the efforts of the workers as they cleaned the house, she felt as if control had been returned to her.

CHAPTER FOUR

Sunday morning had dawned with rain and a limp grayness that seemed to deny the tropical nature of the island. It was not much of a downpour, but it dripped with a persistence that seemed almost inexcusable. Estelle had laid in bed in the large, empty-feeling house and listened to the insistent dripping of the water as it slid off the eaves and plunged to the ground. She had seen in her mind's eye the small, rounded depression made by the weight of that single drop, and her mind had jumped to the north of the country where the craggy hills stood. They, too, must have been rounded once, but each one of those drops tore viciously at the rock, wearing it down, breaking it into pieces, so that the wind, with laughter in its voice, could drag it away. Almost with surprise, she had thought, *One day, it could all be gone.*

The thought was still in her mind now as she sat listening half-attentively to the even cadence of Reverend Gaulson's voice. She looked around the church with limestone walls that gave evidence of its age, for though they had been cleaned in the last two years, the soft, pock-marked stone carried its age like a badge of honor, its whitish cream face showing the dignity of those same soft depressions she had imagined earlier when she had thought of the water falling from her roof. In some ways, though, the church was reassuring. It never changed, and as she glanced around surreptitiously, she took comfort in the fact that this Sunday morning was as always. Half the congregation was fully asleep, and the rest of the congregation was at least half asleep.

Estelle looked at the old man in the pulpit. She was convinced he was at least four hundred years old, or, as Marjorie had once said, that he had come to St Euribius when Adam was in short pants. Gaulson was English, and after fifty-plus years in St. Euribius, he had kept his English accent intact, though he would occasionally speak playfully in the dialect. Estelle thought of him as the Last Englishman. He was the last of a particular breed that had left England long ago to live in the colonies and had never returned. Looking at him now, Estelle wondered what would have prompted that action. Could it be that he had failed in England and could only have been successful in the easy social atmosphere of the colonies? Or was he simply a dedicated servant of God who found the best expression of his faith among those whom, she was sure, he would have thought of as heathens?

From the corner of her eye, she noticed that Anis, who was sitting next to her, had nodded off. It was becoming obvious, for her body had begun that perilous lean forward. Her mouth hung open, and her head had tilted to an imprecise angle of insouciance as her forehead headed with millimetric inevitability toward the back of the bench in front of them. For just a moment, Estelle hesitated, like some devil who should have been banished from God's house, laughing in anticipation of the collision that was about to come. There was something pathetic about the way the rim of Anis' yellow hat started to fold as her head, pressed down by gravity and her unresistant muscles, moved closer to the pew's back rest.

It was Marjorie, sitting on the left side of the aisle and directly across from Estelle, who saved the day. At least she almost did, for she caught Estelle's eye, and under the influence of that furious glance, Estelle almost involuntarily jabbed Anis in the ribs. Now, Anis may have been dreaming, may have been far away in the land of Somnus, laying in green fields. This is not known. What is known is that she came awake with a sudden, jerky motion that moved her body back to the vertical and, aware of the pain in her ribs, she shouted before she was fully aware of her surroundings, "Damn it!"

In that same instant, Estelle became aware of several things. In the first place, looking around, she saw immediately that Anis' yelp had completely re-arranged the geometry of the church, for the congregation had awakened under the urging of that aggrieved voice and now sat in a more upright position. Secondly, Reverend Gaulson had stopped his reading of the text and was staring with the fury of a disturbed gimlet at the two women. The congregation, recognizing where the reverend's anger was directed, now joined him, looking daggers at Anis and Estelle. The latter pulled the broad rim of her black satin hat down over her eyes and slouched in embarrassment.

As the lesson resumed, Estelle avoided Marjorie's eyes and, for the most part, hid behind her thoughts. Occasionally though, she would look at her friend across the aisle and, not for the first time, note with amazement the rapt look on Marjorie's face. *Marjorie is such a contradiction,* she thought. Around her, the congregation, the temporary excitement gone, had slipped back into its usual state, only periodically waking up for the singing of the hymns or falling to their knees when prayer demanded it. Estelle thought, with an internal chuckle, that quite possibly the service was structured with these standings and kneelings to ensure the Sunday morning naps would be periodically interrupted. She almost laughed out loud as she thought of something that had happened in this church several years ago. As if her unexpressed laughter had attracted Marjorie, she felt her glare and held her head down.

The service sauntered its way to an end, and when finally Reverend Gaulson asked the blessing of the Lord upon them, the congregation moved quickly to the doors, animation restored in their awareness of their imminent release. Anis had hurried out and was already in her car when Marjorie caught up with Estelle, prickliness over Anis and Estelle's behavior written all over her body.

"And where that heifer running off to?" she asked, looking after Anis' departing Lexus. Estelle stared after the car which, as it turned right and quickly disappeared behind a hedge that bordered the highway, had what Estelle thought of as a guilty look.

"She's probably embarrassed," Estelle said with a chuckle.

"When the two of you going grow up?"

Marjorie's voice carried upset like a pregnant rain cloud.

"Me? I didn't do anything," Estelle giggled, avoiding Marjorie's eyes.

"The two uh wunna going straight to hell. In fact, the devil got a special section set aside fuh de two uh you. And don't think I didn't see dat look on your face. I know exactly w'at you was t'inking 'bout."

Something shifted in Estelle's eyes, which were partially hidden by her hat, but Marjorie noticed. She hesitated for a while and then ploughed on.

"You did t'inking 'bout Christmas Eve night."

Estelle smiled, a layer of sadness evident, and nodded.

"Dat was w'at? 1964, right?"

"Something like that," Estelle responded, not sure that she wanted to remember.

"It did 1964. Mark did just win he first athletics championship and we, mainly you, invite he to midnight mass."

Estelle nodded, thinking back to that long-ago time. She and Marjorie had both invited him, but it had been she who had manipulated Marjorie into that invitation. Mark had been a churchgoer, but only because his family insisted on it—at least, the family he lived with. His mother had never been around, and his father had left for England at almost the same time Mark had been born. He had essentially been reared by his grandparents, and they insisted on his attending church.

He had accepted the invitation easily, with the nonchalance for which he had been known, only too glad to escape the watchful eyes of his grandparents, who attended the Christian Mission church.

"Do you remember what happened?" Estelle asked her friend.

"Yes. I remember."

Marjorie's voice had ascended to a pitch that sounded aggrieved. Then something struck Estelle. She had, for the last three days, studiously avoided thinking or talking about Mark St. Auburn, and now, here she was encouraging Marjorie to talk about him. Estelle turned away, looking at the solidity of the church. They said it was second only to the one in Holetown, Barbados in its claim to being one of the oldest Anglican churches in the Western Hemisphere. Estelle had never quite understood why the claim was important, but somehow it instilled pride in the parishioners, and so it had proudly been painted on the notice board that stood at the entrance to the drive leading up to the church.

That church had shaped so much of who she was. In spite of what she described as her "objective distance" from the church, it had exerted a powerful influence on her behavior, her selection of friends, and her belief system. *Could Reverend Gaulson, who I criticize both as an individual human being and as a historical category, still be shaping who I am?* she wondered.

Before she had time to answer the question, Marjorie asked, a razor in her voice, "W'at are you t'inking 'bout?"

"How much the church has influenced me."

"Well, it shoulda influence you some more. Imagine you misbehaving in de house uh de Lord. Although I don't know why I should be surprise by dat. It won't be de first time dat you get in trouble in church."

Estelle looked at Marjorie from under the brim of her hat, and when their eyes met, they both laughed. It was a release and a relief, an unburdening of pent-up sound that washed over the parking area like water from a newly opened dam, cascading down in peals of joy. Before long, they were leaning on each other, attracting the unfriendly stares of the devout who felt that the sanctity of the church's environs was being violated. When they had exhausted their irrational gaiety, Marjorie looked closely at Estelle. Then she reached out and lifted the rim of her hat, staring at her face.

"My God. You eyes look terrible. Wha' time you get to sleep?"

Estelle turned away slightly, avoiding Marjorie's penetrating stare. The last of the guests had left around eleven o'clock, and she had told the staff to go home. They could clean and tidy the place on Sunday. She had been tired and wanted to be alone, and she had indicated that to her four friends.

They had spent the whole evening on the balcony. In any other group, this would have been considered rude, but everyone knew Marjorie and fully accepted her, and, by extension, her crowd. She had not wanted their company last night, though, and they had left, making playful remarks about not staying where they were not wanted and having homes of their own. As soon as they had left, she had missed them, but she was not sorry to be alone.

The house had felt empty as she turned the lights off and, before going upstairs, switched the security system on. St. Euribius was no longer the safe, trusting place of her youth, and the security and wrought-iron companies were making a fortune as a result. Still, alone and in the darkness, she had not been able to sleep, and after trying futilely for a while, Estelle had put on a CD of romantic classical music. The first track had been the *Moonlight Sonata,* and as the evocative whispers of Beethoven's flawless tones washed over her, she had sought the illusion of peace in this nocturnal escapade. Try as she might, she could not help thinking about Mark. The thoughts were contradictory. So much had happened to him since that Christmas Eve night in the church—the beginnings of love and disappointment. For some reason, that night had never left her mind, and in its serio-comic recollection, so much of her life seemed framed.

Mark had come to the church that night dressed in a gray pants and a white shirt with a thin tie of indeterminate color and vintage. He had no jacket, and his appearance had caused some sniggers among the boys and girls who were in attendance. Estelle and Marjorie had broken away from their parents and had sat in the balcony at the back of the church. Mark had known nothing of the Anglican protocol but had complained about the constant kneeling and sitting or standing. When, at the end of one particularly long prayer by Reverend Gaulson, Mark had remained kneeling after everyone had arisen and sat, she had thought he was joking around. It was only when the soft buzz of his gentle snore came to her that she had realized he was asleep.

Now, standing in the churchyard, avoiding Marjorie's eye, that night came back to her, and she asked herself, *How do you fall in love with a man like that?*

"You t'inking 'bout he, ain't yuh?"

Marjorie's voice cut into her thoughts like a buzz saw into ice cream.

"What are you talking about, Marjorie?"

"Mark St. Auburn. Dat is who I talking 'bout. You thinking 'bout he. Dat is de only t'ing dat does get that watery-misty, foolishy-foolishy look on you' face."

Estelle felt her anger rise, but it was without the energy to sustain itself, and, turning, she asked, "You think I should go and see him, don't you? Is that what you were talking about last night?"

Marjorie looked on the verge of a smart remark, but, surprisingly, she quelled the instinct and instead said, "Nobody can decide dat except you, Estelle, so don't try and pass dat decision on to me. Only you know wha' going on in you' heart, darling."

"It's not my heart that is the problem, Marge."

"So wha' you worried 'bout, girl? You care wha' people going say? Dey don't have to live you' life."

"But you know there is going to be talk."

"Hell, girl…"

Marjorie stopped, remembering that she was still in the church-yard, then resumed after she had asked God's forgiveness for the recalcitrance of her tongue.

"Look, Estelle, people going talk anyway. Dey talking now. Just not in front uh you. Look, I know dat dere ain't uh single St. Euribian who got any friends nor family in jail. I guess dat mean dat we does only lock up foreigners. But times changin', an' people becomin' more understandin' uh dat sort uh t'ing. Anyway, I ain't standing up in dis churchyard all morning talkin'. Come home wid me, and we can talk dere. And I ain't lettin' you drive. You eyes look like dey goin' shut any minute."

Estelle protested weakly, but she did not have the energy to fight, so after Marjorie said she would send Samuel, her handyman, to pick up Estelle's car, they walked to Marjorie's Mercedes and were soon on their way. For a while, they said nothing, and Estelle listened to the powerful, almost seductive, sound of the German engine. Outside, the fields of half-grown sugar cane waved half-heartedly as the two women slid by. Estelle was slightly turned away from her friend, looking at the landscape as they headed east. Soon, the sugarcanes gave way to the open fields of the cattle growers, and all around she could see the brown and white of the cattle's coats. The cattle brought to mind a funny story, and she turned to Marjorie.

"Do you remember Lester and Pyle?"

Marjorie laughed.

"Of course. Dey had dat small house down on de rocks right next to de sea. Wha' mek you t'ink 'bout dem?"

"The cattle reminded me of a story the workers used to tell about Lester."

"Wha' story?"

"Well, you know they were both fishermen, right?"

"Uh-huh."

"Well, Lester went out fishing one day, and when he had gotten a good spot, he dropped his fishpot. You know how you mark the spot where you drop a fishpot, right?"

Marjorie looked at her friend as if to say, I grew up in the village not in the plantation house like you. Estelle ignored the look.

"Anyway, the way you do it is to identify a marker on the land near or on the horizon because the further out you go in the sea, the further into the land you can see. If you pick an object as soon as it comes into view, that tells you how far out you need to go the next day. The position of the object also gives you your position on a horizontal axis."

Marjorie's face looked skeptical, not because she doubted the logic, but she mistrusted the source. She had never seen Estelle fish a day in her life.

"Only you could tell uh story 'bout fishermen and still manage to slip in uh word like 'horizontal axis.' Dat is why you' stories never seem to got no zing. Yuh can't get speaky-spokey wid dese stories."

"Oh, shut up and let me tell the story," Estelle replied, laughing but mentally adjusting to Marjorie's criticism.

"Where was I? Oh, yes. Lester pick out a spot, check the land object, and head back to shore. De next day, he and Pyle gone out to look for de fishpot, and for a long time Lester checking de land and checking de sea. No fishpot. He rowed 'bout up and down, checking de land and checking de sea. Still no fishpot. Finally…"

Marjorie's eyes rolled at the use of the word, but her body had assumed the tension one sees when a person waits for a punch line.

"Pyle says to Lester, 'Where de fishpot, man?' To which Lester replied, 'I put it down somewhe' 'bout here yesterday.' So Pyle says, 'Wha' you mark it wid?' And Lester looked at Pyle and replied 'A cow.'"

Marjorie's mouth opened wide like a live flying fish that is tossed on the beach and, feeling the absence of its oxygen, begins to gasp for air. This had the unfortunate effect of expanding her enormous breasts, and they pressed into the horn of the Mercedes, the sharp sound acting like a punctuation mark to the story.

"Yuh mean dat asshole... sorry, Lord... dat idiot mark it wid uh cow? He didn't t'ink dat somebody would move de cow by de next day?"

Estelle joined Marjorie, feeling the tension slip out of her as her friend absorbed her offering, letting her worship in the only way that could bring relief, through the ordering of the past. The peals of laughter continued, and though Estelle well understood why her friend extended her umbrella of unity, she was grateful and looked at Marjorie with a love that came from somewhere other, deeper, than friendship. As the large car slid across the ridge that divided the east from the west of the island, Estelle closed her eyes and was soon asleep, safe in the knowledge that her friend would protect her.

CHAPTER FIVE

When Mark St. Auburn had seen the Rasta boy fall, the proximate parabola of his flying locks a universe unto themselves, he had felt an irrational urge to defend the recognition the boy had given his act of rebellion. Later, it would be said that he had acted to defend the boy, but at the moment he had stepped out of the car, he had not been certain of his emotions. Later, it would be said that the guard had turned on him and that he had therefore acted in self-defense, but that too was unclear in Mark St. Auburn's mind. He was much more aware of the brittle silence of the day and the patchy puffs of cloud that sat like fluffy cotton balls in the unnaturally blue sky. He was also aware that the place was empty. All of the cars that it seemed only a minute ago had been backed up were gone, and he wondered, *Could it be that no one had seen this act?* The guard had turned, something like panic and outrage in his face, and, in turning, had raised the billy club almost as a shield. Mark St. Auburn would never be clear about this, but some time later he would be certain it was something he could not quite define but which reminded him of his own face from what seemed a lifetime ago that had come at him like an accusation. He did not remember striking out viciously at that face, only that he had tried to block it out, to rid himself of the pain that suddenly reared up in his soul like a spear thrust.

Then he was looking at two bodies on the ground, and the empty day lay like an illogical question around him. For a moment, he had thought to run, but he knew that too many people had seen him. In any case, where would he run to? The island was tiny, and though the stories of the people were replete with heart-men that no one ever found and at least one escaped convict who had evaded the police for years, there were few ways or places to hide in St. Euribius. As he had looked down on the two bodies, he was struck by their vulnerability, and, irrationally, he had worried about a rain shower soaking these two dead men. So he had walked to the guard's booth and called the security office.

Now, Mark St. Auburn sat on a lumpy bed in a jail half a mile away from the resort. The bed creaked, and he could not help but think of the gap between the bed he had been scheduled to occupy and this rather musty-smelling one on which he sat. He stared straight ahead, his eyes on the single-bolt lock that separated him from thought and action. The police had taken almost everything from him – wallet, watch, belt, even his shoe laces – but they had left him his glasses, and he thought how easy it would be to use them as his means of escape. Almost clinically, he visualized the tumblers in the simple lock, seeing in his mind's eye the configuration of the innards of the almost ancient restraint. It would be no trouble at all. Getting out of the jail would be no problem. For the most part, these people did not expect trouble, and windows were open all over the place. Though he was being held for murder, his demeanor had not been threatening, and he had been cooperative, so the policemen had relaxed around him once their initial anger and officiousness had dissipated. It was not the first time he had used mildness as a means of gaining an advantage.

Mark St. Auburn swung his long legs up on the bed which smelled of some contentious combination of semen, urine, and disinfectant. The pillow was less vile but still contained elements of this effluvium. He noted with curiosity that the three smells did not mix, each occupying its own separate sphere of olfactory influence, and he chuckled, remembering when he was a boy having the same experience. He had to clean the pig pen every morning before going to school, and try as he might to avoid it, the filth would get on his body. He had learned early that when a pig defecated, it was as if it was extruding the evil that dwelt within it, and that evil, made material, carried its inhuman nature in its smell. Nothing could get rid of the vile smell of pig dung, and neither perfumes nor colognes stood a chance against its olfactory preeminence. He would bathe until his black skin had a silvery shine, and then douse himself in cologne, all to no avail. The pig dung and the cologne existed in separate metaphysical spheres and never the twain would meet. He would head off to school, fully aware that he had failed and, in failing, had made things worse, for the overused cologne had become its own weapon of assault while doing nothing to curb the miasmic aggressions of the pig dung. Mark St. Auburn's body shook with the memory, and he wondered about this ability of his mind to separate things, to find in life the essence of death.

Why had he come back here? Was it that, like a homing pigeon, he had flown to where his instincts took him? Or like a salmon, he had simply swum to the traditional point of spawning? Was it that he was finally tired of running, hiding from them and, more importantly, himself? Was he afraid that he could not escape anymore, that those men who lived in the shadows, and were sent by other men who cast even longer shadows, would finally run him to ground? If so, why had he chosen this place, so small that discovery was inevitable, for his last stand? Worse, why had his mind begun to split? Was he going insane? That question had nagged him for weeks now. What were these memories of his past that came not only as remembrances but with a sense of dislocation, as if he were living someone else's life, telling someone else's story? It was as if his lies were real and his reality was a lie. When it came and he recognized it, he hid from the world, locking himself in a dark room, watching the video of his real or imagined life. They had intersected a long time ago, and so he had no firm hold on reality. Madness terrified him, yet he felt no terror when his dislocations came, only a sort of detachment, a sense of being a watcher of another's life.

Why had he come here? Was it to die? If so, why had he killed? Even now, he could understand that the guard was dead, as was the Rasta boy, but it did not feel as if it was a lived experience, but rather a papier-mâché exhibition in his mind. Searching now for the emotion that should accompany his killing of the guard, or even the guard's murder of the boy, he felt only the vacuum of his intellect. Had he already gone mad? What was madness? Was it the inability to find sense in that which is real? If so, then most people were mad. He thought of Dostoevsky's Idiot, wondering if his inability to tell a lie or his willingness to tell only the truth was proof of madness. Could an absolutist be sane in a relativistic universe? In any case, that did not apply to him. He was the most relativistic human he knew. St. Auburn's mind suddenly shifted to the guard, and for a moment, the man was again alive, standing in those ridiculously starched pants and the scuffed shoes, and St. Auburn laughed aloud, thinking how tragedy sat in such comfort next to comedy.

He would not live long now. Those men in the shadows probably already knew where he was, and their reach was long. They cared less about the money than the betrayal or the potential for even greater betrayal. Mark St. Auburn did not mind dying, but he resented the possibility that he could just fade out without a record, the recipient of a temporary sympathy from people who were once his friends but who would be only too happy to move on. He smiled as he thought of where he was now and the confusion that it must be causing in his old circle. It was a pretty cynical crowd, but he felt certain that, even for them, murder would be seen as a breach of etiquette. Four days in this jail and no one had come to see him. He understood why this was so, but still he would have thought Estelle would have come.

Estelle. He thought of her as anger wrapped up in chains. She was a university lecturer now, but he remembered her from an earlier time, when her life had seemed lost in a haze of false friendships and lovers and a kind of self-destructive angst that had created both a passion and a hatred in him. He giggled as he remembered what his uncle used to say: "You know women. You can't live with them, and you can't live...."

Here he would pause, then add "with them." It was certainly true of his relationship with Estelle. Maybe it would be more accurate to say relationships, plural, because they had broken up and gotten back together so frequently that their friends had thought of their relationships as seasonal. It was in one of those off-seasons that Estelle had gotten pregnant. For some odd reason, the child had brought them closer together, though the girl was someone else's child. Where was Heather now? He had no idea, having lost track of her as he had lost so much in his life. He had heard that she had gone to Europe somewhere, but he was not sure of the country. She would not be a girl anymore but a woman in her thirties.

He had been sure that Estelle would come, but she had not. Mark St. Auburn sighed, thinking, *So much time has passed. Why should she come?*

But the question came from some rational part of his brain that did not affect the fire of his anger at her betrayal. *Maybe if I had taken Heather as a legal daughter things would have been different,* he thought. But he knew that was a lie. Estelle's relationship with him lay like a cave drawing from antiquity, suggesting much and confirming nothing. Would a child have freed him of this sense of fading out, of having passed through history without affecting it in any significant way? He was not sure, but as he thought of that first night he had held the child in a darkened room as she had cried for an absent mother, he had felt the oddest combination of tenderness and power. Tenderness and power because the baby had been so small and the lungs seemed to be working so hard to make the piercing screams that had assaulted his ears.

St. Auburn shifted his position on the bed, trying to find some comfort. Outside, the dripping had turned into a downpour, and the shushing sound of the rain sat like a great cover to the earth. It was dark, and the little light that crept in from the outer corridor of the jail felt like a greeting from a distant god. It had been on an evening such as this when he had found Estelle again; and from that moment, his life had changed, for he had grown up in an instant. They had been separated yet again, but this time it had lasted for more than two years as he had sought to make sense of the transition from the irresponsibility of high school to the muted fascism of the "real world." They had broken up after leaving the fifth form and had gone their separate ways. He had heard of her from time to time, but there was no reason for contact since they lived in different circles. Estelle was from a plantation family, one of the few black plantation families in the island, and without the leveling influence of high school, they would never have met. For he had grown up poor, and it was only the power of his grandmother's vision and the government's policy of free education practically from the cradle to the grave that had brought about their meeting.

Their meeting, however, had the quality of magic for him, though he could not always be certain now whether he remembered or imagined that first contact. He had first seen her with her friends when he had been in second form, and she had been in her first year. What had struck him about her immediately was the fact that she had fully developed breasts even at that age, but when he did get around to looking at her face, he was captivated by its complexity, though he had not thought of it that way then. Her face had been round, almost devoid of angles, and it gave her a peaceful, cherubic appearance. It was an appearance that was shattered by her eyes, though, for they stared boldly out, aggressive questions contained in them. He would later learn to fear those eyes, for they could burn with anger or become limpid with hurt. Even today as he thought of her, St. Auburn knew he preferred to deal with her anger, for anger built his defenses. He was helpless before her pain. Yet, even as he thought this, he knew it was a lie or, at least, only half the truth.

He smiled in the dusk, remembering when she had turned those eleven-year-old eyes toward him, and her friends had giggled, telling him what he wanted to know. It had not taken long for them to begin the childish, hesitant conversations that had somehow established in everyone's mind she was his girl. Yet, nothing had been said, and he wondered what alchemy turns a tentative meeting into a relationship. Was it simply a matter of frequency of interaction? Was it the sense of expectation, the searching out on a repeated, regular basis of another? Or was it simply the fact that she kept a seat next to her on the school bus for him since she got on the bus much earlier than he did? He was not sure, but the magic of the change from curiosity about a person to that sense of possession was perplexing and, to him, vaguely uncomfortable. It had lacked definition in his mind, and so her insistence on exclusivity, on being in love, had both perplexed and annoyed him. He smiled in the faded light, thinking that it would not be the last time he would misunderstand a girl's intention. There was something frightening about their ability to isolate so quickly, to find the object of their desire and to pin it, like an etherized rabbit to a dissecting board, illuminated by the searchlight of their eyes. St. Auburn had never become quite comfortable with that. Their capacity for worship had always seemed slightly pagan to him, and when, at eleven, Estelle had turned those dark pools of hope and desire on him, he had felt both power and fear, for even then he understood, in some irrational way, that she would always give but that, try as he might, he could never possess.

"Was that what I wanted? To possess her?" St. Auburn mumbled to himself in the shadowy light.

He did not know even today. Often, he had asked himself if her pregnancy had been a good thing. It certainly had not been for her, and, as a result, he fully understood that she had always been alienated from the child. Motherhood had sat like a burden upon her, and she had resented the restraint and the violation. Those had been her words.

"I feel violated by this pregnancy," she had said to him one evening as they had sat in the darkness, and he had wondered how that could be. Though he had no children and had never wanted any, he remembered how his cousin had described her relationship with her child, and he was struck by the sense of unity in her description. He had never felt that sense of connectedness to anything, and when his cousin had said that she could not find words to describe the feeling, he had prodded her, vaguely fearful of the mysticism in her face.

"It hard to explain. Actually, I di'n't like being pregnant. I did hate to blow up like dat. You know w'at I mean? Feeling yuh body just take over from yuh and become bloated an' widout shape. I partic'ly hated de fact dat my mout' did always springing water, an' I had dis urge to spit all de time. It is disgustin'! But de worst part is de mornin' sickness. Dis feelin' dat yuh goin' always t'row up. De firs' few mont's w'en I did pregnant, I di'n't go now'ere 'cause I always feel like I did goin' t'row up."

St. Auburn remembered being slightly queasy listening to her, but he could not stop himself from asking the question.

"So how you control the sickness? I mean, how did you get things done?"

His cousin had laughed, her hands holding her belly as if some trace memory of the child still existed there. It was something he would notice again and again. Whenever women started to speak of their children in affectionate terms, their hands would unconsciously stray to their belly. When they were upset with them, those arms would keep their distance.

"Only uh man would ask dat question. You don't control mornin' sickness, boy. It does control you. An' as fuh gettin 'tings done, women does always find uh way."

He had been anxious to change the subject, but something deeper than his revulsion at the images she was conjuring up drove him to continue the conversation.

"It sounds pretty horrible to me," he had said with an apologetic laugh. "But if it is so bad, how come you women always talk about the bonding between you and the child? It is hard to see how that happens given the discomfort you are describing."

His cousin had smiled, and immediately he had felt shut out. Her dark, sweaty face had turned beautiful, peaceful, and composed.

"You ain't got no idea," she had said softly. "It is de oddest thin'. It strange, but I don't really remember de birf. My firs' real mem'ry is w'en he put he lips 'pon my breas' to feed fuh de firs' time, an' he did know w'ere to go, even tho' he eyes di'n't open yet. He hands sorta hang on to my breas', and he little toes curl up."

Her eyes, big and bright, had moistened.

"You ain't got no idea, Mark. It did de firs' time dat I feel like somebody love me fuh me. Yuh know wha' I mean? Fuh me. Not fuh somethin' dat I could do, or fuh how I look nor not'in' like dat. He di'n't know if I did black or white, skinny nor fat. He di'n't even know if I smell. But yuh know w'at? He di'n't care."

She had looked away, wiping her eyes. Then, she had said softly, "Yuh nevuh get dat kinda acceptance and love now'ere else."

St. Auburn had never spoken to his cousin about the subject again, but the conversation lay like a weight in his memory, for he knew that it was something beyond him, out of his reach. That is why his reaction on that long-ago evening, standing in a darkened bedroom trying to quiet the screaming child, had been so odd. What had he hoped for in that act? He remembered that, when he had told Aurelius St. John, one of the three Saints, about it, Aury had said it was a surefire way to get a woman to go to bed with you: pay attention to her child. Mark was convinced that was not the case. In fact, though he and Estelle had been in an on-again, off-again relationship for nine years, covering all of his time as a teenager, they had never had sex, so sex should not have been the motivation.

Often, he had wondered if his conversation with his cousin had prompted his action, for it had not been premeditated. He had heard the baby's screams and had walked into the room and picked her up. The baby had gurgled and stopped crying immediately. Estelle had rushed into the bedroom and angrily snatched the child, who had proceeded to cry again. She had then put the child down, and the crying had continued. St. Auburn had picked the child up, and once more the crying had stopped. When Estelle returned, she had a bottle with milk, and she had taken her child to feed it. For a long time, she had said nothing, and he, too, had sat quietly watching the baby feed until the darkness had come, and mother and daughter became only sounds in the night. Almost in sympathetic communication, the others in the beach house had left, and as the quiet and darkness reigned, some oddly constructed bond had formed between them, something different from their youthful fumblings and naive pledges. In this darkness where he could not see her, he finally had seen her. He had sensed her rejection of the child, and something in his heart had rejoiced.

Now, lying on a smelly bed, St. Auburn wondered about this reaction. What had he hoped for? And, ultimately, why had he not gotten it? He was still puzzling out the answer to this question when a policeman came striding up to his cell.

"Somebody here to see you."

St. Auburn nodded and swung his long legs down from the bed, standing and tidying his clothes. In the dimly lit corridor, he could hear the footsteps approaching.

CHAPTER SIX

"He is a yardfowl."

The voice cut through the air, and Anis could almost feel the smoke recoil. She looked at Marjorie, who had placed the long, slim cigarette between her full lips after uttering her statement. Anis watched the end of the cigarette flare into deep red light, then fade as Marjorie put it down in the ashtray. *She's smoking again, and that is not good,* Anis thought, waving her hand in front of her nose to accelerate the dissipation of the smoke. Anis, Maylene, and Marjorie were sitting in Marjorie's den, and Anis looked around, thinking of the house as a temple to excess. It was huge, probably in excess of twenty thousand square feet, and surrounded by the most beautiful gardens in the island. Even the people from the National Botanical Gardens would come by to look at the profusion of species and color. The house was built on a wide marine terrace that overlooked the sea. Marjorie had bought the land over a fifteen-year period and now owned almost a hundred acres of the cliff overlooking the eastern coast. This was not the most friendly coast, but she said it reminded her of the English moors with its isolation and its haunted look. She had spent a fortune moving earth to be able to construct the magnificent gardens that Anis could see glistening in the washed-out afternoon light.

"What exactly is a yardfowl, Marjorie?" Anis asked after the smoke had cleared.

Marjorie's reply was emphatic.

"He is uh exact one. A yardfowl, according to Marjorie's St. Euribian dictionary of standard dialect, is anybody who t'ink dat being able to call de prime minister by he first name is a paycheck. In other words, a total jackass."

Anis was irritated by this and said, "But we are not talking 'bout calling the P.M. anything. We talking 'bout Left Foot's light to white woman."

"Same thing," Marjorie responded glibly. "Any man as black as he who got to find a woman that look like somebody drop she inna barrel uh flour and then dust she off, is, in my humble opinion, a yardfowl."

Before anyone could respond, she added, her voice pitchfork sharp, "An' half he age, too."

Maylene and Anis looked at each other. It did not sound as if Marjorie was talking about Left Foot anymore. She had used her cigarette stub to light another, and she now puffed heavily, creating a gray mist in the den. Anis looked away, somehow embarrassed by her friend's actions. She watched as Marjorie squinted, lowering her hand until the cigarette was perilously close to her dress.

"Why dey like dat though, nuh?"

Maylene stared outside, trying to analyze the raindrops, it seemed. Anis caught Marjorie's eye. She saw the volcano exposed there and said, "Dese men 'bout here only good fuh one thing, so de truth is, I don't waste time trying to make them into what they can't be, nor pretending dat they are what they are not."

"Yeah. We know wha you does do wid dem."

Marjorie's voice, though playful, carried an undertone of bitterness, but Anis, careless of the tone, wiggled her backside in the couch, causing the other two women to laugh. She looked up the stairs and asked, "How long Estelle been sleeping?"

"Ever since we got here from church. She looked so worn out when we did standing in the churchyard, I thought dat I would bring she back here. She came in, and in about twenty minutes said she was going to rest she eyes. Dat was about half past twelve. She been sleeping ever since."

"Dat party must really did tired she out."

"Party, my behind. You know it ain't no party dat put dat dark shadow under she eyes. It is dat good fuh nutting bastard Mark St. Auburn. What she did ever see in he, I can't understand."

Marjorie would later regret the comment, but then, it had burst out of her like a suddenly untapped geyser.

"Shit, Anis, the same thing you used to see in him."

Marjorie had stopped mid-puff, and her shoulders hunched, making her short, fat neck disappear. Her eyes, already squinting to keep out the cigarette smoke, narrowed even further, and her mammoth bosom heaved.

"You sure you want to start wid dat?"

The voice, only a moment ago so officiously lighthearted, was cold like the Atlantic wind on the east coast in December. Anis thought she might retort, but she did not. Instead, she wondered where Mark St. Auburn was right now, and it was with a feeling of satisfaction that she realized she did not care. What Marjorie and the others continued to see in that man, she could not understand. Anis stood up and walked over to a bay window that looked out on the rough seas which, in the gray, fading light, seemed close. She knew it was not. Ever since the night before, she had felt edgy, and she knew what had caused it. It was Marjorie's joking comment that she should forgive Mark St. Auburn after all this time. That had burned her. And though she knew they thought she had run off from church because she was embarrassed at sleeping and then swearing during the sermon, it had not been that. She had been upset with Marjorie, although she had not realized just how upset, when, the night before, Marjorie had been hurting at seeing her ex-husband with that young girl. She knew that Marjorie wanted them to sympathize, was manipulating the conversation to have them understand her grievance, but Anis was not in the mood today.

She had not slept either. When she had gotten home, the boy had been waiting. She had called him from the car, and he had ridden his bike over. She had taken him directly to her bedroom and had pummeled his hard body until the bed had fallen down between the supports of the bedstead, the crisscrossing lathes displaced by her violence. She had grunted and moaned, and, occasionally, she had heard her high-pitched wails, but her body had dammed up, and nothing came. She had felt the nervousness in the boy as he realized that he could do nothing for her, and she felt her customary contempt for the men who labored in her body with the terror of her unfulfilment at the back of their minds. She could always tell when their panic came, for they would bore into her, trying through brute force to do what their spirits could not.

As she watched the rain beat down on the bowed grasses of the marine terrace, she wondered where they had learned that instinct to violence. For it was not love nor even their satisfaction they sought at that moment. *And what did they seek?* she asked herself, clasping her hands behind her back and, in doing so, forcing her tiny buds forward so that they stood like abbreviated points against the loose cotton shirt. (She almost never wore a bra.) What did they seek? To dominate? To force from her the thing she held closest as a gift to be given at her will? They did not know that she could sense the contempt in them when she gave that gift. She could feel their silent laughter when she twisted and moaned under them, feeling their puny triumph in their false kisses and silent lies. So she gave in when she wished, on those rare occasions when they gave her not their inches but themselves. So when they smiled in the darkness that they insisted on, as she bent into a V, thinking that they had won, she urged them on, luring them into that place where their triumph always seemed imminent. Seemed. Then, she would keep calling to them until the panic came like the scent of decay, and their fear hung in the room, the smells mixing, exciting her mind to greater violence and cruelty. In frustration, they would succumb, breathing hard against her left ear. It was always her left ear, as if they thought in that ear she could not hear their whimper and their awareness that they had failed…again.

Last night, the boy had tried to work his magic, and when he had accepted that his violence was useless against her will, he had climbed off her, plunging his face in her sweaty body. For a moment, she had almost laughed, but she knew that would have freed her slave, for man's anger was always his motive and, therefore, his strength. So she had moaned louder, the promise in the decibel, and he had sought solace in that. Another face had stood like a phantom's mask in the night, and when the boy had left, somehow shrunken by the encounter, she knew he would not be back.

Before her, the afternoon lay stretched out like a patient, yet one not incapacitated so much as watchful. She ignored the obvious gray, for along the edge of the northern horizon some strangely refracted light had created a thin slice of ochre that was like a line of hope in the rainy day. She saw, in her mind's eye, the sun to the west, bending around the island, creating this oddity that was difference, this oddity that was beauty. She stared at the anomalous ochre line that seemed to cut the day in half like a zipper of light.

It gave her an idea that was so different from the schlock that was making her living. She painted and sold naïve, romanticized images of the island, seascapes of undifferentiated boats with provocative names like Isanwandl—but not too provocative, because the tourists had to be intrigued by the vague historical images of resistance yet reassured that they had won, were continuing to win. They had to know that when they plunked down their one hundred or two hundred dollars, or even when she half-exerted herself and they paid her thousands, that they were not paying for her vision nor her skill but her service. She often wondered where they put her paintings. Certainly not on the walls with their Picassos nor in spacious rooms that held eighteenth-century Dutch carvings or seventeenth-century Chinese fans. Her work did not fit with golden urns and silver trays that spoke of antiquity and, even more importantly, spoke of their owner's ability to accumulate the past, fitting it layer upon dead layer over the emptiness of their lives, filling up one corner of the world with their collected trophies.

She had been invited to New York a few years ago by a man who had bought one of her most expensive paintings and who had also passed over her body. In his office had been an encased polar bear. He had hunted it in Alaska and spoke of the remote beauty of the landscape and the all-but-invisible people who lived there in harmony with this strange land. Yet, he had gone there with a single, deadly purpose, and now the fruit of that purpose dominated the outer foyer of his large and magnificently appointed office. He had bedded her in that unconsciously harsh way that powerful men take possession of women's bodies, but somehow the dead bear, with its mouth pathetically wide open, had robbed him of his nobility. Outside of the ambiguous context of the island and his temporary descent to humanity, he had seemed empty, unimportant. He had not brought her there just to bed her but had really wanted her to pick out the right place for her giant painting. Anis had looked around that office with its artifacts from every corner of the globe, and she had been torn between flattery and contempt. She had insisted he place her painting in one of the inner offices, almost hidden away. He had looked uncertain, had weakly protested, but he had no faith in his own judgment. The artist was supreme, even here on his throne of power. So she had hidden her seascape from the accusatory, dead eyes of the polar bear. She had not spoken to the man since.

Anis felt the heaviness in her soul, and she clung to the disappearing slice of ochre, letting it sleep in her spirit, storing it against future need. She did not think she would need it for a while. Two days ago, she had started a new painting. It was of a man, but a man constructed of a series of triangles. The triangles had come first, seeming to float around until, as if gently attracted by weak magnets, they had slid together. Suddenly, the painting was there. Now, all she had to do was get it on the canvas. The man's body was dwarfed by the large, triangular head with the base at the top and coming to rest on a precarious apex that sat on a huge neck. The neck looked as if it had been sliced so that the vermilion lay upon it in sharp contrast to the pasty gray of the inverted pointed head. The eyes she had borrowed from the Aztecs, so they were wide and unfocused, staring into a future that carried both surprise and pain. The body had only been sketched out, but she had drawn the monstrous penis that hung like a deformity down to the man's knees, forming two triangles from the bulbous head up to the man's groin.

Standing in the growing dusk, she felt the urge now to modify that penis again, to make it even more monstrous. She crossed her arms and almost thoughtlessly slid her forefinger and middle finger between the first and second button of her blouse, encasing the little lump there. Her left breast sprang to life under her touch, and the right nipple, almost in sympathetic reaction, rose to half-mast. Something filled her throat, and she thought of the cruelty of the man who now was in a jail on the west coast. Why had she let him do it? Why had he laughed? Why did she allow it to affect her so? The bile rose in her, and her thoughts slid back to another night that lay like a dagger in her soul.

It had been Old Year's Night, and they had all gone to a party. Estelle and Mark had been sort of together again, but Estelle's parents had given her a strict curfew. She had to be home by twelve. On Old Year's Night that hardly made any sense, but Estelle's parents were an odd bunch, and they had never been too comfortable with her, Marjorie, and Maylene because they were from the village. Sandra they accepted because Sandra's father had been a judge and was then a successful politician. She, Maylene, and Marjorie were the "Chattel House Gang." That is what Estelle had told them her parents called them. Even today, Estelle had no idea how that had hurt.

On Old Year's Night, 1967, Estelle's parents' oddity had created a dilemma. They had partied at the Crescent Beach Hotel, but if Estelle were to be home by twelve, then someone would have to drive her there. It had been agreed that Mark would use Aurelius St. John's car to do so. Mark had looked so crestfallen at having to leave the party that she had volunteered to go with them and keep him company on the way back. They had driven in silence to the south of the island where Estelle's home had been, and he had unceremoniously dropped her at her steps at the end of the circular driveway. They had returned to Crescent Beach Hotel, but instead of going into the parking lot, Mark had pulled down toward the dark cliffs on which the hotel was built. When he had parked, she had sat in brittle expectation, the gentle music coming from the large, American car like an aphrodisiac, lifting some dark fear in her.

As her two fingers caressed her breast in the growing immateriality caused by the dying light, Anis wondered what had happened. Why had she allowed him to slide his hand between her legs? Why did she sit in a rush of warm hope as he had turned her unresistant head, covering her lips with his full, soft mouth? Why did she feel no sense of betrayal but only a nascent fear when he stripped her and laid her on the long, leather front seat of that huge American car? Why did she not cry out when she felt the iron of him fighting against her bamboo resistance? Even today, she remembered the feel of that splitting apart of her body. She had not wanted to cry nor did she want to stop him, even though the pain had shocked her and he did not seem to care, did not seem to even know she was there. She had thought vaguely about the possibility of becoming pregnant but felt foolish talking to him about it. So he had pushed into her, and she had bit her lip, sinking her fingers into the soft seat of the American car.

When it was over, he had seemed impatient to get back inside with the other two Saints and the girls, but she had discovered the wetness, and when they had turned the light on, they had seen the blood. For the first time, in the light, she had seen his eyes and the disgust that lay there, and something inside her that had started to bud died in those eyes. He had used his underwear to clean the seat, but her dress had been ruined, and he had to take her home.

What, in spite of that look of disgust in his eyes, had raised her hopes? Was it the thrill of taking something from Estelle, who seemed to have everything? Was it that finally someone had looked beyond the flat chest to the warm creature that lay hidden behind the shame and fear? Was it the irrational thrill of having Mark St. Auburn, the star athlete? What had driven her to betray her friend and herself? Mark St. Auburn had promised nothing. In fact, they had almost not said a word. Yet, the next day at school, she had allowed it to be known that Mark was now her boyfriend. It had not taken long for Estelle to get the news, and the confrontation had been ugly. Worse, Mark had come by the school later that afternoon to train with the girls and had ignored her. A slow shudder passed over her body as she thought of the sniggers of the girls, but worse was Estelle's look of triumph and Mark's unawareness of her. Later, she would come to understand that look, but then it had confused her, and she had rushed back into invisibility after that brief moment in the light.

When, after eight weeks, she realized that her "friend" had not come, she had told Marjorie who, even then, seemed the most experienced of the girls. To her credit, Marjorie had never told the girls about what had happened, but somehow she had confronted Mark, making him take responsibility, and he had used his contact with an old chemist who did not want the school's best athlete to be kicked out of school to procure some bitter liquid she had been forced to drink. It had made her sick but had not brought her period on, and she remembered going up a long, dark stairway to a hidden office and laying on her back, her legs raised high, while a kindly, bespectacled old man looked inside her and yanked the life out of her. Mark had arranged it but was too embarrassed to accompany her, so she had laid in the recovery room for an hour or so, bleeding and feeling the hate build.

Completely ignorant of what she would go through, she had agreed to meet him afterwards to go to the cinema. She had done so, and in the darkness, she had almost died from the pain, feeling the waves of fluid rush periodically into the pad the doctor had placed down there. She had thought she would faint, but when he had tried to touch her and had felt the large, obtrusive pad, it was as if, for the first time, the tragedy had been given life, and he had snatched his hand back, scalded by her life. She had felt, almost smelled, the strange combination of embarrassment, disgust, and contempt, and, assaulted by it, she had risen quietly and left the theatre. He had not followed her. It was the last time they had spoken.

When Estelle had married him, she did not attend the wedding, and everyone seemed to understand. She had repaired the relationship with Estelle, but it had never become again what it had been, and she knew that among the grievances she held against Mark St. Auburn was the loss of the trust that had once existed between her and her friend.

The abrupt appearance of light cut into her thoughts, and she turned quickly, her right hand straying guiltily away from her chest. Marjorie had put on a newly re-engineered CD by Miriam Makeba, and as the haunting voice asked plaintively "Where are you going, weary wanderer?" Anis thought to herself that she had no answer, except another refrain that stole into her mind:

"Back to back, belly to belly,
Uh don't give uh damn,
Uh done dead already."

Marjorie's slanted eyes bored into her as she walked toward her.

'You over dere playing wid you'self again? As much as you play wid dem things, somebody would really t'ink you got bubbies to talk 'bout."

Anis laughed and, crossing her arms, covered both of her breasts, saying as she sat, "Nuhbody ain't complaining 'bout dem."

"Nuhbody can't see dem, that's why."

Marjorie's voice was playful, but Anis heard the tang of orange peel in it.

"Dey don't need to. Dey seem to be able to find everyt'ing else."

"You ain't got to tell we dat you pussy ain't got nuh stop sign. We know already."

Anis got up, standing with one hand on her hip and the other held out in front of her, palm facing outward toward the two women. She pantomimed Diana Ross, singing in her high-pitched voice, "Stop, in the name of envy."

They all laughed, and Maylene suddenly said, "You know what we have not done for a long time? Go to Carnival. Why can't we go down to Trinidad in February? That could be fun."

Anis looked at Marjorie, who looked away before saying, "Now why in the name of Jesus would I want to go to Trinidad?"

"Trinidad ain't do you nutting. Just because John from dey, don't mean we can't go."

Marjorie's big lips pouted, giving the impression of a frog about to gulp for air.

"You know why we stop going to Trinidad?"

"Yes."

Maylene laughed, saying, "Anis went out in the parking lot with that Indian fellow and almost got us killed."

"How was I to know he was married?" Anis asked, a grin on her face.

"Well, you coulda ask. Why would you just assume dat a man dat look like him was free?"

"Why should I ask? I didn't want to married him. His wife was he responsibility. He was mine."

The women grinned, Maylene and Marjorie shaking their heads in amazement.

"You don't get frighten that you going catch something, Anis?"

"I ain't chasing after not'in', so why should I catch anything? We is all over fifty now. Fifty-two to be exact. Wunna don't think that is long enough to live?"

Maylene looked at her, disapproval on her face.

"Only God can decide when we is supposed to go, Anis."

"My point exactly, Maylene. None uh we going go before we time."

Marjorie noticed that the playfulness had gone out of Anis' voice, and some vague sense of unease crept into her mind. She dismissed it, as Maylene asked, "You going to talk to Estelle?"

"'Bout what?"

"You know. 'Bout going to see Mark. I think she should go. At least, somebody should go. It don't seem right that nobody should go to see him."

"How you know that nobody ain't going to see him?" Marjorie asked, and they stared at her, a question in their eyes.

Anis asked suspiciously, "You went to see him?"

"No, I didn't," Marjorie replied, her voice all restraint and forbearance. "I called his brother."

"You called Aurelius? Why you had to call him? He know dat he half-brother in jail."

Anis's voice was aggrieved, and they looked at her in surprise when she added, "So what you say to him?"

"I tell he dat he should represent he brother."

Anis shook her head.

"You know dat dat was always a weird relationship. Dose two were good friends, but neither one of dem acknowledged the blood relationship. And yet, everybody knew about it and considered dem brothers."

"The Three Saints," Marjorie said, a wisp of nostalgia in her voice. "'Trouble in triplicate,' deir old headmaster used to call dem. Dem t'ree boys raise more hell dan uh army. You remember w'en dey stole the headmistress car from we school and tek it to de automotive shop at deir school?"

The women started to giggle, girls again in the memory of the boys' mischievousness.

"Yes, yes," Maylene said hurriedly. "Miss Armstrong had no idea what had happened to her car, and she kept the girls late every day after school for a week. Then somebody broke down and told. Do you remember who it was?"

"Yep. Mabel Short," Marjorie said, her voice like an urge in the night.

"That's right, that's right," Maylene continued. "She was Mabel Scantlebury then. She lived out in the north and couldn't get a bus after six o'clock, so she somehow found out who had done it and told the headmistress. The Three Saints got banned from our school for about a year, remember?"

"Not uh year. De headmistress just tell deir headmaster not to let dem come to we Sports Day."

The women laughed louder, slapping their legs. Then Anis said, "Dey came anyway. Late, almost de end uh de day, but dey came."

"You remember what we had done?"

"Absolutely. We kept three seats for them right behind where the headmistress and all the other dignitaries sat so that when the boys came in and the girls started to move about to let them into the seats, the headmistress could not help but turn around. When she saw them, her white face went red like a cherry. Man, she coulda shit a brick."

They were silent for a while, quietly chuckling at their memories. Then Anis said, "Do you realize how long we have been involved with those three men? Sometimes, it seems like forever."

Marjorie grunted.

"So did Aurelius say he was going to see him?"

"You know Aurelius. He wouldn't give you a straight answer if you tell he dat God had ask de question. I don't know if he going or not, but he listened."

"You know w'en I t'ink back, it seem so odd that Mark is de Saint who got into trouble. W'en he did a boy, he seem so much more serious dan de other two. Now, Anderson St. Clair is prime minister and Aurelius St. John is our most respected lawyer. You ever t'ink 'bout that? Yuh never kin tell how t'ings goin' turn out."

Marjorie's voice had the whisper of the grasspiece in it, a suggestion of a love affair between two elements of nature. The two women sensed something in the voice, something they both knew about time and chance and that dimly understood relationship between the two. Something in that voice called to a past that, if not innocent, at least had hope. Now, that voice wondered for them all if that hope had been fulfilled, whether both success and failure had not chased them through time. The silence dragged on, stretching like plasticene, wrapping them together in a unity not of their own making, but as it extended beyond the boundaries of their common contemplation, they broke apart, thinking individually about a life they had shared and yet, somehow, had not.

CHAPTER SEVEN

Upstairs, Estelle had popped awake when Miriam Makeba's voice had asked that searing question, "Where are you going, weary wanderer?" but it was the songbird of Africa's observation that had caught her imagination. When Makeba had sung "I can see by the dust on your feet that you have sorrow in your heart," her eyes had moistened. She had heard the laughter downstairs but had not wanted to leave the warmth of her solitude. The rest had done her good, and the lifelessness that had plagued her earlier was gone. She raised both legs off the bed, suspending them in the air, feeling the tautness in her stomach muscles. That tautness did nothing for the layer of fat she felt as she placed her hands on her stomach. She felt bloated and, not having run today, imagined that she had picked up some weight. Looking around Marjorie's testament to her success, she had the usual feeling that Marjorie had not quite got it right. Sure, the house was big and sat on the one piece of land on this island that she would kill for. Only nobody had seen its beauty before Marjorie had bought practically the whole terrace. The house, however, was not the fitting monument that should have been there. Too close to the cliff in an effort to get the full view of the ocean, it now felt isolated, dwarfed by the expanse of the terrace. The gardens had helped a little, but even they could not make up for the poor location of the house.

Estelle lowered her legs, refreshed by the strain in her abdominal muscles, instantly feeling guilty at her criticism of Marjorie who, in spite of her bullying and crassness, had never been anything but kind. She sat up, but, undecided about whether to go down, she flopped back on the bed, her short hair feeling prickly against her neck. She felt refreshed but no less tense, and the tightness in her stomach was like a fist. It had spasmed as soon as she had awakened, and now it was spasming again. Mark. Why could he not just stay out of her life? She knew her friends downstairs were speculating about whether she should go to him, and she could guess what they had all decided. After all, she had always gone to him when he had called. Why not now? "Murder is different," she whispered to herself.

There was nothing in her makeup, her upbringing, nor her socialization that prepared her for this, and she felt quite stuck, as if her feet were encased in concrete.

"Why should I go, anyway? I have not talked to Mark St. Auburn in twenty years. What do I owe him?"

Even to her ears, her voice sounded plaintive, but she told herself that it was a fair question. What did she owe the man who sat in jail somewhere to the west of where she now lay? Did whatever he had done for her outweigh the repeated betrayals, the loss of faith? What could equal that? *Still,* she wondered, *how do you measure social gifts? Is* every act of kindness, of love, equal to another? Or were some more important? Did her love and its betrayal equal what he had done for her, his act of faith in her when her world had been turned upside down? Or did the fact that he had turned it upside down negate his act of faith? Where would she be now if he had not come back to her after the birth of her child? She had been broken by the pregnancy, for the world had changed around her, and she had felt the madness in the air stinking like the sea when it purged itself. The geology of her social relations had shifted, and she remembered her mother's supercilious voice when she had said, "It is the height of absurdity, Estelle, to love a man who calls himself Blue."

She had stared at her mother, alarmed at the woman's capacity for ignoring the truth. She had told her she was pregnant, and her mother had heard the voices of her friends complaining. They had stood that night in the isolation of Estelle's bedroom, two women who should have known one another but did not, and Estelle had felt the loneliness descend once more upon her.

Even today, she did not know why she had become pregnant with Blue's child. It had not been for lack of experience, nor had he insisted that night, laying in the darkness of the little cove. He had been willing to stop, but something hot and daring had risen in her soul, and she had urged him, almost shamed him, into the act. Even then, he had been willing to pull out of her, but she had held him, almost daring him to stop. He had not. Why? What had driven her to that one act of stupidity? She had often blamed Mark for it, for he had left her after school without even a goodbye, so there had been this hole in the universe, a tear that she had tried to fill with hot nights in dark places.

Her parents had been useless to her, with their obligations of one sort or another, their antiseptic love, and their judgments. Her father had no time, consumed as he had been with "building a business," as he always said, noting that St. Euribius was changing and that, unless sugar growers found something else to do, they would all be paupers in fifty years. He had invested in the then-nascent tourism sector, and his hotels, car rental agency, and tour business had grown with the industry. When he had died, he had left her a good deal of security. Her mother still lived in the plantation house a few miles from her, and in that world of maids and butlers and plantation workers who were resentfully polite, she would live out her days. Aurelius St. John took care of her business affairs, and he was very good at it.

Who had driven her into those hot, dark spaces where life lost its sense of responsibility, and men gave her not the pleasure they thought they did but this other thing, this sense of freedom from restraint? She thought of Anis, who had been so alone when they were girls and who now seemed always to have some man or boy in her bed. Were they opposite faces of the same coin? She did not know. She only knew that when Blue came in her that night, she had been immediately aware that she had been impregnated. Is it any wonder he had resented her afterwards? That he had looked at her in confusion and with a hatred that bordered on madness? She had always blamed him, always felt he had taken something away from her, but had he really? He had been childish, irresponsible, and cruel, but should she have expected more from a boy who was himself young and foolish, from a boy who, for God's sake, called himself Blue? Maybe her mother had been right. Maybe it was absurd to love a man who called himself Blue. She had seen him a few months ago, and it had been remarkable. Nothing had changed about him. He still had the same sly grin that invited women in, and, more surprisingly, as she had surreptitiously watched him work the room, women still responded to his charm. She had wondered briefly if he had ever married but had not cared to find out. It was good that she had seen him because she had seen how small he really was. He had been afraid to speak to her, awed in the light of her social position. That had felt like a breath of fresh air that somehow swept out the putrid smells of those hot, dark nights.

Then, however, she had broken, and the eddies around her had shifted, much as they were shifting now around Mark St. Auburn. He had come to her at an invitation not of her offering, but one that she had learned to treasure. He still had no idea what he had done for her in that time immediately after the birth of the child. He had come like a light in a world that had been shaped for two years by gray, and he had done it not by being sympathetic but with an arrogance that she admired. He had destroyed her self-pity, replacing it with his cynicism and laughter. She lived in the mists of the world, and he lived above it, somehow unaffected by its cruelty, because he was more cruel, and its cynicism, because he was contemptuous. He had taken her on a path she could not have foreseen, filling up her mind and life in ways she had not anticipated. His mind was plastic and his reading eclectic, and when he spoke, she looked at him as if he could not be wrong, could not falter.

Her world had been circumscribed by her mother's instructions about social norms and her father's obsession with social security, and she knew that neither was what she wanted. Mark's voice was the new voice of the nation, recently independent and curious, striving and angry. It sought out targets for its anger and receptacles for its hopes. She knew Mark wanted an audience, and she was the best he had. And when he talked about the world's past and how its future had to be as a result, he imposed order on a mass of facts that had had resonance but no meaning. His mind had captured hers, trapped it even, so that she became confident as his words in her mouth began to convince people of something that she had never known – that she was smart. It was in that recognition she finally was able to separate herself from the social institutions of her parents. They, too, had recognized the change in her, the growing confidence in her own opinion, the relaxation of her inner soul, so that as her fear diminished, she had developed a tentative, careful bond with them, but it had been one constructed on her terms.

They had seen the danger that she did not. Could Mark really have been all she made him out to be, or was he simply a creation of her fear and hope, a man who stood in the center of her whirlpool for a brief moment and did not flinch? He had once said to her that he was the most wonderful piece of fiction she had ever created, that she should not have been a historian but a novelist because he had been her best fictional character. He had said it tongue in cheek, though, for she knew he liked the thought of being a creator, of having made her. In that respect, he was no different from any other man. It was a form of control, but she had used it to construct herself. Maybe he was right, maybe it was all fiction, but it was a fiction that formed the laced network of her consciousness, and that brittle membrane should not be tampered with. Their relationship for that two-year period had been like two fires meeting, Vulcan and Prometheus, the torrid flames licking at each other, a universe of conflict and reconciliation. Funny how, now when she thought of it, she remembered only the good things. She remembered him as kind, which he never was, and attentive to her, which he had been when he was with her, but he was oblivious to her once he left. She would sit at night waiting for him to call, smoking one cigarette after another, mechanically taking care of Heather, the child whom she now thought of as dispossessed. She had robbed Heather of something, and the child had grown up yearning for her attention, an attention she could not give. Why did she do that? Was it that she had felt excluded from her parents' circle and could not find, did not know, the right levers inside herself to pull to love her own child? Or was it the memory of the begetting? Was Blue the one who was being despised in the rejection of the child?

Estelle felt something hard in her soul cracking, and the moisture felt cold on her face. Miriam Makeba's voice had faded into the darkness, ending as she was half aware on that earthy "aieee-uh" which was like a pelvic thrust in the darkness. She could hear the hum of voices again, and, not knowing why, she walked to the door and pulled it wide open, inviting her friends' voices in. It was Maylene's voice she heard first as she stood leaning against the bedroom's door-jamb.

"Wunna ever t'ink 'bout how we move from de village up here in dese heights and terraces?"

There was embarrassed laughter, then Marjorie's brassy voice, hellfire floating at its edges, said, "I ain't move into nuh height nor terrace, girl. I buy the height and the terrace."

There was silence for a moment, then Maylene spoke.

"I serious. Wunna ever t'ink 'bout it? Yuh know, I been t'inking 'bout 'wha Sandra say last night 'bout order being so much an illusion and chaos being just behind it, and I could not shake de feeling dat she did talking 'bout we."

"Who is 'we'?"

"St Euribius, yuh know. Or even we as uh group."

Anis' voice was serious when it came.

"You think she was talking about us, Maylene?"

"I don't know," Maylene replied, following Anis into the structured tones of the language. "But I sometimes get the feeling that all this – you know, Marjorie's big house and her business, my husband's law practice, Estelle's whatever – all of this is the thin veneer of order that

Sandra was thinking about, and somewhere below it is something chaotic and frightening, something we don't understand."

Marjorie's voice sliced in, like an off-cutter on a crumbling wicket. "Dat is bare shite. You...."

But Anis' interruption was like a batsman who had spotted the bowler's long forefinger on the seam of the ball and had anticipated the turn. It was like a cover drive.

"Shut up, Marjorie, and let her finish."

Estelle could hear that Anis had intended the words to be playful, but they had come out like a slap that started in friendly response to a joke but had picked up speed in the air. A little silence ensued before Maylene added, "Well, I remember that while we were on Estelle's balcony, we heard this woman telling someone, probably a daughter, to pick up the clothes because the rain was coming, and we all giggled. Why did we giggle? We all come from the village. Well, except Estelle. Even Sandra lived in the village, although her father had money. So why did we laugh? Why did hearing this woman tell her child to pick up the clothes sound so odd, so foreign?"

No one answered, and after a while Maylene continued, "Except for you, Anis, none of us go into the village anymore. Why is that?"

"I can tell you why I stayed, Maylene. At first, it was because I had no money, so staying at home was the normal thing to do. Interestingly, I had always thought of my grandparents' home as small, but when they died, the house became hollow, an echo of the past, and I needed sounds to fill it up. The village did that for me. You can always hear a voice, somebody yelling well wishes or cussing somebody. There is always sound, always life. Then, after the paintings started to sell and I had a little disposable cash, I found that my inspiration came from the broken lives of the village. I think if I lived out here, I would paint one really beautiful canvas, but after that, I would be able to find nothing. Don't take offence at that, Marjorie. This place is beautiful, but my artistic sensibilities would not live out here on Briar Cliffs. They just wouldn't."

"You are different. You have your hands firmly planted in the soil, Anis. You still go into the gullies to get berries for your paints and still pick dunks and cashews and all that. We don't anymore."

"Look, Maylene." Marjorie's voice was impatient. "You show me a gully I can drive the Benz into and have some girl hand me what I want through a drive-through window, and I would be happy to go to the gully. Until then, give me good roads and solid houses. If you want to be poor again, that is not hard to do."

"You are missing her point, Marjorie. All Maylene is saying is that we are, or may be, losing something of our selves, our souls, in this transformation. She is not talking about wealth and poverty."

"Well, what the hell we went to school for? What was it that we slaved over all those books for every night as God send? Tell me what it was if it was not to make money. Nobody don't give a blast 'bout yuh soul if you don't have some money to back it up."

"In one sense, you are right, but Maylene's point is that, if we lose our souls, then the other things we create may be, will be, in jeopardy as well. And I mean that not in any heavy metaphysical sense, but in material terms."

"I can always tell when you don't know what the fuck you talking about. You always get more speaky-spokey. And why can't Maylene talk for sheself? You is she translator now?"

On the stairs above, Estelle smiled. Marjorie was being Marjorie again. She was the only one of the group who had not gone to university, and so the rhythms of the village lay like a caress on her tones. Her presence in any room was like the smell of fish or raw wetland, black with fertility and pregnant possibilities. So Estelle smiled at the irony of the argument going on below, and yet, she understood the underlying structure of the conflict. They had come very far in a short time. From the village to the terrace had taken Marjorie only half of a lifetime. Her two sons, who were both studying in America, would be lost to the village, would not understand their mother's nuances and would laugh at her quaintness behind her back.

Yet, twenty-five years ago, Marjorie, Maylene, and Anis would not have been commenting on the village but trying to get out of it. They did not realize that the very fact of the discussion meant that it was no longer real to them. They had become nostalgic, and one can never be nostalgic about the present, only the past. Still, the village lay there beneath the brow on which her house stood, quiet yet somehow vaguely threatening. For her, the threat had always existed, for she was a "plantation girl," as the others called her. But for them, it was new, this sense of alienation from what should have been theirs. Each tried to hide her alienation in some way. Sandra protected the village from itself by keeping the predators away from it, though she did it with thumb and forefinger firmly clasping her despairing nostrils. Anis lived with them, pretending that in location came communication. But, years ago, she, too, had placed the wrought-iron bars on her windows. Marjorie hid from them out here on "the moors," as she called them, glorying in her preservation of their speech but brutal to her workers, easily replying when asked why she was so tough, "Somebody got to pay fuh dis house."

And Maylene. Well, Maylene was an unpainted canvas. She was the only one of them to survive in marriage, and Estelle felt that she did this by ignoring most things. Yet, she had raised the question. It was as if she knew something the others did not, could feel the pulsating heart of her past staring at her without recognition.

Estelle thought of her students at the university. They had changed in the time since she was there. She remembered when they worried about Maylene's question, when the reconstruction of the world had a particular meaning. Her survey course in West Indian history still contained the resonances of those meanings. Discovery and Settlement. Enslavement and Transportation. Slavery. Abolition. The Rise of the Free Colored. Labor Riots. Independence. Huge slices of life reduced to an orderly progression, reduced to history. For most of her students now, it was something to get out of the way, a requirement the university still insisted on, though they could not for the life of them figure out why. She remembered once in a discussion, one of her students, on hearing another talk of his father's rise from poverty to the middle class, had dismissed it. It was not that the girl did not believe him. She knew what he had said was true, but she was not interested in the story of the struggle to get there. That she took for granted. Only the succeeding had become important.

Estelle had thought of that for a long time. Was that the measure now? Success? Would glorious failure in the pursuit of a noble cause no longer matter? She had noticed, particularly among the Barbadian students, who were by far the majority at the university, a certain distance from the past and a rapid and unreasoning embrace of the future. How do you teach a history of noble failure to a people whose only measure of success is wealth? Yet, she knew powerful ideas had triumphed in this backwater of a world, this "overcrowded barracoon," as V.S. Naipaul had called it. Had Naipaul been right when he called these islands "flotsam"? Could these people's efforts mean so little in the grand scheme of things? Could her life, with its triumphs and failures, ultimately mean nothing? She felt not, and yet her students seemed to agree with Naipaul, in their actions if not in their words. She knew the conversation going on in Marjorie's den was less about the village than it was about their fear of being disconnected from the soul that had given them life. They would not have agreed with her, but she had felt their fears much longer than they had.

She heard the soft tingle of Marjorie's doorbell and then Duncan, her butler, saying, "Good evening, Mr. St. John. Come in, please."

Estelle moved away from the door, going into the bathroom. As she looked in the mirror, seeing her face staring inquisitively back at her, she thought to herself, *It's not a bad face.* Then, she switched the light off and headed downstairs.

CHAPTER EIGHT

"The man himself," Marjorie said joyously as the tall, dark-skinned man walked up the four steps leading to the smallest of the three sitting rooms in the house.

He bent down and kissed her on the cheek, a smile lighting up his face. It was a good face, hard at the edges, but gentle in the middle, with soft eyes that reminded her of a rabbit, with its gentle stare that seemed to see suspicion in everything. She hugged him, and he said, real warmth in his voice, "I could get used to that."

"I keep telling you to get rid of Beverley, and we could do a deal."

"And I keep telling you, if I ever get rid of Beverley, I'd be broke. I handle too many divorces to fall into that trap. I see some cars outside. Who's here?"

"Anis and Maylene are in the den. Estelle's upstairs sleeping."

She thought she saw something cautious enter those eyes that so many women had looked into, and she thought of a day a long time ago when she had, too. No time for that now. She walked before him into the den, surprised Estelle had joined the other women. Marjorie got them all tea, and they turned to Aurelius St. John, the man they called Saint Two.

Estelle sat just out of his field of vision, as if she did not want him to see her reactions. The others pressed in around him.

"How is he doing?"

Aurelius did not answer immediately, a slight frown on his face. Then he said, "That is a good question. I am not sure. Physically, he's fine, but he seems distracted. No. That's not the right word. He is not detached, either, but maybe sort of disoriented."

"Disoriented?" Marjorie asked.

Aurelius looked away, apparently perplexed. Then, he looked at Estelle.

"Did you know he was in Vietnam?"

At first, she did not understand the question and said, "He traveled a lot, but I don't know where he went."

"No, I mean the war. The American war."

"The American war? In Vietnam? No. I didn't know anything about that. Why?"

Aurelius St. John frowned, rubbing his chin with his forefinger.

"That's all he wants to talk about."

Then, he looked at Estelle and added, "Except for talking about you."

Tension seemed to creep into the room, and Estelle looked down.

"What about Vietnam he talking 'bout?"

Marjorie's voice was a steam engine climbing a hill.

"The truth is, I am not sure. He was all over the place. It was like he was not entirely aware of what had happened."

"Did he talk about what happened?"

"I couldn't get him to focus on it. Every time I brought it up, he smiled and talked about something else. Mostly, he talked about you, Estelle."

They all looked at her, and she looked away, hearing a buzz in her head. Then, Marjorie asked, her voice surprisingly soft, "Are you going go see him, Estelle?"

She was aware of the room, but it had lost its size, had become stifling, and she pulled at the collar of her blouse. Involuntarily, she realized that she had not changed since church that morning. They waited for her answer, but finally she just shrugged, shook her head, and standing, asked, "Did someone bring my car from the church, Marjorie? I think I should go home."

"Sure, dear," Marjorie replied gently, rising to walk her to the front door.

As she waited for the butler to bring the car around, Marjorie hugged her, her huge breasts like clouds on which the wind alighted. Without thought, Estelle turned and kissed her on her cheek.

"What was that for?" Marjorie asked, her voice carrying pleasure like the scent of cinnamon. "Don't tell me you turning funny?"

"No, Marjorie, but thanks for everything."

"Since you so grateful, can I ask my question again?"

"Not now, Marjorie. I can't answer that question now."

"Well, can I say something then?"

Estelle nodded, her head down.

"First, we all are here for you, okay? Call me whenever you need to."

She paused, then added, "But don't spend all your time thinking about this thing. He needs you, too. You know him. It would have taken a lot for him to ask for anything. He asked for you."

Estelle felt something rise in her chest, but she said nothing, only squeezing Marjorie's hands and walking down the steps.

As the black BMW slid through the darkness, Estelle fought the urge toward expectation that repeatedly rose in her breast. He had asked for her, but how had he done it? She saw his face, with its dead eyes that looked like a fish she had once seen thrown up on the beach. The sky had been reflected in the eye, but it had seen nothing. If he had asked for her with those eyes, then she knew she would not really matter to him. It would have been form, not need, that drove the question. Or maybe his eyes had crinkled at the edges as he had grinned, the even teeth exposed, large and horse-like. A predator's teeth. She remembered he used to joke about filing them into points so he would look like a true predator. If he had asked with that face, then he was simply being ironic, letting her know that he was aware of her agony, and that it was as silly as it always had been. Or maybe he had looked earnestly at Aurelius as he spoke. If so, the message was probably for Aurelius himself.

Mark St. Auburn was a chameleon, adept at changing himself to whatever environment surrounded him. It was not that he sought to please. It had never been that. In fact, he was one of the most socially insensitive persons she knew. But in some subtle way, even his insults seemed to fit the situations. People admired him, accepted him, but they were never entirely sure they liked him. Most were convinced he did not like them. At least, that is how it had been at school. All of those girls would take their clothes off for him, but none could be sure that he even liked them. She remembered once she had said to him at the point of another breakup, "Do you know that you hate women?"

And he had smiled, replying, his voice serious, "No. It is only that I like the part of women that they hate in themselves, and I despise that which they love in themselves."

She had been stumped, could not follow up, so she had lit a cigarette and sworn at him, knowing her anger only made him more remote, less available. She could not hurt him, and that made her angry, and the angrier she became, the more shielded he was. He had asked for her? She hated herself for allowing a flush of pleasure that made the gray, rain-soaked road seem less defined, and she slowed down, letting the powerful car drift through the night, almost like a horse that knew its way home and did not need to be guided. The highway was empty, people held inside by the rain and the sanctity of Sunday, and she was glad of this, for the world itself felt empty, filled only by her thoughts.

In the beginning, there was the word. Word and form. How could the ancients have grasped that idea so easily? Word and form, thought and reality, inextricably linked. God had given form to the universe through a word, a word presumably reflective of a thought. Plato, too, had deciphered what the ancient Hebrews understood. Reality existed in a non-material form, and what we called reality was but a shadow.

Estelle realized what she was doing, intellectualizing her emotions to avoid the pain, but it always worked, and as the black car pushed aside the light mist, she succeeded in doing it again. Her thoughts structured the world, gave order to the chaos of her feelings. Memory was disorder, but history imposed reason on the disorder, so she thought of their past, trying to provide structure to it, and when the contradiction popped up like a jack-in-the-box, its red tongue stuck out, laughing at her trial, she pushed it down gently, ignoring anything but the order she tried to impose. Order, however, involves choice, and Estelle was not sure which things to discard. Was there really a relationship, a progression, if you will, between his gentleness with the child and his occasional cruelty to her? Was there really a connection between the softness of his kiss and the violence of the slap he had once given her? Where was the order? *Order came from knowing,* she thought, *and did one person really know another?* If she did not assign motive to his actions, the memory was simply a catalogue of facts, but if she did, would it be anything other than her mental map laid on his actions? *Why do men act as they do?* she wondered to herself. A car passed, waking her from her reverie for a moment.

His "thing," whatever it had been with Anis, had been inexplicable to her, and Anis still hated him for it. She had been more ashamed than angry at his fooling around with Anis, and it had broken them up once again. She still remembered his look and his words. He had denied it at first, trying to make Anis out as delusional, but the other girls had already told her what time he had gotten back to Crescent Beach Hotel. He had explained that Anis had gotten sleepy, and he had taken her home, but he could not help but allow the smallest grin to escape for the benefit of the other two Saints. The girls understood the grin, so when Anis had mentioned her liaison with Mark, no one could figure out why she had done that, given Mark's reputation and his relationship with Estelle. The girls had rallied around Estelle, rejecting Anis, but Estelle had seen little point in that since she knew the rejections carried their own guilt. Marjorie had once said to her with a big laugh, "De truth is, girl, Mark St. Auburn is guilty of being screwed more than he is of screwing. I think Shakespeare said that."

So she had not shut Anis out once the initial anger had passed, for Mark was like the beacon in a lighthouse. Light then darkness. Sight then blindness. When the light came, it illuminated whatever was in front of it without partiality or prejudice. It was what made him so incredibly kind one moment and so horribly cruel the next. The girls, who had remained friends as women, now thought him irresponsible. They thought he should grow up, but he had never changed, had never given any indication or made any promise that he would. In his mind, he was still twelve years old, she knew, and when her eyes had caught his, he only knew what he saw and wanted. It was silly, she understood, but it was who he had always been. His kindness was unconscious, like that of a dumb animal, and proceeded from instinct. When the other two Saints laughed at their conquests, they called him the cobra, silent and deadly, because you never heard him coming, but he was always calculating, always seeing the weakness.

She did not believe this. Mark St. Auburn was instinctual, and women warmed to that. It was precisely the lack of calculation in him that they liked. So after two years of absence, when he had come into that dark bedroom on that long-ago evening, his act had been natural. He had picked the child up, and it was as if she had felt the lack of perturbation in the big man. Heather had stopped crying immediately. She had never told him this, but it was not anger so much as jealousy that had made her snatch the baby from him. She had been trying for an hour before he came to quieten the child, but as if it sensed something tumultuous in her, it had continued to cry. She had not known that he had come in and, at first, when the baby had stopped crying so abruptly, a dart of fear had shot through her, and she had rushed to the bedroom. Finding him there with the child held gently against his breast had brought out something deepseated and vicious in her, a sulphurous combination of frustration, anger, dislike, and jealousy, all of which had been contained in the words, "Give me my child."

What had caused those feelings to this day she could not fully explain, but Marjorie, who always had an answer for everyone's emotional problems but her own, had explained that the outburst had been prompted by her anger that Mark was not the child's father. She did not think this was the case but had no sound explanation for her actions.

Mark had become the tenuous link between her and the child who had grown so attached to him that Estelle had been drawn along by their inarticulate attraction to each other. The love she could not feel for the child, she poured into him, and though later she would wonder if it had really been love, his obvious attachment to the child became confused with her love for him, and she grew to believe that she, too, loved the child. Heather had not been fooled. She would gurgle when her mother picked her up, but at the first opportunity, she would scamper away to Mark's willing and open arms. Gradually, a different kind of dislike had grown as she realized that Mark was so open and relaxed with the child but so unconsciously inattentive to her.

The marriage had been quietly done, without the hundreds of guests her parents had envisaged; in fact, she had not told them until she and Mark had returned from Grenada, where they had spent their short honeymoon. They had never forgiven her for this, and her father, on his deathbed, had talked of his one disappointment: that he had not had the opportunity to give her away. If, however, her parents' disappointment hurt, the long weekend in Grenada, which was all Mark could afford, had been like a dose of energy for her. In her mind's eye, she saw the small villa on Cinnamon Hill overlooking Grand Anse Beach where, for the first time in her life, she had lived in space that felt like her own. It had been a two-story villa with the bedrooms on the first floor. The living room had opened out to a balcony that overlooked the beach and exposed the beauty of the eastern hills. She would leave Mark asleep in the mornings and watch the sun rise over the hills of the Spice Island, each day a new one, as if God were creating afresh.

But the honeymoon had ended, and she had gone back to St. Euribius with a glow that was obvious to everyone surrounding her. *Where has that glow gone?* she now asked herself, swinging off the main road and slowing even more as she approached the village. It was odd that they still thought of it as "the village" given that there was no distinct edge to it anymore. Houses were springing up everywhere, and borders were disappearing as people moved outwards in the island, converting agricultural land to settlement. In her first-year class, she taught this as an act of repossession, black people buying up land that they had slaved on for so long. The land-owners were getting a second round of value out of their property. No longer maximally supportive of sugarcane, it was now being converted into lots. Lots, however, she taught in her history lecture, give the possibility of permanent possession. The only problem was that land no longer constituted wealth. They were getting it two hundred years too late. Wealth had changed its face in that time. The students understood this, and while they studied with the thought of home ownership and, therefore, land ownership as their motive, their minds had accepted this other, less visible wealth that now moved around the world at the speed of light. The village had no place in that world, and so those young students were reshaping it, making it more modern and connected.

She passed the old, wooden church as she had passed it so many times, thinking of the joyous sounds of belief that emanated from there on Sundays and on Wednesday nights. It had been in this spot since she was a child. It never grew, and it always seemed as if the same people were attending. When she was a child, the congregants who would stand outside gossiping after Sunday service would raise their hats or bow slightly when her father drove by on his way from the Anglican church on the west coast. It occurred to her that no one bowed anymore. Instead, the eyes slid onto the BMW like slime after a slug had passed. So, whereas her father, who had driven the workers as hard as need be to create the wealth she had inherited, had been respected as a "hard but fair" man, she lived in that ambiguous world of resented privilege. On the rare occasions she walked through the village, she felt their eyes on her, carrying that volatile combination of hostility and contempt. Now, the shadows frightened her. High on the hill, she could see the beckoning light of her home, but here in the dimness of the rain-soaked village, she no longer felt safe.

The people had always liked Mark. He had that easy way of being with them. Yet, even as she thought this, she immediately qualified it. He had not really been with them, but he seemed to be of them in a way that she did not. When their childhood romance was going well, she would come to him on Saturdays, meeting him on the beach. She was always pleased that everyone seemed to know him, seemed to be wishing him well. Mark carried a book everywhere, and people seemed to see much in that. They commented on it admiringly, calling him "the doctor", claiming him and his aspirations as theirs. He would be their success. Most of those people were dead, but Estelle wondered what Mark must feel like now with this killing. Oddly, she also wondered how those old people would feel if they could see where he was or, more importantly, what he had done. The guard he had killed had lived in the village, and though Estelle did not know him, she remembered his mother, who, like so many in the village, had worked in one of her father's hotels and though she did not know this for sure, the guard's grandparents had probably worked in her father's fields.

She stopped the car, making sure the doors were locked. As the car's wipers stopped, the world became first blurred, then soon obscured. Around her, the lights danced as the raindrops slid down the glass of the expensive car. The edges of the small houses disappeared, and Estelle saw only the huge darkness, interspersed with the wavering, uneven lights that looked like malevolent eyes in the night.

CHAPTER NINE

Aurelius St. John waited as the tall iron gates of Spirals, as the prime minister's residence was affectionately called, swung open. As the car eased forward, his face was thoughtful, even worried. He had not stayed long at Marjorie's home, leaving soon after Estelle. He had called her at home, but the butler had said she had not yet returned. He had left a message to have her call him. She looked a wreck. *Everyone is taking the situation with Mark pretty hard, but, God, she looks like she is already dead,* he thought as the attendant brought an umbrella down the steps for him.

Inside, he handed his raincoat to the butler and walked swiftly towards the back of the residence, where he knew Anderson St. Clair, the prime minister, would be. He was no stranger to the residence. The house had been constructed to impress foreign visitors, and, once again, Aurelius marveled at the brass scones and the beautiful, ornate marble fountain that gushed gently in the middle of the open reception room. The chairs, he knew, had been imported from Italy and the gilded mirrors from a small but exclusive factory in the English Midlands. Except for the few palms that lay still in the chill of the rainy evening, nothing was from St. Euribius, and Aurelius smiled. He had handled the legal work on the construction of the residence fifteen years ago. Still, he thought the effect of the whole was pleasingly harmonious. As he crossed the foyer, he could see the prime minister standing on the back patio, his round, compact body short and pugnacious like a cannon's shell. The man turned, his face alight with a smile of genuine pleasure.

"The man himself," he said in their boyhood greeting, handing Aurelius a drink which he immediately sipped.

The vodka and tonic slid down his throat, leaving a faint trail of fire.

"I thought you would be back before now," the P.M. said, signaling Aurelius to sit.

"I went by Marjorie's house before I came here. She had called me to give me hell about not seeing Mark. You know how she is."

The P.M. laughed, his whole body shaking.

"I sure do. I assume you allowed her to believe that you went as a result of her call."

Aurelius watched the hard, sly eyes and, not for the first time, thought that Anderson St. Clair looked like a fox. A very fat fox. He nodded, and the man across from him said, "Good. Good. Dis is a very troublesome t'ing, man."

Aurelius felt just a breath of irritation rise in him, and he said, "He seems all right."

"Seems? What do you mean 'seems'?"

"I think there is a problem somewhere. Did you know he fought in Vietnam?"

The prime minister hesitated just a fraction, then said, "Yes."

Aurelius waited, but the man did not continue.

"Well, that's all he wants to talk about. I tried to get him to talk about the case, but he just smiled and talked about Vietnam."

"What was he saying about Vietnam?" the prime minister asked casually, the clear drink, Ron Rico, probably, going up to his mouth.

"He kept reminding me of various engagements he had been involved in, almost as if he felt I had been there with him."

"What kind of engagements?"

"Fights. You know, battles. What I don't understand is how he could have been in Vietnam, though. When did he leave St. Euribius?"

"The same year you left to go to England to university—1968," the prime minister replied, and a knowing look passed between the two men.

"But wasn't Mark supposed to be going to university on a scholarship? When I mentioned Vietnam tonight, Estelle didn't seem to know anything. She just left."

"Poor Estelle," the prime minister said with genuine sympathy. "She is a real trooper. She hung in there with him for a long time. That is one strange relationship, eh?"

Aurelius did not want to talk about that, so he persisted.

"So when did he go to Vietnam? Why didn't he go to university as he was supposed to?"

"He was on an athletic scholarship. Apparently, he pulled his hamstring pretty badly his first year and did not perform very well, so he lost his scholarship. He didn't want to come back here, so somehow he ended up in the American army or marines or something."

"So he never got a degree? Never went to university? Everyone thinks he's got a master's. How did that happen?"

"Can't say, man. You know Mark. Remember his seventy/twenty/ten rule?"

"Yeah," Aurelius laughed. "Your life is seventy percent imagination, twenty percent inspiration, and ten percent perspiration."

"Maybe," the prime minister responded, "Mark was just living out his rule."

"You mean, he made up all that about the master's and university and all the other stuff? That doesn't sound like him. How long have you known about Vietnam?"

The prime minister hesitated, and his fat face became like blown glass in muted light. Aurelius had seen that look many times. Anderson St. Clair was worried.

"I found out today."

"Today? How? Did you talk to Mark?"

"No. I got a visit from Van Stiles."

"William Van Stiles? The American ambassador?"

Anderson St. Clair nodded slowly, sipping his drink.

"The real man himself," Aurelius said. "What did he want?"

It was impossible not to note the slight edge to his voice. The Americans were not loved at the moment, and as Aurelius looked at his friend's face, he had the sneaky suspicion something unpleasant was coming.

The prime minister stood, walked over to a small, ornate desk that Aurelius knew had been a gift from the Taiwanese and unlocked the drawer. He pulled out a thin envelope and placed it on the desk. He hesitated, then reached in again and pulled out a large packet. He carefully relocked the drawer and brought the packets over. Even before the prime minister handed over the two packets, Aurelius could make out the eagle on the envelopes. The prime minister said, "Read the small one first."

Aurelius quickly skimmed the short note, ignoring the diplomatic language.

"Extradition?" he asked, looking at the prime minister in confusion. "They say he is wanted in America for murder. Whom did he kill? This letter does not say."

The prime minister shrugged.

"I have no idea. Van Stiles is supposed to come by tomorrow. In the meantime, you might want to read this file on your client. He is your client, right? There is a lot we don't know about Saint One."

Aurelius looked at the larger packet, but his mind was somewhere else.

"You can't let them extradite him."

The face of blown glass shimmered in front of him.

"Why not?"

"He is St. Euribian."

Aurelius' voice had hardened a bit.

"Is he?" the prime minister replied blankly. "He carries an American passport. When was the last time he was here? Thirty-one years ago? As far as I can tell, he does not even have a St. Euribian passport. What's my basis for claiming sovereignty here?"

Aurelius did not reply immediately, surprised by the rush of anger that had pushed the blood into his ears so that he heard what sounded like the constant crash of small waves against the rocks. He did not want to overreact, but something beyond reason seemed to be pushing him.

"The sovereignty argument is not that hard to make, Andy," he finally said. "Have you thought of what the people in the village will say? There is a lot of anger over these two deaths. These people are going to want satisfaction. If you give him up to the Americans, there is going to be hell to pay. You know this, so what are we talking about here?"

As Aurelius had spoken, the prime minister had listened carefully, his eyes almost hidden inside the slits made by the lids. He had sipped, but now he put the glass to his mouth and gulped the drink down. He placed the glass on the table and filled it again with the Puerto Rican rum, looking a question at Aurelius, who shook his head.

"It gets more complicated, Aury."

"What do you mean?"

"Deighton Cox called today, too."

"You mean Ras Man? What did he want?"

"He is part of your hell to pay. Apparently, the community he speaks for wants Mark freed. They think he was simply defending the Rasta boy. They want a quick trial and his exoneration."

Aurelius could see the complication. He knew the Rastas now dominated the informal economy of the island, living on the fringes of the tourist industry. For a long time, they had been an inchoate, angry, but largely powerless group. The fact that they had become more than this could be attributed to one man: Ras Man. He had recently stopped using the name, reverting to his old name, Deighton Cox, but he had given up none of his fire in defending the group. Like Aurelius, Deighton Cox was a lawyer, and he, too, had made good in the expanding economy of St. Euribius. He had inherited a good deal of land from his family and had watched its value, in the 1990s, escalate to unimaginable heights during the land boom. He had given up his law practice and had gone into the land-development business, becoming very wealthy as a result. He had not left his Rasta roots, though, and for the first time, the group had a champion who could influence the highest levels of government. Yes, Aurelius could see why the prime minister had that glassy look.

"I hope you pointed out that, under our present system of government, you can guarantee the trial but not the outcome," Aurelius said, laughing.

The prime minister did not join him, and, again, he felt that uneasiness crawl into his mind.

"Read the file, and talk to me tomorrow afternoon. Come by government headquarters. I'll be there. You want another drink before you leave?"

Aurelius shook his head and rose, his long body still athletic, and the prime minister watched him both in admiration and envy. Aurelius worked hard to keep that look. He ran every day and played squash three times a week. *Too much effort for too little result,* the prime minister thought, rising to walk his friend to the door. As they got to the steps, the warm rain still poured down, and, suddenly, the prime minister, making a sweeping gesture that included the house and the night, said, "Aury, do you ever get the feeling that all of this is just a shadow? That it could crumble any minute?"

Aurelius laughed, saying, "I have told you to stay away from the Americans."

CHAPTER TEN

Estelle awoke with a start, aware of the huge face staring down on her. It was distorted and ghoulish, and she drew back into the resistant leather of the BMW's seat. It took her a second to realize where she was and to recognize the face that was mouthing words she could not hear. It was Mr. Cox, Maylene's father-in-law. She rolled the window down, an embarrassed smile on her face.

"Good morning, Mr. Cox."

"Good morning, Miss Estelle. You awright? I see de car park here an' I dint know dat somebody did in it at first. You awright?"

"Yes. I am fine. I was out with the girls last night and must have had too much to drink. I guess I parked here because I got sleepy."

His eyes got glassy at the explanation, but he said nothing, and she sat up, placing her hand purposefully on the steering wheel. The old man was dressed in faded but clean khaki pants and shirt, and Estelle thought, *Jeans have not yet penetrated his consciousness. He is still, at the foundation, British.* She smiled at the thought, and the old man returned the smile.

"Can I give you a lift somewhere, Mr. Cox?"

"No need, Miss Estelle. I goin' by de quarter ground."

"Come on. Jump in. Let me take you over there."

As the big car slid through the slight chill of the early morning, Estelle noticed the stir in the canes and the tremor in the leaves. The man's land was about a mile away, so it did not take long to get there, but the morning felt new, and a line slid into her head from a Cat Stevens song.

"Morning has broken, like the first morning."

There was something new about this feel to the land at dawn and just after. The rain had stopped, but the heavy scent of the earth's fecundity lay like a blanket upon the land. *Echoes of the past,* she thought, not sure why that came to mind. The road was winding, and she remembered a story her father had told her about the many unnecessary bends in the roads of St. Euribius. Slaves had built the original roads and, though the land was flat with few natural obstacles to avoid, they had built the one natural obstacle to being seen that they could. When a road bent, they became invisible for a while. It had allowed them to slow down from the backbreaking work for a moment when they might be out of sight of the overseer. Estelle smiled until the thought suddenly occurred to her that the overseers belonged to her now. The old man's voice cut into her thoughts.

"It is uh shame 'bout Lemuel, ain't it?"

"I am sorry, Mr. Cox. Who?"

"Lemuel. De guard dat get kill down by Shady Lane."

Estelle groaned. She had forgotten the man's name, but the sudden tightening of her stomach was not only for that reason.

"Yes. It is a mess. Did you know him?"

"Yes, yes. He did Mabel Greaves boy. Nice boy, too. Always spick an' span. He dress real nice, an' really did good to he mudder. She goin' have uh hard time now 'cause she don't work. De cancer, you know."

"Miss Greaves got cancer?"

"Yes, yes. They dia'nose she 'most a year ago now. De boy did taking good care uh she. I did too glad when he get dat little pick down at Shady Lane, because I kno' fuh a fac' dat t'ings got easier after dat. Now he gone. Boy, yuh never can tell what goin' happen, yeah?"

Estelle felt aggrieved, sorry that she had picked the old man up. Though her mind told her he was just talking, she felt as if his comments were aimed at her, and a cloud descended upon the morning, turning the smell of the land fetid and the mist into a shifting, wraithlike creature within which the phantoms prowled. She kept the smile on her face.

"So who is going to help she now?" she asked, taking a half step toward the dialect.

"I really doan know, to tell yuh de truth. She might have to go in de almshouse 'cause dere really aint nobody to help. I mean, we in de village will try to help out, but you know how dat is. Now dat de young people moving out and buying all of dese new houses all about, nuhbody ain't got much help dese days. So I really doan know wha' she goin' do."

Estelle slowed, knowing she was approaching his small quarter-acre plot—the "quarter ground," as he had referred to it.

"Well, thanks fuh de lif', Miss Estelle. You doan have to turn. I can walk back dere."

As the car stopped, he looked admiringly at the dashboard, and then, his soft eyes asking permission, he ran his hand over the upholstery, saying, "Boy, St. Euribius come uh long way, eh, Miss Estelle? 'Course you family always had money, but I think 'bout Maylene and Deighton. None uh we dint had nuttin'. Dey grow up widout much t'ings, and Deighton dint have nuh steady place to live. Just moving from pillar to post, from pillar to post. We try to mek sure that Maylene get to go to high school 'cause we did know dat t'ings did changing."

He paused, and the smell of guava was on his breath. Estelle sat with the engine idling, feeling both the warmth and the distance in his words.

"I glad dat wunna girls is still friends. Lot uh changes eh, Miss Estelle, but dat still de same. Dat is uh good t'ing."

As she drove back along the winding road to her home, Estelle thought of the old man's last words. The unchanging things were a good thing, he thought, though the past had meant hard work and little pay. But what had really changed? He still walked to his "quarter ground" every morning, finding meaning in creating life in a plot of land that her father or his father had probably given the man for some now unknown service. What would that service have been? Not simply doing his job. Everyone in the village would have done that, so why had this particular man gotten land? The question lay like a scythe paused over ripe grass, pushing Estelle into a relationship with the village that she had ignored. What was that relationship, and why was she now afraid of it? All of her friends – Marjorie, Maylene, Anis, Mark, Aurelius, Sandra, and Anderson – had come out of these villages. She had not. She was the "plantation girl," a part of, yet somehow separate.

Around her now, she could see the women bending in the land, their heads tied with white cloths. There was something both obscene and pathetic about the way their backsides stuck up in the air, like they were exposed, vulnerable, open to the air and whatever else passed by. For a moment, the world went out of focus, and Estelle rubbed her eyes. She did not like that the guard had become real to her. In the newspaper, he had been anonymous, the facts given about him holding him in stasis, somehow artificial, bloodless. There was a faint sense of distant recognition as the name of the village, Prescod's Bottom, had been given, and a hint of connection, since the village's name was her family's name. The Prescods, her family, had owned these lands since the end of the eighteenth century, an oddity in this land of harsh slavery and debilitating colonialism. And those women, their backsides raised like the prow of an ocean-going ship, had bent like that on Prescod land since that time. Her mind slid to the other ways in which they had bent as well, and her heart called out in some agonized way to a universe that had put on its best raiment. The sun was climbing out of the ground, having survived another night's journey, and the earth rejoiced. Estelle saw, but did not notice, the beauty of the day as she drove past her house, heading further east.

"What is the matter with me?" she asked, trying, in the presence of her voice, to push away the shadows surrounding her heart.

She still had not succeeded when she pulled into the long drive of the old plantation house. It looked like a fortress. She drove around the house to the back, marveling at the unchanging nature of the world. Even this early, the yard was busy as men scurried around, moving equipment, walking horses, washing large pans. Was it her imagination or did they seem to become more diligent as her car slid into the yard? Her mother's old Austin was parked in the garage, and she thought about how much that symbolized about the plantation.

Inside, she greeted Nello, the cook, who was busy in the kitchen, but she did not stop to talk. Upstairs in her old room, Estelle was surprised at how little had changed in that room, almost as if her mother was consciously preserving the past. She had not been to the house since the killing and had not spoken to her mother about it. She was not looking forward to the conversation. So why had she come? Estelle lay across the bed fully clothed and closed her eyes. Behind the lids, the images played hide and seek. She was so tired.

She was not aware that she had fallen asleep until Nello's hands shook her gently. She opened her eyes to the kind, round face.

"Wake up, Miss Estelle. You mudduh want you to eat breakfast wid she."

Estelle sat up, yawning and rubbing her eyes.

"What time is it?"

"Goin' on nine o'clock."

"Thanks, Nello."

Estelle went to the bathroom, washing her face and trying to put her hair into something approximating order. Two hundred dollars a week, and Faye could not give her something that survived a night without a comb. She rummaged through the medicine cabinet and found a small comb. Her hair changed from anarchy to disorder, and, giving up, she dried her face and went downstairs.

Her mother sat out on the patio, her breakfast table shaded by a large umbrella. Before them, the land stretched away in waves, the young sugarcanes moving gently like a green ocean. The long line of palms that guarded the driveway were militant sentinels in this peaceful scene. Far in the distance, Estelle could see the ridge where, legend had it, the English had forced the slaves to kill off the last Caribs who lived on the island. The bodies had been thrown off the ridge into the gully. According to the old people, a hurricane had come that night, the giant waves pushing the water up the seams of the island into the rivers and streams and finally into the gully where the Indians' bodies lay. The sea had taken them and then retreated. To the east of the island were twelve rocks that stood out from the ocean, constantly pounded by the surf. These were the last of the Indians who had given their name to the region but who could not fight off the inexorable march of history.

"Well, you do look a fright."

Her mother's voice, urbane, cultured, and emotionally distant, cut into her thoughts.

"Good morning, Mother," Estelle responded, her voice resigned. She was now fifty-two, but her mother's voice always made her feel fifteen.

"Apparently, it has not been a good morning for you. I understand you slept in your car in the village last night."

The village semaphore. She was not surprised. Probably Nello had seen the car on her way to work.

"You ought to be more careful, Estelle."

Something inside of her warmed a little at her mother's concern but dissipated as the older woman added, "Your reputation is not all that sound as it is, and reputations are like cold sores. They never heal."

Estelle sighed loudly, but her mother ignored it, delicately buttering a piece of toast cut into a perfect triangle with the crust sliced from the edges. *So familiar,* Estelle thought. The teapot, white china with a floral pattern, sat in the middle of the table, two matching cups and saucers standing guard. Two grapefruit halves were in a glass dish, and two eggs—one boiled for her mother, and the other scrambled for her—sat in front of them. The freshly squeezed orange juice squatted like a yellow stain in the glass jar. Estelle picked at her egg, trying to avoid comments about her not eating. Something heavy weighed on her soul, like a man waiting to be hung.

"Well, are you going to introduce the subject or shall I?"

Estelle stared at the line of palm trees in the distance, aware that she had wanted something when she came here, but also knowing she would not get it in this house. Still, the powerful presence of her mother's decaying hand was a counter to any harshness that welled up in her. The hands and arms had changed, assuming a dried-out muscleless flabbiness on the skeleton that had become so obvious to Estelle's eyes. *She is becoming skin and bone,* Estelle thought, looking up to her mother's face. This, too, had changed, and Estelle felt a distant surprise in the recognition. As the old woman placed the toast carefully in her mouth, Estelle noticed the slightly yellowed false teeth that seemed an entity separate from that mouth which, in spite of the wrinkles that started on her high cheeks and converged like streams of mercury on the corners of her mouth, still had force. Mrs. Gweneth Prescod fought the world with that mouth. It was small and had a precision to it that was like a barrier, or maybe a slicer and dicer, willing, ready, and able to destroy. So Estelle said, "I have not been to see him, Mother."

"Quite right, too. It's good to know you can show some sense once in a while. This, dear, is what comes of ignoring your parents. Mr. St. Auburn comes of bad stock. His end was inevitable."

Estelle felt the thunderbolt hovering behind her, and something must have changed in her face because her mother's own face turned stern, the hard planes of the almost fleshless visage tightening into a mask that seemed to say, "Don't you dare look at me in that tone of voice."

Why those words came to her, she could not tell. Of course, her mother would never say that. It was something Marjorie's mother used to say. The thought of Marjorie calmed her, and she said, "Mother, there is nothing wrong with Mark's stock. We all come from the same stock."

"Don't be foolish, girl."

Her words carried their own explanation, and Estelle was silenced by the sultry breeze that came across the center of the island, still carrying the pregnant smell of the wet soil.

"You never believed this, Estelle, but breeding is important. That is why Mr. St. Auburn was so wrong for you. It broke your father's heart when the marriage happened, you know. Of course, you would have known nothing about that. You were too happy."

The last word came out with the smell of rotted fish, and Estelle, feeling defenseless, replied plaintively, "I was happy, Mother. Isn't that important to you?"

"No, Estelle, you were not happy. You were excited. The two emotions occasionally overlap, but they are not the same. You were always a little foolish, particularly about Mr. St. Auburn."

Estelle put down the delicate cup with the tea in it, measuring her mother's words, finally deciding why she had come.

"So you won't help, Mother?"

The old woman's mouth slid to a point, closing up like a sea anemone sensing approaching danger.

"No, Estelle. I will not help. Nor should you. Why don't you accept that your husband is careless of everyone's life. I do not speak of this latest unfortunate incident. He kills everything. He's killed you."

"No, Mother," Estelle responded, her voice intense, like escaping steam under high pressure. "No. He did not kill me, Mother. Mark saved me from…."

"From what, dear? That silly business of the child? That could have been taken care of but for your foolishness. It was your insane desire to hurt us that made that decision for you. In any case, Mr. St. Auburn was only taking care of his responsibility."

Estelle almost laughed at that point. She had forgotten that her mother had never believed Heather was not Mark's child. Blue had never been a frequent visitor to the plantation, and there had been little talk of him, so in spite of what everyone else knew, her mother had refused to believe that Mark had no responsibility.

She was never sure why he had married her, but she knew it was not out of a sense of responsibility. Once, when he had been in one of those cold moods that seemed to descend on him out of nowhere, he had said to her, "Don't irritate me with your love. It is like sticky paper. It imprisons rather than liberates." She knew he was harsh from time to time, almost as if he could not help it, but the words had sucked the life out of her. When she had asked why he had married her then, he had looked annoyed, replying, "Isn't friendship enough?"

But friendship had not been enough. Not for her, anyway. She was not like him, self-contained and self-sufficient. She needed the contact, the proof of someone's love. She looked at her mother, who had continued eating, slowly placing one section of the grapefruit in her mouth, chewing carefully, then swallowing. Estelle wondered if she had a specific number of chews for each grapefruit segment. Even as she watched that mouth, though, she thought of the implications of those lines, and a heaviness fell on her spirit, making her want to touch those increasingly flabby, though thin, arms. She did not. Her mother would not understand it. She did not like intimacy, and the touch would frighten her.

Where did that fear come from? Who had hurt this woman so that she did not trust feelings? Estelle thought of her father: big, perfect, a huge shadow in her world. Could she have misunderstood the violence in that relationship? It had always seemed to her that her mother dominated the marriage, her voice like a scalpel before which her father had retreated. As a child, she had always taken her father's side, going to him after an argument between her parents ended. He had seemed soothed by her touch and her childish affection, as if he, too, yearned for something. Still, looking at her mother now, she wondered if her eyes had missed something more subtle than the violence of her mother's icy voice.

Estelle wished she could settle her feelings for her mother once and for all. At fifty-two, she still had the same uncertainty in her presence, slipping back and forth across that invisible line between love and hate.

"Aurelius went to see him yesterday."

Her mother stopped, her hand halfway to her mouth.

"Did he? And why would he do that? Does Mr. St. John plan to defend him?"

There was something irritating about the way her mother referred to all her friends by their last name, as if giving them the social respect they had achieved while denying them all intimacy. Gweneth Prescod called her daughter, her servants, and a very small number of intimates by their first name.

"I believe so. Marjorie told him he had to."

"Do you think Mr. St. John will represent him because Mrs. Andrews told him he had to? If he went to see Mr. St. Auburn, then the prime minister told him to. Mr. St. John does not move unless the prime minister says it's okay. You should know that."

It occurred to Estelle that Anderson St. Clair, the prime minister, had said he would call her. She had not heard from him, but then, she had not been home. She wondered at what her mother had said. She was probably right. The three Saints would stick together, but the prime minister could not be seen consorting with a murderer. He would have to keep his distance, as she herself was doing.

"Have you been to see Mrs. Greaves?"

"Who?"

"The mother of the young man who was killed. Her name is Clotelle Greaves. She suffers from cancer. Have you been to see her?"

Estelle frowned, her face a question.

"You are as irresponsible as he is. You have no sense of your position. Do you understand why the village is called Prescod's Bottom?"

Estelle did not answer, her soul becoming unbearably heavy.

"It is called that, Estelle, not because we own it, but because it is our responsibility. I can tell by your face that you have not even thought of it. All you think about is that man. No thought for the woman whose son is dead, a woman who worked for us most of her life. You do not even know her, do you?"

Estelle wanted to say yes, but the lie choked her, stilling her tongue. Finally, she croaked, "What should I do, Mother?"

Gweneth Prescod looked at her, something alive in her eyes.

"An odd question, Estelle. I am surprised that you must ask."

Estelle felt the old rejection, and she stood. As she straightened her body, though, her knees struck the table, and the white, floral-patterned teapot tipped over, spilling the warm tea on the glass top. The black liquid crawled to the edge, slipping over and plunging into her mother's lap, immediately casting a dark shadow between her legs. The old woman never moved as the tea continued to drip on her, and, later, in the car as she headed for her house, Estelle could only remember her mother's eyes. They were full of disappointment.

CHAPTER ELEVEN

The angel hung in the upper corner of the cell where the ceiling met the walls. Mark St. Auburn knew she had been watching him for a long time, and now, so as not to disturb her, he watched through almost closed eyes, the lashes of which divided the world into hazy lines. The angel was clear, though. Her long wings hung down, covering her body as she attached herself to the ceiling. She had been there for a long time. He had seen when she had first arrived in the shape of a blackbird. She had pecked at the window until it had opened, and, once inside, she had assumed her normal shape. Now, she stood looking down on him, her unblinking, lidless eyes like the surface of a lake. She had not changed since Vietnam, her placid face giving evidence of her caring and concern for him. She had come to him a lot that day at Cam Ne. Mark closed his eyes completely, knowing the angel would be there when he opened them again. In fact, she was becoming a fixture since he had been placed in the jail. She had seen so much that he wondered how her eyes remained so clear, so placid.

Even she had blinked at Cam Ne, though. They had come in after the helicopters had told the Vietnamese to get out. If the marines found them there, they would be considered VC. He had been with the 9th Regiment, U.S. Marines, and they had taken fire two days before. Their lieutenant, some white boy from South Carolina, had been killed, so the 9th was pretty pissed off. Command had told them not to take any shit, and if even a single round was fired at them, they should destroy the village. As usual, the blacks had been up front, and when they entered the village, he remembered Ray's eyes. He had the killing madness, and Mark had moved a little further away from him. Shit just happened in

'Nam, and the enemy was not always on the other side. He could see the other bloods had moved away from Ray, as well, and while alert to the huts that surrounded him, he kept a part of his mind on Ray.

He was still not quite sure what had started it, but Ray had yelled "VC," and the world had turned yellow and red. The 9th had shot everything in sight, and the place had turned smoky, so that men were indistinct in the mist of the gun smoke. When the figures had appeared in front of him, he had swung the M-16 on them, watching the bodies buck as the lead ate into them. Six kills. The exhilaration had shot through him, and he had moved on, looking for targets. All that had confronted him were empty huts, and these he had burned as they were instructed to do. Suddenly, the guns had stopped. Fear and excitement receded, and the machines of death in the mist became men again. Slowly, the mist had cleared, and as they stood in the center of the village, only six bodies were down. A quick voice check told them that everyone in the 9th was okay. Ray had run to him, yelling his congratulations. He had the only kills in the village, and the adrenaline had still been pumping through him when he went back to the edge of the village where the kills had taken place. He had lost his lunch that day. The six bodies lay sprawled on the ground, and the horror had crawled into his mind. There had been a man, a woman, and four young girls, the eldest he had guessed to be about twelve and the youngest around three. Their bodies had lain in the grotesque angles of the dead, and for the first time, the angel had come outside his head and had stood among the dead, her eyes remote and unquestioning. Mark still remembered Ray's brutal laugh and his words, "A fucking cherry."

After Cam Ne, the angel had wandered in and out of his head, protecting him, being his eyes and ears. She was more beautiful now that she could escape from his mind, and sometimes her face changed, and he would see others from his past in her. Today, though, she had her own look, serene and beautiful. They had burned the bodies in the sweltering jungle and had reported six VC kills to headquarters, but sometimes, when the angel was not in a good mood, she would take on the faces of those young girls he had met and dispatched so abruptly in that faraway jungle.

Mark opened his eyes. She was still there, but her face had changed to that of Estelle's, and Mark shook his head, not wanting the images to coalesce. The motion dislodged the angel, and she disappeared.

"Just as well," Mark said out loud, changing his position on the bed and covering his eyes with his arm. Immediately, he saw Estelle's face, then the rest of her. It was night, and the starless darkness made him feel like he was underground, covered by something heavy. They were in her parents' garden, and she was teetering between anger and fear. They walked deeper into the darkness created by the huge spreading mango tree that was, at the moment, barren. The wind whispered in the leaves as if some spirit lived there.

"You don't want me?"

Her voice was heavy like molten lead, but the upper registers carried a hint of hysteria.

"How come you have never wanted me?"

He had sighed loudly, thinking once again, caught between a desire to explain and the will to hurt. Finally, he said, "Don't mistake the issue. It has nothing to do with want. It does not make sense."

"What did they tell you about me?"

"Who?"

"You know who. All the others. Did they tell you about me seeing a psychiatrist? Do you think I am crazy? Is that why you won't touch me?"

He had felt the fetid combination of guilt and anger, and his reply had sought to push the conversation away from intimacy.

"Well, you sure are acting crazy now."

The darkness had swirled, and he sensed rather than saw the hand. He had moved just in time, and the slap had exploded against his shoulder. Immediately he had become calm, knowing this would infuriate her.

"Don't you think you have enough trouble as it is?"

"I am taking care of my trouble, Mark. I want to know why you think I am disgusting."

He knew what she wanted, and a simple denial would have solved everything, but he could not do it. Something rebellious rose in him at the thought that his emotions were being manipulated, and she became empty, nothing to him. She was the other competitor in a game which he would win, and the affection which she craved, he would deny. So he said, knowing exactly what he was doing, "I don't find you disgusting, Estelle, merely desperate, and desperation is never attractive."

He had rather like that phrase, had worked on it for days, waiting for an opportunity to deliver it. Now, it had been said, and he had heard her breath catch in the night. He waited for her, knowing she would speak first, but that catch of her breath had taken some of the joy out of the phrase, and he wished she would fight him with the weapons that he chose. Her tears ate at his heart, weakening his will, giving her the victory though he had won, and sometimes he hated her for that.

In the end, he had pulled her head against his half-bared chest and allowed her to cry against him.

"Listen, Estelle, it is not that I don't want to, but I should not. You are still in a very fragile place."

"I am not as fragile as they seem to think. Did Dr. Myrick talk to you?"

He had considered lying but did not see the point of it.

"Yes. He called a while ago."

"What did he say?"

"Nothing personal about you. He did say to me that he knew about our relationship and, given that we had been friends for so long, I could be good for you. He did warn me, though, that if I was not in for the long haul, then I shouldn't start up with you again."

Estelle had been quiet for a while.

"Did he tell you what is wrong with me?"

"There is nothing wrong with you, my sweet. You are just distraught and tired."

"No. I have been diagnosed as mildly manic-depressive."

"What does that mean?"

"I can't control my emotions. I go from being very high emotionally to being very low. I have to take medicine for it and the therapy."

"You will be fine," he replied, not sure of what he was saying.

"So are you going to make love to me?" she had asked, and immediately the tension had come back.

The truth was, he had been afraid, both of the mental instability and the warning about a long-term commitment. Mark had felt certain he could sustain a supportive friendship for as long as she needed it. It was this other thing that sex introduced that had frightened him. In spite of his reputation, sex was a mystery that he approached with a great deal of trepidation. A complex of fears, not the least of which was the fear of a child, held him back. Above all, though, was the fact that she had outgrown him in the two years since school. He had created a whole lifetime of sexual experiences for her in his mind, and in this world, he had felt inadequate. She had somehow become a woman, and he had remained a boy. His reluctance, therefore, sprang from deepseated fears about his inadequacy. He had poured himself into the child, substituting her for the mother to whom he gave the lukewarm gift of his intellect. This she had gulped down, starved as she was for both knowledge and attention, but the other had never been right between them. So that night, he had said, "Take what I can give, please."

He let her hear the plea in his voice, knowing she would warm to this victory of sorts. She had hugged him tightly, believing that, in the end, he would give way.

Mark St. Auburn opened his eyes. The angel was gone, hiding somewhere in his mind, and he was glad, for she had taken with her the faces from Cam Ne.

CHAPTER TWELVE

"I can't even see de crack in my backside."

Marjorie's voice carried a vague grievance as she twisted, looking with difficulty over her shoulder at the exercise pants she wore.

"At least they fit," Sandra's voice responded sultrily, her eyes watching the other woman's middle.

"Fit" may have been an overstatement. The pants had stretched themselves around Marjorie's distended middle and protruding rear, and the needlework showed the stress. Sandra, Maylene, and Anis watched as Marjorie walked around, the soft swish of the material sounding like an accusation as her giant legs rubbed. From the night of Estelle's party a week ago, she had been talking about losing weight, and Sandra, who was a fanatic about her daily workouts, had agreed to help. It had been she who had arranged to have the exercise outfits made for her friend, knowing that, left to her own devices, Marjorie would never go beyond talk. Now, Marjorie was venturing out on her first walk. Anis and Maylene had come by for support, but as Anis had said, exercising after the sun came up always struck her as pagan.

"I look like uh idiot wid my ass bulging out like dat."

"No, you don't. And anyway, nobody going to see you out here. You own all de land in dis place."

This seemed to convince Marjorie, and she picked up a broad, straw hat and walked to the door. The day was beautiful, with that crispness of a perfect tropical day. A thin fringe of startlingly white cloud sat on the horizon like a giant hen on eggs, but other than that, the sky was clear, the blueness of it shocking. The rains of the last few days had disappeared and with it, that fertile smell of the land. Instead, the land breathed something that seemed to come from an opened, mysterious jar of perfume in a closed room. Standing high above on the cliffs, they could hear the soft, rounded boom of the breakers hitting the shore, and in the air they could feel the soft spray from that wild ocean. It was so different from the other side of the island, where the water sat like silvered glass, with only the gentle sound of the tide, moving the small shells and rocks that formed a permeable border between sand and sea, giving the sense of movement. Here on the eastern side, below Marjorie's enormous house, it was all sound and fury, the crashing waves a constant refrain.

Marjorie started out briskly, the others following with inquiring looks. By the time she had reached the end of the long approach to the house and had turned onto the road she had put in to connect her to the main road over two miles away, she had slowed. In the tracksuit, with her head covered by the wide-brimmed hat, she looked like a parade elephant out on a morning walk. At first, the women had been quiet, but as the pace slowed to accommodate Marjorie's accelerated breathing, Anis asked, "How come Estelle didn't come? Dis is right up she alley."

Sandra looked at Marjorie, asking, "You talk to her since last Sunday?"

Marjorie was not too happy with this sudden curiosity because they had reached a slight rise in the road, and she had leaned forward into the hill, her breathing becoming more labored. She managed to gasp, "Yes. I talk to she on Wednesday. She didn't sound too good."

"What do you mean?"

Anis' voice sounded a little anxious.

"She went to see she mother on Monday," Marjorie responded, and the other women groaned.

"Wha' happen?"

"She mother tell she that she did stupid for marriding Mark and dat she shouldn't go to see him now."

"Jesus. Dat woman can carry a grudge," Maylene said, her voice fading into the warm wind.

"So Estelle is messed up now, right? I ain' never see a mother and daughter that seem to hate one another so."

"I don't think they hate each other. They just don't know how to love each other. Remember how Estelle always used to say when we were in school that she could not get close to her mother? That's not hate. That is frustrated love."

The women were quiet for a moment, thinking about Sandra's words. In some ways, this was not simply Estelle's problem. They all suffered in one way or another with this alienation, but Estelle's was special. They knew it had hurt the girl for as long as they could remember. Estelle had adored her father, and they knew that was a source of some of the rejection she got from her mother. Why this should be so, they had no idea.

"It funny, though, you know. Estelle can't build uh relationship with she mother, and Heather can't build a relationship wid Estelle. Ain't it funny how t'ings does work out?"

"It's more predictable than funny, Maylene. What, to me, is remarkable is that we are attached to our children, not that we reject them."

They had reached the top of the hill, and Marjorie stopped to catch her breath. They all waited for her, milling around. After a while, Marjorie asked, "What you talking 'bout, Sandra? All uh we got children, except you and Anis. We don't have any problems wid we children."

"That's for the most part true, but don't you ever wonder how, with all the pain and discomfort of pregnancy and birth, we have anything except hatred for them? Then there is this brief period of bliss which comes with their total dependence on us, making us useful, relevant, but then that, too, is gone, and the scars develop as they make us angry, and we have to chastise them. So after a while, all you feel is frustration at the distance between you. It is almost as if the moment they can say 'I love you, mummy,' it becomes a lie."

"I am sorry, Sandra, but I dint feel dat way 'bout any of my three children. And w'at dis got to do wid Estelle anyway?" Marjorie, her breathing restored to normal, asked irritably.

"Maybe nothing, Marjorie, but we always assume that Mrs. Prescod just doesn't like Estelle. We never assume that Estelle doesn't like Heather. Why is that? We are willing to see Estelle's side because she is our friend, but we never ask why Mrs. Prescod is the way she is."

Marjorie, like a bloodhound after a scent, asked, "You remember de stories 'bout Mrs. Prescod when she did young?"

"Yeah," Maylene answered, a queer excitement in her voice. "She poisoned she brother, Elmer, dint she?"

"Well, she dint poison he. She almost poison he," Marjorie chimed in.

"What you mean 'almost'? She poison he. He just dint dead, dat's all. Dey had to pump he stomach an' everything. At least, dat is wha I hear my mother say."

"What are you talking about?" Sandra asked curiously.

"You never hear the stories 'bout Mrs. Prescod? Well, no wonder. You grow up in de village, but not of de village. I guess dey dint talk 'bout dem kinda t'ings in you house. Anyway, Mrs. Prescod ain't grow up 'bout here. She from de north end uh de island. Dat is why she still does talk in that differenty-differenty way. You know, wid dat up and down accent."

At this point, Maylene fixed a prissy look on her face and said in a strained, artificially cultured voice, "Wunna gine up?"

The heavy accent on "gine" gave the question a wavy motion, like watching water make a back and forth movement in a bowl. The women laughed, recognizing the accent of the north.

"Get back to the story. What did Mrs. Prescod do?" Sandra asked between breaths of laughter.

"Well, I ain't too sure how true dis is, but she brother Elmer apparently used to feel she up at night and, from what I understand, even used to get 'pon top she. She tek it for a while, but one day, she put Jeyes Fluid in he food, and it nearly kill he."

"Jesus. She is a mean ole bitch, ain't she?" Marjorie asked no one in particular. Then, she quickly added, "He deserve it, though. Fancy he getting 'pon top uh he sister. Wha' ever happen to he?"

"I tink I hear dat dey send he to England. I don't know wha' become uh he up dere," Maylene responded.

"Anyhow, dey marri'd Mrs. Prescod off quick-quick to de plantation boy dat did like she. Dat is how she get up here in the plantation house near de village."

She paused for a while, then added, "I sure dat de rest of wunna hear dis, but since Sandra din't know nutting 'bout de story, maybe she ain't hear dis neither. Dere was de rumor dat Estelle dint Prescod chile neither."

"Whose child is she supposed to be then?"

"Elmer."

"That's rubbish," Sandra responded angrily.

"I was only telling you wha' people use to say. I don't know none of dis fuh sure. Anyway, you is de one dat say we don't try to understand Mrs. Prescod. De story would explain uh lot, won't it?"

Marjorie could see upset in Sandra's face and, seeking to avoid a blow up, asked, "How far you t'ink we come?"

"About half a mile. You tired?" Sandra replied, absentmindedly.

"No. Let we go a little further and den turn back. I got some salt-fish fritters calling my name at de house."

"If this is to work, Marjorie, you will have to change your diet, too. No salt-fish fritters."

"So how I goin' get the energy to do dis every day? You trying to kill me?"

Sandra looked at the huge body and said dryly, "We've got a long way to go to get there."

CHAPTER THIRTEEN

It was a full two hours before the women got back to the house, and Marjorie felt very proud of herself. Now, her friends lay sprawled on her patio which stretched like a crescent moon around the house, overlooking the turbulent sea. The patio was built on the second of the three floors of the house and gave a panoramic view of the surrounding land, with its brownish-gray shrub and protruding rocks. They had all eaten a light breakfast and now talked desultorily, allowing the warm breath of the ocean to soothe away the discomfort of their world.

Maylene had taken a book and gone to the end of the patio, and she now reclined in a lounge chair. She was not reading, though she held the book to her face. Her thoughts were elsewhere. She wondered what Mark was doing and why it was so hard for them to talk openly about him. She felt as if they were doing everything to keep their minds off their old friend and lover. They had all had some brief interlude with him, and for some reason, it lived with them, controlling their responses now. It was as if they all felt connected to him and, through him, to each other, in a way that was so intimate they feared it.

Unlike the others, she had not been able to go directly to sixth form, so she had gone to work in a bookshop. She had always loved reading, so it seemed the most natural thing in the world. For the first time in her life, she had fallen in love—with the smell of new books. There was something so deeply pleasurable about that smell that, even today, she could arouse herself by closing her eyes and thinking of those early days in the bookshop. Maylene closed her eyes, laying the half-finished novel on her well-proportioned bosom. *My pride and joy,* she thought. She had been lucky. Though heavy-breasted, she had not, as so many did, had to watch her breasts head for her stomach. She worked out five days a week to make sure they did not sag, that they did not "bre'k deir necks," as the boys used to say. So far, it had worked, and she swished in the large chair, feeling with pleasure the tautness in her chest and her behind. Mark had liked her breasts. In fact, he was like a little boy with them. He treated them like a baby would, instinctively touching, kissing, and sucking them. He had reduced her embarrassment at their size because he saw them as a luxury, a gift from the gods, and because he did, she, too, learned to see them as such. He was the only man who had brought her to a climax simply by sucking her breasts, leaving sharp, blue-red marks on them from the pressure of his teeth. There had been nothing sophisticated about him, no extraordinary technique that had made her insides melt and made her ask, "What are you doing to me?"

He had reminded her of a child feeding, a hungry mouth that was so single-minded she had fed her breasts to him, almost choking him.

Why was it so hard for them to see him now? She turned to look at the other women who seemed to be half-asleep after their walk. So many secrets. This island was one big secret whose flag was a lie. Now, the new secrets were growing like a cancer in a body. She had seen the look that passed between Marjorie and Sandra when they had wondered if Sandra would get the case, and she had immediately put two and two together. The story about Estelle's mother, too, had started something in her, something that made her nervous and restless.

Below the cliff, the sea looked heavy, like a woman about to deliver, and the sonorous boom of the waves was like a giant sigh. She thought of her husband, and her heart constricted. Another secret. Since the killings, he had been having secret meetings at the house, and she worried about that. Deighton was the most honorable man she knew, but she also knew where that honor could lead him. She had never seen him so angry as after the word had gotten out that Mark had killed the guard after the guard had killed the Rasta boy. He had been torn because he did not like Mark and, therefore, hated what he knew he had to do. She had always been nervous about Deighton's attachment to the Rastas because it brought an element into her house she did not like. She could not help feeling nervous when she saw the long, dark locks that reminded her of a lion's mane and the wild look in their blood-shot eyes. They never looked her in the face but stared at the ground, and she was convinced it had nothing to do with shyness, but that they could not stand her. Why Deighton had gotten involved with them, she did not understand. His practice had been successful, so he did not really need this low-end legal work. Something had changed in him after they had been married, and, though, as things go, hers was a successful marriage, she had no idea why he had suddenly begun to grow locks in his late thirties. He had cut them off only a year or so ago, but the young men with the smell of herb still came by.

She and Deighton had become quite successful since the value of the land had skyrocketed. Instead of selling for what had seemed like easy money in the nineties, he had gotten backers to develop the land, believing that to sell was a betrayal. The gamble had worked, and he now had a number of developments around the country. The rich and famous could not seem to get enough of the place, and land that, twenty years ago, no one could figure out what to do with, had suddenly become very valuable. Deighton bought everything that was for sale, and, for a while, their every penny had been mortgaged, paying off the debt on the purchased land. They had turned the corner three years ago, and now, money seemed to be everywhere. She had finally persuaded Deighton to get rid of the locks, convincing him that the people he wanted to court did not understand what those long, hanging rolls of hair meant. She had pleaded with him for years, and finally, for her fiftieth birthday, he had cut them as a gift. Her heart had lifted the moment he had walked into the bedroom. It had been late, and she had already been in bed, a kind of low-grade anger burning in her soul because he had forgotten her birthday. When he had walked in with the single flower and the long, dark bottle of champagne, she had been first surprised, then elated. They had not touched the champagne that night.

Why had the last year been so good? She had told herself that, without the money worries, Deighton was more attentive. But in her heart, she knew that was not the case. She had changed. What had shifted inside her, making her more accepting of her life, a life she had fought against for so long? True, her children had both gotten out of university in the last two years, and that had been a relief. They both now worked in the development company and had recently bought their own townhouse, sharing space and just about everything else, it seemed.

Still, she knew it was not that either. It was something more internal, as if she had finally found peace, not because of action taken, but just as a process of acceptance of things as they are. She was different from the others in many respects, not the least of which was her staying at home to build her family. She had not worked since her marriage and had quickly discovered that those things her friends complained about, she did not mind. It was not that she liked the monotony of domestic work, but as long as she could play in her gardens, it all seemed worthwhile. Her friends were so busy that they often appeared to have forgotten who they were, chasing something they had not defined and would not be able to recognize if it were found. She did not want their success, that world of frantic meetings and hurried meals. Even Anis, in spite of her artistic temperament, had become caught up in this chase. She still had the same insouciant voice, but now her success as an artist was important. She no longer painted for herself but for the money that seemed to be flowing in in ever-increasing amounts. She knew Anis hated her work, was forever criticizing it, but she could not stop turning out the very thing she hated.

For years, she had worried that her friends had overshadowed her, but as she looked around at them, she wondered. Marjorie had lost her husband to her work. She was certainly rich, but what did it mean? She was still raw and hurting from John's walking out. Of course, Marjorie would tell anyone that John's eyes and much else had strayed, but the truth was that she had had no time for him, whatever she might say now. Anis had never married and now lived in that frenzied world of beds and beaches, boasting about a pleasure that Maylene was sure she did not feel. She had seen her eyes and felt sure there was no hunger there, only a tired kind of sadness at her hopeless search. Sandra was an enigma, even to the girls who had known her for so long. She was distant, yet friendly, even loving. She occasionally had a man around, but her eyes never seemed to embrace him. It was not that she was like Anis, using them as playthings, but, if indeed she used them, they were so obviously dispensable. And then there was Estelle, who had given her heart once at eleven years old and had never had the strength to take it back.

No. She did not envy them anymore. Their freedom had collapsed rather quickly, and she knew they were rapidly becoming what they had despised in so many other women. They clustered around each other, hanging on for support like drowning swimmers clinging to the closest thing they could find. She did not envy them anymore. Once, they had seemed like birds soaring beyond the reach of men. She no longer thought that. When Deighton had come home a year ago with his locks shorn, and he had given her the gift of himself, she had fallen in love all over again, and that act of sacrifice had kept her in a place of golden sunlight. Until now. In the last week, the fears had returned. When Sandra had talked of the chaos that lay behind the appearance of order, she had been frightened, for she had seen that disorder, and it lay in the killings. Deighton's gift had fallen in a place of shadow, and he had been missing again, though still home. Mark St. Auburn's name had started a strand of memory, and Deighton had reacted to the strand. Maylene sighed, turning on the lounge chair. The sun had changed positions in the sky, and now the rays were on her feet. She pulled up her legs, bringing her feet into the shade again.

"Do you love him?"

She still remembered the tone in Deighton's voice that evening thirty-two years ago, with its poisonous combination of hurt, anger, and hope. She had tried to touch him, but he had pulled back as if afraid to be contaminated. They had been married three years, and she had then been twenty. Mark had come back from America, a cold swagger in his walk and a powerful confidence in his voice. He had spoken a strange language, one that she had not heard before, a language of anger that was righteous and a love of his skin that infected her soul. He had the smell of new books about him, and she had thrilled to that scent of newness and fire and constrained anger. His accent had shifted, and he spoke with the pungent lyricism of the black American, suggesting hipness and awareness. He had told her stories of a world she had not understood, had not thought to explore, and when he spoke of vengeance for past ills, her heart had thrilled, for in his words, the frustration of her soul had found release.

Maylene opened her eyes, looking searchingly at the barren emptiness of the landscape. Every time Marjorie spoke of her "moors," she almost laughed because they had called this land the same thing. Except then, it had been theirs—empty of life, yet so full of possibilities. She had fought to find time to see him, nervous of discovery or betrayal, yet drawn like a moth to his flame. It had not been the sex—though she had given herself to that with an abandon that surprised her—but this other thing that lay in her mind. He had not seemed the young boy she remembered from a short three years before, but something bigger, more real and unreachable. She had felt that he had reached down for her, drawing her up to some glorious land that he inhabited alone. So she played Jane to his Heathcliff, and little did she understand how true that image would be.

When he had taken her there that first evening as the last rays of the sun had stretched from the horizon, she had fallen in love with something. It had never been clear, was not clear even today, that it had been him. But some association of the dying light and the hard flame in her had illuminated him, creating a thing bigger than he was. It was a thing that stood above her, looking intently at the dying light and growing greyness of the surging sea, aware of her, yet somehow remote, impervious to her suggestions. She had sat, her legs tucked under her flaring skirt, fully aware of the pain in her breasts and the slight pounding behind them, and she had seen that he knew too. As the sun died, the cool silence had come, and she wondered why, in the darkness, she was not afraid of this man she had known but did not know. She had watched him merge into the night, a shadow, insubstantial yet evocative, throwing small stones carelessly into the sea. That image would stay with her forever, this man, lost in shadow, flinging the land into the sea. In their short affair, much had happened, but somehow this image was insulated from the pain and shame that was to come. He had kissed her that night, without any other touch. And she had known it was wrong, but few things in her life had felt so right. Like an angel, he had kissed her, cool, remote, with the distant fire burning deep inside him, and her imagination had nursed that fire, building it inside her as if she were a hearth on which this ember lay.

They had been bound to be discovered. Her frequent absences from home could not be intelligently explained, and in her ears the excuses sounded empty, transparent. Deighton had looked at her strangely, his eyes aglow with a suspicion he could not voice.

In the end, she had betrayed herself. After a few months, Mark had found Estelle yet again, and he had begun to neglect Maylene. She had fought back, all the while recognizing the absurdity of her position. She was married and had no intention of giving up her marriage. She was comfortable, and, if it lacked fire and shadow, it was substantial and real. It lived in the midday sun, unlike Mark who only seemed to be real when in shadow.

The sunlight had found her feet again, and she drew her legs up so that she was now laying in an almost fetal position. It had not felt like infidelity. It had not felt wrong. There was an innocence to him, to the meetings that seemed devoid of guilt. So she had taken more risks because they had not felt like risks. His relationship with Estelle should not have mattered, just as her marriage did not, but Estelle had come with tears and fear and an all-consuming need for proof of something. Estelle's child had lanced through her like a permanent pain, a statement of her anger at so much and so many. Maylene knew that Estelle's anger had backfired. Whom had she wanted to hurt anyway? She was sure that Estelle could not have said, but it was evident she had hurt only herself. When the girls had begun to worry about her sanity, they had encouraged her to see a psychiatrist, a friend of Marjorie's, but Estelle had become more bitter and spiteful, spurning the friendship of the women, yet desperate to be recognized by them.

Heather, her daughter, had suffered during this time, for Estelle had been a reluctant mother. They had all pitched in to nurture the child, and even today, Heather was more affectionate with the girls, particularly Anis and Marjorie, than she was with her mother, whom she watched like a lost fawn, hope now gone, but still wondering.

It had been Marjorie's idea to bring Mark to the beach house where they gathered on Saturdays. Maylene remembered how she had been a bundle of nerves, not sure of how to act with him in the presence of the others. It had been dusk when he had arrived, striding in that loose-limbed way that he had practiced as a boy. It was as if the wind had come in with him, and, for a while, she could not hear what was being said. He had been so cool, so reserved, almost invisible, a voice with laughter and a foreign lilt that had caused the others to titter and exchange amused glances. Then, the baby had started bawling and, uninvited, he has walked off into the darkened passageway.

In some ways, he had never returned, and she had betrayed herself. She had begun to write him letters, pouring out her need to him, but he had been, as he always was, remote, almost invisible. She still could not explain why she had left one of her unmailed letters in her jewelry drawer. Was it that she had wanted to be caught, wanted to resolve her conflict, in this one act of careless aggression? What could she have hoped would be resolved? Certainly not Mark's feelings. He was like a hummingbird, all unconscious motion and feeding. Did she perhaps think it would force a confrontation with Deighton and thus force her to choose? She had never had any doubt as to what that choice would be. Loving Mark was like loving a cloud—it would always change. He had substance, but it was the substance of tar. An imprint would last for a while, but, slowly, it would disappear, returning to its original, unperturbed state, showing no signs that it had been disturbed.

Deighton had found the letter with her infantile outpouring. How does one answer a question that seeks not merely information but reassurance? She had seen his eyes, shaded red in anger, and the flaring nostrils that showed the beginnings of panic, but the worst part had been the voice. The voice had striven for command, had been too loud for the question, as if it had been surprised in mid-flight and had veered away from its purpose. What do you answer when asked with such hope and fear?

"No. I don't love him."

It had been as if this had released Deighton from his thrall, and she had watched with a kind of abstracted curiosity as the anger overtook the fear. The confirmation of his hope had destroyed his fear, and in that rearranged landscape, his anger had flowed out like a dam that had burst. His hands had spasmed into fists, and his face had lost its humanity, becoming the expression of a will as old as man himself. She had been sure he was going to beat her, and she had been prepared for it, had almost welcomed it as a penance, not for her wrong, but for her stupidity.

Deighton had not hit her, and a little piece of her had gone into the deep, a tiny slice of her mind that wondered if he had not loved her enough to fight. When he had stalked out of the house, she was not sure if she would see him again, and she had fallen to the couch, crying in confusion and not at all sure why her tears had come.

Then, a year ago, he had cut his hair, and some of the lightness had come back into their relationship. Until a week ago. The news that Mark was in St. Euribius and in trouble had brought back that shuttered look, the wild question of thirty-two years ago. Deighton had begun to come home later, and when he was home, the Rastas were there, the smell of their herb like a shield against her will. Secrets. Would they never leave this island?

"What you ovah dere mumbling 'bout? You playing wid yuhself or just goin' mad?" Marjorie's voice was playful with an undertone of malice, and Maylene turned over, facing her friends.

"Oh, my God! You are crying? Wha' happen?"

Instantly, Marjorie's voice had changed, becoming gentle, soft like a wooddove's breast. Maylene rubbed her eyes, surprised.

"Oh, nothin'. I did just t'inking, tha's all."

"'Bout what, darling? Wha you t'inking 'bout dat would mek you cry?"

Marjorie sat on a chair next to Maylene, who looked at her bulbous face, thinking that Marjorie was such a good person despite her mouth, which seemed not to have a "governor." No restraint at all. Yet Marjorie was always the first to feel what they each felt from time to time.

"The past. I did t'inking 'bout the past."

The other woman looked at her closely and slowly said, "It seem like a lot of people doing that these days."

Maylene nodded, looking over to where Anis and Sandra lay, apparently asleep, and asked, "You hear from Estelle?"

"No. She must be still recovering from going to see she mother last week."

They both laughed, the sound immediately snatched by the breeze that blew constantly on this side of the island, but in their laughter a faint note of darkness hung like a scythe over defenseless grass.

CHAPTER FOURTEEN

Estelle was, at that moment, approaching an old shed-roof house that was located on the edge of the village. She noticed the three Rastas who sat in quiet observance as she approached. One was eating a mango and another was whittling a piece of wood, and from the way he sliced into the wood, she could tell it was an act of purposeless creativity. The third leaned against the tree, pulling at the scraggly beard that looked tangled from where she was. Estelle was sorry she had not asked Anis to come with her. Anis was much more comfortable in the village than she was.

The houses stood in haphazard order all around her. The village was built around the road, and on each side stood the small homes, a few now gaily painted in preparation for Christmas. Once upon a time, the whole village would have been painted. Made of wood the termites seemed to take particular pleasure in boring into, these fragile homes were preserved by the paint. Christmas was the traditional excuse for doing what was necessary, and when she had been a child, she remembered driving through the village and seeing the men on their wooden ladders making the village beautiful for the birthday of the Christ. The children had dragged the marl from her father's gully, and the residue of the limestone he sold spread a gritty, white carpet along the pathways. There had been few Christmas lights in the village then because so few of the homes had electricity. Now, all of them had electricity, but the bright, blinking lights that had replaced the multi-colored strips of twisted paper that had then been the Christmas decoration adorning the homes seemed shabby and predictable by comparison. Many of the houses looked as if they were giving birth to some foreign species, as chattel houses were being gradually–"as the money afforded itself," as the old people said—transformed from wood to concrete. *The sign of social arrival,* she thought. *The acquisition of a "wall" house.*

"Can I help you?"

The voice jolted Estelle out of her daydream. The Rasta who had been reclining against the tree had straightened up, a machete hanging like an extension of his arm. She felt a slight tremor run along her back, and she wondered, *when did I become afraid of these boys? Why am I afraid?*

As if he had divined her thoughts, the tall, gangly boy put down the cutlass and watched her compose herself.

"I am looking for Mrs.Greaves. Clotelle Greaves."

He pointed down an alley between two freshly painted homes.

"She live in de back. When you get dere, just go in. She can't get up. At least, she don't like to, so when people come by, dey just go inside. She does left de door open."

"Thank you," Estelle said, looking worriedly at the little alley between the houses.

Chastising herself, she turned into the alley, her ankles twisting over the uneven, rocky ground. Once she was past the row of houses that fronted the main thoroughfare through the village, the order disappeared, and small, unpainted houses seemed to be everywhere. There was no one about, and, for a moment, Estelle just stood, confused at the sudden collapse in the arrangement of the village. The haphazard nature of the layout stumped her, and she realized she had assumed only one house would have been back there. She looked around in perplexity, trying to decide, almost to intuit, which house to approach.

It was the open door that caught her eye, and she walked uncertainly to it. The house was made up of two rectangular spaces topped by a triangular roof. It had not been painted for a while, and the flakes of dried paint stood off from the spottily rotted wood as if to deny its acquaintance. One room, the bedroom, she guessed, had glass windows. They had been carelessly installed, and Estelle could see the flecks of paint from some long-ago attempt at beautification and protection of the wood. The putty that had been used to hold the glass in place had dried, and, breaking into cracks, had, in places, fallen away, leaving the impression of missing teeth. The rest of the house had wooden windows.

Estelle knocked timidly on the open door, calling softly, "Mrs. Greaves?"

Inside, she heard something that sounded like a response, and, emboldened by the voice and the Rasta's instructions, she walked in. The front rectangle had been divided into two parts: the bedroom she had seen as she had approached and a tiny sitting room. The second rectangle was what looked like a combined kitchen and dining room. The old woman — at least she seemed old to Estelle — was reclining in a chair that looked like a hammock. Estelle could see it had been cleverly constructed of mahogany, with a canvas seat that stretched from the top, which was just above her head, to some twelve inches beyond her slippered feet.

"Come in. Come in. Siddown over dere whe' I kin see yuh. It does hurt w'en I haf to turn 'round."

Estelle walked gingerly across the springy floor and sat in another mahogany chair with an intricate design of laced cane.

Nobody makes these anymore, Estelle thought. *This chair must be at least fifty years old.*

The old woman allowed Estelle to settle herself, and then, laying her hands across her protruding stomach, she asked gently, "Wha can I do fuh you, miss?"

It was a better question than the old woman knew.

"Do you know me, Mrs. Greaves?"

"Yuh voice seem familiar, but I can't see too good nuh more."

"It is Estelle. Mr. Prescod's daughter."

"I know dat I did know de voice. Yuh sound just like you muddah."

Before she could control herself, Estelle asked, surprised, "I do?"

"Yeah. Nuhbody never tell you so before? But den, they ain't too many 'bout here who did know she before she married you fadduh."

"You knew her before?"

"Yes. All two uh we come from up in de north."

Estelle wanted to ask more, but she knew that was not the reason she had come, and that any attempt at intimacy made her task that much more difficult. She was about to speak when the old woman straightened, her fragile body looking brittle with its sudden tension.

"Wait a minute. You is Estelle. You is de one dat marrid de boy who kill my son, right?"

In spite of her preparation for this moment, the question slid beneath her defenses, creating a feeling of sympathy for the old woman and anger at Mark for having placed her in this position.

"I am. That is why I.... come by to see how you is." The dialect sounded false and obvious in her ears. "I sorry dat I dint come by before, but I was...."

Estelle caught herself, realizing that, if she finished that sentence, the old woman would have no reason to talk to her. How do you become too busy to provide aid to a grieving, dying soul?

"Out of the country," she lied, hoping that no one who spoke to the old woman would contradict her.

"Who had de party at you house las' Saturday night?"

The voice was stiff, aggrieved, and contained what Estelle imagined was a sneer. Desperately, Estelle plunged on.

"I plan it before. Dey call me back to Barbados where I does work. I dint want to cancel it."

The old woman's body relaxed a little, and she asked, "So what you want wid me now?"

Estelle hesitated, then answered, "I only want to see if I can do anyt'ing fuh you. If you want me to buy somet'ing or whatever. I not so sure myself, Mrs. Greaves."

Estelle was near to tears, and she sat wringing her hands and crossing and uncrossing her ankles. The old woman's mouth, already twisted by some internal pain, tightened, and Estelle held her breath. Even as she waited for the response, though, Estelle could not help noticing the glossy shine on the woman's face, like a plastic mask placed there to disguise her true features. *She must have been very pretty once,* Estelle thought, feeling the revulsion rise in her throat at the thought of the cancer that was devouring this woman's womb. Estelle looked surreptitiously at the bulging stomach, searching inside herself for some feeling of connection to that womb, but whatever maternal similarity had existed between them was gone. She could not help but see those voracious expanding cells.

"Look, Miss T'ing. I don't know wha you want wid me, but whatever it is, don't look fuh it here. Dat wutless man uh yours gone an kill my son, my onliest chile, and he goin' swing for it."

The voice carried the finality of an avenging angel, and Estelle wanted to protest that "the wutless man uh yours" did not apply, had not applied for over twenty years. Instead, she said nothing, held silent by the tears that had sprung from the woman's eyes.

"I so sorry, Mrs. Greaves. If dey did somet'ing I could do to bring he back, I would do it. I so sorry."

Estelle's voice caught on the last word, and suddenly something broke in her, and she began to sob, her face in her hands. The sobbing went beyond the old woman's sorrow, Estelle knew. Somewhere inside her, something was giving way before the old woman's hurt, which had joined hers, making it more poignant. Her chest was full, her breathing came in gasps, and an acidic sensation made her nostrils burn. A thousand images flitted through her head, and Mark and Mrs. Greaves, Heather and this woman's son became all mixed up, piling one emotion on top of another until she felt sheared, like a rotten branch in a high wind. The woman in front of her cried for her son, but when the images began to make sense to her, she was surprised to find Heather's face with its big, inquisitive eyes staring back at her. Something in the forlornness of those eyes stabbed at her heart, and she sobbed even harder, feeling a cold hand cup her heart and begin to squeeze. She felt as if she were dying and, later, would swear she would have if a voice had not plunged into her mind.

"Do stop the bawling, dear. For once, show some restraint."

She looked around and into her mother's face. At seventy-six, Gweneth Prescod still walked with her back straight as a post, giving the impression of rejecting any suggestion from the world that she ought to bend to anything. She wore a flowered dress, belted at the waist by a brown, ornately embroidered belt and a broad-brimmed felt hat. The tan-colored gloves both irritated and embarrassed Estelle. Why did a black woman have to protect her hands from the sun? Involuntarily, she had stood when her mother entered the room, and Gweneth Prescod took the seat, accepting it as her due. Estelle now noticed that Nello had accompanied her mother and carried a small lunch basket made of bamboo.

"Well, Clotelle, how are you feeling today?"

"So-so, Gwen. De pain killers workin' de magic. How you?"

"I got up this morning, so it is a good day."

As Nello laid out the food of mashed white potatoes, mashed yams, and what smelled like flying fish but looked like a paste, Estelle watched in astonishment as her mother gently ran a cloth over the sick woman's face, removing the shine. The intimacy surprised her, and the fact that the dying woman had called her mother by her first name was even more surprising. Gweneth Prescod did not encourage familiarity. Not for the first time, Estelle felt as if she were seeing the world through a shimmering mist in which the real and unreal merged, dancing like sprites that were indefinably threatening. Estelle had stepped back from the intimate circle created by the three old women and watched the feeding like a spectator, her back pressed hard against the wooden partition.

The dying woman, it seemed, had used up her energy with her emotional outburst at Estelle and ate very little, her eyelids drooping as they tried to feed her. Her body slid further and further down the canvas chair until it was impossible to get anything down her throat. Then, Estelle's mother looked over her shoulder, asking irritably, "Are you going to help us or just stand there?"

Estelle rushed forward, not sure what was demanded of her but willing to do anything to still that voice. They got the old woman into a rickety bed, and after seeing that she was comfortable, Estelle's mother turned to go.

"Nello, you had better stay here until she is feeling better. You, Estelle, come with me."

Estelle followed her out, crossing the small grassy area to the dark alley. Once on the road, Estelle looked for the Rastas, but they were gone. Still, she knew her comfort came not simply from that, but the fact that her mother stood with her in the road.

"What did you say to upset her?"

"I didn't say anything, Mother. I just wanted to help."

"Well, I see you were as effective as you usually are."

The anger came like a north wind, cold, slicing like a saber into her mind.

"Can't you, for once, say something good about me? I didn't do a damned thing, I tell you."

Her mother stiffened at the swear word, the square shoulders seeming to snap back. When she spoke her voice was low but pregnant with fury.

"Don't you speak to me in that tone of voice. I will say something good when I see it. Until then, I will speak the truth."

"Whose truth, Mother? Yours? I am good, Mother. Much better than you give me credit for."

Gweneth Prescod walked toward the car where her chauffeur was waiting with the door half-opened. The old woman stepped in, not looking back at her daughter, who stood, the tears bundled in her eyes. As the car reached the end of the road and disappeared to the right, Estelle said with quiet insistence, "I am."

CHAPTER FIFTEEN

Aurelius St. John leaned back in the leather swivel chair, his thumb and forefinger pressed into his tired eyes. When he took the pressure off, the little motes of darkness danced for a while. The Saturday afternoon sunlight lay like a translucent cowl upon the earth. He could hear the voices of his two children playing outside, and, for a while, he hung on to that, wishing for the realism of this house, his children, and that seductive sun to give him his bearings in a world he did not understand. Aurelius looked at the papers on his desk and shook his head in amazement, for the man who had emerged from those pages was not someone he knew. It was certainly not the gently ironic boy who had left St. Euribius for America thirty-six years ago. Why had he gone into the United States military? Why the secrecy about it? Aurelius could get no answers from Mark, who seemed stuck in a moment in time, or rather a block of time somewhere between 1967 and some undetermined time in the 1970s. He was aware that he had killed the guard, but he did not seem to think of it as something that had happened recently, instead merging that with his stories about Vietnam.

Aurelius picked up a sheet of paper and re-read it. When he replaced it, a look of wonder was in his eyes. Mark was a highly decorated soldier, had won two Bronze Stars, a Purple Heart, and the Medal of Honor. Why had no one heard of this? The commendations read like something from a John Wayne film, and were it not for the official nature of the documents, Aurelius would have dismissed them as something made up. Where was the preparation for this violence? Where in Mark's soul could there have been the undercurrent for this reckless bravery? He thought of an evening when they had stood on the rocks near the village where Mark lived, waiting for the "skeets" to swim by. Every evening, this family of manta rays could be seen moving like a black stain in the water, their fluid, flapping motions disguising the vicious, slashing power of their rapier-like tails. He remembered one evening shaking with fear as Mark had dared him to jump into the middle of them as they swam by. He had wanted to, but his muscles had not cooperated, and he had watched in shame as Mark had jumped in their midst. The water had boiled with those swishing, deadly tails, but Mark had climbed back onto the rocks, laughing and untouched. Is that where his bravery came from? This sense of having the luck to escape danger? Still, he knew Mark was not always brave, for he had talked of the fear of the night and the wind that walked like a shadow when the lights were out. He had asked the prison guards to keep his light on at night, but they had refused, and he had pulled the thin sheet off the bed and leaned the mattress against the wall, leaving a space for himself. He had slept on the sheet placed on the bare concrete. When he had been told of this, Aurelius had called the commissioner of police, who was also a high school friend, and had gotten Mark his light.

He was insane, of course, and that would have to be his plea, but Aurelius wondered about this country's reaction to a plea of insanity based on something they had never heard of: post-traumatic stress syndrome. In many respects, St. Euribians were a very simple people, seeing the world in stark, almost Mosaic terms. An eye for an eye made perfect sense to them. As he had driven around the country last week, it was as if there had been only one murder: that of the guard. After the initial furor about the two killings, the country had practically dismissed the boy's, their anger somehow transmitted to the second, Mark's killing of the guard. It was almost as if they had accepted that the boy somehow deserved it because he was trespassing, and in any case, his death had already been avenged. Yet, ironically, none of the goodness of that vengeance, such as it was, seemed to be transmitted to Mark, and many in the country had concentrated their anger on him.

Deighton Cox had not. The man had been everywhere in the last week making a case for Mark's innocence. He was provocative and confrontational, and people were reacting to him with nods and a chorus of "dat is true, man." The air was being tainted, and although Aurelius should have been happy since Deighton was, in a sense, on his side, the undercurrent of violence worried him. The country was being split along a fault line of which Mark was the center. Whatever the outcome of the trial, that did not augur well.

He had spoken to the prime minister, and it was evident that the Americans were applying a considerable amount of pressure to effect the extradition. Aurelius looked at the papers again. So much was missing from those pages. There was a good deal of detail from the years 1968 to 1970, the years when Mark had been in the marines. He knew Mark had returned to St. Euribius in 1970 and had gotten married to Estelle sometime in 1971. He had left again in 1973. As far as he could tell, no one in the island had had any contact with him since then. According to the file, Mark had gone back into the marines, but there was little about what he had done after that. He had been posted around Duc Pho, had had his share of battles, but seemed to have gotten into trouble with his superiors as well. After South Vietnam had fallen to the Communists, he had disappeared. At least, the file seemed to have nothing on his whereabouts until 1999 when he had re-surfaced to commit the murder for which the United States was now insisting on his extradition.

How could a man disappear for twenty-four years like that? Aurelius wondered. Mark was no help. He seemed to have no interest in talking about the murder in the United States, and Aurelius' calls to New York gave him nothing. Mark had no bank accounts, no home address, no debts, no driver's license, nothing that normally attached a person to society. To all intents and purposes, he was dead or, at least, he was invisible, and Aurelius knew in this age of giant computer databases that was a feat almost impossible to accomplish.

More perplexing was that Mark was not poor. When Aurelius had broached the subject of the cost of his defense, he had been told to talk to Estelle, that she had been given Mark's money. He had not called Estelle yet, but he had no reason to doubt Mark.

Curiouser and curiouser, Aurelius thought. He needed to have a psychiatric evaluation of his client if insanity was going to be the defense, and he could not see what else would be. He made a note to arrange that on Monday. Also, he had to check on the autopsy results from the coroner's office. He was just about to jot another note down when the phone rang.

"Hello. Aurelius St. John here," he said, a little irritated at the interruption.

The irritation disappeared when he heard the voice. It was Sandra Mahoney.

"Hi, Sandra. To what do I owe the pleasure? You girls decide to give us a chance again?"

"You fellows always had a chance. You just never seem to know what to do with it. Actually, I am calling about something that affects your client."

"Which one? Mark?"

"Yes. The man himself just called. I am going to be the judge."

"The P.M. called you about this? That's damned unorthodox. What's he got to do with it?"

Even as he asked the question, though, he knew he was simply going through a formality. Sandra understood how things worked in St. Euribius.

"Beats me, Aurelius. He called about ten minutes ago and told me the chief judge will be assigning the case to me."

He sensed that something was not being said, so he said, "Thanks for letting me know. Are you asking me if I see a conflict here? Actually, I don't. We all know Mark. Except for the really young judges, everyone knows or knows about him. You were never any closer to him than the rest of us, right?"

"No. Not really. In fact, the rest of you were actually closer to him than I was when we were in school."

He sensed the hesitation again, so he asked, "Something bothering you, Sandra?"

"Well, yes. I am a little concerned that the P.M. made this call. I know we are all friends, but it smacks of interference. It was also something he said."

"What's that?"

"He said he knew I would do the right thing."

"And you will. Everyone respects your professionalism."

She was quiet for a moment, then said, "Thanks, Aurelius. Maybe I'm too sensitive. This thing with Mark has everybody a little off-balance."

"Tell me about it. I was preparing for the case when you called. I guess we can't discuss it now that you are going to be the judge, but he's had one hell of a life, and none of us knew anything about it."

"Yes. We had better not go too far down that road. I will probably have the hearing on Wednesday next week. Anyway, good luck."

"Thanks for the heads up, Sandra. Enjoy the rest of the day."

Aurelius slowly put the phone down, his face frowning. He was much more disturbed than he had let on. The prime minister had no right to call a sitting judge on a case. Worse, he had called Sandra before he had called him. It was not clear what Anderson St. Clair was playing at, but Aurelius knew he had better find out. Shoving the papers into an orderly pile, he dialed the number at the prime minister's residence. Martin, the butler, answered the phone.

"Hi, Martin. This is Aurelius St. John. Is the man around?"

"Ah, Mr. St. John. The Prime Minister is at home, but he is in a meeting at the moment."

"Anything important or something I can break into?"

"Mr. Van Stiles came by. Shall I say that you are on the phone, sir?"

Aurelius thought for a moment, then said, "No. Would you be good enough to have him give me a call later? I'll be in the office upstairs, so have him use that number rather than the house number."

"Very good, sir, and have a good day."

Aurelius hung up with a vaguely uncomfortable feeling that things were going on around him about which he knew very little.

Looking out the large bay window, he could see the house of his neighbor, and he smiled. He had bought the property almost twenty years ago, when it was rab land—all "gullies and grasspiece," as his father used to say. Now, it had been turned into a first-rate golf course with multi-million dollar homes on it. Aurelius shook his head, smiling. Below him, on the well-clipped lawn, he could see his two sons, Andy and Llewllyn, running around, chasing each other, and he was surprised at the emotion that sprang up in him. Why had he not had that as a child? The emotion swept over him unbidden, a sudden rush of feeling that tightened his chest and sent the tears into overload.

"Damned fool," he said to himself, squeezing his eyes shut to push the dampness out and thinking how relieved he always felt after these emotional surges that led to a single sob and modest tears. *Would I be better off if I cried more?* he asked himself, but the thought made him smile. He could just see the effect of his breaking down in court, pouring out his heart. A restlessness had come over him, and he picked up the car keys and walked downstairs. Beverley, his wife, was reading and put the book down as he came into the room, looking at him closely.

"I am going down to the jail for a while. You all right, or do you need anything while I am out?"

"I'm good. I may take the children over to my mother's later. Any idea how long you will be gone?"

"Probably a couple of hours. If the P.M. calls on the office phone, have him call me on my cell."

"Okay."

He stood, uncertain of what to do, and she watched him, aware of his discomfort but knowing she could not speak first unless she wanted to destroy the emotion she guessed he was feeling. If she asked a question, she knew he would counter with either another question or give some logical answer, so she waited for him, knowing what was bothering him probably better than he did. When, after a while, he said nothing, but continued standing in the entrance to the sunken den, fidgeting, she asked, too casually, "Have you seen your father lately?"

He turned to look at her, his eyes searching for something in her face.

"That's uncanny. That's exactly who I was thinking about. I should take you to the horse track. We could make a fortune."

They both laughed. Then, he continued.

"I have not spoken to him for almost a month. Maybe I should drop by after I leave the jail. Well, if you think of anything you want, call me."

He turned, and Beverley thought, *Men and their feelings. So strange and yet so manageable.* Aurelius left the house thinking his decision to go and see his father was his idea.

Not for the first time, he marveled at the monstrosities around him. When the golf course had been built, he had instructed them to leave his house off the fairway so, although it wound around him, he could not see it from his home. His house was still isolated, still had the original feel of being in the rab land that he had originally bought.

The course, very popular with the newly monied class and the tourists, provided a solid income. He had a deal with Gweneth Prescod, Estelle's mother, to direct the guests at her hotels to the course, and that also helped to attract a steady flow of players.

Soon, he was on the highway, and around him, the world buzzed. *So many cars now,* he thought, remembering the world in which he had grown up.

Aurelius did not go to the jail. Almost unconsciously, the car headed east, and within half an hour, he was on the long, bumpy approach to Marjorie's house. By the time he parked in the circle of her driveway, she had come out and was standing on the top step of the verandah.

"The man himself," she shouted, her voice booming like the ocean which sent its reciprocal message back to her.

Aurelius laughed and hugged her, kissing her on the cheek.

"Boy, don't start nuttin' you can't finish. I liable to kill yuh. You want uh drink?"

"Absolutely," he replied, sitting down heavily on a leather reclining chair.

As the butler fixed his drink, Aurelius sat in silence, watching the heavy motion of the sea, its blue-gray surface like the smile of a fiend.

"What's with the tracksuit?" he asked.

"Oh, this? Those skinny-ass women in town getting on my nerves, dat's all. I goin' lose some weight. De girls did over here dis mornin' walking wid me. You like?"

Marjorie turned, showing off her full figure and the tracksuit.

"I like very much. What about diet?"

"Dey got me eating so much damned rabbit food, I feel like my top front teeth getting longer."

Aurelius laughed as Marjorie imitated a rabbit's munching, tiny chopping actions.

"You don't make a very good rabbit, Marjorie."

"No, honey. I was always more of a cat," she responded, her eyes suggestive.

Aurelius shook his head. He had heard about John showing up at Estelle's party with some young girl, and he knew Marjorie's exercise and diet routine would last precisely as long as she thought about her ex-husband and the girl. He also knew she needed reassurance now about herself, and he said, "You were always a beautiful cat to me, babe."

She laughed as the butler handed him his drink, and she asked, "Where Beverley and de children?"

"Home. She said she may take them over to her mother's home."

For a moment, the afternoon teetered on the sword point of a possibility, but the moment passed, and Marjorie collapsed into a chair next to him.

"How de case goin'?"

"I don't know. This is very strange. It is hard for me to deal with Mark like this."

"How you mean?"

"Well, I see him now. I know what I know from the records I have, but I still can't get the Mark I knew out of my head. You know, until all this craziness started, I had not seen him since 1968 when I left for England. Soon after, he left for the States. When he was back here in the early seventies, I was still in England. I have not seen him or heard from him in thirty-six years, Marjorie."

The big woman turned to him, her eyes soft but alert.

"He was devastated when you left."

"Mark? He is not the kind to be devastated by anything. Saint One is the most remote person I know."

"You men can be so blind. As a boy, he adored you, Aury."

"What do you mean? He was as popular as I was. He was the one with the fast feet, and everyone loved the boys with the fast feet."

"They loved the cricket boys more, and that's what you were good at, Aury. Everybody loved you. You were friendly to everyone, and people had a certain comfort with you."

"You mean I was not threatening," he replied with a laugh.

"No," she answered in kind. "You tek off mo'e panties dan most boys, so I ain't talking bout dat, but you had the looks and the confidence that he never had. I think that Mark both adored and resented you for that."

For a while he was silent, not fully aware of the breeze that had shifted to the northeast, suggesting that more rain was in store for them. Finally, he said, "It feels like Mark is becoming a different person right in front of me, like he is changing all the time."

"I don't think Mark is changing. You just never looked very closely at him, Aurelius. You know, when he was here for those couple of years in the seventies, we used to talk a lot. He really would open up, and I was surprised at who he was. He talked about you quite a bit."

"About me? Why? What was there to talk about?"

"Mark is very sensitive, Aury. He told me once that the most painful moment in his life was when your father sent for you to come to England. That tore him apart."

"Well, he didn't miss anything. England was hell. I didn't get along with my father, and after the initial excitement of having me there was gone, he quickly discovered he didn't really want to be a father. He was too busy chasing English women."

There was a bitterness in Aurelius' voice that surprised them both, but Marjorie didn't want to be distracted.

"That may be, Aury, but think of his situation. Mark had lived with this horrible ambiguity his whole life. Rejected, or at least not acknowledged, by his father, yet taken in by his father's family, having no affection from him, but being constantly asked by his family to forgive a man who had denied him. And you were part of that, Aury."

"Me? What did I have to do with it?"

"Even as a boy, you did what everyone else did. You ignored the subject, even though it was there like the air, everywhere around you. You pretended, too, that there was no connection, that you were just friends."

"Why are you laying it on me? He did the same thing."

"Yes. He did. But you were older, and you had been claimed by your father. However much you may have found that experience unpleasant or uncomfortable or unfulfilling, you had your father. He always had only the ambiguity."

Trying to lighten the tone of the conversation, Aurelius laughed, saying, "You getting awfully speaky-spokey."

Marjorie did not laugh. She sipped her drink in silence for a moment, then said, "Do you think you can defend him?"

"What do you mean? Can I get him off? I don't know. Murder is a pretty serious offense, Marjorie."

"That's not what I mean, Aury. I mean, can you defend him? Can you argue a case for a man you don't know?"

"Of course. I do it all the time."

"It is not all the time that the man is your brother."

"That does not matter. The law is the law."

"If you really think that, then Mark is in trouble."

Aurelius' tone signaled his irritation.

"Why should he be in trouble?"

"Because I don't think this case is going to be about guilt or innocence. This is going to be as much about you and the rest of us as it will be about him. Except for you, not one of us has gone to see Mark. Why is that? I suppose each one of us could give you a reason if pressed, but I have been wondering over the last week if we are not doing what we have always done. We admired him, liked to be associated with him – at least, once he had become well-known – but we always kept him at a distance. You know, except for Estelle, no one remembers much about him before he became a well-known athlete. Estelle remembers things and used to tell us all these stories about Mark doing this and Mark doing that, but we could never remember. We remember what we want to. Basically, that amounts to the fact that he had fast feet, mistreated Estelle, and screwed everybody. That's it. You, on the other hand, we remember. You we have stories about from the time you were about five. Why is that?"

"First, I don't know that what you are saying is true. You are asserting...."

"Oh, cut the shit. Don't run away with your intellect. I am talking about your feelings here."

Aurelius subsided into the chair, a small node of anger growing in him. Finally, he said, "I had better go. I have to meet Beverley at her mother's."

Marjorie smiled, standing herself and leaning forward to hug him. Her breasts brushed against his chest and again the afternoon shimmered, but he pulled away and walked down the long, fan-shaped steps.

CHAPTER SIXTEEN

Marjorie heard the phone ringing as she watched Aurelius' Toyota bump its way down the road leading to the highway.

Good luck, she thought, a sigh escaping her as she turned to face the butler.

"There is a Mr. Bryan Edwards on the phone, ma'am."

"Who?"

"Mr. Bryan Edwards. He said he was at Mrs. St. Auburn's party last week."

"Oh, yes, I remember him," she said, hurrying into the house.

The English voice on the other end of the line was water after a midday run.

"Good day, Ms. Andrews. How are you?"

"Quite well. And you?"

"The same. I am sorry. I know it is the last minute, but I have been invited to a reception this evening. It's a small affair in the west of the island. I am somewhat intimidated to go alone, so I was wondering if you had some time this evening...."

"Sure. I am not doing anything. Where are you going?"

"Actually," came the embarrassed reply, "I don't know where I am going. The family's name is McCordle."

"Oh, sure. I know them. They live in Lytton's Bay. Do you want me to pick you up?"

"I know this is terribly ungallant, but if you don't mind, I'd prefer that. I still can't find my way around this island."

"You know what they say. St. Euribius is small, but designed to get you lost. What time?"

"I'd say seven would be good enough."

"Seven it is."

"And thank you very much."

She hung up, a faint tingling running along the surface of her skin. She had thought about the tall, graying white man a couple of times during the week but had stored the thought since she was not sure she would see him again. Her watch said it was four-thirty.

Just enough time to get ready, she thought, climbing the spiral staircase to the second floor. Within minutes, her bed was overflowing as she selected, critiqued, and discarded one outfit after another. Finally, she settled on a smoky gray suit with the shoulders cut square and padded. The pants were snug, but the long Edwardian jacket came down to her knees and was so beautifully tailored it disguised most of her stomach. It made her look strong but not overpowering, and this she could pull off given the man's height. She grabbed the clothes and took them to another bedroom, leaving the mess in the first.

When Marjorie stepped out to her car a couple of hours later, she felt ready, protected by an armor of expensive clothes and perfume against the malicious eyes she knew would follow her that night. Bryan Edwards did not live far from her, and as she pulled into the tiny entrance of the guesthouse where he had rented rooms, she saw him standing in the shadows of the steps. He wore a shirt with the collar open, and peeking through, Marjorie could see the gray and black hairs of his chest.

"Good evening. Thanks for being so understanding," he said as he slid into the Mercedes.

He had a bottle of wine in his hand and a single rose, which he gave to her.

"No trouble at all. How come you didn't call Estelle? She would have done it, too."

"Actually, I didn't call her because of the situation with her husband."

"Nobody considers Mark her husband anymore, even though they are still married. He has been gone for a long time."

"What caused the breakup?"

"That's a very good question. There is no one thing anybody can point to, and Estelle never said anything. They did have a big blow up before he left, but I was never sure if that was the cause."

"What was the blow up about?"

"You probably haven't heard, but Mark was an athlete. He was a good one, too. Represented the country and everything. Well, when he came back from America in 1970, he started working out again, preparing for the '72 Olympics. I am not sure of everything that happened, but, apparently, some girl on a visiting team took a liking to him, and Mark being Mark, he responded. Estelle got wind of it and went uninvited to a reception for the teams. It seems Mark had already agreed to take the foreign girl back to her hotel, and, naturally, Estelle objected. There was some kind of fuss between them, and he slapped her in the face. Then, he left her standing there and went off with the girl."

"Wow! This Mark sounds like a real Neanderthal."

Marjorie hesitated, aware that she did not like the thought of this foreigner criticizing Mark.

"Actually," she responded, "he can be, but he is a bit of a contradiction. He can be very kind, too."

"He doesn't sound too kind to me. He sounds like the kind who just takes people for granted. Were the two of you close?"

"Good question. You know, I don't think anybody has ever been very close to Mark, except Estelle. Their relationship is still talked about in our circles."

"Why?"

"It's been going on since 1963. Over forty years. She was eleven when they first met, and it was love at first sight. Mark had a ton of women all through high school, but, in some way, everybody always felt he belonged to Estelle. I know she always felt that she belonged to him."

She could hear the wistful quality in her voice, but she did not care. Estelle and Mark's relationship was tragic, with its pain and missed opportunities, but there was something wonderfully romantic about it, too. She had seen Estelle when the relationship was going well, and it was as if something divine had entered her. Even Mark, with his gently ironic stance on the relationship, was more human when Estelle's influence was on him. She was just thinking that it was her awareness of that cocoon of magic around them that had ruined her interest in Mark when the man next to her said, "You could be of great assistance to me in the research I am doing."

"What exactly are you doing? Estelle said it was sociological."

"Actually, it's more psychiatric than sociological."

"Are you a psychiatrist?"

"A research psychologist. I am at the University of London hospital."

"I thought Estelle said you were at Oxford."

"I also do some work there."

"What exactly are you studying about St. Euribius?"

"Mental health."

Marjorie laughed a big laugh that filled the car.

"You won't find too much uh dat 'bout here. Everybody know dat St. Euribians mad as hell."

The tall man chuckled, saying, "Actually, you are not too far wrong. Do you know that West Indians have a very high incidence of mental illness in the UK?"

"Really? It must be the cold."

She was really thinking that it must be the result of being around white people all the time but, uncharacteristically, did not say it.

"We are not sure of the reason, but we are studying it."

"In St. Euribius?"

"Actually, we are conducting the study in three places: Birmingham, London, and here. St. Euribius is the control group."

"What is a control group?"

"Your incidence of mental illness is not very high in your own country, yet it is extraordinarily high in the UK. We'd like to find out why. That's why I am here."

"I see," Marjorie said, her mind slipping to what Aurelius had said about Mark not being all there and seeming to be stuck in the past.

They were, however, approaching Lytton's Bay, and she concentrated to be sure not to miss the turn-off.

The McCordle's home sat on the graceful arc of Lytton's Bay, and they had illuminated the water with electric lights in the shape of tapers, so there was something slightly pagan about the place. Alex and Brenda McCordle met them at the door, each in turn hugging her. She had met them through Anis, and her eyes darted around to see if her friend was there. She did not see her. A drink materialized in her hands, and she found herself giving Bryan Edwards a short biography of everyone in the room, often in the form of humorous anecdotes. As she talked and drank, she found herself warming to the man who laughed at her jokes and was attentive to her needs. He did not compliment her in obvious ways, but his eyes, which strayed in boyish discomfort to her body from time to time, devoured her, making her feel desirable and sexual. He encouraged her to talk, listening carefully and asking lots of questions, but saying little. Marjorie found this attention flattering, and instinctively she restrained herself, almost pulling in her personality, modulating her voice and adjusting her spirit to his. The party slipped away from them as they sat on the terrace that had been built out over the sea, sipping drinks that appeared magically when needed. The host came over, inviting them to view some new piece of art he had painted. Both of the McCordles were artists, although it was rumored that Brenda McCordle could afford this lifestyle because of what she had gotten after her divorce from her second husband, who still lived in England.

Downstairs, in the display room, the work was laid out. It was clear immediately that Alex had talent, even though his subjects appeared naïve. Brenda strove for complexity, and there was an intellectual density to her work that overwhelmed her art. Marjorie and Bryan Edwards took their time looking at the pieces, particularly after Alex McCordle left them alone. The man guided her eyes, showing her the differences in the quality of the paintings, leading her through the smooth, gently unified brush strokes of the one and the lack of continuity in the other. Marjorie cared little about the paintings, did not like either artist's work, but she found the certainty of Bryan Edward's voice reassuring and his attention to her, bewitching. So it seemed the most natural thing in the world that, when she turned to ask him a question and found his steady, smoldering eyes upon her, she should lean toward him. They kissed, and Marjorie felt something frightening, yet inevitable, rise in her soul. As her heart pounded out its insane tattoo, a voice told her to stop this man, that she was being foolish, but the aridity of her soul cried out for drink, and she drank.

On the way home, she called, giving the servants the night off, so that when she arrived at the house on the moors, it was deserted. She could have pretended, maybe should have pretended, but the slow drip in her spirit was a prelude to a larger deluge that she could not stop. She remembered that she had left one bedroom a mess and took the tall man into another room. Her clothes seemed to disintegrate off her. For a moment, she felt the tremor of fear, and her suspicious eyes searched his face for the laughter that her reason told her must be there. She found none, and, sighing with relief and anticipation, she allowed herself to be taken to the bed.

Somewhere above her was a shimmering light, but the man extinguished it. He was an artist, and his lips, seeking the most hidden recesses of her body, were like brushstrokes that were inexorably creating art. She felt the building of pressure behind her loins as his lips moistened her, making her body light and girlish again. His hands cupped her in forbidden ways, and Marjorie understood that she should feel shame, but her borders had been breached by an army of pagans who neither knew nor cared about her rules. When he moved upward over her, she opened up to him, feeling the sharp discomfort of his entry. He attempted to pull back, sensing her flinch, but she would not let him, luxuriating in the painful stretching of her inner body. When finally he was through her walls, she laughed and cried and called his name, her ungainly body suddenly a magical wisp that tossed him and herself upon the stormy sea. She came with a deep shudder that started midway between her navel and her spine, then pressed itself outward to her pelvis, which was in spasms. She held on to the man who, in silence, ploughed her field, and when finally she felt him grow and harden in her, she let go, gasping at that collapsing feeling of air going out of a balloon. He lay on her, breathing hard, his lips nuzzling her face and shoulder. Marjorie closed her eyes, aware of the tears that were streaming down her cheeks, and she moved her hand away and surreptitiously wiped her face. As she fell asleep, she silenced the cautionary voice that was trying to be heard. She would listen in the morning. For now, she was content to feel young again and loved.

CHAPTER SEVENTEEN

Aurelius stared at the face of the man before him as if he were something alien, incomprehensible. He had come to the jail to see Mark with very bad news and had nerved himself for the anger or despondency he had seen in his clients so often when their hopes were dashed. He looked away, taking in the dreary surroundings of Dathorne Prison. It had been built as a fort in 1818, after a slave rebellion had terrified the slave owners of St. Euribius. It was large, much larger than the population of the country would justify had it been built only for prisoners. It was to have been the slave owners' last stand if the island went up in flames. It was an unusual prison in that respect, but it had some advantages. One of these was the availability of separate quarters that were somewhat more comfortable than the main prison cells. It was here that Mark was housed. They had moved him from the smaller jail on the west coast only the day before, after the commissioner of police had called Aurelius, indicating that groups of Rasta youth had been seen congregating on the beach near the jail. Word had gotten to the station sergeant that they were planning something. No one was sure what, so they had moved Mark to Dathorne.

Aurelius had also filed the motion to have his client psychologically examined the day before. Late that day, a courier had brought a letter to his office, and inside, he had found the reason that had brought him to the prison this morning. The American Embassy had entered a request to the court blocking the psychiatric evaluation. At first, Aurelius had been angry, but then, the anger subsided into perplexity and a growing sense that something was happening that he did not understand. Now, Mark had just told him it did not matter because he intended to plead guilty anyway. So Aurelius looked at him closely, searching for any sign that he was in one of his crazy phases today. But Mark had never seemed more sane since this whole thing had begun. There was no talk of Vietnam or Estelle today. There was a kind of icy awareness of his circumstances, an awareness that seemed tinged with irony.

"Is your evaluation complete, Aury?"

The voice carried a faint hint of laughter.

"You can't plead guilty, Mark. You will hang if you do."

"Is that so bad, Saint Two? 'Death comes to every man, but no man knows his time.' Isn't that what they taught us in school, old boy? Or didn't you believe in all that?"

"This is madness, Mark. I can get you off. An insanity plea stands a very good chance of succeeding. If you plead guilty, then you will hang."

The man in front of him chuckled.

"But you are trying to prove me mad, are you not? Why should I not, therefore, act as if I am? If I were to be found innocent because of insanity, what would they do? Put me in the psychiatric hospital for the rest of my life? What makes you think that is better?"

"Is that it? You are afraid to be locked up, so you would rather die?"

"How disappointing, Saint Two. Don't you find that a little obvious? There are so many kinds of deaths. Do you think me innocent?"

Aurelius noted that Mark's accent had shifted, losing the rich lilt of the American black and assuming a more clipped, vaguely British tone. Still, he had never asked the question about Mark's innocence, neither of Mark nor of himself. Before he could answer, Mark continued.

"It does not matter to you, I know, but don't you, on occasion, wonder why your system places such faith in competition? If you have a contest of ideas, then the better argument wins. Ipso facto, justice prevails. Don't you ever question that? Don't you ever wonder about innocence and guilt?"

"This is not getting us very far, Mark. Sometime when the case is over, we can argue the merits of our judicial system. In the meantime, it is what we have, and one would have to be a fool not to use it."

"Or insane," Mark responded with a chuckle.

They were both silent for a while, and Aurelius looked around the spare, barely furnished rooms. How many times had he been in these places? The very density of the stone walls was oppressive. In this one sense, St. Euribius had not changed. The old fort still protected the society from some vague, undetermined creature that lurked out there, hiding in the shadows cast by sunlight. Mark had had to be placed in this isolated section because of the generalized threat that lay among the inmates. The sense of grievance these people carried like cancer in their souls was even more concentrated in the prison, for the prison shielded the society from the hatreds contained within itself. Long ago, Aurelius had heard stories of the horror of this place, what it did to men, how it seemed to live at night, moving, crawling in the darkness with the screams of dying men and the grunts of bulls climbing cows. Men discovered their tops and their bottoms in this place and were never the same again. Reform after reform had provided some creature comforts, but they could do nothing about the spirit of Dathorne Prison, that spirit which was abroad in the night and now seemed to be floating on the breezes that cooled the island.

"I can't defend you if you insist on this, Mark."

Mark laughed.

"I never asked for your defense of me, Aurelius. I simply accepted your representation."

"You don't want me to defend you?"

Mark was serious for a moment. Then, he ran his forefinger across his chapped lip, replying, "When have you ever defended me, Aurelius?"

"What the hell are you talking about?"

"Defending me. Isn't that what you wanted to talk about?"

"Yes, but not this. I want to talk about your legal defense."

"Let's forget your law. Let's talk about morality. When have you defended me, Aurelius? Do you remember Tomping Gully?"

"Yes. It is up the hill from where you grew up. What about it?"

"Don't you remember what happened there? Do you remember the wild dogs?"

"Yes, but...."

"You encouraged the boys to tie me to a tree and leave me there."

"No, I didn't. And anyway, that was a thousand years ago. What's that to do with now?"

"It's got to do with defending me. For you, it is the past, but it still lives with me."

Mark slowly pulled up his pants leg and shoved the sock down. "Look."

Aurelius could see a scar about three inches in diameter on the man's leg, and a memory hit him. He had urged the boys to tie Mark to a tree, knowing it would frighten him since a pack of wild dogs haunted the gully. They had pulled the long vines from the few remaining fig trees and had lashed him to a green-heart tree. Then, they had run away laughing. It was not until later that evening he had heard that Mark had been bitten by a dog and had been saved by one of the workers in the fields who had heard the dogs and, guessing that they had someone trapped, had rushed into the gully, machete swinging. Aurelius looked at the scar, the day merging with those long-ago memories, and after a while, he turned away, looking at but not seeing the policeman at the end of the corridor who guarded this solitary prisoner. After a while, feeling tired, he said, "Why do the Americans care so much about you?"

"It's a democracy," Mark laughed. "It's supposed to care about its citizens."

"You know what I mean, Mark. They are trying to block your psychiatric evaluation. Why would they do that? You are accused of a murder in the States. It should not matter if you are evaluated here. I can understand the extradition request, but this is beyond reason. It makes no sense."

Mark's eyes became hooded, yet his face smiled more broadly.

"Who understands America? 'Why, man, he doth bestride the world like a colossus.'"

Aurelius recognized the line. They had both studied Julius Caesar in fifth form. He did not want to pursue that line, however, and he asked the question that had been nagging him for a while now.

"Mark, do you want to die?"

Again, Mark's face changed, and Aurelius thought for a moment that he looked unbelievably old. When he answered, his voice was faint, with an edge of pathos.

"Have I ever been alive, Aury?"

Aurelius had no answer, and he looked intently at the man, trying desperately to see some hint of the boy with the flashing feet that had made them laugh and given so much joy, but that boy was hidden behind the hooded eyes and the pathetic voice. The question reminded Aurelius of his conversation with Marjorie, and he now wondered if his life and Mark's were destined to be in conflict. They sat in silence, two men apparently lost in their own memories, and before long, Aurelius stood, hurrying from the place, promising to return the next day.

Outside, he drove hurriedly, as if trying to outrun something that pursued him. "Have I ever been alive, Aury?" The question plunged into his brain, creating cascades of pain that were like little drills, almost blinding him. He pulled off the highway and drove down a dilapidated road to a small beach. He had lost track of where he was, but it didn't matter. He parked, feeling the glint of the mid-morning sun bounce off the water and into his brain, adding to the streaks of pain. Aurelius closed his eyes and leaned back, listening to the slow, gentle swish of the tiny waves as they shoved the small pebbles around.

Marjorie had said that Mark had lived with ambiguity, but so had he. He was as much a bastard as Mark had been, and his father—their father—had ignored him as thoroughly. Why was Mark the victim here? His father had been irresponsible and, occasionally, hateful, not just to Mark, but to him as well. Until the surprise letter that had invited him to come to England, the man's relationship with him had been haphazard, consisting of an occasional letter and an even rarer pound note. He had written letters to his father at his mother's insistence, but there had been no real attachment until he went to England. Even in England, the attachment had been warped. He had spent his first year with his father, but then his mother had come to England as well, and he had gone to live with her in Tottenham. Though his father did not live too far away in Wood Green, he saw him only occasionally. Mark had not missed anything by having to stay in St. Euribius. London had been cold and damp, and the buildings had closed in on him. He had missed the open spaces and the sugarcane fields, the startlingly blue sky and the sea.

He probably would have gone mad had it not been for Beverley. They had both gone to the London School of Economics, and it was there that he had fallen in love for the first time. She had become his refuge from a mother who was too tired from working in the kitchen of a large hotel and a father who was too busy with his social life. Both had left him alone for their own reasons, and it was only the university and Beverley that had given some structure to his life. No, Mark had not missed anything.

Still, even as he thought this, Aurelius was honest enough to know that Mark's situation had been a little different. At least he had been acknowledged. Mark had never been, and that fact shaped attitudes toward him. It was not that Mark was so different from so many of the boys, but somehow he wore his bastardy like a brand of shame. They had never actually been in a class together since he was two years older, but he remembered hearing about the time when all the boys were asked about their parents in class. This was not unusual; in fact, it happened at the beginning of every term. The boys had made fun of Mark because he had lied, saying that his parents were married. He had been teased mercilessly about it, and Aurelius had joined the others.

He twisted uncomfortably in the car and opened his eyes. The headache had abated, and he raised the seat he had reclined. A few children had come to the beach and were splashing water on each other. Using the heels of their hands, they pushed the water with fluid but precise movements, forcing the water to jump forward, a gush of spray that the two boys on the other side ducked from while punching their own water spray back at the smaller boys. He could see that the taller boys, more coordinated and stronger, were winning, and before long, the smaller boys surrendered, running out of the sea and scampering up the rocks to escape the watery assault. His headache gone, Aurelius smiled at the playfulness. He stretched and turned on the engine. He still had to prepare for the case even if Mark wanted to plead guilty. The car jolted its way back to the highway, and he had just swung into the traffic, heading back to town when the phone rang.

"Aurelius St. John," he said absently, his mind on the boys in the water and Mark in school.

"It's Estelle, Aury. You had better come to the house. I think I have a problem."

CHAPTER EIGHTEEN

Marjorie watched carefully as the maid placed the salad on the table set for two. She wanted everything to be perfect. Bryan Edwards had agreed to come by for lunch, and she had come home from the office early to supervise the preparations. Even from where she stood, the beef and broccoli looked terrific. She had given instructions for the preparation of a French sauce and could smell the saliva-inducing aroma from across the room.

She walked out to the verandah, satisfied that everything was in order. Outside, the sun was like molten gold, blinding and making the blue waters sparkle like incandescent creatures of the night. The moors stretched in all directions around her, running up against the next marine terrace that was to the rear of the house. Everywhere, the short, tough-looking, gray sage rose like stunted men peeking out from the ground, curious at the goings-on. Marjorie sat in a chair next to a small table and watched the road. The heat waves shimmered, creating dancing ghosts in the distance. She was not sure what had happened to her, but for the first time since her divorce, she felt alive, expectant, as if the future held something. Bryan Edwards was kind and gentle. He was attentive and curious about everything. He helped her to overcome the one fear she had, and that was of feeling inadequate. He listened when she spoke, and he asked about everything. It was not like with the girls where she imposed her opinions whether the girls wanted them or not. Every one of them was better educated than she, and she was not always sure they were not laughing behind their acceptance of her gentle bullying. In four days, Bryan had pushed all that aside, and she thought, with a little surprise, that she had not spoken to any of them since they had left on Saturday. He had come over every night since Saturday, and she had waited in a kind of tremulous expectation each time. He was experienced at this, and though some part of her wondered at the source of that skill, she pushed it from her mind, content to follow the dictates of her body and the sweet sense of acceptance that he brought. The servants knew he was sleeping over, but she did not care even when they lowered their eyes as she passed.

Her heart leapt as she saw the light glinting off the car as it wound its way down the long connector to the highway. He was right on time, and that thought stayed with her until he had parked and was ascending the steps.

"Good day," he said with an easy formality that somehow seemed to elevate her.

"Hi," she responded, hearing, to her chagrin, a hint of diffidence in her voice.

He bent down and kissed her cheek, and she threw her arms around his neck, hugging him close. He laughed and squeezed her.

"I hope you are hungry," she said, rising and leading him into the house.

"Famished."

They sat quickly and were served. Marjorie whispered to him.

"The staff must think I am crazy. I never take time in the middle of the day. You are ruining me."

"You probably have enough money, anyhow. Why work so hard?"

"I have never not worked hard, Bryan. I don't know how not to. I grew up in the village, just below Estelle's house. You had to drive past it to get to her party. No one in the village had anything, and just about everyone worked either in the fields or the hotels. We all worked, no matter how young you were."

"Did all of the women in your group grow up together?"

"Yes. All except Estelle grew up in the village. Sandra's father had some money, but the rest of us—Anis, Maylene, and me—we all came from laboring stock. Anyway, I am always talking about me. What about you? Did your family have money?"

"Not really. My father worked as a steel executive in Sheffield. We were comfortable, but not particularly well-off. How did Estelle's family get its money?"

"They are actually a pretty interesting family. On her father's side, they trace their family back to slavery. I think Estelle said in 1799 her great-great-great grandfather bought his way out of slavery."

"Fascinating. And they have had wealth since the eighteenth century? That's very unusual for a black family, isn't it?"

"You bet. She is very proud of that fact. They own nearly all the land around here. Now that everyone is building homes, they are making a fortune. They also own hotels and other businesses in town."

"Why does she lecture at the university then? You would think she would be busy enough with all her business affairs."

Marjorie laughed, spearing a piece of lettuce and placing it delicately into her mouth. She was trying to stick to her diet, and even though today was a serious temptation, she was succeeding.

"Estelle ain't got no head for business."

Marjorie caught herself slipping into the dialect and, not ready for that, added, "Most of us think that she took the job in Barbados to get as far away from her mother as possible."

"Really," Bryan Edwards laughed. "They don't quite fancy each other, eh?"

"Oil and water." Marjorie returned the laughter.

"But if Estelle does not take care of the business, who does? Her mother?"

"To some extent, yes. But mostly it is Aurelius St. John who handles things for the family."

"The lawyer?"

"Uh-huh. Do you know him?"

"Yes. We met at Estelle's party."

"Couldn't have been. He was not at the party."

Bryan Edwards tilted his head back, shielding his face and draining the glass. When he put it down, he looked at the bottle.

"That's a good wine. California?"

"Yes. Estelle is trying to convince us that the Americans have culture, too."

They both laughed at this like two conspiratorial children making fun of a terrifying schoolmaster behind his back.

"Do Estelle and St. John have a relationship?"

"No. Aurelius is happily married. Why are you asking so many questions about Estelle anyway?"

"You introduced her, but, apart from that, I am curious about her."

"Why?"

"I know she saw a psychiatrist for a while, and...."

"Wait a minute. How do you know about that?"

Bryan reached out and touched her hand.

"I told you I am studying mental illness in St. Euribius."

"Yes, but how would you get access to Estelle's records? Very few people, even here, know about that episode."

Edwards' face was sympathetic.

"Her name was among a group that I requested information on before I came here. Since I have been using people in England who left St. Euribius in the 1960s as part of the study, my control group is from the same period."

"Does she know?"

"No. None of the people know."

"Well, I hope I am not part of some control group."

"My dear lady, there is only one way I have any desire to control you."

Marjorie giggled, looking into his playfully earnest eyes. She dropped her fork on the salad plate with a tiny, clinking sound and said, "You want to try controlling me now?"

"By all means, madam."

They were both laughing as they headed upstairs.

CHAPTER NINETEEN

Aurelius watched the prime minister's face as the man's portly but powerful hand slammed down on the table.

"He can't do that. If he does that, he hangs."

Aurelius could not quite tell if he was hearing a threat or simply an observation, but he was surprised at the P.M's response.

"You got to stop 'im," he said slowly, his finger pointing at Aurelius.

"Andy, I am speaking to Mark, but when all is said and done, I represent him. If he wants to enter a guilty plea, then he can. I can advise. I can't command."

"He cannot do it. You stop him."

The voice was angry, and the prime minister was pacing about his office. Aurelius looked at him closely, searching for the signs he knew so well that would indicate the man he had called friend for so long was acting. He could see no evidence of it.

"Wha goin' on wid you, man?" he asked, a little worried and also wondering how the prime minister would react when he told him about Estelle.

He had not expected this outburst; in fact, he had not expected much of a reaction at all. He had just meant to bring the prime minister up to date as a courtesy. The man, however, had turned red, his chubby face seeming to balloon up, and had exploded. Now he appeared to be agitated beyond reason.

"What's going on?" Aurelius repeated when there was no answer.

The prime minister stopped and looked at him, his eyes porcine and flecked. He seemed to be trying to decide something. Finally, he said, his voice still raised, "We can't find him guilty. We have to find him innocent and turn him over."

Something turned in Aurelius' stomach, and he sat further back in the chair across from the prime minister's desk, his eyes narrowing.

"Turn him over?" he asked quietly.

"Yes. The Americans have prior jurisdiction. He committed the murder in New York before he killed the fellow here. That gives them prior jurisdiction."

Aurelius sought a way to respond, suddenly aware of his friend's position. They had never observed the niceties of protocol except in public, but now, unbidden, those burdens of social position were slipping into place.

"Has the attorney general agreed to the extradition?" Aurelius asked quietly, and the prime minister looked at him. With a start, Aurelius realized there was fear in his friend's eyes.

"No. No official decision has been made."

Aurelius was aware of the phrasing, so he asked, "But you have decided to honor the Americans' request?"

There was no immediate answer. Then, the prime minister asked, apparently inconsequentially, "Did you read today's paper?"

"No. It's in the car, but I haven't had a chance. Why?"

"Deighton Cox is having an open-air meeting tonight. He is rallying support for Mark's cause."

Aurelius shrugged, uncomprehending.

"Deighton has to be given time to get the message out, Aury. He can persuade people of Mark's innocence. That's what you want, isn't it?"

The question startled him. What did he want? He had not thought about the trial in this personal way, only as a problem to be solved. Tactics, not feelings, solved problems, so he had kept his feelings at bay. Yet, Saturday's conversation with Marjorie and this morning's with Mark had begun to eat at those walls he had placed around his feelings. What *did* he want? There did not seem any possibility that Mark could escape his fate. He had killed, maybe even murdered, two men, at least. Every instinct in him said Mark should be punished for that. Why, then, this hesitation? He could see where Anderson was headed with his reasoning, but it was flawed. More importantly, it was dangerous. Still, if Mark was insane, then he would be found innocent. This attempt at manipulating the justice system worried him, and he said so.

"There are practical considerations here, Aury. An innocent verdict in this atmosphere threatens us all. There is an anger at this killing that

I have not seen before. I was in Mango Valley yesterday at a political rally, and the mood is ugly. You should get off the golf course once in a while and talk to the people, Aury. There is something that's a little frightening out there."

"And the Americans?"

The prime minister looked at him sharply.

"Leave the Americans to me."

Aurelius, however, could not quite see how he could do that. He had had a short stint as the minister for foreign affairs in the nineties, and he had found dealing with the Americans even then to be a source of great discomfort. They carried their power like a drawn sword, and he had become aware of just how impotent a small country was in those corridors of power.

"What are you going to do, Andy?" he asked.

"Not sure yet. If we can get the temperature in the country down, then the best solution seems a quick verdict of Mark's innocence of the guard's murder, then permission to extradite. Not that I will interfere in the judicial process," he added with a significant look at Aurelius.

"You realize Sandra will not brook any interference in her court-room, right? You did have her chosen, didn't you?"

"Her reputation will be a shield. The people like her and trust her judgment. If he is found innocent in her court, there will be fewer voices raised against the judgment."

His voice had become quiet, almost as if he were talking to himself, and Aurelius could almost see the man's brain processing the problem, dividing the issue into assets and liabilities. Anderson St. Clair was a rarity, a brilliant intellect with unerring political instincts and a way with the common man. He was equally comfortable in the dignified air of a ball in London or a rum shop in the island. He had undoubtedly been the most popular politician in the country for almost two decades, and most of the people who voted for him referred to him as the "village P.M." in spite of the fact that he was the third of his family to be in the House of Parliament. He had grown up comfortably but had early established his relationships among the poor. Those who knew him said he learned that comfort as a boy in the cane fields with an unending variety of women who worked for his father. Whatever it was, he had been admired for his ability to mix with all classes, particularly among the poor, who were acutely aware of their historical isolation from the privileged. As a result, he had been returned to the House of Parliament with increasing majorities for almost twenty years.

In the last week and a half, though, something had soured, and the incipient anger that lay in the bellies of the poor which had always been deflected from him on to less skillful politicians had expanded to include him. Accustomed to being lionized, Anderson St. Clair was showing uncertainty now.

The Americans obviously complicated the matter since they were clearly exerting an enormous amount of pressure both to silence and to extradite Mark. What could have caused this interest in one of their own war heroes who had obviously gone bad? As if the man had read his mind, the P.M. said, "Mark's really gone, isn't he? I heard about what happened with Estelle. Why would he do that?"

"I haven't spoken to him yet, but we don't know that the twenty million is not his money."

"Come on, Aury. Where would Mark get twenty million dollars?"

Aurelius shrugged, having no answer. When he had arrived at Estelle's home, he had been surprised to see two police cars and a transport jeep in her driveway, and he had rushed out of the car, fearful something had happened to her. Inside, she had been sitting quietly on a sofa, waiting for him to come. The five policemen stood, uncomfortable in the elegant sitting room, talking desultorily to each other.

"What's going on?" Aurelius had demanded, and she had looked at him, fear in her face.

"They say I have stolen twenty million dollars."

Aurelius had almost laughed, but her face had stopped him, and turning to the sergeant, he raised his eyebrows.

"We have not accused her of theft, sir, but there are certain improprieties which we are investigating."

"What improprieties?" he had asked sharply.

The man hesitated, and Aurelius said, "I represent Mrs. St. Auburn's interests. Speak up, man."

"There was a large transfer of funds from an account in the Caymans to Mrs. St. Auburn's account at the Canadian Imperial Bank of Commerce in town."

Aurelius shrugged, saying, "So what?"

"Mr. St. John, with all due respect, we are not here to answer your questions. We are here to question Mrs. St. Auburn."

"She is not saying anything until I know what is going on."

"Then we will have to continue this down at the station, sir."

They had placed Estelle under arrest, and he had called Sandra, letting her know what had happened. Bail had quickly been arranged, and

Estelle was home, clearly frightened. Now, the prime minister was jumping to conclusions about the source of the money.

"I haven't had time to check anything yet. I wanted to fill you in. But it doesn't look as if it is Mark's doing, anyway."

"What do you mean?"

"According to the charges, the account in Miami is Estelle's. No one seems certain about the source of the funds. The police are working with Miami to track down where the money was coming from. Of course, Estelle swears she doesn't know anything about a Miami account."

"What do you think?"

"I have been handling her family's affairs for a long time, Andy. If something like this was going on, I would know about it."

"Yes," the prime minister said, looking out the window at the startlingly blue water. Outside, a small sailboat slid across the marine picture framed by the window, and Aurelius thought, in the growing silence, how beautiful this bay was. How many visitors got beyond this beauty? How many saw beyond the smiles on the people's faces? He was not like so many who simply saw the widening gap between the poor and the rich, the "poor man" and the "higher up and better off," as the people said. They had made tremendous progress since independence. One quick drive around the country would show that, and the traditional indices of progress would indicate their success. What those indices did not capture was a certain hopelessness that he now sensed in the poor. It had not always been so. Most of his friends had grown up poor, had fought their way out from the village through their own and the government's efforts. What had changed? He had no retained servants, a decision he had made a long time ago, uncomfortable with the idea of holding a man or woman so close to his service and yet separate from his family. He had watched, with a growing discomfort, his friends assume the privileges they had confronted with such resentment only forty years ago. He thought of Marjorie's house, built out there by itself, isolated and large beyond all reason. *What are we hiding from?* he wondered.

"You say something?"

The prime minister's voice slid into his thoughts, shattering the image of Marjorie's house and bringing the brilliant bay back into focus.

"No. I was just thinking about when we were boys."

The prime minister turned around smiling, a little of the tension going out of his body.

"What were you thinking about?"

Aurelius realized he could not say exactly what he had been think-ing, so he said, "Just how simple things seemed then."

"Yes. Simple. A huge mass of poor, ignorant people who accepted what their masters told them, and tightened their belts to avoid their burning hunger. There was nothing simple about our childhood, Aury. Don't romanticize it."

Aurelius did not answer, his thoughts pushed around by his friend's comments. Finally, he said, "I have to get going. I want to go back and see Estelle, and there is a lot that needs to be done to get an investiga-tion going."

He stood and headed for the door. As his fingers grasped the brass knob, the prime minister said, "Go to the meeting tonight. Deighton Cox is speaking at Wither's Gully."

Aurelius nodded, walking out. As he was walking down the corri-dor, he saw two white men coming into the building. One he recog-nized as Van Stiles, the American ambassador, the other was a tall, graying man he did not know.

CHAPTER TWENTY

Estelle stood on the balcony of her home, looking out to the long, southeastern plain of St. Euribius. Her emotions were alternating between fear, anger, and embarrassment, but it was the last that dominated. Her mother had called, and, though she had said little, listening to Estelle's teary explanations, Estelle could almost hear the condemnation in her silence. She had not called any of her friends, not sure of what to say. She did not know where the money had come from, but the trail it had traveled was suggestive and frightening. Apparently, the St. Euribian police had been watching the movement of the money for a while. No one had said where it originated – it was not clear that they knew – but it had gone through a bank in Panama City, Panama, had worked its way through Managua, Nicaragua, then the Caymans, and finally into her account in St. Euribius. Aurelius had said there was no question that the money was being laundered, and that raised the question as to its origin. Where had the twenty million come from? Was it a payment to someone for something? Panama City and Managua frightened her, although she only had vague ideas about their role in the movement of Columbian drug money. That, however, had been the first thing to come to mind, followed by the scary thought that Mark was involved in that business. Estelle thought of the man she knew, finding it hard to accept the logic of her own reasoning.

Mark hated drugs or any other form of intoxicant. She remembered that, when the other boys had been experimenting with alcohol and cigarettes, he had had too much to drink once and had gotten drunk. It was as if the one experience had been enough, and, without any comment, he had never drunk alcohol again. The same had been true with cigarettes. She had been with him the day he had developed the curiosity about them. They had gone to a small grocery shop, and while she had ordered gum, distracting the shopkeeper, he had stolen a pack of cigarettes from the open stand. They had both run up the hill above the village to smoke. Mark had quickly realized that he had little interest, but, having stolen the pack, it was as if he had felt duty-bound to smoke them. He had finished the box, smoking one cigarette after the other, and getting sick later that day. She knew his mother had beaten him for smoking, but he had never told his mother where he had gotten the cigarettes, as far as Estelle knew, though the threat of repeated punishments had hung over him.

Estelle threw the thought out of her mind angrily. Mark had always been trouble for her, and even now, when she had had nothing to do with him for more than twenty years, he was still a source of pain. She had called the chancellor of the university to let him know she might not be returning for the term beginning in January. The police had taken her passport, forbidding her to leave the island.

"Why would Mark do this to me?" she said out loud, staring down into the small clump of trees below the balcony. Her eye caught a spider's web, in the middle of which a large, grayish-black spider lay. She seemed so calm, so complacent in the bed of the web, that Estelle for a moment envied her. Then, she said, "But she is a woman, too, and probably has her own problems."

Her spirit seemed without purpose, and pictures kept flashing through her mind, frightening her. Not infrequently, Estelle saw herself falling off the cliffs that stood in front of Marjorie's house, into that angry, dark sea that would pound her broken body into pulp against the rocks. Her mother's face stood like an accusatory finger in her mind, and even the sympathetic faces of her friends hid the malice and contempt they felt. She was preternaturally aware of her embarrassment and tried to tell herself that she had done nothing, was guilty of no wrong, but her mind could not hold that thought, and it slipped back to the secret, laughing faces that she feared would follow her.

Something caught her eye, and she turned, seeing the sunlight reflect off the top of the car that had left the highway and had turned into the long road that led to the village. She had planned to go and see Mrs. Greaves today but had been too ashamed to go into the village. Though her arrest would not be in the papers until the next day, she was well aware of the village semaphore and was sure that everyone there knew her business.

She had sent the servants home, unable to stand their looks of bland acceptance that carried neither condemnation nor pity, and she wondered where the loyalty in the servants, so noticeable in her father's house, had gone. The relationship had changed since the country's independence from Britain, and the bond now lacked all emotional association, being a pure exchange of labour and payment. For a moment, Estelle was confused, not sure what to think. In her history courses, she taught that this change was a good thing, the regularization of the relationship of labour and capital. She called it the destruction of the chattels. It was the new arrangement of the interaction between men, a rough proxy of equality, built, depending on your point of view, on mutual exploitation or the mutual gift of a resource. She paid her servants well, much better than Marjorie, who often accused her of not appreciating the value of a dollar. Yet, today, when the police had come, she had been disappointed to see the emotional vacuity that had been their response. What had gone wrong in their attachment to her? Why had she lost what her father had so obviously had? She had sent them home, unable to accept their detachment.

The car had reached the village but had not stopped, so she knew it must be coming to her home. Estelle walked into the oppressive silence of the house, its size now overpowering, and descended the long, fan-shaped staircase. As she pulled the door opened, Aurelius' car came to a stop in the driveway. She watched as the long, athletic body uncoiled from behind the wheel, and she thought how much he and Mark resembled each other and what a pity it was that the shadow of the past kept them from acknowledging what everyone knew and had long accepted.

"How are you holding up?" he asked, with a wide but somehow still reserved smile. She thought it must be his professional face, and for the first time, Estelle felt like a client. She shrugged, leading him up the stairs and out to the balcony which, in the late afternoon, was the coolest part of the house.

"Did you talk to Mark?" she asked as he sat.

She stood in the nearby alcove where the butler, before he left, had placed their drinks.

"I just came from Dathorne, but I wouldn't say I talked to him."

Estelle turned, her face a question.

"Well, today he was not very communicative. He seemed not to understand where he was. He kept mentioning an angel, and he was back in Vietnam again. You sure he never mentioned any of this before?"

"Aury, Mark has been gone since 1972. I have not seen him since. Anything could have happened in that time. I don't know him anymore."

"I understand. Don't get upset, Estelle. I have to ask you this. The accounts in Panama City, Managua, and the Caymans, they are not yours, right?"

She looked at Aurelius in surprise and anger, her eyes narrowing and her nostrils flaring.

"You think I had something to do with whatever that money represents? If you think so, you can leave now."

Aurelius held up his hand, smiling reassuringly.

"Calm down, Estelle. I have to prepare for your hearing, so I have to ask these questions. You understand?"

She turned away, but not before Aurelius saw the tears in her eyes.

"You say you have not seen Mark in more than thirty years. Any idea why he would create accounts in your name all around the world?"

She shrugged again, not answering, and Aurelius walked to her side, placing his arm around her shoulder.

"Estelle, we will get through this. I don't believe that you had anything to do with laundering money, but we have to be clear about everything."

"I don't know why Mark would create accounts in my name."

"Actually, it almost seems silly that he would use his own name. There is not much of a disguise in the 'St. Auburn,' since both of you use the same last name."

"You know, I have been thinking about that. Mark is a lot of things, but he's not stupid."

Aurelius paused, then responded.

"No, not stupid, but he is really disoriented sometimes. Like today. I don't think he knew I was there. Kept addressing me as the angel. Then again, a few days ago, he and I had a perfectly rational conversation."

"What did you talk about?" Estelle asked, without knowing why.

"He started talking about when we were boys. He said I never defended him against the other boys."

The slightly nervous laughter suggested he wanted her denial of Mark's assertion, but Estelle was silent, and Aurelius felt a weight in the pit of his stomach.

"We have a bit of a situation," he said, looking at her. "You know nothing of the accounts, but they are in your name, with your signature approving the movement of the funds. Mark is not responding to my questions, and the police are building a case against you. You sure there is nothing you can tell me?"

"No. When Mark left here in 1972, he didn't have any money. I don't know where he would have gotten all of that money."

"You two got married, and less than two years later, Mark went back to the States. Why didn't you go with him?"

Estelle walked a few steps away from him, looking down on the village from which came a mixture of sounds. Some choir on the radio was belting out:

"Hark the herald angels sing
Glory to the newborn king."

Alongside that comforting song, she also heard the heavy throb of a reggae beat she did not recognize, but a group of boys evidently did because she could hear their disembodied, young voices singing along with the refrain.

A series of answers went through her mind, and she weighed each, one by one, finding them wanting.

"I didn't go because he didn't want me."

The words were heavy, like lead pellets dropped in water, and they sank between them.

"Mark is a child. He sees things; he wants them. Then, he loses interest. When he loses interest, he begins to hate the thing he wanted only a moment ago. I couldn't live with that…that…uncertainty."

He had some idea of what she meant, having seen that same flightiness in Mark. As a boy, Mark had been incapable of seeing the anguish he caused, and he would move from person to person, group to group, charming enough to force his way into whatever situation presented itself but, ultimately, standing outside, watchful and ironic. He had treated high school the same way. Smart, he had found things easy, but a lack of discipline had caused his failure. Mark had been a very poor student, though he had seemed to know everything there was to know about the world. He had read constantly and failed repeatedly. Aurelius thought he understood what Estelle meant.

In fact, he did not. He could not fully understand what she meant by "uncertainty," for the word carried much more freight than it denoted. The first few months of the marriage had been a wonder to her, and Estelle had gloried in the fact of the union. She was obsessed with Mark, and he seemed equally available and open. He had gone to work at the port and, since he was on the night shift, that gave him days off.

She had converted day to night, keeping the curtains drawn and turning lights on for him to read to her. It was the closest she came to that sexual fulfillment that the girls talked of. He read everything to her that he was reading, and, gradually, history, literature, mysticism, and geography—the things to which she had paid little attention—became important to her. What amazed her most was that he never talked down to her, accepting that her instinct would understand what her mind did not. It was not the words that conveyed meaning to her, but his voice, which carried emotion so easily that she felt Paul Morel's pain and Lolita's bewitching quality. In bed, they would lay, he on his back, absorbed by the book yet somehow aware of her, holding her to him. He did not mind being touched as long as it was not an interruption. Mark never seemed to mind if she fell asleep. He would continue reading silently until she awoke, slightly embarrassed. He never commented but would hug her close and begin reading aloud again wherever he happened to be in the book.

Her father had given them the house on the beach, and they would spend whole weekends walking and talking in the sand. Heather was always in tow, and, gradually, Estelle saw the bond between her and the child fracture even more as Mark became the child's object of affection. He was extraordinarily gentle with the girl, and though he never commented on it, she sensed that in his attention lay a rebuke. It was the only ripple on the placid pond of their love. At least, it was in the first year.

Nineteen seventy-two had dawned with an ugly rainstorm, and the waves had pounded the beaches with a violence that frightened her. As the day had progressed, the water had crept closer to the beach house, each wave seeming to reach further into the land like the tongue of a dragon seeking food. The child, frightened by the waves, had cried all morning, and she had held her, feeling a vague annoyance. By ten o'clock, he had not come home, and the time seemed to stretch out, each tick of the bedroom clock like a nail in her consciousness. She had called the port but had been told that he had left, and she had sat, holding the child, listening to the tires of the cars rushing by making that peculiar squishy sound, and trying to distinguish Mark's tires. By midday, he still had not come nor had he called. She had called Marjorie, who had said she had not heard from Mark and had offered to come by later. Hanging up the phone, Estelle had had the awful feeling of her stomach sinking into her pelvis, almost as if she were pregnant again.

Mark had called at twenty after three, laughter in his voice and the noise of the boys playing dominoes in the background. He had not apologized, only said that he was at Saint Too's house and the fellows were playing.

"I'll get there later," he had said.

Estelle had put the phone down, a darkness before her eyes. Placing the child in her cradle, she had slowly undressed, taking each piece of clothing and folding it carefully, then placing it on a chair. She had kept her panties on. With each removal, the darkness intensified something that hovered in her mind like a bat in a cave. It was not a headache but a sense of being trapped inside herself, of having no outlet for that fierce, hot anger that burned in the pit of her stomach. It was like death coming on a silent wind, this darkening of her mind. She must have lit a cigarette because, in some far distant place, she had felt her hand burn. Her fingers still carried the scar from that singeing. Fortunately, the cigarette had fallen to the floor and burned itself out. As the depression sucked the life out of her, leaving her limp, lost in a land of shadow and darkness, she had wondered about the child, but its face had merged with Mark's just before all became black.

She had awakened to find Mark lying next to her, his arm like a gentle cloth bringing warmth. She still remembered the look of disappointment on his face when she had asked for a cigarette. She had had no idea then, but was later told that she had been unconscious for hours. Apparently, Marjorie, recognizing something in Estelle's voice, had driven over and found her almost naked and the baby crying. She had tried to wake Estelle but to no avail, so she had called Maylene, Anis, and Sandra, and they had called around until they found Mark.

Estelle sighed now as she remembered the first moments of her awakening, and even today, a confusion reigned about those moments. She was sure that she had been dying, could see the welcoming darkness. She had wanted to give up, to stop this thing called life, with its pain and confusion. She was told that the girls had shaken her and yelled her name in panic, but she had not responded. They had called Larry, the psychiatrist, and he had arrived before Mark, but his ministrations had been equally ineffective. He had been on the verge of calling an ambulance when Mark had walked in, ordering them all out of the bedroom. He had taken his shirt off and laid beside her, stroking her back and nuzzling her neck. He later told her that he had not spoken, but she knew, somewhere in the darkness of the approaching peace, his voice had come like a strand of light, and she had followed that beacon.

That act had somehow transformed their relationship. Though he had never actually said it, she knew that he felt he had given her life and that had confirmed something for him. She remembered the little book he had read quietly after that. It had been titled *The Three Magic Words,* and those words were "you are God." She was sure Mark had believed that, had sought consciously to find within himself the power he believed to be there. In that act on that wet, dark evening when he had called her from the darkness and she had come, choosing him over her peace, he had proved to himself that he was God.

"Children make very poor gods."

She was not aware that she had spoken until Aurelius, who had stood patiently watching her, said, "That's an odd thing to say."

"What did I say?" she asked, surprised.

"It sounded like 'Children make very poor gods.' What were you thinking?"

"About your question. Why did Mark leave…." She hesitated, then added in a childlike voice, "me."

"And that's your answer? Children make very poor gods?"

She smiled, and he had the distinct impression that she thought him a fool.

"My relationship with Mark is very complicated. More so than you could ever know."

Aurelius looked at the woman closely, noticing the odd combination of features. From her eyes down to her chin the face was round, almost cherubic, but from the eyes to the crown of her head, there was the impression of squareness. He had never noticed this before, and he thought how this woman, whom he had known since she was eleven, had always seemed hidden, somehow unavailable. Looking at her now, he thought her beautiful, but a kind of madness lurked behind the beauty, and the frantic light in her eyes belied the cool voice of the historian she had become. An odd thought struck him for a moment, that maybe both she and Mark were mad, but then the thought was gone.

"Mark's going to plead guilty, Estelle."

She struggled to control her face, and, for a moment, she almost succeeded, but then it crumbled, and the tears washed down her cheeks, pausing for a moment, then plunging on.

"They are going to kill him, Aury."

"No one is going to kill Mark if I have anything to say about it. He's not right. If I could get the damned psychiatric evaluation, I am sure I could have him declared incompetent, but the Americans are trying to block that."

The woman was on the verge of a reply when his cell phone rang.

"Aurelius St. John here."

Estelle watched as a look of perplexity came over his face. He spoke for a short while, then hung up.

"That was Sandra. She wants me to meet her at the attorney general's office. She didn't say what it was about. I am going to have to run. You goin' be awright?"

Estelle nodded, wiping her face. It was not until Aurelius' car was sliding by on the narrow access road below her balcony that it occurred to her that Sandra had not asked to speak to her.

CHAPTER TWENTY-ONE

The angel had not left his side all day. She was playing games, Mark knew, constantly changing faces, but she could not hide from him; he knew all of her disguises. Earlier today, she had tried to hide behind Aurelius' face, but he had found her out quickly enough, and when he had laughingly addressed her, she had left, taking Aurelius' face with her. Now, she had placed herself between the iron bars of the cell, and her face was squeezed between two of them, gazing at him, her eyes calm but welcoming. He rubbed his hands across his eyes, wishing she would go away for a while, but she was leaving less and less now. When he moved his hand from his eyes, she was still there, and he swatted at her helplessly, saying, "You won't forget, will you?"

The face was unmoved, not answering. Mark stood, walking toward the door to the cell, and the angel's face changed, a threat appearing in her eyes. He stopped. In her eyes, he could see an image, and he peered at it, thinking back to the place of that image.

It had rained all night, and they had pushed north from Cu Chi, seeking the enemy. The Vietnamese jungle had dripped on them, soaking them to the bone as the residue of the day's heat was washed away. There were five of them on a recon mission. They were not supposed to engage the enemy, but word had come from Danang that there had been heavy movement to the north of Cu Chi, and the 9th Cav had ferried them in. There had been no word of when anyone would come for them. They were specialists and lived off the land. Sometimes that meant living like animals, and as they had slipped further north, they had escaped the bounds of humanity. Mark looked at the four men with him. No one carried any insignia of rank. In their work, rank was the enemy. Ray, six-foot, four-inches of rage, found Vietnam much to his liking. From some hellhole on Chicago's south side, he was free for the first time in his life. He had power, and men, white men particularly, walked around him. Mark knew Ray killed for fun, and it did not much matter who the target was. Many had guessed why the lieutenants, all white, never seemed to last in this platoon, but few speculated out loud. In 'Nam, if you talked about a man, you had better be prepared to kill him. Ray had that dark light around him, and Mark had known Ray would not be killed. Gary, the one white guy in the group, hung with Ray, as if he thought Ray's magic would protect him, and sometimes in the night, Mark would hear him squeal as Ray ploughed into him. It was the ultimate act of dominance, and Ray understood dominance. The other two, Samson and Heartache, were boys, eighteen and nineteen, and both had come from West Philadelphia.

They had each been part of a regular platoon once, but when each had been the only survivor of his platoon on three separate occasions, the brass had made them into a special unit. Mark, like Ray, had been made sergeant once, but whenever they went back to Danang, they were so wild that, by the end of leave, they would be privates again. So they traveled and fought as one, no one with any rank above private. Ray was the acknowledged battle leader and Gary carried the radio, their contact with the hell to the south of them that was South Vietnam. Their job was to seek out and report. Then Puff the Magic Dragon would come, lighting up the night, and leaving the sharp, acrid smell of kerosene and burnt flesh.

On that morning, as the rain had continued to pour down, they had come to a break in the jungle and squatted, eyes fixed on the darkness of the trees on the other side. They were alert but not tense. For one thing, four of them knew who would take the point. It was always Ray, walking in that dark magic light. Mark looked at him, sitting apart, caressing the M-16 like a lover. His other hand caressed the white boy's long, dark hair, and Mark wondered if Ray, in his state, could tell the difference. He could see Ray was juiced. He had been smoking all night under the low tarp they had erected to keep out the worst of the rain. The smell and the glow were a dead give-away, but no one instructed Ray, who often said, "I is a invisible nigguh. VC can't see me. He will kill you other motherfuckers though." Mark smiled, thinking that Ray was not given to pep talks. They did not like each other, and Mark always made sure he stayed behind Ray in a firefight. Since Cam Ne, Ray had watched him with that hunger he saw in the man before a battle. There were no rules in Vietnam. Men developed a code of morality that was based on its value as a survival tool, but sometimes the code of the world, that frightening place, would break through, and soldiers would become men for a brief moment. Then, they did what he had done when he had seen the girl fall. Her long, black hair had flown in a graceful, flowing arc, like a halo about her head, and she had fallen heavily. When he went back to the center of the village, she was still alive, holding her stomach in with her hands. She had been mouthing something, but no words came, and he had vomited. When his paroxysm was over, he had turned back to find Ray, his pants down, on top of the girl, his lean hips pumping with a diabolical fury. Something had broken in him, and he had swung the M-16 at Ray's head, but the man was like a wild animal, and something had warned him of the attack. He had spun off the girl, his long dick bent like a mallet in the humid air, reaching for his gun, but he had frozen at the sound of the cocked M-16 in Mark's hand. It was what the group called "the moment." Ray had looked at him, the madness clear, his body red from the girl's blood and his cock having a chafed look. Everything in Mark said he should kill him, but the world had looked in, and Ray had laughed.

"Say, bro. You go' kill me over a dead VC?"

Sanity had returned, and they had burned that village, but he never stood in front of Ray.

That morning, north of Cu Chi, they had watched as Ray had stepped into the clearing, his long body almost instantly lost in the black light that protected him. The mists came off the water that morning, and Mark could feel the tug of the mud as he slipped and slid forward. He knew that Ray was ahead of him because of the smell. Ray carried the souvenirs of his kills with him, the ears of the dead VC that he cut off and strung around his waist like a belt. It was another reason that the others, Gary excepted, stayed away from Ray. The smell was in their imaginations, Ray would say with a cold laugh. The Viet Cong knew him and seemed to run away from the smell of the decomposing ears of their brethren.

That misty morning, however, they were not VC, but North Vietnamese regulars who had been hiding on the other side of the clearing. Mark had felt the air around him grow light, and the slow beat of the angel's wings had surrounded him. They had been issued little clickers that sounded like crickets, and he had clicked his. Though he could not see the men around him, he could imagine what was happening. Each man had squatted in the tall grasses of the bog and had made his way back to the other side. Inside the trees, they had regrouped, and Ray had hissed, "Now what the fuck is it, cherry?"

"There is regular North Vietnamese Army on the other side."

"How you know dat?"

"They are there. Call in Puff."

For a moment, it had looked as if Ray might argue, but then he shrugged and nodded to Gary, the radio man. As the coordinates were called in, they pulled back further to the south. The flyboys were known to make mistakes.

Twenty minutes later, they heard the sweet sound of American engineering as the planes had come in low and fast. As the world had turned to hellfire and the nasty smell of man and oil had mixed in death, Mark's eyes had watered. It must have been from the chemicals in the air. As they had moved rapidly back south to their extraction point, Ray had slid up next to him, the stink nauseating.

"That's twice, motherfucker. Third time lucky. Got it?"

Mark had nodded in the way that dead men do, but Ray had laughed and clapped him on the back.

Now, he looked at the jail bars where the angel's face still hung, and he said, "Thank you."

CHAPTER TWENTY-TWO

Aurelius walked into the attorney general's office just as most of the workers were showing that restlessness that signaled the end of the day. Some waved or said hello as he walked through the building, ascending to the third floor where the attorney general's office was located. He felt tired and a little distracted as the secretary welcomed him and led him into the inner office. Three persons were in the room, and Aurelius felt a sinking in his stomach. Something was wrong. Sandra stood as he came in, and Aurelius thought, not for the first time, that it was odd how such an attractive woman was still unattached. The other men in the room he also knew. First was Neville Francis, the attorney general, a short dapper man, who regardless of the heat, always wore a full suit with a white handkerchief showing its triangular tongue from the jacket pocket. The other man was Sir Aaron Harmon, the last of the old, black gentlemen from the pre-independence period. He was chief justice of St. Euribius. When the attorney general spoke, Aurelius could see the slight frown on the chief justice's face. He did not much care for informality.

"Hello, Neville," Aurelius responded, shaking hands all around.

"How is Estelle?" the chief justice asked, and Aurelius shrugged.

"As well as you might expect. She's frightened."

"Yes, of course. Gweneth Prescod must be beside herself. Such a private woman. Now this. First, the murder that her son-in-law commits...."

"Alleged," Aurelius responded, a little annoyance in his voice. Everyone looked at him closely.

"Yes, of course. Alleged. For Gweneth Prescod, of course, the distinction is meaningless. She is of the old school. Dignity above all else. Now her daughter is involved in this sordid alleged money laundering. She does not entertain much and even less does she accept invitations. This will certainly keep her on that plantation for what is left of her life."

Aurelius looked at the stiff, slightly sour face of the chief justice, wondering if he was simply describing his own response. In a moment of perversity, he said, "You probably know her best. She is part of your circle, isn't she?"

He watched with amusement as the chief justice's face twisted out of shape, the lines on his cheeks and neck sliding around to accommodate the weak muscles underneath. When this tectonic shift was complete, something like a dignified sneer had taken up its post on the old man's face.

"Hardly, dear boy. She moved into our group because of Leslie, but she was hardly of our circle. She came from the north, you know."

This was said as if it constituted a full explanation of the preceding statement, and Aurelius smiled, the thought occurring to him that it would be good when this generation was gone. He was immediately contrite, however. It was, after all, the chief justice's generation that had clamored and fought for independence from Britain. In fact, this man before him had led the legal charge in the 1950s and 60s. It seemed to Aurelius, though, that once the political separation from England was complete, these men had been lost, seeking in the cultural attributes of the old metropolis the certainty they desired. They—people like the chief justice and Estelle's mother—were out of step with where the country was headed, with the youth following the pell-mell rush toward the siren song of the United States. Aurelius could hear it everywhere in the shifting accents of the island. *The chief justice's generation is comic in its brittle assumption of English form,* he thought, *but at least it had been assured.* Now, the country seemed to be reaching around in desperation for a center. He did not say this, though.

"Yes. I had heard she came from the very end of the island. Was she one of the Yardes?"

This was one of the better-off families in the north.

"Good heavens, no. Gweneth Prescod came from one of the small villages somewhere down there. There are a few old stories about her family. Apparently, Leslie saw her one day when he was having a look at some land he wanted to buy down there. Love at first sight and all that. It caused quite a fuss, I can tell you. The family threatened to throw him out, but he persisted. They never fully accepted Gweneth. Isn't it odd that Estelle should have made the same choices her father did?"

The mention of Estelle's name changed the evolving atmosphere, and Aurelius asked, falsely playfully, "Why have I been summoned?"

The other two looked at the attorney general, who fixed his pants seam before responding.

"We wanted you to know before it became news that we are ruling in favor of the Americans' legal challenge to the psychiatric examination."

"What? Why? There is no legal rationale for it."

"Actually, there is, Aury. Inniss vs. Payne in 1961. The issues were the same. England was granted the same right."

"St. Euribius was a colony then," he responded angrily. "Sandra, you and I have argued this in moot court for the law students. You don't believe that Inniss vs Payne applies anymore than I do. Why are we doing this?"

Sandra looked away, not answering, and the smooth voice of the attorney general cut in. "The law's the law, Aury. Precedent is precedent. We cannot give to the English what we would deny the Americans."

"Law, my ass. This is about politics, not law."

The chief justice's face had changed again, a peculiar type of distaste evident in the down-turned corners of his mouth.

"Come now, my boy. No need to be uncultured. Neville is correct. The law does not support you. Find another strategy. I remember...."

Aurelius was not interested in his memories, and he cut him off, appealing to the attorney general.

"Neville, Mark is going to be hung without the insanity plea."

The A.G.'s eyes turned sly as he responded, "As I understand it, Aury, the insanity plea is your idea. Doesn't your client want to plead guilty?"

Aurelius immediately realized he had been a fool to think the prime minister would not tell these three about his conversation. Still, he felt betrayed. He had told the P.M. as a friend, not as Mark's counsel. He was angry now, and, knowing the potential situation, he asked coldly, "Do you want me to enter the guilty plea tomorrow then?"

The faces interested him. Sandra's looked strained, as if she might be having a particularly stressful bowel movement. The chief justice blanched, his light skin seeming to stretch to cover the skull beneath. Neville Francis merely smiled, his eyes soft, like quicksand.

"No. There will be no hearing tomorrow. Nor the day after that. Don't pretend to be naive, Aury. You know what is happening here."

"What is happening here, Neville? What I see is my client being shoved to the gallows or some American hellhole or worse. That's what I see happening here."

"Don't let emotion cloud your judgment, Aury. These are dangerous times. I have never seen the country so split on an issue. Deighton Cox has been very effective in turning this into a cause. It is no longer the Rastas against the world. In some strange, alchemic way, he has made this case a referendum on the government. The prime minister will not be brought down by this. You understand?"

Aurelius thought of the prime minister's open palm slapping the oak table at the residence and knew that he understood only too well. For a moment, he felt some sympathy for them. So much of who they were, how they evaluated their worth, was tied up in the possession of the government and the power that brought, so he understood their nervousness. He was not, as the prime minister had suggested, so isolated not to have felt and seen the change in the mood of the people. Unlike them, however, he did trust the system and the people. If the trial went forward, he was convinced the people would accept the verdict. Mark's membership in the ruling class was, at best, transient, yet he had become a symbol of that class's isolation, their lack of caring about what happened to the little people.

In truth, Mark was one of the little people himself, his marriage to Estelle notwithstanding. Deighton Cox was trying to portray Mark as a village boy who had defended a poor Rasta boy. Many had accepted that characterization, but the majority saw a rich plantation owner who could afford the ten-thousand-dollars-a-night resort from which they were excluded, and someone who had not even been satisfied to live in St. Euribius. This complex set of circumstances had mixed with their own, until now, inchoate sense of displacement and deprivation, and what the government now had was a political situation they could not control.

Deighton Cox's voice had become more strident with each passing day, and he was gaining converts to Mark's cause. The government hoped to diffuse the tension by allowing Cox to drain away the anger the village people felt, convincing them that Mark had merely acted to defend a helpless boy. Cox was shrewd. He had not attacked the guard Mark had killed, but rather the establishment, the resort hotel that had made the guard necessary. In this way, he had gradually been shifting the anger away from Mark. The prime minister, Aurelius knew, wanted to buy enough time to allow this emotional shift to occur. Then, there would be a quick trial at which Mark would be found innocent and quietly handed over to the Americans. Problem solved. They were calculating that once the Rasta's death was vindicated in Mark's release, Deighton Cox would be satisfied, and the extradition could take place without too much social turmoil. Aurelius did not know what arrangement had been made between the Americans and the prime minister, but he was sure it would be something big.

"Aury."

The attorney general's voice was soft, insinuating.

"Aury. We must have some time. If this place explodes, we all lose. There is no benefit in that. Mark must not be allowed to plead guilty because he cannot be hung here in these circumstances. The Americans' request will be honored, and Mark will be out of our hair."

When the bile rose in Aurelius' throat, he was not at first sure why, but as the anger grew, blinding him, a thought coalesced in his mind. They were talking about his brother, and the only reason Neville and Sandra could see him as an ally was because Mark was right. He had never defended Mark against the boys, so why should he be expected to defend him now? A rush of hot shame flowed over him, causing him to feel slightly faint, seeing in the faces of the three something hated. Aurelius bowed his head, hoping to hide his feelings, but the tension in his shoulders was a signal, and he gave up.

"I am not going to let you sacrifice him. Not to the crowds and not to the Americans. Have you looked at the file on Mark they gave the prime minister? Aren't you concerned about the holes in it? With all their resources, the Americans are unable to find any substantive information on Mark after the early eighties except for this murder in 1999. Then he disappears again until he shows up here, and the Americans immediately begin the pressure to extradite him, making sure there is no psychiatric analysis. I am surprised they are allowing him to have counsel. Doesn't it strike you as odd that they should want to silence a man who seems to have no life since the early eighties? How does a man disappear for twenty years, Neville?"

The attorney general's face was unchanged.

"None of that matters, Aury."

The voice said that decisions had been made, and there was little he could do about them. Maybe it was the sense of helplessness that fueled the anger burning in his soul. He would never know. But something shaped the words that came from him, something that was wild and frightened him.

"I won't let you get away with this."

The attorney general looked at Sandra and the chief justice before he replied, but when he did, his voice had lost all warmth.

"There was another thing, Aury."

"What?"

"Your conflict of interest."

"My what?"

"Your conflict of interest. You are now representing an accused murderer who is implicitly accused by another of your clients of fraud. You will have to abandon one or the other case."

Aurelius knew Neville Francis always spoke with precision, so the use of the word "abandon" was intentional. He stood, nodding to the three, and left the room.

CHAPTER TWENTY-THREE

The crowds started about a mile away from the open-air meeting in Wither's Gully. The gully was an odd geological feature, a split that ran for miles along the central hills. It had been a source of stories of necromancy and fear, of women disappeared and children lost when Aurelius had been a youth. But in the last twenty years, it had lost the magic. Some enterprising soul had built a road that now led to an aquarium, and the ghosts had receded under the insistent tread of commerce. The lights in the gully itself could be seen from where he was. There were few cars but lots of foot traffic, and Aurelius, following his instinct, parked his car and walked in the crowd, trying to merge in. He had worn a pair of blue jeans and a golf shirt, and with a cap pulled low over his face in the uncertain light of Wither's Gully, he hoped not to be recognized.

Banks of speakers had been erected, and he could hear the testing of the sound going on. From time to time, Deighton Cox's voice could be heard as the technicians tested for sound levels. *So different from when I was a boy, when the political rallies would set up in no time, and the sound would be so bad that only those close to the dais would understand anything,* he thought. Now, the sound was clear, and it occurred to him that he did not need to go all the way into the gully. Around him, the silent crowds made their way down, but he slid out of the center, seeking the edge and looking for the small hills he knew were in the gully. Finally out of the press of the bodies, Aurelius looked around. He was still a good distance from the dais, but he could hear, and that was more important than seeing. After all, he knew who would be there. He did wonder, though, if Maylene would be with her husband. He had not seen her since the day at Marjorie's house, and he wondered how this campaign to save Mark was going in that household. He knew Maylene and Deighton had almost broken up because of Mark, and he smiled at the irony of this meeting. *What motivated men?* he wondered. What would drive Deighton to save a man he despised? He had never forgiven Mark, had expressed his disdain for him to Aurelius more than once, almost as if daring him to defend the man. Aurelius could find nothing to defend. Mark's behavior had been execrable, yet so typically Mark. Deighton never referred to the incident itself, stepping around it like a man with an already sliced foot avoiding broken glass, but he had not forgotten, and it took only the mildest reference to Mark to get him going about the man's moral vacuity.

Aurelius found the mound for which he had been searching and quickly climbed to the top. He could see the harsh light of the dais and could make out the small figures moving about in the distance. Already the crowd had grown quite large, and, seeing it, something crawled along his spine. They were quiet, and that frightened him. The size of the crowd also frightened him. He had not known that Deighton Cox had this kind of appeal. He thought of the prime minister's face as his hand had come down on the table, and Aurelius understood what he had seen was fear. In the silence before him, in that attentive silence, was the core of the issue that confounded them.

He searched around for a comfortable spot and sat, regretting that he had not thought to bring a cushion. Still, if from time to time he moved his weight from cheek to cheek, it was not too bad. Aurelius watched as the crowds filed past, a dark mass that seemed purposeful, drawn to this place and this moment by something beyond them. *How had Mark become this catalyst?* he wondered. Mark, who was so uninvolved that most thought him cold. Who was the man in the cell now? He did not seem familiar, was not the Mark he remembered. In school, they had argued for independence, running the corridors to stir up the boys. At sixteen, the battle for independence had consumed him, and Mark had gone along, not sure of what it all meant, but not willing to be left out of the biggest event in his life. *I,* Aurelius thought with a smile, *had been passionate.* He had written short tracts at school and circulated them. Those teachers who were uncertain whether St. Euribius could survive on its own separated from Britain—and there had been several—had been castigated in these tracts, which were insulting but funny. The boys had been uniformly pro-independence, so neither threat nor cajoling had induced a single boy to betray him. Even today as men, boys from that time would speak with pride of "the secret."

Mark had gone along, but he had never shown much enthusiasm for the struggle. What got his juices flowing was not St. Euribian independence, which Aurelius had always suspected Mark saw as an irony, but the role of Britain and, at that time, an emerging America, around the world. His real excitement came from the conversations of Smith in Rhodesia and apartheid in South Africa, Lumumba's assassination in the Congo and Nasser in Egypt. Aurelius remembered that Mark had once said to him that they were part of something bigger, and unless St. Euribian independence were understood in this context, it would mean nothing. He remembered this now because the comment had been made at the strangest time, at a time when Mark's mind should have been on pleasure not politics, but he had always been odd in that sense.

They had gone to the beach to meet Marjorie and Estelle. He had taken the bus to Mark's village by the sea, and they had walked along the beach for three miles to where they had agreed to meet the girls. Mark had been fifteen at the time, and Aurelius almost seventeen. Both girls were fourteen. There had been a tensile hypersensitivity to Mark that day as he had walked along, occasionally breaking into a splashing run at the edge of the water. The sea, kicked into the sunlight, had broken into rainbow globules that lived for a moment, then died, falling back to the ocean. Aurelius, although older, had felt younger that day, as the two of them had gone by the hotels that were just beginning to appear along the coast. Tourism had still not fully arrived, and the large stone homes along the beach—bay-houses they were called—sat like miniature castles, the NO TRESSPASSING signs a signal of their difference. Most had dogs that barked as the boys had passed, and Mark had walked close to the low walls that kept the dogs in, irritating them into a frenzy. Sometimes, he would stand, staring into the wild eyes of the dogs, who, affronted at the insult, barked more furiously, until at one house a white man had come out, shooing the boys away. Mark had run along, his laughter disappearing into the sounds of the breaking waves. Then, he had run back to Aurelius shouting, "Let we go to Miramar's jetty."

Aurelius had objected, knowing the new hotel had made it a policy to keep the boys off the jetty. It had been reserved for tourists. Someone had told Mark that the hotel could not do that since, according to St. Euribian law, the jetty was an extension of the beach, not the hotel, and all beach land and its extensions were public property.

The boys played cricket nearby in a grove of coconut trees called the Coconut Walk, and whenever Mark walked by, he would go on the jetty, daring the guard to say anything to him. Aurelius smiled, remembering a later date when Mark got into trouble for that trespass. But that day, they had walked by after Mark had made his obligatory saunter to the end of the jetty and back. The girls called, and they had hurried along the beach, passing Colony's Rest and Coral Waters, and later, Shady Lane. These hotels were still there, still storing North Americans and Europeans for the winter.

It had been an odd day. The brittle silence had created a sense of suspended time, the sharp gold of the sun, ethereal. Sound had traveled easily, and, as a result, distance felt shortened as voices without bodies came through the air like past lives revisited. The tourists had retreated before the heat, and they had felt as if the land had been repossessed, as if it had been free of the blood of conquest, still possessed of Arawak voices. Sometimes, the disembodied voices were incomprehensible, and Aurelius had wondered whether they were real.

The girls had spread a blanket in the sand under the shade of the sea-grape trees whose broad, green leaves trembled slightly at the violation. Mark had been with Estelle then, and he had fallen heavily in his frenetic, playful manner next to her. They had been late, but Mark never worried about that. He had grown accustomed to her waiting. It had not taken long for the two couples to find the dim coolness created by the sea-grape trees, and though the girls had firm rules about how far the boys could go, it did not matter, the very possibility of the forbidden being stimulus enough. The afternoon had passed slowly, as if the sky above watched these four, savoring their guilty acts of discovery.

It had all gone quite well for a while, Aurelius thought with a chuckle. Then they had gone into the sea, and he and Mark had swum out, matching each other stroke for stroke. He was not sure when it had become a competition, but at some moment it did, and neither could stop. They breathed on opposite sides so each breath forced their eyes to lock, and the urge to dominance became clear. Mark's eyes had become hard pinpricks of flint, the white bow-wave created by his head slicing through the water falling along his sleek body, creating the impression of a dark seal. Their arms were weary when they stopped, treading water and squirting it from their mouths in apparent nonchalance. They had stopped at the identical moment, their frightened eyes communicating their need to end the insanity. They had swum beyond the bluish-green water of the inner sea and now treaded in the darker navy blue of the deep. High up in the hills they could see the scattered houses and the smoke from the wood fires. The green of the fields was a surprise that stretched from horizon to horizon. The gully in which he now sat could be seen like a creamy-white scar across the middle of the island, where its innards had been exposed as man had taken the limestone to build homes. The girls were tiny dots on the beach when they started back, this time using a comfortable breast stroke. Aurelius had sensed the mischief brewing in Mark as they made their way slowly back to the shore, but he was still surprised when the boy had slid his cool, wet body next to Marjorie's. What happened next still confused Aurelius. It was as if the magic of the day itself had given them license, as if it had removed their restraints. They had slid back into the cool of the sea-grape trees, a world of mottled light, and seeking the privacy of distance, they had gone beyond their previous bounds, pushed on by an odd madness that the shadows themselves seemed to create.

Later, as the sun was disappearing, they had emerged, the triumphant smile of the boys smothering the girls' look of perplexed shame. It was the only time he had had sex with Estelle, and though he had never talked about it, he had never forgotten. Occasionally, when he saw Marjorie and Estelle together, he wondered if they still remembered, but he had never had the nerve to ask. He suspected Mark did because there was something about him that suggested all events were recorded for future use. As Aurelius sat on the small mound waiting for the meeting to begin, he wondered what had motivated Mark that day. Was it innocence, that desire to explore everything, regardless of the cost? Or was there something else hidden in the boy, some fiery-eyed wolf that would occasionally creep out to hurt and destroy, only to crawl back into the shell of innocence that the boy had created? He was cruel. There was no question about that. But what moved him, what drove him to these acts of cruelty, this apparent lack of caring for another soul? He had killed at least two men, but he seemed not really aware of these as acts of moral contravention.

"Killing is easy," he had said, and now Aurelius wondered if this had been a statement about his skill or his morality. Why had Mark killed the guard? No one knew. Deighton Cox was arguing that Mark had defended the Rasta boy. He, Aurelius, was arguing that Mark was insane, but Mark did not seem to agree with either of them, asserting that he was guilty.

Aurelius knew he could not allow Mark to plead guilty. He looked at the surging, silent crowd before him, wondering what energy lay within that beast. Deighton Cox had started to speak, warming the crowd up with a series of jokes designed to get them on his side. The laughter, however, did not go through the entire crowd, and Aurelius sat up, a disturbing thought going through his mind. This crowd was not all here to support Deighton. The silent surge that he had sensed earlier and could powerfully feel now was the latent energy of opposition.

Immediately, he stood up, his instincts alive. There were few people where he had stopped, and he descended the hill quickly, walking towards his car. Upon reaching it, he got his cell phone and dialed the commissioner of police.

"Hi, Patrick. I am at that meeting Deighton Cox is holding at Wither's Gully. You had better get some more people out here. I think you've got a problem."

Before the commissioner could respond, Aurelius heard something loud, like a car backfiring, and he started the car, turning quickly and heading toward the exit. Behind him, a roar had erupted, climbing out of the gully and assaulting the suddenly dark sky.

CHAPTER TWENTY-FOUR

"I think you gone mad."

Marjorie's voice was surprisingly quiet as she stood back, staring in perplexity at the unfinished painting Anis had uncovered. It was the kind of painting that would attract attention, for it stood in stark contrast to the other stock that lay in untidy distribution around the rooms of the house. There was little order in this room full of empty canvasses, easels, and finished paintings. The paintings were immediately recognizable as Anis', possessing a kind of vapid romanticism that made the poverty of the island a bloodless beauty. There were locally made boats of extravagant colors, little boys chasing bicycle tires, chattel houses of unimaginable grace and beauty, all trapped in history, recalling a time and place now irretrievable, lost. Marjorie thought it all a lie because the surface rendition of the society never seemed to capture the spirit of the country but simply reflected some image that an outsider saw. She knew Anis hated most of this work though it sold well enough.

The painting she had just exposed was nothing like the rest of the work. Marjorie was not sure what it was, but it was clear Anis had spent a lot of time on it. What caught her attention immediately was the oversized penis that hung like an abomination down to the figure's knees. On it, she had painted a variety of knobs and ulcers, and the bulbous head that seemed to dissect the knees showed signs of what Marjorie could only interpret as a kind of scaly rot. The body, however, was perfect, an athlete's body with a ridged stomach and a gently flaring chest that seemed as welcoming as a lullaby. Marjorie continued to stare, feeling the confusion she was sure the painting was designed to evoke.

As her eyes slid up past the perfectly proportioned, angled neck, she encountered the unfinished face. Here, too, Anis had striven for contradiction. The right side of the face was finished, and the forehead flared nobly skyward, trapping the short, curly hair. The one eye seemed amused, curious beneath the slightly arched brow. Marjorie stared at that eye for a long time, her eyes consciously avoiding the rest of the right side of the face. Inevitably, however, her eyes were pulled downward to the jaw, which was a bloody skeleton. The painting gave the feeling that the flesh had recently been pulled off, and the large canines and molars lay exposed, except for the brilliant scarlet that adorned them.

"I t'ink you gone mad, Anis," Marjorie repeated softly, repulsed yet unable to take her eyes from the picture of human destruction before her.

Anis sat on a stool in front of the painting, a peculiar look of forced serenity on her face.

"Maybe."

Her voice was equally quiet, and Marjorie looked at her curiously. The last few days had been hard, and the girls had not gotten together. In fact, today was the first time she had seen Anis in almost a week. It seemed as if suddenly everyone was busy. She had become absorbed with Bryan Edwards, who was now a fixture at her house. Sandra, now that she had been given the case involving Mark, had practically sequestered herself, and no one seemed to have seen her. Estelle, the money-laundering charge hanging over her, had done what Estelle always did when threatened. She had isolated herself and had neither been answering nor returning calls. Anis had not come around either, evidently having been engaged by this new horror of a painting. And now Maylene had been shocked by the attempt on Deighton's life.

Marjorie looked at the newspaper in her hands with the headline "RIOT." This is what had brought her to Anis' house, but before she could say anything, Anis had rushed her through the darkened, untidy house to see the painting. Now, she was waiting to hear what Marjorie thought. Marjorie could think of nothing, so she unfolded the newspaper and shook it flat.

"You see dis?" she asked, shoving the paper in front of Anis' nose.

Anis, a trifle annoyed that Marjorie had said nothing about the painting, took the paper and, reading the first lines of the article, said, "Dis happen las' night?"

"Uh-huh. I hear dat almost twenty people get hurt, and somebody shoot at Deighton."

"Wha' somebody shoot at Deighton fuh?"

"A lot of people don't like de fac' dat he trying to get Mark off."

Marjorie's voice petered out as she remembered that Anis would not be opposed to Mark being found guilty, either. Anis turned back to the painting saying, "Actually, I find Deighton's actions just a little confusing, too. I would t'ink that he would be de last one to defend Mark St. Auburn. Perticully after what Mark do to he."

Marjorie was reluctant to answer, but finally she said, "Dat happen a long time ago, Anis. Maybe Deighton is a bigger man dan you t'ink."

For a second, Anis' face turned nasty, and she seemed on the verge of saying something but did not.

"Dis t'ing getting dangerous, Anis. You know when I did driving in de village just now, I see de Rasta boys, 'bout ten of dem, standin' under de mango tree. All of dem had cutlasses."

"Yeah. Dey been a couple of fights between the Rastas and some of the other fellows in de village. People pissed off that de Rastas trying to get he off. Most people 'bout here feel dat he should hang."

Marjorie wondered about the "most people," but said nothing. Anis continued to read.

"It just seem so strange to have people 'bout here so upset dat dey shooting at people. Deighton could've been killed."

Anis shrugged, but she did not reply.

"We should go and see Maylene. See how she doing."

Anis hesitated, then said, "Okay. Wha 'bout Estelle? You talk to she?"

"No. You want to go up there?"

"We might as well. You know how she is. Unless somebody reach out, she just goin' go in a shell. Lemme change."

She handed the paper back to Marjorie and walked out of the room. Soon, Marjorie heard the shower, and she looked once again at the painting, surprised at its violence. When she had awoken that morning, Bryan had already left, but the indentation in the pillow next to hers was a cradle, and she had turned into it. It had been redolent of that smell, so different from her own that she was always aware of his difference. She felt happy for the first time in a while, and her feelings had moved so quickly that she had been frightened by them. He was like rainwater to her parched soul, and the moisture of him had fertilized her so that now she felt as if she were growing. It had been a long time since she had wanted to do something for a man, the bitterness engendered by John's betrayal too deep to allow anyone close. Bryan had come without artifice and with an innocence and curiosity that swept aside her defenses, making her vulnerable, open, and responsive. Had her friends not suddenly gotten all caught up with their own circumstances, she would have been boasting. She had even picked out the phrase she wanted to use. She had wanted to talk about "her regular man," but everyone now seemed preoccupied with their own troubles. Marjorie felt cheated, thinking that only a couple of weeks ago, the girls were getting together three of four times a week, and they would have been teasing her were it not for this murder that had set the country on edge.

Her mind turned to Mark, and she said out loud, "He did always de cause of trouble."

She had not heard Anis come back into the room, and she started when the voice said, "You bet your ass. He did never no good, and I say good riddance to bad rubbish."

She turned as Anis was pulling a thin, white cotton T-shirt over her head, the little nubs of her breasts exposed for a moment. Anis' lack of breasts fascinated Marjorie, and she stared even as they had disappeared, the bra-less little points sticking out at her like two marbles that had been shaved.

"You like dem?" Anis asked, now laughing, and Marjorie, glad of the change of mood, responded, "Dey ain't nutting dey to like, sugar. Wha' you need is a handful like dese."

She cupped her huge breasts, realizing in this act that the week of walking and dieting had actually begun to work. She had lost about seven pounds in the last week.

"Dey is only a distraction, hon. I ain't find a man yet who kin keep he mind 'pon dem. Dey always itching to move on to something else. Dey is only a gate-stop dat men got to get past."

Both women laughed, the mood lightening with their banter. As they walked out the house, Marjorie asked, "What you been doing de last few days?"

"Mostly working on de painting. Some uh de village folk been coming by to talk 'bout de case."

"No recent conquests?" Marjorie asked with a grin.

Anis did not join her, instead replying with something like surprise in her voice, "No, come to t'ink of it. I don't believe I had none since de night of Estelle's party. I had a real strange feeling dat night. You know, like dat boy did killin' heself 'pon top uh me, and it didn't make no difference to me nor to he. You ever get dat feeling?"

Marjorie, filled with her recently rediscovered passion, could not agree, so she said, "You need love, girl. Dat is w'en it does mek a difference. You know since I have been seeing Bryan, t'ings so different. It feel like fun again."

Anis looked at Marjorie slyly as she pulled her door shut. Anis never locked her house, and most people knew that. No one ever stole anything from her. It was as if they knew she had chosen them over the Heights and Terraces, and the village was grateful, accepting her idiosyncrasies as simply local color. Marjorie thought of all the locks on the doors of her businesses and the elaborate security system at her home, and she felt a slight envy at Anis' security. They climbed into Marjorie's car and pulled out, moving slowly through the village. Anis did not reply to Marjorie's comment until they were moving.

"Love? I waiting to find uh man wid a ego small enough to love. Dis Bryan, you t'ink he is de real t'ing? You know dat he only here to study somet'ing or other, right?"

Marjorie understood the question. It carried a lifetime of experience, much of it painful. Bryan would leave at some point, and her friend did not want her to be hurt.

"I know, but it really don't mek no difference. I need to do dis. You know what de most amazing t'ing is? I did believing dat I did ugly fuh so long, dat I forget how to see beauty in other people, Anis. Bryan mek me feel beautiful, you know? So de world look more beautiful to me now."

Anis looked at her friend, the acid retort dying on her lips.

Marjorie is pretty, she thought. *She only let sheself get fat after John started messing up.* Anis reached across and rested her hand on Marjorie's briefly.

"I happy fuh you, girl, but be careful. I don't know a single man who understan' wha' we want or need. Dey does pay attention w'en it suits dem, and next t'ing yuh know, dey gone. I ain't trying to mess up you head, okay? Just be careful."

"I know, girl. I can't depend on dis going anywhere, but I goin' ride it til it gone. You know what I mean?"

Anis laughed, nodding as she replied archly, "Well, let it ride you sometimes, too. No point doing all de work."

"You too bad, girl."

They had turned into the long, uphill drive leading to Estelle's home, and as if that act had sobered them, they fell silent.

"Ain't that Aurelius' car in front de house?" Marjorie asked as they approached the circular drive which bent around a fountain.

She parked, and they walked quickly to the door which opened as they approached. The smiling face of the butler greeted them.

"Aurelius here?" Marjorie asked, brushing past the smiling man.

Anis said hello and spoke with him familiarly as they climbed the long, fan-like staircase. Estelle and Aurelius had been deep in conversation but broke off as the women approached.

"Well, well. Wha' de two uh wunna doing out here? Wunna whizzy-whizzying like wunna having an affair. I goin' tell Beverley unless somebody mek it worth my while to keep quiet. And you ain' bound to say nutting, Estelle. What you got, I don't want."

Marjorie's voice boomed, laden with good humor, and everyone laughed, although Estelle's smile looked forced. Aurelius stood, kissing both women. Estelle looked at Marjorie, saying, "You lost weight. And from what I hear, you don't need anything from me nor Aury. Word is, you getting more than you can handle."

"And straight and regular, too," Anis chimed in, laughing and taking a seat next to Estelle, who reached out and took her hand gently.

Marjorie laughed loudly, happy to be the center of attention. Aurelius looked perplexed and asked, "What are you nuts talking about?"

"You ain't hear? Marjorie got a new man." Anis paused, then added significantly, "A white man."

Aurelius looked at Marjorie, who was preening, and laughed, asking, "You got a St. Euribian white man?"

"No," Anis answered. "This is over-and-away white meat."

"Yeah? Who is this?"

"It's a researcher from Oxford who is here studying mental illness in St. Euribius," Estelle answered.

"Really. Is there something special about our mental illness?"

"Well, you know what they say. All St. Euribians totally mental."

"So when are we going to meet this fellow?"

"When Marjorie untie he from she bedpost," Anis responded, laughing. "Wunna know dat she ain't been getting none fuh a while, so dat poor man got to pay de piper. I suppose when he come up for air, she goin' introduce he to her friends."

Marjorie laughed, replying, "Dat cud be a while, darling."

She turned away, her eyes catching the newspaper neatly folded on the table between Estelle and Aurelius. The black headline—"RIOT"— stared at her, and she said, "What de two uh wunna mek of what happen las' night?"

"Aury was just telling me he was down there when the whole thing started," Estelle responded, and the three women looked at Aurelius inquiringly.

He nodded slowly, saying, "Yes. It was very strange. I never thought we would see such an undercurrent of violence here in St. Euribius. But let me tell you, the mood was weird last night. Both factions showed up, and it was like a political rally, except that it was too quiet at first, almost as if everyone was waiting for something. I felt it and got out of there as quickly as I could."

"I don't know wha' dis place coming to. Who woulda thought dat dere would come a day when people would get shoot at fuh speaking deir mind in dis place. You know, it beginning to sound like Jamaica or Haiti or some such place."

There was a hint of anger tinged with disappointment in Marjorie's voice, and the others nodded in sympathetic understanding.

"De papers say dat de police get dere just in time, or it could've been worse," Marjorie added.

"True. I called Patrick as soon as I noticed that there were two separate groups down there, and he must have sent more police out immediately. Actually, I might have heard the shot. I thought it was something backfiring, but it must have been the shot."

"It look like de police got a description of the man who fired at Deighton, but dey can't find he."

"Yes. I talked to Patrick this morning. He tells me that they are on high alert all over the country. It seems there were a couple of fights in the north, as well, over the same thing."

Estelle had been silent, alone in her thoughts. She really did not want to think of the confusion that seemed to be springing from the very air. She did not want to think of Mark, since her anger flared every time she did. She looked at Anis: thin, compact, yet seeming to possess a tremulous energy that surrounded her like a patina. Anis' face was wooden, and Estelle could guess her thoughts. She, too, did not want to have to think about Mark and probably wished him ill. She was not sure how she felt. Mark had certainly hurt her time and again and now seemed to have enmeshed her in some unsavory deal in which he was engaged, but she could not quite bring herself to hate him.

I must be one of those women who bond forever, she thought. *Why could I not have been born like Anis, with the capacity for eternal hate?* Mark had hurt Anis when she was seventeen, and she had maintained her resentment for thirty-seven years. Thirty-seven years! Did Mark know how much the woman hated him? Would he have cared had he known? *I wish I could be like Anis, not caring so much,* she thought with a soft sigh.

The others had continued talking about the riot the night before, generally wondering what it signified. Then, Aurelius stood up, saying that he needed to go to the prison.

"Think about what I told you, Estelle."

She nodded, not sure what her answer would be. Then suddenly, she asked, "Aury, do you think I should go and see Mark?"

Everyone stopped talking, looking first at Estelle, then Aurelius.

"No. Not now. Your defense is based on not having any relationship with Mark for the last thirty years. It would be odd if you suddenly started seeing him now. It wouldn't do your case any good."

"I feel so guilty about your not representing him."

"What you two talking 'bout?" Marjorie asked, suspicion in her voice.

"Aurelius has a conflict of interest. He can't represent both me and Mark since I may be defending myself against Mark."

"Why?" Marjorie asked a little angrily.

"Well, we think the money Estelle is accused of moving around actually belongs to Mark, and he simply used her name to cover his activity."

"Why would he do that, Aury? Why would he set up an account in his own last name if he wanted to hide it? That make sense to you?"

"Ordinarily, no, Marjorie, but you haven't seen him. He is not all there. He seems to be drifting in and out of awareness. He could have done anything."

Marjorie looked unconvinced, and when she spoke, her voice was chilly.

"So you are going to give him up?"

"I can't represent both of them," Aurelius responded, the strain evident in his voice.

Marjorie looked at him for a long time, her eyes both hurt and accusatory. Then, Anis said, "So you t'ink Aury should leave Estelle to fend fuh sheself? He got to choose, and fuh my money, he should stick wid people who been loyal to he for such a long time."

Aurelius looked at Anis, gratitude in his eyes, then said, "I have to go and talk to Mark. I hope he can understand me today. Yesterday, he was a total blank."

He turned and walked out, the three pairs of eyes following him, each reflecting their own thoughts. For a while, the women sat quietly. Before them, the St. Euribian day shone, its sparkling beauty unaware of their lives. Marjorie watched a sparrow as it grabbed a piece of twig and darted back to a tree where its nest was. In the fustic tree, she could see the half-finished nest, and she thought of the story she had heard as a young girl—the warning to the know-it-all. When Blackbird and Sparrow first came to St. Euribius, Blackbird quickly learned how to build a nest made of twigs. Sparrow tried but could not build one. Finally, Sparrow swallowed his pride and asked Blackbird to show him how to build a nest. Blackbird agreed, but each time Blackbird would say "do it this way," Sparrow would reply, "I know." Finally, when the nest was half-finished, Blackbird, fed up with Sparrow's prideful response, said, "Okay, if you know so much, finish the nest yourself," and flew away. The nest was only half-made. From that day, Sparrow and Blackbird were enemies, and Sparrow never learned how to build a full nest. It was still half the size of a blackbird's nest.

She watched as the grey-feathered bird hopped around, taking its time to arrange the twig. *It must be getting ready to lay eggs,* she thought.

The fustic tree stood tall, its forbidding thorns sticking out like a warning. It was the only tree she knew that had thorns from its base all the way to its crown and, therefore, could not be climbed. The tree also reminded her of Mark, and she smiled. They must have been around twelve or thirteen years old and had been in the hills hunting down fat porks and dunks that hung in edenic abundance all along the walking paths. He had stopped so suddenly that she had bumped into him with a curse. He had been transfixed, and the fear had spread through her mind, filled with wild dogs, heartmen, and baccus. It had been none of these that had arrested Mark's flight, though. On the ground was a tiny sparrow, so young that the gray of its feathers was still streaked with yellow. It had evidently fallen from its nest and was feebly flopping around. Mark stood holding her back with one outstretched arm, his eyes darting from the tiny bird to the nest high up in the tree. There was no way to climb the fustic tree because the long thorns would shred the skin. The mother had built her nest out of the reach of walking predators, but now it was also out of the reach of one who wanted to help. Mark had reached down, gently picking the bird up and then looking forlornly upward. There was no way to climb that tree. Carrying the bird, he had searched for another nest in the nearby clammy-cherry tree, but none was to be found.

In the meantime, the mother had returned and was buzzing Mark's head, her shrieks of outrage joining the squeaks of fear from the baby sparrow. She had watched, fascinated by the caring he had shown that day. Finally, he had put it on the ground, and they had walked a little way off, hiding in the trees. She still remembered the sense of cool mystery those trees had created, the large over-spreading machineel tree dominating the space like a supreme god. They had watched, fascinated, as the mother had tried to pick the chick up with her beak, but the weight had been too much.

The sob had caught her by surprise, and when she had turned around, the tears had streaked Mark's face. Before she could say anything, he had walked out of the trees, frightening the mother bird away. She had watched, mesmerized, as he had walked like an automaton to the little sparrow. When the action came, it was so swift that she did not have time to protest, only to look in horror at the boy. He had brought his foot down in a short crushing motion, and she had heard the bones crack in the bird. The silence had descended with the sharpness of a knife slicing through butter, as the mother had flown back to the top of the tree, hopping frenetically from branch to branch.

She had run to where Mark stood, a violent protest on her lips, but his face had stopped her. It was wooden, remote, devoid of remorse or cruelty. Moreover, the cry-water still cascaded down his cheeks. Marjorie had stood watching, confused by so many things, but, above all, one thought. It was the first time she had seen Mark cry.

After that, the day had lost its lustre, and they had trudged home in silence. She had come to visit her aunt in Mark's village, and it was not until she had reached her aunt's home that she had broken the heavy silence that had fallen between them.

"Why you do that, Mark?"

Her soul had trembled at his answer, which was said in a voice totally devoid of emotion.

"It would have died anyway."

"What you crying 'bout?"

Anis' voice cut into her memory, shattering the image of that flawed day, like a stone thrown through a glass window. It took her a little while to remember where she was, but then she looked at Estelle and said, "I did thinking 'bout Mark. I see he kill a bird one time."

Anis' face soured, but Estelle smiled.

"You mean the day up in the hills? When the bird fell out of the fustic tree?"

Marjorie felt a sense of violation rise in her.

"You know 'bout it?" she asked.

"Yeah. Mark told me a long time ago. He always said he was so hurt by the bird's helplessness and his inability to help that he thought it best not to let it suffer."

Marjorie continued to look at Estelle, her memory of that day at odds with Estelle's explanation.

"I hated him that day. He didn't look human. De way he raise up he foot and bring it down on dat poor bird…"

She shuddered, and the others looked at her. The looks were very different though. Anis' face said that Marjorie was justified in hating him, except that she should not have limited it to that single day. Estelle's face showed a kind of pasty horror at Marjorie's words. No one said anything for a while. Then Anis sucked her teeth and stood up.

"Let we go and see Maylene. I ain't got no time to waste t'inking 'bout Mark St. Auburn."

The tone was discordant, but Marjorie and Estelle rose quickly, as if anxious to rid themselves of their thoughts.

CHAPTER TWENTY-FIVE

The cell had gotten smaller, and Mark sat, his back to the wall, watching the simple, bolt-secured lock that kept him in. In his mind, the picture of the tumblers was sharp, and he felt certain he could leave whenever he wanted to. He was in an isolated part of the prison, away from the general population that he could hear now as they made use of their illusory freedom in the yard. Aurelius had told him that his life would be in danger if he ventured out among that crowd, as their sympathies for the dead guard had been expressed. The news of the murder and, later, Mark's transfer to Dathorne Prison was common knowledge among the inmates, and they had talked about avenging the guard. Since so many of them had come from the village, they knew both the dead man and the dying mother, so the emotions were raw.

Mark was not too concerned with the inmates. If the occasion ever presented itself, he would deal with it as it came. What really worried him was the absence of the angel. She had not come around all day, and he watched both the cell door and the small window to see when she would come. He had been waiting all day. Also, he had seen the face of the man whom he had killed, and a leaden sorrow had now descended on his soul, for the face carried a boyish innocence that haunted him. He wished the angel would come so that he could gaze upon her peaceful face. Instead, he saw the medium-height man with the rigidly starched khakis leaning into his car as he stopped at the entrance, waiting to gain admittance to the hotel. After that, it was a blur, but he remembered the cruel clubbing action of the guard and his own response. It had been the young boy's hair that had triggered a long-buried memory in him, as it had flared out, making a halo of snake-like strands around the boy's head. His action had been almost involuntary, and the single chop to the larynx had folded the guard in on himself.

"Why did I do that?" Mark mumbled to himself.

At the far end of the corridor, the guard looked up, staring at the cell where the crazy man was held. Mark saw the alertness in the man and pretended to be half-asleep. Soon, the guard slipped back into his usual daydreaming. Mark had not seen Aurelius for four days, and he understood that his half-brother was no longer his lawyer. They had sent another lawyer, but he had not wanted to talk to him, and the man had left, carrying his irritating disappointment with him. Aurelius had explained that he could not represent both Mark and Estelle and, like so many times in the past, Aurelius had chosen someone else. Mark worked this around in his mind, but no emotion came with it. In fact, it had been rather amusing to see how uncomfortable Aurelius had been. Mark had said nothing, keeping his eye firmly fixed on the angel who had stood behind Aurelius, her slim, white body exposed, as her wings, outspread, covered Aurelius. Aurelius had not known she was there, and Mark and the angel had laughed in secret conspiracy.

Aurelius was worried but had no idea what surrounded him. Of course, Mark had had nothing to do with the money trail that had been laid so obviously. He would have been ashamed to do something so childish, but he knew who was behind it, and the purpose was obvious. His imprisonment protected him, at least for the moment, so they were going after someone they believed to be close to him. He had no family and, unless his teenage relationships counted, no friends. Estelle was all they had with which to threaten him. And it was a threat. In fact, it was more than a threat. It was an exact duplication of a mission he had run in Haiti. In that case, the general had not cooperated, and the wife had died, hacked into pieces by a gang of apparently mindless criminals. The criminals had never been found. So he knew they were sending him a message. He had asked Aurelius to have Estelle come to him, but she had refused. He wanted to tell her everything, to free his soul of the weight that pressed the darkness down on him. Today, that darkness had lifted, but he knew the angel was never far away, and she always brought her shroud. He wanted to talk to Estelle. Something in his heart had cried out for her. That is why he had come to this place where he could so easily be found. It did not matter anyway. He was going to die, and maybe that was a good thing. Long ago, he had lost the ability to live in the world, the normal associations of memory, place, and feeling torn apart by his years in the jungle. The jungles of Vietnam had provided freedom, a world in which law was dead, and he had thrived in that world, seeing in it a perfect complement to his shattered emotions. When had he lost his humanity? When had he and Ray become one? Ray lived comfortably outside the law, a god who made his own rules, who conformed to no man's wish. All the hatred he had brought from the Chicago ghetto that had spawned him was given free rein in Vietnam. It had been he who had first said to Mark, "It is easy to kill," and, in some way, had transformed death from an experience to an image. He was not sorry about Ray.

Even in the slime of the jungle, though, there had been a star in the darkness, and when the angel's shroud had threatened to overwhelm him, he had fixed his eyes on that dim, distant light and had hung on. The darkness of the jungle's night was not peaceful. It moved like sinuous snakes in a barrel. Nothing was still, movement was everywhere, and when it became too much to bear, he sought out the enemy, sometimes hunting apart from the group, anxious to kill, to find meaning in this endless slog of mud and insects and water and trees. Killing had become a form of sanity. It gave purpose to his life and the endless movement. He remembered Ray's face that day in Cam Ne when he had vomited on seeing the girl's body, her guts spilled out and her lips moving in a silent request. She had fallen when he had cut her in half, the lead tipped bullets making a neat stitch across her torso. Then, her guts had spilled out. When Ray had gotten off her, he had at first thought she was dead, but she had twitched, and her eyes, gray scales in her face, had opened. He had shot her twice in the head. Then, the darkness had descended, and the jungle had welcomed him. He had known that he was going mad, but madness had seemed like normality then. Insanity made the nights shorter, and killing gave them purpose. He had held on to the dim light of Estelle's memory like a lifeline, something that kept him moored to the shore.

When he had left after two tours and had headed back to St. Euribius, it was towards that light that had shone so fiercely in the jungle. She had come to him, with a child he wanted to protect, and in that protection, to find his humanity. He had never talked about Vietnam, never wanted to, even when he awoke at night, the sweat pouring off him because something, a dog perhaps, had moved in the night. He had lived with fear: fear that the jungle would return and fear that it would not. For the gentleness he gave to the child was a lie, a profound act of self-deception. The darkness still claimed him, and the angel still sat in attendance of his act, watching and smiling. He had married Estelle, hoping to trap that light that had guided him for so long, but it had not worked, and he had led her from innocence to depravity, in pursuit of the emotional charge the jungle had created. It had not worked. His soul had been lost in the darkness, and she could not lead him out of it. Their life had become a descent into a sexual hell of frenzy and experimentation. He knew she could sense his desperation and tried to give him what he wanted, but her body or her mind had betrayed her, and she took her satisfaction like a saint, with a smile of sacrifice.

She was not a saint, and though she had tried, her will would frequently falter, and the stark anger could be seen lurking behind the adoration in her eyes. It was not that she had not loved him. She had, but the brutality he brought to her bed soured her, and her body had dried up, absorbing his nocturnal descent into the proxy for the jungle.

In the end, he could not take her sacrifice, and he had enticed her to make love to him with threesomes and foursomes, discovering her nether self and finding himself filled with both contempt and self-loathing. She had never given him what he had wanted, that sweet, satisfying song of fulfillment, of confirmation, and so he had sought it elsewhere. At first, he had been discreet, but soon he gave up all caution, not caring, even willing the discovery. Estelle had been dazed by the rapid shifts in his personality. One moment, he could lay with her head on his chest, reading to her, creating that feeling of warmth that, for her, was the closest she came to ecstasy. When he read, he knew she had heard not only the story, but his love of words, and the magic of the interplay between the words and the voice had soothed her. He had always known about this magic of the sound of words, and he managed her this way, giving himself in these acts of unconscious love. Conscious love, however, had been denied her and him, for that act of connecting brought the jungle close, and when she whispered her desperate words of affection, searching urgently for some response, the picture of a young girl falling, her hair splayed out like a halo, would snag his mind, cutting off the words.

She had unconsciously encouraged his betrayal of her, for her anger was always tinged by tears, and that strengthened him. He had started to enjoy her pain, and their life became a reciprocal act of violence, a violence that had, at its center, a certain bitterness. He had watched the deep darkness emerge under her eyes, a stark contrast to the soft, doe-like look that had become her trademark. Even their violence had had an operatic quality, she behaving in repeated ways as if her actions had been scripted. Neither could quite figure out how to get off the treadmill of emotional violence, and their lives had become desperate, an orgy of emotional blasts and recovery.

Lana had broken the cycle of violence and response, love and anger. Mark could not remember her last name nor her face, but her first name had stuck. Lana had been a match for him, for she, too, lived off others' pain, feeding from the trough of their shattered souls. She had come to St. Euribius from Canada, a white Russian whose family had escaped Stalin's venom, carrying nothing with them into the dark Siberian night. In Canada, the family had prospered, and Lana, restless and free, traveled the world for excitement. She had had a husband somewhere, a dim figure who was more legend than fact.

He remembered the first time their eyes had met, and in that meeting was an understanding. So when she had casually invited him to join her and a friend at a beach club that night, the predictable had happened, and he had ended up at her house. Several people had been there, and they had smoked quite a bit. Throughout the night, he remembered exchanging bodies that fell on him like vampire bats, until, exhausted, he had fallen asleep. Much later, the sound of soft sniffling had awakened him. A little girl, no more than five or six, was walking among the naked bodies that lay around the floor. He had later found out it was Lana's daughter. She had been searching for her mother among the bodies, her forefinger in her nose. That image had stayed with him a long time. A young child lost among their depravity.

It had been late morning when he had gotten home, and the house had been empty, echoing with the sound of guilt. In the bedroom, a surprise had awaited him. He had found all his clothes folded neatly on the floor, and he had laughed. It was only after he had picked each piece up to find it had been disfigured in some way, usually with a knife slash, that the smile had faded. Something in that cool, quiet act of vengeance had sent a chill through him, and then a hot, dark anger had arisen. It was an anger only the jungle could satiate, and he had soon left St. Euribius, heading back to the Marine Corps and into the dark, soulless bowels of the Vietnamese jungle. They had welcomed him; and once they were sure his old instincts were intact, they had sent him back to that gray, musty world of uncertain enemies and even less sure friends. The angel lived with him, her wings outspread in protection, and her magic always worked. He was reunited with Ray, the only survivor from their group of two years before, and they had created their legend.

The star that had guided him on his first two tours had gone out, and in the lost light, Estelle's ghost had lived. They had written to each other for a while, but he could not muster the energy to find the reality of which she spoke. Her memories, on paper, became knife wounds, and, after a while, he had stopped answering, allowing the darkness to absorb him. His bond of hate with Ray had grown with his respect for the man's ability to survive, for Ray's magic light still illuminated him. They were decorated several times, but no one ever tried to promote them. They were good for one thing: destroying the enemy. And if, occasionally, they got confused about who the enemy was, officers turned a blind eye because they were the frontline. Mark smiled as he remembered how they were treated whenever they were brought out of hell for a few days to some frighteningly normal place like Danang. Ray wore his belt of rotting ears, the trophies of his kills, everywhere, and the stink sat on him. When they entered a bar, two tall men with the devil's mark upon them, hardened veterans had walked out silently, for they recognized that look they called devil's fire. They lived alone, drank alone, and occasionally they took the whores that had flooded Danang. They did it with a noisy violence that some officer always paid a tavern keeper to hush up. They were the elite of Satan's army, and they marched with pride.

Nixon's pullout had left both of them purposeless, and Mark had taken his pay and gone to New York, hiding in a small apartment on Flatbush Avenue. He went out only when he had to and kept the apartment in darkness. He was cold in the winter and hot in the summer, but that suited him fine. Sooner or later, they would find another jungle, and he would be ready.

He had been on the verge of dying when the letter had come to him. It was from Estelle. She had written it months ago, and it had made its way through a variety of military stops. The marines had finally found an address for him. He had not opened the letter for several days, worried about the fact that he had been found at all. He had left the apartment and had never returned, moving deeper into Brooklyn, hiding from the eyes that had searched him out. When finally he had opened the letter, he had been surprised to find that Estelle was in New York. She was studying for her doctorate in history. It had been ten years since he had seen her. He had been back from Vietnam for seven years, living like an animal, trying to find a hole deep enough to hide from the sun.

He had called the number she had written in the letter, and a man had answered. He could tell it was a white man, and something flared in him. He had felt this with a kind of wonder, for feelings had left him a long time ago. She had called back, and Mark had been surprised at the joy he felt at hearing her voice. He could not see her immediately, for even in his insanity, he understood that he could not present himself in the condition he was in. He found out that she was living with the man who had answered the phone, and a fierce competitiveness rose in him. It was not the right of marriage that motivated him—Indeed, he had forgotten that he had married her—but something primal stirred in him at the thought of another man possessing her. So the slyness had risen in him, and he had drawn her in, touching again, with words, the gateway to her soul.

It had been almost four months before they met. She had sent the man away to his parents in upstate New York, telling him the truth, that she had something to work out with her husband. Joe, good soul that he was, had left her alone in his apartment, and Mark had come. Their meeting had been awkward, for it felt as if it were a beginning, but a beginning with a painful and complicated history. They could not quite find the starting point, and he had watched her frustration turn to anger and then to something like desperate hatred that night. It was around Christmas, he remembered, and the oversized Christmas tree had seemed like an intrusion in the small apartment. They had talked desultorily but could not find the emotional bond they had had. He had wanted to touch her, but that had seemed too much of a commitment.

Finally, her body tight with anger, she had gone into the bedroom, the sharp click of the lock sounding a note of finality. Ironically, he had fallen asleep easily that night, and the dreams that left him fearful and drained had not come. When his survival instinct had been activated, he had known upon waking that it was too late. The luminous dial of the clock had said two thirty-two in red numbers, and outside he could hear the swish of tires, far below, on wet pavement. The Christmas tree flashed its three cycles of light: red, then darkness; green, then darkness; white, then darkness. The cycle seemed unending, and he had said into the darkness, "Are you going to do it?"

Mark twitched in the cell now, as he remembered the woman standing over him, her black body assuming the shades of the Christmas tree, alternately red, green, and white, and after each color, fading into the sharp, temporary darkness of the room. He had watched her right hand, in which there was a long knife that flashed silvery in the light. She was silent, the tears streaking her face, forming a mask that had been cut into three pieces. He had felt no fear. In fact, an odd calmness had pervaded his soul. In that moment, at that time, it had seemed right that she should be the one to end this death that he had been living. So, he had watched, welcoming the pure slice of the blade as it penetrated his skin, then his flesh, and finally some vital organ. Like most amateurs, she would go for the stomach, the biggest target, as if instinctively understanding that there, one could inflict the most pain, make the victim suffer longest. He had waited in the flashing light, watching the horror of her face, like a Halloween mask in the night.

She had not struck the deathblow. Instead, she had dropped the knife, a look of desperate confusion on her face. He could remember the look of her body through the nightgown she had worn. The flashing lights had given that body magic, a mystery he had never seen before. As she had stood over him, the water falling from her face to the rise of her chest, he had felt as if he had found the perfect moment, as if the many parts of his self had come together. Violence had been the stimulus of their lovemaking that night, but they had not been violent. Instead, they had lain in a soft blanket, their bodies incidental to this act of love. It was a sacrament and a leave-taking, an act that begged for forgiveness and said goodbye. He still remembered the salt of the tears when he had kissed her face and the oddly tangy smell of cigarettes that lay upon her breath. He had found his humanity in that moment, in that sweet act of giving. Ultimately, though, the frustration had built in him, for she had given herself with a wildness that promised much but had denied everything. From a long ways off, he could hear her cries that were an encouragement but, in the end, sounded like thinly disguised laughter. It pulled him on, hinting at an ecstasy that had never been his gift, a perfect complement to the heat in her touches. She had learned much in the ten years he had been missing, and he took the fruits of that knowledge with pleasure and with bitterness, his mind seeking the cause.

Somewhere along the way, she had stopped crying, and her eyes had bored into his. Their color changed with the flashing light, and she had seemed inhuman then, a creature that stared out from some other world that he did not know, could not understand. They had both been locked in their own world, connected by their strange, tactile association that, in the end, mattered little. Neither had felt any satisfaction in the act, and when, finally, he had arisen, the heavy hurt in his loins, he understood that he had lost touch with humanity. He had dressed silently and slowly. She had turned her naked body to lay facing the back of the couch. He could see the sweat on her, and something in him had softened at the thought of her chill. He had placed a blanket over her and, after picking up the knife from the floor, had walked out into the cold New York night, his senses alert to the streets, yet carrying with him the pungent smell of the woman.

Mark stood up in the cell, the movement catching the attention of the drowsy guard. Mark waved at him, and the man waved back. He felt sorry for the guard who was as condemned to solitary as he was. Feeling listless, he sought to energize himself by doing push-ups. He did a hundred, then did five hundred sit-ups. That done, he started to stretch, loosening his body. Outside, the sun was disappearing, and the cell had taken on the mysterious gray of evening.

Suddenly, he was alert, the hair rising at the back of his neck. A tall, graying man had walked into the cell block and was speaking quietly to the guard, who took what looked like an envelope from him and quickly scanned it. He started to escort the man towards Mark's cell, but the man stopped him with a smile and a nonchalant wave of his hand. Mark came to the cell door, his hands gripping the bars. As the man approached, he gauged the movement of his body but could detect no sign of strain. Finally, the man stood before the cell.

"Hello, Mark," he said, his voice casual, almost laughing. "You have given us quite a run."

Mark looked at the familiar face, the memories flooding his mind. He sensed the angel's presence on the outside, but though he could hear her flapping wings, she did not come in. He was glad because with this man, he needed to be clearheaded. After a while, Mark said, his voice careful, "Good evening, Colonel."

CHAPTER TWENTY-SIX

Aurelius watched the approaching lights of the airport with a sense of relief. He had been in three countries in three days and was bone-tired. Trying to backtrack the flow of money, he had been to the Caymans, Managua, and Panama City to meet with the bankers: discreet, cautious men who understood how to keep a secret. He had verified that the twenty million had, in fact, flowed through the banks, and the movement had been authorized by Estelle's signature. The trail ended abruptly in Panama City, the initial deposits having been made there over some twenty years. He had seen the deposits, which had begun in 1982, starting with amounts in the tens of thousands, then later growing to hundreds of thousands per deposit.

Where would Estelle have gotten that money from? The only thing that made any sense was drug trafficking, but he could not bring himself to accept this explanation. Estelle was too conscious of her social position, in fact, maybe too insecure in it to allow herself to be tempted in this way. He had handled her business for more than twenty years. Could she have been involved in something he knew nothing about? He did not think so. Yet, the money, with its uncertain origins, was there, and so was her signature. What would be the advantage of someone trying to place her in this compromising position?

His first thought had been that Mark had done it, but now he was not so sure. He remembered the look in Mark's eyes when he had asked for Estelle. He had wanted her to come to him, and his disappointment was obvious when she had refused. Could he be playing a part, pretending to want her while playing out some sick act of vengeance? He was not all there, that much was obvious. But what would motivate him to hurt Estelle in this way? Then there was the issue of the American involvement. What was their interest in Mark? He may have committed a murder in the United States, but that did not justify the extraordinary lengths to which the government had gone to keep him out of court and to get him out of St. Euribius. There had to be a connection between these two things, but for the life of him, he could not figure it out.

His last two conversations with Mark had been useless, the man lost in some fog that Aurelius' voice could not seem to penetrate. Yet, something lay in Mark's mind that he felt connected these things. He no longer represented Mark – that thought sent a shot of guilt through him – but he had to see him, had to have him make sense of this conundrum.

The plane touched down with a bump and a sharp, short shriek of tires, and soon he was walking quickly toward the terminal. He was still quite well-known, so he headed towards the DIPLOMATS ONLY line, though that particular designation no longer applied to him. He was soon in his car, heading home. He needed a shower and a rest, and his eyes were closing as the car headed east along the dimly-lit highway.

Within half an hour, he was home. Beverley had evidently taken the children to her mother's home, and the house was pleasantly dark and welcoming. He quickly showered and donning a knee-length robe, went up to his office on the second floor. The message light was blinking on the telephone, and for a moment, he thought of not answering. Finally, with a sigh, he pressed the replay button, sitting at the same time and sifting through a pile of bills and other letters. The fourth message was from the prime minister, asking him to call back as soon as he got in. Aurelius hit the stop button and quickly dialed the prime minister.

"Hey, Aury," Anderson St. Clair's voice said cautiously. "How was your trip?"

"Tiring, man. Worse, I didn't find anything to help Estelle. The banks were already aware of the trouble and had had the signature verified by experts. I did wire it to London to get my own verification. I am not optimistic, though. What's been going on here the last three days?"

"We had a small flare-up two nights ago, but nothing serious."

"How about Deighton? He still out campaigning or did the shooting scare him?"

The prime minister laughed.

"You know Deighton. He wouldn't back down from God himself. He now has police protection, though. I can't afford to have him hurt. Anyway, that's not the reason I had called. It's about Estelle."

Aurelius' stomach tightened slightly.

"What about Estelle?"

"You told the police and she confirmed that she had not seen Mark since 1972, right?"

"Yes. Why?"

"Then you have a problem, Aury. The police have evidence she was seeing Mark again in 1982. I am sure since your trip to Panama City you recognize the importance of that year."

"The year the deposits began. What are you saying, Andy?"

"Nothing at all. Just wanted you to know that Estelle is on record as having lied about her relationship with Mark. Didn't want you to be blindsided by this. That's all."

Aurelius hung up, wondering why the prime minister would give him information about a police investigation. Then he thought his question uncharitable. Anderson St. Clair was, after all, Estelle's friend, too. Maybe he was just trying to be helpful. Still, it was unusual for Anderson to expose himself in this way.

Aurelius dialed Estelle's number, but there was no answer. That was unusual because one of the servants would normally answer the phone. He hung up and called Beverley at his mother-in-law's home. The excitement in her voice was like a balm, and he spoke for a while with her and the two boys. She would be home within the hour, and Aurelius turned the desk lamp off and laid on the coach. In five minutes, he was asleep.

CHAPTER TWENTY-SEVEN

Estelle awoke abruptly with that sharp separation of unawareness and sentience that was the marvel of sleep. She lay still in the darkened house, but outside, she could see the reflected brightness of the security lights. She tried to remember what had awakened her from the vaguely remembered dream that had fled upon her return to consciousness. Something beyond reason kept her unmoving on the bed, a dimly understood feeling that, if she moved, she would betray her position. She was just about to dismiss this thought when she heard a low whisper, and the muscles in her body tightened. Someone was in the gardens. Her bedroom sat at the back of the house, and from the patio, she could view her gardens. Her senses fully alert and her heart pounding, she slipped quietly off the side of the bed, keeping her head below the window. The blinds had only been partially pulled, so if she stood up, anyone outside would be able to see her figure outlined in the light from outside. After a while, she cautiously raised her head, pulling the blind slowly back and hoping that whoever was outside would not notice the movement. At first, the darkness of the lime trees was all she could see beyond the penumbra of the light. The stillness sat upon the land with a brittle insistence, and she felt alone in the world except for the memory of the whisper she had heard. She stared at the bushes for a long time, aware of her fear, but with some part of her mind thinking that she was foolish.

There is nothing out there, she thought. *I am just tense since the riot, that's all.*

Still, she continued to stare, squinting at the smoky darkness of the lime trees. She was just about to drop the drapes back into place when she saw the man move. Her heart almost stopped as the figure stepped away from the deeper darkness of the trees, and the tall, skinny silhouette was visible for a moment. She recognized the figure. It was the tall Rasta boy from the village who had carried the cutlass like an extension of his arm. Estelle turned and sat abruptly, wondering what he was doing there. He had been polite on the few occasions she had gone back to the village to see Mrs. Greaves, the dead guard's mother. Why was he standing outside her bedroom, that long cutlass in his hand? Her breathing had accelerated, and she sat on the carpet, thinking. What should she do? She was sure there was someone else out there. If she turned on the light, would that frighten them away? Would the light precipitate some action that they were contemplating? Not sure what to do, Estelle hugged her knees to her chest, that act of making her body smaller somehow creating the illusion of invisibility.

Still, she knew she had to do something. Thinking that maybe they were gone, Estelle rose slowly again, peeking out between the partially drawn blinds. The tall figure was more visible now, his back to the house, and he was evidently saying something to another figure who was hidden in the trees. The light occasionally glinted off the cutlass. Estelle withdrew, trying to remember where she had placed the phone. She had taken it out of the cradle earlier and had brought it into the bedroom. She swept her hand over the nightstand in the darkness but only encountered the base of the lamp and a glass with the remnants of her drink in it. Where was the phone? She slid up to the bed and carefully ran her hand over it. She found the phone tucked under a pillow, and she snatched it up, punching the "frequent contacts" button and scrolling through to Aurelius' number. She punched the send button and waited while the phone rang at the other end. Aurelius' wife, Beverley, picked up the phone, and Estelle whispered, "Beverley, is Aury at home?"

The woman on the other end was still half asleep, and it took a little while for her to understand the urgency in Estelle's voice. Soon, Aurelius' sleepy voice was in her ears.

"Aury, there are men outside in my garden."

"Men? In the garden? What are they doing?"

"I don't know," she whispered. "They just seem to be standing there, watching the house."

Aurelius thought for a moment, then said, "Stay where you are. I am going to call Patrick and have him send a couple of his fellows over to check it out. I am going to be there in twenty minutes. Stay where you are, and don't turn on any lights. Okay?"

Estelle answered in the affirmative and hung up, slumping back to the floor and leaning against the bed. Time seemed not to be moving, and, for some reason, now that she had called, she was more afraid to look outside. It seemed like an eternity, but finally, she heard a squealing car turn into the driveway and quick, heavy movement up the steps leading to the back of the house. Reassured by these sounds, she stood, looking through the space in the blinds. Two uniformed policemen were moving through the gardens. Involuntarily, Estelle hoped they would not step on her roses. The two men disappeared into the trees. She quickly dressed and, turning the light on, walked downstairs. As she reached the door, Aurelius was pulling up into the circle before the house. He jumped out as she was opening the door.

"You all right?" he asked, concern evident in his face.

Estelle craned her neck around the doorjamb, looking towards the back of the house where the policemen were walking slowly back to the driveway, their searchlights making short arcs in the night. She waited until they had come to the door, then asked, "You see anybody?"

"No," the stockier of the two policemen replied. "But somebody was definitely out dere. You kin still see de footprints in de dirt."

The four retired to the inside of the house, where Estelle gave a short statement to the police. Aurelius watched her closely, aware of the two sharp lines that had appeared in her face in the last couple of weeks. She was taking this whole thing hard. She had fought her feelings when Mark had been arrested for murder, but her own arrest had shattered her, causing her to withdraw. Always somewhat reserved, she had become reclusive, almost unable to function socially. When pressed, she would still engage in conversation, but it was as if she were acting on instinct, and once the necessity was gone, she slipped back into a sort of stasis. He was worried about her. He still remembered the time she had gone into what Marjorie had called a trance, and nobody could get her to react—except Mark. And Mark had his own mental problems now.

His mind jumped to Estelle's comment about the white man who had become Marjorie's boyfriend almost overnight. She had said he was here to study mental illness in St. Euribius, and thinking of his two friends, Aurelius was inclined to believe there was something special about the insanity of this island. He had joked about that when Estelle had told him of the man's research, but now he was not so sure.

Aurelius looked at her as she gave the statement, and seeing her face with its fear, perplexity, and wonderment, he knew that she could have nothing to do with drug trafficking or money laundering. Still, his natural lawyer's caution held at least the question in front of him. Could the fear be for something other than what he thought? No. Estelle was a good person; a little uptight, but fundamentally decent. Mark had enmeshed her in something that neither Aurelius nor she fully understood. A fierce anger rose in him at Mark for his callousness.

Still, Anderson St. Clair had said she had lied about seeing Mark after he had left the island. She had said more than once that she had not seen him since he had walked away from their marriage in 1972. Why would she lie about seeing him ten years later, the very time the money had appeared in the Panamanian bank account? A small vein throbbed at the side of her head, and he noticed how tenderly she touched the spot.

She must have a headache, Aurelius thought, leaning back on the couch, waiting for her to finish the statement. Finally, the policeman closed his small notebook, saying, "Well, if there is nothing else, Mrs. St. Auburn, we will go out to the jeep. De boss say we should stay around 'til morning."

Estelle nodded wearily, and the two men left. Alone, they sat silent for a while, Aurelius weighing whether she could stand the questions he knew he had to ask. He was not aware that he had drifted away until she said softly, "You had better call Beverley, Aury, and let her know that it's all right."

Aurelius nodded, rising. His wife had, indeed, been waiting, and he indicated that he would be home before daybreak. The children expected him to be there to open the gifts. He returned to the couch thinking how strange this Christmas was. The world he knew was disturbed, set on edge by a single, unexplained act that seemed to have pulled everyone into its vortex. Everything had changed in two weeks, the orderly pace of his life and of those around him, broken by suspicion, anger, and a vague sense of being out of control of their circumstances. He remembered the prime minister's voice a couple weeks ago, when he had asked him if he sometimes felt that all of their lives were an illusion, a chimerical vision that they accepted as real. And Estelle, the historian, the one who ordered inchoate events, the most likely of innocents, was caught in this race of events that seemed to have spun out of control so quickly and without any warning.

"Is something wrong, Aury?"

The voice surprised him, and he looked at her, a hint of guilt on his face. He hesitated for a moment, then answered, "Actually, there is."

Her face closed, and he hated what he had to say, but he had to know if he was going to be any help to her.

"I spoke with Anderson tonight after I came back, and he said the police have got some evidence that you were seeing Mark sometime in 1982. You told the police that you had not seen him since 1972."

Aurelius watched as her face went through a series of transformations. First, her eyes opened wide; then, her face went blank. Finally, she made an inarticulate cry and collapsed, her face in her hands. Aurelius crossed the room quickly and sat next to her. She was shaking.

"What's the matter, Estelle?"

She shook her head, leaning forward. Her exposed neck, showing just a hint of looseness in the flesh, looked vulnerable. Aurelius placed his hand gently on her shoulders. After a while, she said, "Don't make me think of that, Aury."

"Sorry, Estelle. We've got to talk about it. That lie, if it is a lie, could send you to jail."

"Why? I just didn't want to talk about it, that's all."

"Why?"

She paused, then said, her voice neutral, "It hurts too much."

"But you two were together in 1982?"

Estelle nodded, and Aurelius exhaled slowly.

"The problem, Estelle, is that deposits to the bank account began in the same year that you were seeing Mark. Can you imagine how that looks to the police?"

She looked at him, her eyes a little fearful.

"Aury, I swear I don't know anything about the money. I don't know how anyone would be able to forge my signature like that. It must be Mark. He is the only one who would have had my signature on anything."

"And you have no idea what Mark was in to?"

"No. I saw him in New York that one time when I was at Columbia."

"What happened? Why didn't you see him again?"

Estelle looked away, but not before he caught the wild look in her eyes.

"What happened, Estelle?"

When she spoke, her voice was small.

"I almost killed him."

"You what? What do you mean you almost killed him?"

"Have you ever wanted something so much you felt that, if you took away its will, its ability to act, you would have it?"

Aurelius could not say that he had, but the woman really did not want an answer from him, so he kept quiet.

"I wanted him dead. I had waited so long for that day. We had written to each other and talked on the phone for four months before Mark came. I was living with someone, but from the moment Mark called, I wanted to see him. Do you believe in fate, Aury? I felt Mark was made for me, you know! I was eleven years old when I first saw him, and I knew even then. God! God! God!"

The cry came from somewhere in her bowels, and Aurelius could feel the pain in his own.

"Aury, Mark put me through so much."

Aurelius looked at her, surprised at her total lack of reserve. He was both fascinated and repulsed by it. As if she sensed this, Estelle looked at him sharply, her eyes, wild and fearful, seeking the rejection. Aurelius composed his face, and she continued.

"You know, I sometimes wonder what changed him. When he left here, he wasn't like that. Mark was never the most sensitive man in the world, but he could feel things that other people didn't. That was why all those girls liked him."

"Well, his fast feet helped, too," Aurelius said, laughing to lighten the mood.

"No," Estelle said sharply. "Most people think that was the reason, but it wasn't that. Mark is… Mark is a… an… emotional chameleon. He can feel what you feel, and you know that he's feeling it. Women like to be understood more than anything. More even than loved. Although, there may be little difference between the two. That is what Mark had that most boys didn't."

She paused, and Aurelius was aware of an odd feeling. He was surprised to find he resented this description of Mark since it made him feel less accomplished, almost ordinary. Estelle's blindness annoyed him, for he saw in Mark a liar of the worst sort: one who so believed his lie, he thought it was the truth, so others did too. Mark was nothing like Estelle saw. Her voice interrupted his thought.

"He so envied you."

"Me? Why would Mark envy me? He was the one with the fast feet and the huge following."

"Sometimes boys, even men, can be so blind."

Aurelius noticed that she was getting her emotions under control.

"Mark wanted to be you before he had fast feet and a huge following, and he never got over that. You were the one with the light skin and pretty hair and the angelic face. Everybody liked you and would come to see you play cricket long before he discovered he had speed.

You mostly ignored him, almost as if you were ashamed of him. Were you ashamed of him, Aury?"

"Why would I be ashamed of Mark?" Aurelius asked, a deep discomfort settling in the pit of his stomach. He could hear the hollowness in his voice, and his mouth felt dry.

"His poverty, how he dressed, maybe his black skin. Who knows? I only know that you kept him at arms length. Why did you two never acknowledge that you were brothers?"

"I don't know. Neither of us was comfortable with it, I guess."

"And yet you were together a lot, particularly after he became better known than you. Everybody but you thought how odd it was that you two could be friends but not brothers, especially since everybody else thought of you as brothers."

"Mark was too proud. He would never admit it. Even today he has never talked to our father. He still hates him, and, deep down, I feel that he hates me, too. I don't know how to deal with that."

Estelle was quiet for a while, and both realized they had drifted away from their primary concern: the lie she had told which now threatened to trap her. But something pulled them on to this examination of their past. It was as if their separate truths could only be given meaning in this examination of the man who tantalized their lives. Aurelius felt an insubstantial anger, the reason for which he could not locate, for it lay deep in the core of him, hidden from his own eyes. Estelle, more accustomed to opening herself to this ghost that was her husband, fought the pain, explaining away Aurelius' blindness as a proxy of her own. Finally, she continued.

"He wanted you to like him."

"Why would he have cared?"

"Because, Aury, if you had liked him, then he would have had the statement that he wanted. That your father was his father. That he had a place. Don't you understand?" Aurelius sighed, shaking his head.

"He has always felt deserted, Aury. His father never accepted him, and his mother, for the longest time, treated him like a nuisance. She left him with whoever would take him. She did not want him either."

"I think you are imagining this, Estelle. Or simply repeating things he told you. Nobody ever deserted him. My father told me that it was Mark's grandmother who thought my father was not good enough for her daughter. That's why he never had anything to do with Mark."

"I wonder who is imagining things now, Aury."

The night had been slipping away, and Aurelius looked significantly at his watch. Estelle saw the gesture and smiled. Then, she heard the sound of a powerful engine coming down the driveway, and she looked anxiously at the door, her eyes, which had lost their wild look, flaring again.

"That must be Marjorie. I asked her to come over, and you know she lives up behind God's back."

Aurelius stood as he was speaking, heading downstairs to the door. Outside, he saw the policemen approaching the driver's window of Marjorie's black Mercedes. They both recognized her and greeted her in official tones. The big woman dragged her body out of the car, practically ignoring the respectful constables, and lumbered up the steps.

"Whe' she is?" she asked, out of breath.

The workouts evidently had their limits. Aurelius pointed upstairs as she pushed past him, a mother elephant rushing after her endangered young. Before she reached the top of the circular staircase, her voice rang out.

"You awright?"

Estelle nodded, her face warming to her friend's outrage.

"Yuh know, nuhbody ain't safe 'bout here nuh mo'e. I wish I did here wid yuh. I wouda…"

Aurelius, tiring of the drama, said archly, "Wha' you did goin' do? Sit down `pon dem?"

Seeing the hint of a smile blossom on Estelle's face, he grinned broadly. Marjorie turned on him.

"Dis aint nuh laffing mattuh, Aury. 'Bout here getting too blasted dangerous."

Aurelius, properly chastened, became serious. Marjorie, meanwhile, dropped like a lead weight on to the couch beside Estelle, her arms circling the smaller woman's shoulders. Aurelius felt suddenly excluded, and he said, "Well, now that the cavalry has arrived, I am going home. The two policemen will be here until morning, and tomorrow we can talk about if you want to arrange for a guard. Meanwhile, try to get some sleep. We still need to figure out how to handle that other business."

Estelle's face immediately looked haggard again, but she answered bravely, and Aurelius walked out, feeling a little confused about what had happened before Marjorie walked in. He felt that Estelle should have been angry with Mark for getting her into this mess, yet she had turned on him, almost accusing him of some vaguely defined betrayal of Mark. He was tired, though, and would think about it later.

CHAPTER TWENTY-EIGHT

Inside the house, the two women sat, comfortable in the warmth of their magic circle. Then, Estelle said, "Thanks for coming. I really don't want to be alone."

Marjorie hugged her tightly for a second but did not say anything. Outside, the early Christmas morning was chilly, a northeast wind having sprung up. Through the glass doors leading to the patio, she could see the trees waving in apparent diffidence. Estelle thought of the two policemen outside in the wind, and she stood, heading to the kitchen. Marjorie followed her, and as the water boiled, the two women continued in silence. Estelle's fear had retreated, and now, looking back on the scene of a couple of hours ago, it felt unreal, registering in her mind as if she were a voyeur, stealing emotions from another's experience. The police did not know about the boy with the cutlass. Why had she held back? Some instinct had stopped her. The boy had frightened her, but by the time the police had arrived, her reaction had felt a little foolish. She had thought of the boy's politeness when she had gone to the village, and that seemed so different from what she had first thought on seeing him outside her bedroom, she had hesitated.

She and Marjorie each took a cup of tea out to the two policemen who sat in the jeep. They accepted the men's grateful thanks and went back inside.

"I am sleepy, girl. How you feel? T'ink you kin sleep?"

"I am not sure, but you should go to bed. I am all right now, and the policemen are outside. You can use the bedroom next to mine."

They walked upstairs to the two bedrooms with a connecting door that Estelle opened. She saw the bed depress in soundless protest as Marjorie sat, fluffing up the pillows.

It is good that she decided to lose weight, Estelle thought, a warm feeling of affection surging in her. Marjorie's bark was worse than her bite, though she had a hell of a bark.

Estelle changed slowly, feeling exposed with the door open, yet more comfortable because of her friend's presence. Marjorie turned off the light, laying down in the same motion. Estelle slipped under the thin covers, immediately feeling the warmth descend on her. In the darkness, Marjorie's voice, when it came, was small, disguising the woman's size.

"Estelle, I want you to know dat all de girls behind you. Nobody ain't believe none uh dat foolishness. I just want you to know dat. Okay?"

Estelle felt the tears in her eyes, and she did not immediately answer. When she did, it was not directly to Marjorie's comment.

"Do you think people ever really change, Marjorie?"

"Well, you remember Mabel Gittens? She change. She used to screw everything around here, and den she get Jesus, remembuh? And she would walk 'bout in dem long, foolish clothes, saying to everybody who trouble she, 'I rebuke you in the name uh de Lord.' Remembuh?"

In spite of herself, Estelle laughed. Mabel had been a riot. Marjorie was not done, however.

"And you remember Tempest. He used to steal everything that wasn't nailed down. They say he was such a good pimp dat one night Elbert did screwing Anis 'pon de bay, and he t'ing slip out. Tempest did so close he put it back in, and both Anis and Elbert thought de other one did do it. Den Tempest started to go church and would help de police track down thieves. I suppose it tek one to know one."

Estelle giggled, replying, "I don't think that Tempest changing had anything to do with church. It was de lash dat Chanta give he wid de bull pistle. Dey say dat when he hit Tempest wid it, Tempest open he mout wide, wide, but nuh sound dint come out, and he pee straight."

Both women were now laughing in the darkness like little girls, and, for a moment, the world seemed normal. Marjorie had a stock of old stories, and they rolled off her tongue now, at first stimulating the latent laughter in Estelle's spirit then, as she relaxed, lulling her to sleep. The voice was soft, rhythmic, with the cadences of the island, and Estelle felt something lifting off her as her head slipped to the side of the pillow.

When Marjorie was sure that Estelle was asleep, she stopped talking, satisfied with her gift of friendship. She had been awake when Aurelius had called, for Bryan had been expected, but he had not come. It was the first time in the last two weeks that she had been alone, and the house had felt empty and a little overpowering. At eleven, she had left for the church to attend midnight mass and had felt some relief when all the girls had shown up. The service usually stimulated her, the story of the baby Jesus an oil that calmed the turbulent waters of her soul. Tonight, though, those waters had remained choppy, and her mind had been unable to hold the reverend's lesson. Reverend Gaulson had gone through the service with the usual effect so that, by one o'clock, everyone had nodded off, raised to life again only by the periodic irritation of the servers who passed the offering baskets with an alacrity quite out of keeping with the general state of the energy in the church. Reverend Gaulson's monotonous voice ensured that the heightened state of excitement caused by the offering did not last long. She had not taken communion, a certain hesitancy because of her relationship with Bryan having crept into her submission to the church.

Marjorie had been sitting on the front porch when Aurelius had called, still watching the occasional light flare when a car passed on the distant highway, hoping against hope that it would turn off into the long road that led to her home. Each car's lights had blazed briefly and then disappeared into the darkness, carrying her flagging hopes with them. She had called his rented apartment several times, but there had been no answer, and she had had to fight the urge to drive by. They still had not developed that level of intimacy where showing up without notice was accepted.

Now, she lay on the bed, wondering where he was. When Estelle's voice came out of the darkness, it surprised her.

"Girl, your sighing keep waking me up. What's the matter?"

"It's Bryan. He was supposed to come by tonight, and I never hear from he."

Estelle heard both the worry and the fear in Marjorie's voice, and she prayed silently that this would not turn out to be a problem. Marjorie had been desperate after John had left, and they had worried about what she might do. She had, however, directed that emotional energy into her businesses, and they had grown. Still, her collapse in the first months of the breakup had been frightening to watch. Remembering what had happened at her party three weeks ago, Estelle knew that the woman in the next room was still raw and vulnerable. She had let her guard down with this man, but her fear of desertion was still palpable.

"Maybe he got busy with something. You know how we highfa-lutin' scholars are. We get our heads into something, and we forget the world."

"Yeah. Dat mus' be it," Marjorie said uncertainly. "Nobody don't own nobody else, right?"

"You've been the happiest of us over the last couple of weeks, you know. It was as if everybody's life got turned upside down."

"Yeah. I been t'inking how strange dat is. Everyt'ing happ'ning at de same time."

The darkness gave a strange quality to their conversation, almost as if it were pure thought, unattached to minds that felt and saw and hurt. It was an illusion. Yet, the darkness created an intimacy that the women exploited, and the present brought to mind their past, since the two lay in the same cradle, twin curses that screamed in the night. These were not unhappy women. Both had found joy in life, and when that life had jumped up and kicked them in the teeth, they had fallen but had gotten back up, fighting each day on its own merits.

"Estelle, you tell Heather wha' going on?"

The sound of her daughter's name caused a flood of conflicting emotions in Estelle.

"No."

"Yuh should, you know. She should know 'bout dis. Not dat I t'ink anyt'ing going happen to you, but yuh know how she feel 'bout Mark."

Estelle sighed loudly. Marjorie had a closer relationship with Heather than did she, and she always dreaded her conversations with her daughter. The girl had grown up with her face and Blue's height. She had lost the diffidence since going to Europe, and the last time she had been in St. Euribius, Estelle had been stunned at how she looked. Gone had been the clumsy stockiness of Heather's teenage years. She had been wearing a form-fitting mini-skirt of golden knit and a match-ing jacket, and Estelle had stared at her, unable to comprehend the change. Heather was making money modeling part-time, and though Estelle had known this, she had not been prepared for the elegant crea-ture who had walked off the airplane, a stylish bag slung nonchalantly over her shoulder. Worse had been the girl's – the woman's, for Heather was now thirty-three - self-possession. Estelle had expected awkward-ness but had assumed that Heather would be the one experiencing it. She had expected Heather to be what she had been, unsure of the rela-tionship with her mother, and, therefore, a little insecure. She had been prepared to be generous with her time, to make a special effort to be with the young woman. What she had not been prepared for was to be tolerated, to be patronized and, occasionally, ignored. Somewhere in the last decade since the girl had gone to Europe, she had outgrown not only her diffidence but her mother as well. Estelle had watched as the girl lavished attention on her grandmother, and she had felt a powerful sense of exclusion from their circle. In the end, frustrated with the girl's polite non-responsiveness, she had claimed that she had to return to the university early and had left the two. The girl had not come to the airport to see her off.

Their conversations, subsequently, had been infrequent and stilted. They called to celebrate the formal interruptions in the natural flow of their lives like birthdays and holidays and to report the deaths of people that the other might know, but there was no affection, and Estelle was aware of a profound loss that she had no idea how to correct. She did not want to admit that she had given up, but, in fact, she had. Maybe she had given up long ago, and it was only her pride that was now offended by the girl's rejection.

Heather had never rejected Mark, though he had walked out of their lives as casually as he had walked in. It was amazing. He had been with her for the first two years of her life and had written her from time to time, and yet, he lived in her imagination as someone important. She had completely ignored her mother's side of the argument, and in her eyes lay the accusation: Estelle had sent Mark away. Heather still asked about him whenever they spoke, although Estelle had the distinct impression it was more to upset her than with any expectation that she would have information.

She had not called Heather because, in some strange way, she was still snatching her daughter from Mark in a darkened bedroom.

"You gone back to sleep?" Marjorie asked.

"No. I was thinking about my relationship with Heather and about how I really missed my chance with her."

Marjorie did not respond immediately, but when she did, her voice was soft and cautious.

"You can't change wha' happen when you did young. Everybody does mek mistakes, and all yuh kin do is hope fuh de best. Heather goin' come 'round."

"It's strange, you know, but I only just thought about how hurt she must have been as a child. I remember once we were going somewhere, and I had some friends here from America on vacation. The car was going to be pretty full, you know, and Heather was standing on the verandah while we were going down the steps. For some reason, I looked at her, and she said 'There ain't going to be any room for me, right?' It nearly broke my heart, Marjorie. It was not the question so much as it was the tone, the assumption that she would be the one to be left out, that tore at my guts. I don't know what I've done to that child, but I hope some day she can see her way toward forgiving me."

"You did young, Estelle. There ain't nothing to forgive, except maybe you need to forgive yourself. You di'nt prepared for nuh chile, and it showed. But you did your best fuh dat girl, and no matter how she act now, she goin' realize it sooner or later."

Estelle hoped that Marjorie was right. She had never felt more lonely than in the last few weeks since the murder. Her mother had become, if anything, more distant, so she had been reluctant to go over to the plantation. She had begun visiting Mrs. Greaves, and the woman, although gruff with her at first, had gradually warmed. After her second visit, Estelle had realized that she was going to visit as much for her benefit as the woman's.

"You know what's the oddest thing?" Estelle asked, turning on her side and facing the dark, adjoining bedroom. "My mother has been visiting Mrs. Greaves, taking her food and so on. And Mrs. Greaves calls her by her first name. How odd is that?"

Marjorie chuckled in the darkness.

"You mudder ain't the ogre dat you t'ink she is, yuh know. I don't know wha' wrong wid de two of you, but most people don't see your mudder de way you see she. I remember when we did really young, we had what people call de famine. Dat was when de rice crops from Guyana – it was British Guiana den – fail, and people 'bout here did starving. It did you mudder dat open up de plantation to the village, and people went an' dig potatoes and yams from you-all ground fuh free. You remember dat? It must uh been 1960 or sometime 'bout dere."

"Dat was my father who open the plantation to the village," Estelle responded a little petulantly.

"No. Dat ain't true. I remember because de old people still talk 'bout how Mrs. Prescod convince she husband to let de poor people get de ground provisions fuh free. I don't know how you don't remember dat."

Estelle was silent. She was sure that Marjorie was wrong. Or was she?

"Marjorie, are you sure that it was my mother, not my father?"

"Absolutely. My mudder used to talk 'bout it all the time."

She paused, then added cautiously, "You know, you should try and patch t'ings up wid you mudder. She getting old, and you don't want to be sorry for anyt'ing later."

"Why should I patch anything up? I've tried to please her, but nothing I do seems to make any difference."

Marjorie heard the petulance in her friend's voice and wondered if she should continue. She decided it was important to.

"You know, we all used to envy you when we did at school. You would come sometimes in dat big, black car and wid you mudder who always look like she did just come from a tea party. Back in dem days, we couldn't come to you home, so we used to imagine wha' it did like to live in dat big plantation house, wid servants and everyt'ing. It seem to we dat you mudder doted on you den. She use to treat you like you did so special. And you loved it. We did so jealous."

Marjorie chuckled in the darkness, then added, "Yes. We did so jealous of you. De little princess."

Estelle allowed herself to think back to her days at the elementary school in the village. It was true that had been a special time, but she always remembered her father driving her to school, not her mother. Could she be wrong? She so seldom thought of those days now. It was almost as if her life began in high school, and by then her memories were less of home and family and more of the girls and Mark. She closed her eyes in the darkness, allowing the pictures of that past to form in her mind. In those images, Mark's thirteen-year-old eyes stared back at her, the first look that seemed so all-embracing, so possessive, and so haunted. He had looked her over, and something in her eleven-year-old soul had started like a frightened rabbit smelling danger. She was not sure what had actually brought them together, but she felt sure that he must have made the first move. Already, at thirteen, he was clearly the leader of his group of five or so boys, the ones the girls secretly giggled about. Young as she was, she had sensed something in him, something that both attracted and frightened her. Later, she would think of that quality as tragic, but then he simply seemed self-possessed and somewhat callous. She had taken a risk by talking to him because it seemed to her that most of the girls had also sensed that remoteness in him and did not like him. In some ways, he had been shabby, and his poverty had been obvious. Not that many of the girls had means, but his poverty was extraordinary, and he never seemed to have even the lunch money the other children had. She remembered that the girls used to laugh at the shiny surface of his khaki pants. Too many washings and pressings.

Yet, something in her heart had quickened at his attention and his brittle confidence. For her twelfth birthday, he had saved all his money and had bought her a present: a cheap, pink comb and brush set. She had known that it had not cost much, but she had treated it like gold. He had not known how to make the gesture and had shoved it at her with a grunt after school on a day when the sun had peaked through rain-laden clouds. The brilliant, roseate clouds in the west had felt not like approaching evening, but like a new day. She had kept that set until she left for university at twenty-four. While she had been away, her mother had renovated the house, and her comb and brush set had been lost. It was the first time she had confronted her mother.

"Marjorie, have you thought how strange it is that Mark should have ended up in the American army? You remember how opposed he was to England, and by the time we left school, how angry he was about America, too?"

"I don't remember anything 'bout America, but I know he hated St. Euribius' relationship wid England. He did always talking 'bout colonialism dis and colonialism dat. I remember he was all fuh independence."

"You remember after independence how he got into trouble for pushing that guard at Miramar into the water?"

Marjorie laughed.

"Dat was so funny. I sorry dat I din't dere. He, Aurelius and Anderson did together dat day. Some people say dat is how Aury and Anderson political careers start out."

The three boys had been in trouble before for going on to the jetty the hotel had built. Whenever the guard would come to chase them off, the boys would jump into the water, leaving the frustrated village-man screaming at them. The boys would laugh and shout insults back before swimming away. The white tourists would look in amusement or perplexity at this war being fought on their behalf. Then one day, Mark had not jumped off the jetty. The guard had been confused for a moment at this change in tactics, and Mark's boldness had grown. He had smiled, and the guard had charged at him, still expecting him to jump into the water. Mark, instead of retreating from the threatening figure, had charged at him, ducking under the swinging club, and both had fallen into the sea. Surprisingly, the guard had been a poor swimmer, and he had panicked, flapping around and swallowing half the ocean before he realized it was shallow and he could stand. Mark had followed him to the beach and had walked back on the jetty. By then, the whites had been fleeing.

When the police had come, Mark had been taken to the station and held until his mother came. The hotel had pressed charges, but a local lawyer had taken Mark's case pro-bono and had won not only Mark's freedom, but a precedent-setting case. The courts had determined that since, by law, all beaches were public, and since jetties were an extension of the beach, the jetties themselves were also public. For a while, Mark had been hailed as a hero for the local cause, but eventually, the fuss had died down when the hotel agreed to build a second jetty which the boys could use and not bother the tourists. The victory, however, had been complete, and the boys had accepted the second jetty without giving up their right to the first. Slowly, both jetties had fallen into disrepair as the whites shifted their base of operations. Estelle had walked by the jetties a few months ago, and both were now practically destroyed, victims of the occasionally angry sea and the hotel's neglect.

Now she asked, "Marjorie, how could someone who was willing to fight Miramar Hotel over access to the jetty enlist in the American army just a couple of years later? That does not seem to make sense."

"Girl, who kin tell why people do t'ings? Mark always seemed to be marching to a different drummer anyway. Maybe dat was de only way he could survive in America."

Estelle thought for a moment, not convinced. Finally, however, she said, "Maybe you are right. It just seems so unlike Mark to have lied about finishing university and all that; and, also, fighting in a war he had expressed such anger at before he left here in 1968."

They lay in silence for a while, each absorbed in her own thoughts. Outside, the darkness had been lightening for some time, and in the distance, Marjorie heard the disembodied crowing of an early rising cock. Another, equally distant but coming from a different direction, answered. It was Christmas Day.

Marjorie thought about what she had just said, knowing that she was not entirely truthful. She had always felt it was hurt that had driven Mark more than anything. After Aurelius had gone to England to study, Mark had almost gone mad with some combination of envy and anger, but, driven by these, he had trained harder, and his times had improved. The scholarship had been both an opportunity to study and an escape from the shame she knew he felt at being left behind. When, in the last couple of weeks, she had heard that he had never finished university, she had not been surprised because she had always known that America had been more about proving his equality to Aurelius than it was about studying. His scholarship at an American university had matched, in his mind, Aurelius' father – also his father – sending Aurelius to an Eng-

lish university. That particular need fulfilled, she could easily understand the lost motivation. Still, he would have had to remain in America to sustain the illusion. What better place than the American army?
It made perfect sense to her.

Outside, the cocks' voices had multiplied, and into her mind
popped the first line of an old Cat Stevens' song.

"Morning has broken, like the first morning."

The soft, lyrical refrain filled her mind as the cacophony outside
gradually increased. It was Christmas Day. It could be the first day. She
hoped Bryan would call. Later today, all the girls would come by for
Christmas lunch at her house, so she had better get a little sleep. In the
next room, she could hear the gentle snoring coming from Estelle, and
she was glad that her friend had found rest. She should, too. Marjorie
turned on her side, away from the connecting door, and closed her eyes.

CHAPTER TWENTY-NINE

Mark had been writing for hours. The guard had brought him the writing pads and pens, one of which had already been written dry. He was racing the angel, for she was there again, her fingers scratching against the pane of Plexiglas outside the window bars. She had become more insistent in the last few hours, and he knew that soon he would have to let her in. She had been changing, becoming darker, more insistent, and he had had to fight her last night, keeping her away, pushing back the darkness she brought. He had written a letter that he had asked the guard to post for him, and he hoped the man had done it. How would she respond? He hoped she would come. Now, however, he had to write so that Aurelius would understand. He could not let the angel in just yet.

He had had a difficult time figuring out where to start. There was so much Aurelius did not understand. How could he explain it to anyone else? Mark stopped, his mind lost. He had not been surprised to see the colonel. St. Euribius had not been intended as a hiding place, anyway. Coming out of the shadows, he had known they would be on to him within hours. There was little that these men did not know. The constant chatter between Virginia and Maryland, the homes of the CIA and the NSA, ensured that. He had known it would be the colonel who would come, for neither of them existed in any record anywhere, and everyone else from that other world was dead. Mark chuckled. It must have driven them crazy when his real name had turned up on a commercial plane's passenger list. He had ceased to be Mark St. Auburn for so long that they must have hesitated. Yet, from what he had gathered, the colonel had been in St. Euribius the same day he had arrived. They were still efficient.

Mark's hand had continued to move as he thought, but instead of words, he had been unconsciously making long, squiggly lines. He noticed and stopped, concentrating again. Staring around the corner, down the long corridor, he tried to see the guard, but he could not. Idly, he wondered if the guard was honest or if he had been bought. They had the power to corrupt anyone, and few realized how much the working of any system depended on the lowest-paid people. He hoped they had not gotten to the guard. He needed to have his letter delivered.

He wrote on the pad, "What Is Madness?" and smiled, not sure anymore. Had he been mad to go into the Marines or had he gone mad in Vietnam? Had be been mad not to try to make a go of it with Estelle in 1982, or had the madness been to seek out the dark world again? He was not sure. Things were mixed up in his mind, and his actions had, after a while, lost all semblance of rationality. At least, they did looking back from this vantage point. Then, they had been all too rational. The dark world had seemed the only place where the angel laughed, where she became less insistent. She seemed to agree with him in his choices, and she had sharpened his instincts. He had been a perfect fit.

Five men, all survivors from black operations in Vietnam. Five men whose lives were dedicated to training and killing, all in the name of protecting democracy and freedom, in the name of keeping America and her principles safe. Five men who did not know if they were sane or mad, but who fought in the shadows in the name of a set of beliefs they could not articulate. Why had they done it? Certainly not patriotism. Nor idealism. If asked, he doubted if they could have said. It did not matter. They were good at what they were needed to do, and each man, with the exception of the colonel, had cut himself off from the world. They had been, in truth, good for one thing, and at this, they were very good.

Ray had been one of these men. If anything, he had become more vicious than in Vietnam, as his re-entry to American society had restrained him even more than he had been before he left. He talked constantly about racism and the corrosive effect it had on his and "the black man's" soul. He always used that term, "the black man," intentionally setting himself apart, carrying his special grudge like a cancer. Mark was not a "black man"; he was foreign, and Ray made sure he understood that. They were wrapped up in each other, and there was no one that Mark trusted more in battle. Ray understood the shadows, could see in the darkness. He lived in that world with a certitude it would have been foolish to ignore and almost suicidal not to take advantage of. Even that mantle of protection, however, could not negate Nicaragua.

Mark stopped doodling, leaning back in the chair, his eyes closed, thinking of another land far away. Their unit had been there to train a group high in the mountains of Cordillera Isabella. They were not supposed to be in the country, and Mark had never been sure whom they were training or why. The colonel had brought the mission, and they had left Florida, flying to Costa Rica. They had picked up Route 1 out of San Jose heading north. Just past Lago de Nicaragua, they had left Route 1 at San Benito and had picked up Route 7, heading east, leaving the road at Mount Grande.

They should have known something was wrong. There had been too many soldiers and too few civilians, but they had ignored the signs. Seeking to be inconspicuous, they had cut back to the west and had picked up Route 1 again, this time taking it as far as Sebaco. From there, they had gone east again to Matagalpa and then into the mountains. The army had been waiting for them, and they had barely found the group they were supposed to train when the attack came. They had slipped back deeper and deeper into the mountains, each day losing more men. It was not that the Nicaraguan army was particularly effective, but that the group they had come to train seemed to melt into the silent greenery until, on the fifth night, they had been alone, all the would-be rebels gone except for one boy, about sixteen, who had stayed. Mark was never sure why he had not run away, but all night the boy had sat hunched against the dirt which formed the wall of their hole. Mark could see that he was afraid, and Ray, who leaned in the same position, had calmed him by spitting in his face when he had trembled too much.

"Be quiet, mosquito," he had hissed, and the boy, who seemed not to have minded the spit, had turned away as if avoiding the smell of Ray's mouth.

Behind the shadows of his eyelids, Mark could see the scene clearly. The night had been long and tense, and from time to time, the soldiers below would fire up the hill, keeping the tension high among their trapped victims. It was close to morning when the boy, who had shifted to take the numbness out of his buttocks, dropped his gun. Ray had moved much closer to him and whispered fiercely, "You make any more noise, I'll kill you myself."

Mark could not yet see the boy's face, but he could feel his own dislike of Ray rise like a giant wave in his chest. Down below, his ears had picked up the sound of the soldiers' laughter. It had seemed stupid to remain quiet when everyone knew where they were.

"Senōr, why are they waiting?" the boy had whispered to Mark.

It was clear he had not expected an answer but wanted to hear his own voice. Ray had responded with an evil laugh.

"They want the sun to come up. They want to see your stupid face when the bullets smash into it. That's why they are waiting."

Mark had been angry, and though he seldom crossed Ray, he had said, his voice quiet, "Leave the boy alone, Ray. Can't you see he is scared?"

In the silence that followed his statement, they could hear the boy sniffling, the half-concealed cry bringing the fear up like a summer cloud, sudden and black, obliterating all sense.

"No use crying, mosquito. You die anyway."

Ray's voice had been passionless, and Mark, from the corner of his eye, could see the cadaverous grin on the man's face. The boy was staring at Ray's face, and he tried to make his own face look harder, more assertive, as if he thought this would help him face death more bravely. It was almost as if he were wishing he was like Ray. Then, the voice, soft, alluring, and carrying an undertone of laughter, had called out, "Hola, rebels. You want to give up?"

Below, the soldiers had laughed. Someone then repeated the question in conscious mimicry, and the laughter had flared up. Beside him, Mark could hear the boy sobbing. He must have said something because Ray said, "Shut up."

The voice had been savage.

Mark could see the gradual lightening of the sky, and he raised his head to look to the east where the outlines of the mountains stood. He must have been visible for a moment, but no one shot at him. From below, a sing-song voice had shouted, "You are afraid, aren't you?"

And the laughter had followed. Ray, raising the semi-automatic, squeezed off a shot downhill without sighting. There was swearing, and the laughter had stopped. Mark could hear the air snapping as the volley of gunshots had rung out from below, and he had burrowed, animal-like, into the uncompromising dirt. Between them, the boy's shoulders had been shaking as the tears of fear rolled down his cheeks.

Just before dawn, they had slipped away, heading north through the mountains. The Cordillera Isabella is not the world's most hospitable spot, and the going had been rough. Mark had wanted to let the boy go. Apart from them, he could fade into the mountains, finding refuge in one of the villages. With them, if they were caught, he would almost certainly be killed. Ray had been more pragmatic. The boy knew the mountains, and he would help them move north towards the Honduran border. They had been lucky. For some reason, the army had pursued them only as far as the Rio Coco and then had broken off the pursuit. From there, they had worked their way towards Octocal.

It had been just south of Octocal that the trouble had begun. That far north, the boy's knowledge had been exhausted, and Ray had wanted to be rid of him. Mark had argued that they should just let him go, but Ray had turned his rifle on the boy. If he were dead, there was no chance he could say anything to the Nicaraguan authorities if he were caught. They had been a free-ranging cohort with no clear command structure, though Ray's directions were generally followed. The other two men in the group, Sanders and Cohn, had stood back, allowing the older men to decide, but Mark had known something they did not. The struggle had not been about the boy. Rather, it was an unresolved problem of a dying girl in another jungle on the other side of the world. Another set of words had stood between the two men, words that had promised death. No one had been watching the boy, and when he shot at Ray, the surprise had been total. He had missed, but it had been as if he had unleashed the killing rage that had been bottled up in the men after their days of running and hiding. When the smoke had cleared, Saunders, Cohn, and the boy were lying dead, and Ray had disappeared. Mark had never been clear about what had happened in that small clearing on an evening that was like dark velvet— dark velvet stained with blood.

When Ray had run into the jungle, he had left a briefcase containing a very important set of codes, codes that gave access to almost one hundred million dollars spread around numbered accounts in Switzerland, the Caymans, and even more secret and reputable banks in Paris. Mark had made his way to Tegucigalpa and from there had flown to Panama City where the codes had worked their magic, and he had left Panama for Columbia, his retirement intact. Retirement was easy on a hundred million dollars, and Columbia offered plenty of protection even from the kind of men who would pursue him. All one had to do was pay the asking price, and he was able to pay.

Mark stood up in the cell now, stretching the muscles in his lower back. Outside, the sunlight could be seen refracted through the Plexiglas. It was Christmas Day. That thought sent a sliver of longing through him. He remembered another Christmas filled with black great cake, coconut bread, baked ham, and fried dovepeas. He smiled briefly, allowing the remnants of the smells to live in his memory. The smile, however, soon disappeared.

It had taken Ray three years to find him, and when he came, Mark had known that it was no mission; it was personal. Somehow, the army that protected Mark had understood this, too, and they had signaled that this was a matter of honor he should handle himself. They had been careful, checking everything within their vast network to ensure that Ray acted alone, and when they were satisfied, they had allowed him to come. Mark and Ray had fought as only men who had killed together could fight, with a brutality that had surprised even the hard men who had guarded him. When it was over, Ray had lain dead, his neck broken. In death, there had been a kind of boyish innocence to his face. Unlike the movies, the fight had not resulted in cuts and bruises. For the uninitiated, it would have been boring, for at this level of combat, few punches were thrown. The two men had sparred, each waiting for the opening that would spell disaster and death for the other. The brutality had not been in the actual violence, but in their single-minded commitment to each other's death. Ray had over-committed on a straight-fingered thrust to the eyes, and Mark had spun him into a Chinese chokehold, breaking his neck before the screaming lungs could die from lack of oxygen. It could have been a quiet kill, a body thrown in the Columbian jungle to rot in anonymity, but the innocent look on the dead body's face – an innocence that Mark had not seen when Ray was alive – had changed something in him, and he had sent the body to an address in Virginia.

That had been four years ago, and he had lived in the safety of Medellin since then, until a few weeks ago. The darkness had come back, and he had begun to flit in and out of awareness. A German specialist had been flown in and had found out that he had a rare form of brain cancer. It was inoperable, and the doctor had told him he was not sure how long he would live. So, he had started to put his affairs in order. He had activated the account he had kept in Estelle's name for more than twenty years. The money in those accounts was clean, having nothing to do with the stolen money nor the drug fortune that he had built with the help of certain men for whom he had once performed services. At this thought, Mark laughed.

"Clean," he said to himself, the chuckle shaking his shoulders. "Interesting way to describe money paid for other men's deaths."

The guard had heard his voice and yelled down the corridor, asking him if he was all right. Mark answered that he was, and the man settled back in his chair.

At least, Estelle is out of danger now, he thought, placing his head in his hands. They had followed the money, of course. Once he had moved it, they had simply done what he would have done: notified the St. Euribian authorities with a hint about drug involvement. That was all that was necessary to keep him where he was. They had no interest in Estelle. They wanted their money and his silence. She had been his good conduct card. Now, they had their money. He had given the colonel the means to get their two hundred million dollars back – four years of interest, the colonel had said – so all that was necessary was his silence. The colonel was clear that Estelle would pay for any indiscretion on his part, and if he had said anything about the world he had once lived in to his lawyer, he would be silenced as well.

It had been an unnecessary warning. Mark knew these men and would never have intentionally said anything about them. That is why he had to plead guilty. Aurelius did not understand that he was protecting them all. Still, what if he talked during one of the dark spells? He was never sure what he said when the angel came and the darkness descended. Anyway, one thing at a time. The colonel had said that Estelle's legal troubles would disappear now that the money had been returned. He remembered the man's cultured voice as he had said, smiling broadly, his handsome face relaxed, "As a goodwill gesture."

Mark picked up the pen again. He understood their goodwill gestures. He had been a part of their so-called goodwill for a long time, and he knew what the man meant. The legal troubles would go away in return for the money, but Estelle and Aurelius would still be held hostage to his silence. Mark had been surprised that the colonel seemed to know nothing of his illness. He was sure if he did, Aurelius would probably be dead already. Fortunately, the angel had retreated while he had spoken with the colonel.

Mark searched his feelings, wondering if he felt any animosity towards the man and found that he did not. He would have done much the same had the circumstances been reversed. Yet, he knew if Estelle were hurt, this silly jail would not hold him nor would time nor distance protect the man who had sat in front of him. There had been no need to say this. They were both professionals. They understood. Mark looked to the window where the scratching had started up again, then bent to his writing, knowing there was not much time.

CHAPTER THIRTY

"How Deighton holding up, girl?"

Marjorie's voice was solicitous, and the other women turned towards Maylene, who smiled as she walked up. They had all come, as tradition had demanded, to Marjorie's home for Christmas lunch. She had been fussing about for the last couple of hours, her body showing no signs of the sleepless night. In fact, there was a kind of energy to her. In the background, the soft, mellow voice of Johnny Mathis was singing "The Little Drummer Boy," and she sometimes hummed along. Now, she walked up and hugged the latest arriving of the group. Maylene held her for a moment, then said, "Deighton fine. But let me tell you, wid them police around, I am always putting on fresh panties now."

The women laughed, and she continued, "It really strange having dem 'bout de place all de time, but I suppose it fuh de best."

The others had been lounging around the patio, and now that she had been welcomed, they returned to their insouciance. They were all in that state of semi-sleepiness, having attended midnight mass the night before. Suddenly, Anis said, "You know, I thought Reverend Gaulson was better last night."

She stood up and tucked her hands in the holes of her sleeveless blouse. Rocking back and forth for a moment and turning the corners of her mouth down, she said in a fake, but credible, English accent, "And on that night...ahem...as they approached the city of Bethlehem... ahem... there was no room at the inn...ahem...ahem."

She continued to rock back and forth as the women laughed. Marjorie said, "De devil goin' have a special plot fuh you in hell."

"Don't believe in hell, unless you mean de one dat we smelling right here 'pon earth."

"No blasphemy in my house `pon Christmas day, girl."

"Praise the Lord," Anis said ironically.

"I am surprised Anis even knows what Reverend Gaulson sounds like. She's always asleep."

This was from Sandra, who had come out today for the first time in weeks.

"How de hell can anybody not sleep through that man's sermons? And anyway, how come we still got an English reverend? You all can't find a St. Euribian fuh dat job?"

There was a short silence, and then Maylene said with a grin, "Well, listen to Miss Malcolm X."

"No, it is true, though. How come we still have an Englishman in our church?"

"Reverend Gaulson has been dere since forever."

"Exactly my point. Time fuh uh change," Anis responded.

"Why you care? Yuh hardly evah go to church unless we drag yuh out, an den we'n yuh get dere, yuh does fall asleep. I surprise you know who de reverend is."

Marjorie looked around for support, and the other women laughed. Encouraged, she continued.

"It could be worse, chile. We could've had uh American. One uh dem Southern ones."

"At least an American would be modern."

"What modern got to do wid de scriptures? Nuttin' aint changin'."

"Well," Sandra said, "you can guarantee that if America was involved, things would change."

"But not always fuh de better," Marjorie responded a little too quickly.

"Isn't it strange how we have changed in the way we feel about America? When I was a girl, I wanted so much to be there. Everything interesting – toys, scientific advances, the moon trip – seemed to be coming out of there. We all wanted to be American then. Now, things are so different. It's amazing how quickly that happened."

"Deir mout get too big, especially since dis nine-eleven t'ing," Anis responded.

"No," Sandra said thoughtfully. "It was before that. It was as if, in the fifties when we were growing up, even the first half of the sixties, America was the place of perpetual light. Then, by the end of the sixties, a kind of darkness had come over the place."

"I t'ink dat was when we see dem black people there catching deir ass. Dat is what turn we off. Dem pictures dat we used to see in de papers wid black people gettin' attack by dogs dat white people set 'pon dem mustah had some effect 'pon we."

"Some uh dem white people real terrible. Dey just can't live wid we. It like dey don't know how to share nuttin'. And de ones 'bout heah in dis island ain't much bettuh."

"Well, at least the ones here don't have any real power. The American ones do, though."

"You know, it amazing how much dat country does talk 'bout de right t'ings, and how little dey actually do dem. I look at all dem children who left heah and go to live in New York and whe' ever. Almost all uh dem does come back wid a yankee accent, fancy clothes and jewelry and not a shite in deir heads. It like dat place does turn dem foolish. And uh lot uh de new-fangled crime 'bout heah getting commit by dem ones dat coming back from America. Right, Sandra?"

Sandra nodded slowly, saying, "At least, the style of crime is becoming more American. More violent, more premeditated. And there is a kind of hardness to them that suggests prison is no threat. It is the main difference I see between the native St. Euribian and these ones who are coming back from America."

The conversation had been going on between Sandra, Maylene, and Anis. Marjorie and Estelle had fallen silent, each hearing in the observations sentiments that caused some discomfort. As the butler and maid laid the table, Marjorie got up to supervise, and Estelle lay, with her eyes half-closed, listening to the voices go back and forth. Were they thinking of her? In spite of Marjorie's confirmation the night before, she could not be sure that her friends did not have their secret doubts about her. How could she have been placed in this situation? She, who had always lived so carefully, so sure-footed in her avoidance of scandal since her single mistake thirty-three years ago.

She had called Heather earlier that morning, and the girl had still been half-asleep. It must have been about one in the afternoon in France then. She had immediately come awake when Estelle had mentioned the trouble Mark was in. Estelle had offered to fly her home, and Heather had immediately agreed. She was to call back later to indicate the specifics of her flight plans. Estelle had not mentioned her own troubles, fearful that the girl's reaction would have been one of neutrality. She could not have handled that after Heather's emotional outburst at hearing about Mark.

Why did the girl love him so? Could it be that his playfulness with her, even at that young age, had somehow created a bond that neither of them fully understood? Heather had met her father only once, on a day Estelle had taken her to the horse races, and he had been on the grounds. She had introduced them, and the girl had been polite, but there was no reaching out, and she had never asked about him. It was as if Blue had sensed his exclusion, and he, too, had avoided Heather. Sometimes in the night, Estelle would burn with anger at the man's desertion of his daughter, but when the anger cooled, she always knew that she was as much to blame as he. Mark had remained in her imagination like a real father, though he was as much absent as Blue had ever been.

"Look like the rest starting to show up."

Maylene's voice sliced into her thoughts. Two cars were coming down the long, bumpy road that led to Marjorie's house. They were still too far away for her to tell whose they were, but Maylene said, "That's Deighton and the girls in front. I am not sure who the second car belong to."

Marjorie squinted hopefully into the bright sunlight, but Estelle suspected her wishes would not come true this day. So far, only Estelle knew that Bryan had not come the night before, and she had watched this morning as Marjorie had frantically gone through her messages. In the end, she had slumped. He had not called. Now, Marjorie was hoping again. Estelle said, "I think that's Aurelius' car."

"I hope those two boys uh his goin' behave today," Anis said, standing and smoothing her loose cotton dress over her slim hips.

"You just don't like children, Anis," Maylene said laughing. "If you had your own, you'd understand."

"If I had my own, I couldn't keep this gorgeous body, girl."

Maylene rolled her eyes, looking down the road at the approaching cars. Soon, they were there, and Maylene walked down the steps to hug her two girls. Aurelius, in the meantime, had gotten out of the car, a huge smile on his face. His two boys and wife followed him as he came bounding up the steps. Estelle waved, but he came straight to her and, reaching into his pocket, handed her an envelope. Sandra had walked over, though she looked uncomfortable. Aurelius noticed and, giving her a hug, said, "Don't worry, Sandra. It's all right. I got two separate validations today that the signatures are false."

"What do you mean 'false'?" Sandra asked.

"Well, the signatures are real enough, but both London and now, apparently, the FBI as well, are saying the signatures were lifted from somewhere and affixed to the bank's affidavits. Estelle never had anything to do with the authorizations."

Sandra stared at the letter from the Metropolitan Police, looking perplexed.

"But if Estelle didn't authorize the transfers, who did?"

Aurelius smile widened.

"Mark did, apparently. I am going by to see him after lunch. From what I can guess, he must have set up the account twenty years ago. That's when the deposits started. The account was always in Estelle's name."

The others had gathered around, and Estelle took the letter back from Sandra, holding it to her chest. Her body felt light, and the tears had come unbidden. Marjorie and Anis came to her. Sandra continued to look confused.

"Aury, did you say this was validated by the FBI, as well? Did you get a letter from them, too?"

"No. I got a call from Anderson."

"The prime minister called you about this?"

"Yes. He's been checking on things for me. Apparently, he got a call from the American ambassador today."

"Uh huh."

She pulled Aurelius away from the group around Estelle.

"You got confirmation on Christmas day from London, and the prime minister gets a call from the American ambassador. Doesn't that strike you as odd?"

He looked closely at her, not wanting to think what she was thinking. He just wanted to be happy. With this information, Estelle's case would be thrown out, and he could go back to representing Mark—if he would have him. Finally, he said, "The oddity has struck me, Sandra. I don't want to look too closely into it."

"So you would just accept this was all a St. Euribian mix-up that London and Washington cleared up on the same day? A little too neat, don't you think?"

"I am willing to let it go. A bonus is that, if the twenty million is not shown to be the proceeds of illegal activity, Estelle actually gets the money."

Sandra nodded, saying, "What Estelle needs, money won't buy. I think now that this is cleared up, you should encourage her to see Mark. She wants to, anyway."

Aurelius nodded, saying, "I still need to get Mark a psychiatric evaluation."

"Aury, you know better than that. I can't talk to you about Mark's case."

"Sorry. I sometimes forget who you are."

"Nice try, counselor," she responded, laughing and walking away.

Estelle, meanwhile, had accepted the congratulations of the women, and now walked over to Aurelius, who was leaning against the rail. She stood in front of him, her eyes searching his face.

"Thank you."

Her voice was small and broke on the last word. He smiled down at her.

"I didn't do that much really. We got lucky. Justice won out."

"Does this mean this is all over?"

He hesitated, not blaming her for thinking of herself.

"Well, Mark's still on trial for murder."

Her hand involuntarily slapped her leg.

"I didn't mean...."

"I know, Estelle."

She hesitated, then said, "I heard what Sandra was saying to you. It is strange, isn't it? I mean that both the London police and the FBI would get back to you on Christmas day?"

"Yes. It is odd, but sometimes things just work out that way. You shouldn't look a gift horse in the mouth."

"I suppose I shouldn't," she said thoughtfully, looking out towards the steely-gray sea. "But I can't help thinking Mark is responsible for this somehow."

Aurelius looked at her sharply.

"Why do you say that?"

"I don't know. It's just a feeling, that's all."

He shrugged, then said, "Are you going to see him now? I'll have this charge against you cleared up in a couple of days. After that, there is no reason not to see him. If you want to, that is."

Estelle stared off in the distance, aware of the buzz around her, the women talking, the children running about, Deighton sitting flipping through a magazine, the vague sounds of cutlery coming from somewhere deep in the bowels of the house. The lunch had been set up on the southeastern side of the patio, thus allowing a full view of the end of the eastern coast with its harsh, yet alluring, beauty. She could feel the racing of her heart, and below that, the slight thrill of expectation. She would see him, she knew. Estelle looked over to where Deighton was sitting by himself, reading and occasionally glancing over at the children who played noisily. She touched Aurelius affectionately on the shoulder and walked over to Deighton. He looked up, a smile on his face.

"Hi, Estelle. Congrats."

"Thanks. There is something I wanted to ask you. Have you heard that there was some excitement at my house last night?"

He shook his head, his face asking the question.

"Last night, the police had to come to my house. There was a boy outside my bedroom with a cutlass."

Deighton's face showed alarm. Then, something changed in his eyes.

"A Rastafarian?" he asked cautiously.

Estelle nodded, watching him closely.

"Did you get a good look at him?"

"Yes. He is always in Prescod's Bottom, although I don't think he is from the village. He always has that cutlass."

Deighton nodded slowly.

"Ras Tyla. Tall, skinny fellow with sharp features and sort of reddish hair?"

Estelle nodded.

"Yes. That's Ras Tyla, all right, but he wouldn't hurt a fly. He is a very nice kid. I didn't hear of any of my people being arrested."

"I didn't tell the police who it was. At least, not yet."

"Why not?"

She hesitated, feeling foolish, then said softly, "He has been polite to me whenever I went to the village."

He looked at her, perplexed, and then understanding dawned.

"I'll talk to him. I'll let you know what he says."

"I also thought there was someone else with him. I didn't see the person, though. He was back in the trees."

Deighton noticed the look on her face and smiled.

"And you thought it was me. It wasn't. I operate within the law, Estelle. I know this place has become a little weird in the last couple of weeks, but I am defending Mark only because he defended one of my boys. I don't think he should go to jail nor lose his life for that. But don't confuse that with affection. I still think Mark is a selfish, thoughtless bastard, and I wouldn't lift a finger to help him in his other troubles. He did, however, try to protect one of us, and for that, I think he deserves my help. But don't think for a minute I would take his side against you. I realize you are the primary witness against him in this money laundering business, but that is your and his business, not ours."

Before she could answer, Marjorie shouted, "Wha' de two uh you plotting over dere? We just about ready to eat. Come."

Marjorie did not believe in separating the children from the adults, so they all ate together, the children taking most of the attention. Estelle watched Maylene and Beverly with their respective children, noting the affection between them and feeling a little jealous. The conversation, when it was not about homework or behavior, circled around the topics that were uppermost in their minds. She could see the slight tension between Maylene and her husband, the tightness in Anis' jaw, Aurelius' occasional distraction, and the slight nervousness in Marjorie, and she thought of the causes. Even Sandra, who always seemed to be above their normal irritations, appeared more reserved and self-contained.

They are all tied up with Mark, she thought. *It is just like when we were children. How is this all going to end?* Estelle wondered how they would feel if Mark was condemned to death. She knew he intended to plead guilty and wondered why he would do that. Could it be that he suffered from a sense of guilt? He could have argued that he had been protecting the boy, which is what Aurelius wanted his defense to be. Why had he changed his mind after he had agreed initially to the psychiatric defense? It was as if he had been willing to go along until he had heard that the Americans were blocking the evaluation. Then, he had changed his mind. Why had he done that? And this secret life in America. It all pointed to something she did not feel at all comfortable with. Now, it looked as if two police forces in two different countries had, apparently coincidentally, agreed on her innocence, when only yesterday, everything had been leaning toward her guilt and possible imprisonment. She knew that the individual acts of men often lacked logic, yet, historians like herself always imposed order on these events, taking facts and making them part of an orderly advance of man from past to present.

Am I doing the same thing now? she asked herself. She had read, almost a year ago, a book on quantum mechanics and had been struck by something called the principle of uncertainty. She had immediately seen its applicability to history and had struggled to find a comparable description of the historical process. She had been frustrated because, ultimately, she was engaged in the business of imposing order on the disparate tendencies of human actions. It was not that she hoped to eliminate contradictions, but if the historical analysis was sufficiently remote, it accounted for the contradictions in the same way that God was omniscient. He had to be remote to be omniscient since involvement reduced perspective.

Yet, she could see no logic in the activities of the last two weeks. She had been caught up in the raging waters of a waterfall. Her actions had made no difference, and it was the very randomness that alarmed her. How could a single act of cruelty or generosity cause the effects of the last two weeks? She thought of the worn-out metaphor of the butterfly flapping its wings in Asia and causing a hurricane in Florida, and she wondered, given what had happened to her and the others, whether this was not very possible.

Estelle became aware of the eyes on her before she realized that she had stopped eating.

"What is it?" she said to the room.

"I asked if you didn't like my food," Marjorie responded in mock outrage, looking around the table for support.

"Sorry. I was daydreaming. The food's delicious, as usual."

"What you daydreaming 'bout?"

"Historical uncertainty. The principle of randomness."

"Oh, God. It's Christmas. You can't t'ink 'bout something else less eggheady?" Marjorie asked, still falsely offended, and everyone laughed.

"Actually," Sandra said seriously, "I have been thinking of something similar. Chance. So much of what happens to us seems to be determined simply by chance. Even the things we think we control. Even...."

"Jesus. Not you, too," Marjorie groaned, leaning her large body into Sandra's. "It's bad enough having to listen to the professor."

"No, no. I am serious. Think about it. A month ago, who could have predicted any of these things that have happened? I am sitting in judgment of Mark; Estelle is first accused, then cleared of a crime; Aurelius is pulled back and forth between her and Mark, and so on. Yet, none of it has anything to do with our actions. It seems totally random. As Estelle was saying, it leads to the principle of historical uncertainty."

The table was silent for a while, then Deighton said, "I don't see any randomness. I see a definite historical act and then, a series of choices. Each one of us chooses to react to that historical act, the murder of the guard and the Rasta boy –his name was Ellis, by the way – in our own way."

Sandra turned towards Deighton, who was sitting at the far end of the long table. She thought he still looked strange without his dreadlocks.

"Let's grant that the initial reaction expresses volition. What about the secondary reactions? For example, did you intend to create this much tension in the island? I doubt it. You simply wanted to defend Mark. What proceeded from that was largely a function of randomness."

Estelle watched Sandra, smiling, admiring her cogency. She had always had that quality in school and had been one of the few girls who would argue with the boys when they were having their political discussions. She still had that instinct. Estelle looked at Marjorie, who rolled her eyes, and said, "You see wha' you start. Another good meal ruined wid wunna talk 'bout wha'ever it is wunna talking 'bout dat nuhbody can't understand."

She looked at Aurelius' fifteen-year-old son, asking, "Evan, you know what dese people talkin' 'bout?"

Evan smiled and shook his head.

"Yuh see?" Marjorie continued, "Wunna borin' everybody."

By this time, however, the servants had begun to remove the plates from the table, and Marjorie said, "I hope wunna save some room fuh dessert. I mek some rum cake."

"I thought you did 'pon a diet," Anis said with a grin.

"I am, but today, in honor uh my friends, I will sacrifice my body," Marjorie responded pompously.

"You mean you going sacrifice dat cake," Anis replied, and a general laughter ensued.

The cake having been placed on the table, silence descended, as the clink of knives, forks, and china filled the air. It was only when the port was brought out that the conversation once more began. Anis got it going.

"Hey, Marjorie. How come de prime minister ain't coming by dis year? It ain't like he to miss a meal."

Marjorie laughed, responding, "Our two stars, Estelle and Amstel, can't share de same space. Maybe Amstel convinced he dat he shou'nt come. Even dis house ain't big enough fuh de two uh dem."

They all knew of the animosity between Estelle and Amstel, and they laughed, looking at Estelle, who pretended irritation.

"Look, dey ain't uh ting wrong wid me and Amstel. Dat is all in wunna mind."

"Well, dat prob'ly explains why you invitations to the residence always getting lost or misplace or somet'ing."

Even Deighton, Estelle noticed, who was usually so serious, laughed at that one.

"Well, I prob'ly go to the residence, as you all it, too much any-way."

Marjorie clapped her hands for attention.

"Aury, Deighton, let we get dese lil children out uh here. Look," she said, waving her hands at the children, "go and play. Take some uh de fruit wid yuh."

The children, glad to be released, scampered off.

"Okay. Now dat dem gone, let me tell you de real reason dem two can't get along. Amstel did always frighten dat Anderson did want Estelle."

"Marjorie, stop it," Estelle said, not amused.

"Stop what? It almost happen, didn't it? I tellin' lies, Aury?"

Aurelius raised both hands in surrender.

"No, you don't. I aint got nutting to do wid it."

"Yuh lie. You had a lot to do wid it. Just after we lef school, before you went to England. You thought dat Mark was too irresponsible, and you started carrying Estelle and Anderson 'bout wid you, hoping dat somet'ing would catch between dem. Didn't work though, but Amstel been pissed wid de two uh dem ever since."

Marjorie finished with a loud guffaw, and the others joined her. Satisfied that the audience was hers, she continued.

"Estelle always like to mek out that she is uh angel, but she ain't as timid as she look. Deighton, you remember how Anderson get to be Saint Too?"

Deighton looked up, smiling and shaking his head.

"Well," Marjorie continued, practically ignoring the man of whom she had asked the question, "Lil Miss Innocent here is de one who give he dat nickname. Aurelius know dis is true 'cause he did dere. Anyway, you know dat we used to call Mark, Saint One, and Aurelius, Saint Two. Well, since Anderson's last name was St. Clair, he asked Estelle how come he wasn't a Saint too, and Miss T'ing here says in her snooti-est voice, 'Are you a Saint too?' Well, dat was pretty much the end of Aury's matchmaking. And the worse part of it was, the nickname stuck."

Deighton, smiling, said, "I always wondered how come both Aury and the prime minister were called Saint Two. I now get it. Anderson is not Saint Two, but Saint Too. I wonder how many people know that?"

"Not too many, but I kin tell you dat neither Amstel nor Anderson ever forget dat."

Estelle shook her head, thinking that it had been a strange time. Mark had gone off with some other girl — she could not even remember who — and she and Anderson had flirted for a minute, mostly, as Marjorie had said, at Aurelius' urging. Even she and Aurelius had had a short liaison. She looked at him now, wondering if they could have made it. He seemed so content with Beverley and his children. She really admired him. He had gone down the route so many of the boys had followed and had pursued a political career in addition to law, but then had suddenly quit to be home more. So unusual in the men of her generation. An old memory of a late afternoon on the beach with Marjorie, Aurelius, and Mark flashed through her mind, and she felt the embarrassment rise in her.

I wonder if he even remembers that afternoon, she wondered. It had been so weird, exchanging partners like that, but in spite of her hurt at Mark's drifting over to Marjorie, that day had a special quality that had made it forgivable. She, normally so jealous of Mark, had accepted that day as somehow right because it had been so magical. She had not talked to anyone about it, and even Marjorie, whose mouth had no cover, had been secretive about that day. They had talked about it only once. Coming from the beach, after the two boys had left to return to the village, Estelle had been quiet, staring at the ground. Finally, she had asked, "What just happened, Marjorie?"

The girl, her eyes like fire in the afternoon's sunlight, had smiled, and said, "I t'ink dat we just got used so dat dem two could mek love to each other."

The statement had stayed with Estelle ever since. Even during that horrible second year of the marriage when Mark had seemed to want to drag her down into some bottomless pit of excess, when he had wanted to find her, it seemed, only through sharing her, she had thought of Marjorie's statement. She had closed her mind to the embarrassment, accepting his depravity because it seemed, for however brief a moment, to connect him to her. It had not worked. She had gone into the depths with him, but instead of the light she had hoped for, there she had found only more depths. Those depths had almost drowned her, so she had flogged her body into behaving in ways she believed necessary. Her body had never cooperated, and he had lived within a hot mist of resentment because she could not give him what he thought he wanted. She had learned to hate the act, though not him, and they had lived in this odd attachment that was a contradiction until he had shattered her soul with the cold, angry words, "Making love to you is like climbing a mountain without climbing boots."

The words had stripped away the fiction, had given voice to all her fears about inadequacy and had emphasized her feelings of uselessness. It had been a cruel thing to say to her, but she had blamed herself, as she had done with so many other things that Mark accused her of.

"Go ahead and let it out, girl. We understand."

Estelle looked around, aware that they were staring at her again. Marjorie's moon-like face was the very essence of sympathy.

"What?" Estelle asked tentatively, as she became aware of the wetness on her face.

"We know what a relief it must be to be out from under a cloud, so you just go ahead and cry."

Estelle laughed, embarrassed.

"I am sorry. I seem to be a wreck today."

"Dat's okay, dear. Uh lot happen to you in the last few days."

Estelle nodded, rising and heading into the house.

The day passed slowly, and by late afternoon, the group was beginning to break up. Deighton promised to call her later that evening after he had spoken to the Rasta boy. As Aurelius was packing his family into the car, Marjorie's phone rang, and the butler indicated that the prime minister was on the line. Remembering their earlier conversation, they all giggled. Marjorie walked into the house, and they could hear her loud, abrasive voice going on at the man at the other end. Aurelius and Estelle stood on the verandah, looking at the darkening sea.

"Are you going home tonight? I didn't get a chance to talk to you, but I have arranged with Patrick to have an off-duty policeman stay over by the house for the next few nights. You will pay him, of course."

"I know who the man was outside my bedroom. I don't know why I didn't tell you."

"Yes. Deighton told me. He's going to talk to the boy. Don't worry. Deighton's a pain sometimes with his counter-cultural ideas, but he is very honest, Estelle. If he says that he will get to the bottom of it, he will."

"I know. I was thinking it's funny how, even though Maylene is so much a part of our group, Deighton never seemed to want to be any part of it."

"The same could be said for my wife. Beverley says we seemed like planets spinning around a star. If another planet came in, it would mess up the constellation."

Estelle smiled, responding, "Beverley said that?"

Inside, Marjorie yelled Aurelius' name and, smiling wryly, he walked inside, saying as he went, "Earth Mother calls."

Estelle walked down the steps to where Beverley waited in the car, trying to keep the boys quiet. The translucent beauty of the woman shone through her lost figure and slightly chubby face and, watching her, Estelle felt a profound sense of loss. The woman covered Estelle's hand when she rested it on the car's window and said, "I am so happy everything seems to be working out for you. Aurelius hasn't slept much in the last few weeks since this thing started."

"Thanks, Beverley. He's been like a rock."

"You know, I think for the first time, he has had to think about his relationship to Mark. I always felt Aury thought that was an unresolved issue in his life, but you know how men are, stubborn as anything. But I think this whole thing now has him thinking. It was really difficult when he had to choose between you and Mark. Sometimes, you know, I don't think he makes a distinction between you two. It's almost as if he sees you as one."

"What an extraordinary thing to say. And yet, in some strange way, I understand what you mean. Thanks, Bev."

Aurelius had exited the house and was coming purposefully down the steps.

"That was Anderson," he said, walking up. "I am going to take you guys home, and then I have to go by the residence for a while."

He kissed Estelle on the cheek, and she watched as the car bumped its way down the road until it disappeared in the distance. Then, she walked back up to the verandah, her head bowed in thought.

CHAPTER THIRTY-ONE

Christmas evening was sultry, with a quiet that seemed like a presence. The wind had died down, and now the silence pressed against the ear like a soundless voice, whispering something profound yet undefined. Aurelius had put his glass down and watched as the ring of condensation surrounded it on the glass top of the table. *So much like the island,* he thought. He and the prime minister had been talking for a while, but in the last several minutes, the silence had descended as Aurelius had tried to understand. Actually, he did understand, but he struggled to accept what the prime minister had said. Worse, he was struggling with the last question he had been asked.

"What difference does it make to you?" the prime minister had said, without any real perplexity, no upset in his voice.

He glanced at the chubby man who sat in the dusk watching the darkness come. The bougainvillea trees, five of them, spread their branches over the whole area in his field of vision, their red flowers, normally ablaze, now almost lost in the impending gloom. Aurelius turned in the chair, facing the prime minister.

"You are willing to sacrifice him, Anderson?"

The prime minister sipped slowly, enjoying the soft taste of the Puerto Rican rum.

"It is not exactly a sacrifice, Aury. Mark did kill the guard and is accused of killing someone in the U.S. By any standard of justice, he deserves punishment. I know how you feel about the death penalty, but as you know, I don't feel the same way. We have to find a way to give him to the Americans."

Aurelius paused. He was not naïve, but he felt that Anderson was too willing to give Mark up.

"Why is this so important to you, Anderson?"

"Listen, Aury. You have been here, too. You know how the Americans work."

Indeed, he did. America was a country with enormous faith in its own capacity to do good, and that faith occasionally led to seeing the ends as justifying the means. The victims of its actions, though, often could see only the means, and, therefore, America's instinct toward doing good was often derailed. Its enemies tended to multiply, thus making the superpower even more self-protective. Aurelius knew the World Trade Towers disaster had shaken America's confidence in its invulnerability, and while many had castigated the president for lashing out, he had understood the strategy. It was not so much revenge, as many said, as it was the need to recreate, as quickly as possible, the false umbrella of invulnerability. He had been to the United States early in 2002, and he had been shocked at the loss of confidence among the population. Fear had sat like a cloud on New York, and he had had no doubt that the rest of the country felt similarly. The American division of the world into enemies and friends, with no one allowed to sit on the fence, had shifted the politics of the world dramatically, and the behaviors of most nations reflected their fear of the superpower. Yes, he did know how the Americans worked, but he did not see how it applied here, so he asked, "Why do the Americans want Mark, Anderson? The files you gave me don't say, but that in itself is significant. What is Mark to them?"

The prime minister did not turn but looked into the deepening dark. When he finally spoke, his voice sounded hollow.

"I don't know for sure, Aury, but his silence is very important to them. I don't think you can save him."

"What is it they are holding over you that you so easily want to give him up?"

Aurelius' voice had risen as the hot anger clawed at his throat, causing a tightness in his chest and a burning sensation high in his nostrils. He felt as if tears were forming and shook his head abruptly.

"Nothing in the way you mean it, Aury," the prime minister replied, his voice resigned. "There is nothing specific, only a vague sense of threat. There are so many things we need: Trade, tourism, loans. You name it. I don't have to tell you that the success we have enjoyed over the last decade was in no small part due to American investment. They could shut that down, Aury."

"But they have made no specific threat?"

"No. No specific threat. They don't have to."

Aurelius leaned forward, resting his elbows on his knees and cupping his chin in his hands.

"It is not right, Andy."

"Come on, Aury. He is guilty as hell, and you know it. What difference does it make who has him? If we hang him, does that make it somehow better? Particularly in light of tensions here now? We are always boasting about our stability, but you, better than anyone, understand how that stability is purchased. The mood out there is more sour than I have ever seen it. I won't let that boil over, Aury."

Aurelius picked up the drink, diluted now by the melted ice, and gulped it down. He understood Anderson's dilemma, but his every instinct told him that the action to be taken was wrong. He did not know what Mark had done for the United States government, but he fully appreciated the official emptiness of the man's life for the last twenty-odd years. If the Americans had no record of him, it could mean only one thing: that what they knew was far too sensitive for official records. He thought of the man sitting in jail, fewer than ten miles away, his mind on the brink of disintegration, and he knew, without a shadow of a doubt, that Mark would die for certain if he were extradited. He wondered if the Americans knew of the mental illness. Something told him they did not because, if they did, then Mark would be even more of a threat.

Suddenly, he straightened up, his body rigid and his eyes fixed on some point in the darkness.

"Wha' wrong wid you?"

The prime minister's voice gave evidence of some irritation.

"Andy, did you tell the American ambassador about Mark's delusional episodes?"

"What delusional episodes?"

Aurelius looked towards the chubby man.

"I didn't tell you that Mark sometimes seems to be floating in and out of reality?"

"Yes, but I assumed that was a legal defense. I didn't think it was real. You mean he is really going off?"

Aurelius exhaled slowly, feeling some relief.

"Yes. And Andy, you absolutely cannot tell the ambassador about this."

"Why?"

"Because I think Mark has things in his head that, if they believed he could involuntarily say, then they would have to get rid of him."

The prime minister laughed.

"Are you sure dat you not de one wid t'ings in your head? You t'ink Mark did a spy or something?"

"I don't know what he was, but I know his disappearance from the official world is strange, and the Americans' interest in shutting him up is very strange."

The prime minister was quiet for a while, and the silence had that pregnant quality, as if he were weighing something. After a while, he said, "It is not the American ambassador who worries me. It is that fellow who showed up just before Estelle's party."

"What fellow?"

"Tall white fellow. Graying at the sides. Estelle said he was from Oxford and was doing research on mental illness. He is actually very close to the American ambassador. He's been here a couple of times in the last two weeks with him, and believe me, he is a very different sort here than the person I met at Estelle's party."

"What do you mean?"

"In my office, I got the feeling he was watching, able to look through me to see if I was holding anything from them. It was a very strange feeling."

"Did you know he was having some kind of relationship with Marjorie?"

"With Marjorie? Good for her," he laughed, then stopped suddenly. Aurelius could almost feel him thinking, and he stood, quickly walking to the nearby phone. Marjorie answered at the first ring.

"Hi, Marjorie. Aurelius here. I have an odd question for you. Your friend. I can't remember his name. The one you met at Estelle's party…Yes. Bryan. Did he mention being associated with the American ambassador?…No. I don't know that anything is wrong, but I am with Anderson, and we are trying to figure some things out. …No. I don't know that it has anything to do with Bryan for sure. It is just that Anderson told me that he had sat in with the ambassador on two conversations about Mark. …Sure. I guess it could have had something to do with the mental health issue. By the way, did you tell him anything about Mark having Vietnam episodes, the flashbacks, I mean?…Okay, okay. I know you two had better things to do than to talk about Mark's flashbacks… What is that? Estelle? Why was he always asking about Estelle?…Yes. I could well imagine that you would get a little pissed off. …Did he now? Knew about Estelle's psychiatric episodes in the eighties? What did you tell him? ...Okay. I know Estelle is your friend, and you wouldn't betray her confidence even if you getting some on a regular basis. Okay. Thanks. By the way, where is Bryan now? ...You haven't seen him in two days? Isn't that unusual?"

Aurelius listened for a while, then said, "Thanks. Hang in there. Did Estelle go home or is she still there? ...Okay."

He hung the phone up slowly and walked back to his chair. The prime minister was staring at him.

"That was Marjorie."

"Yeah. I figured that out. What were you driving at?"

"Marjorie said she did not see the fellow yesterday or today."

The prime minister shrugged in the darkness.

"Doesn't it strike you as odd that he disappears the same time we get confirmation about the forgery of Estelle's signature? And on Christmas day to boot?"

"Well, not seeing Marjorie and disappearing are two different things. She can be a little hard to take, although she is the salt of the earth when taken in small doses."

"No, Andy. I don't know what is going on, but I have the feeling all of these things are connected."

"Look, Aury. I don't mean to be cruel, but the truth is, Mark is not my primary concern. If I can help without hurting the country or the party, I will, but don't expect me to go out on a limb for Mark."

Aurelius was quiet for a while, then he said softly, "You never really liked him, did you?"

The prime minister did not answer immediately, but when he did, there was something steely in his voice.

"Not much, Aury."

"Why? Is it that foolishness with Estelle a thousand years ago? That was more my fault than his."

The prime minister sighed, then replied, "I was never really a Saint, was I?"

Aurelius stared at the man's face and, not for the first time, he wondered what had driven Anderson St. Clair to this position of power, prestige, and authority. He thought of the man's words, knowing they were true, so he said, "No. You were as much a Saint as I was. In some ways, we were all appendages to him."

"You have no idea how much it pissed me off to be an appendage. You always included me, but he didn't care. It was not even that he disliked me. He just didn't care. It may have been Estelle that gave me the nickname 'Saint Too,' but Mark was the one who kept it alive with his laughter."

The prime minister paused, then asked quizzically, as if only then getting the significance of Aurelius' comment.

"Did you feel that way, too? I thought it was only me."

"No. My brother is the most self-absorbed person I know. I think it hurts us because there is no malice or forethought. You were more right than you know when you said he didn't care. That is not a metaphor for malice, anger, or disdain. He quite literally does not care. That is why most of us feel the way you do, Andy."

He stopped, and they sat quietly in the darkness for a while. Then, the prime minister said softly, "You know, that is the first time I've heard you call him your brother."

Aurelius did not immediately answer since he felt the emotion well up in him. His eyes swam in the darkness, and his chest felt tight.

"If you give him to them, they will kill him. You know that, don't you?"

"Yes."

The silence was noticeable as the prime minister stretched the word out. Aurelius also heard something else. Anderson St. Clair would do nothing to help Mark. He also knew that pleading would make no difference. It was confusing how a man that so many seemed to be involved with could simultaneously be so expendable. Except for himself and the lawyer who had replaced him, no one had been to see Mark in the three weeks he had been in jail. Why was that? How could a man that had been missing from their lives for more than thirty years create this kind of turmoil, a confusion so profound that they all seemed to be spinning away from him, flying off into some dark, unexplored spaces in their souls?

Aurelius stood, feeling the prime minister's eyes following him as he walked down the short flight of steps to the lighted fountain. The water flowed in its repetitive, unending cycle, its color created by the prisms over which it flowed. He remembered when Amstel had picked it out. They had been on a buying trip to Paris, and Beverley and Amstel had gone off together, returning with the catalogue that had promised this fountain. It had been a good choice. The fountain gave the bower a serenity and unity that even their disturbed spirits could not undermine. Aurelius turned back to the short, corpulent man in the darkness.

"You knew, didn't you?" he asked quietly, his eyes alight.

"Yes. I knew."

"How could you put Estelle through that, knowing she had nothing to do with money laundering? I can understand your abandoning Mark. He, after all, has committed a real crime. But why Estelle?"

"They told me no harm would come to her, Aury. And they were exploiting the tensions here. Didn't you wonder about how quickly the factions seemed to have gotten organized? Deighton may have been acting without any evil intent, but once he created the Rastafarian resistance, it was easy for them to create a counter voice. The threat was always there. If I didn't cooperate, they could turn this place into a hellhole."

"Why didn't you tell Deighton what was going on? He could have backed off."

The prime minister laughed.

"You are asking me to trust Deighton's discretion. Never trust an idealist, Aury. He wouldn't have believed me."

Deep down, Aurelius knew this to be true, but his anger still burned.

"You should have tried, Andy."

"I did. What do you think caused the riot? Who do you think fired the shot at Deighton? They had come to my office that day. In fact, it was immediately after a meeting I had with you. I objected to what they were doing, threatened to stop cooperating if someone other than Mark was going to be sucked in. They showed me how important I was. The riot was a warning. They could do the same thing on a much larger scale if they wanted. After that, I pretty much went along."

"The boy who was outside Estelle's bedroom last night. Did you have anything to do with that?"

"No. I was as surprised as you to hear about that. The commissioner called me."

They could hear a phone ringing somewhere in the house, and Aurelius guessed it must be in the office because the house phone next to him was silent. Soon, they heard the soft pad of the butler's footsteps. The call was for Aurelius. He followed the dignified, old man back into the house. It was Deighton.

"Hi, Deighton. What's up?"

"It's about what happened last night. I spoke with Ras Tyla. I think you should hear this from him."

He put the boy on the phone, and Aurelius was surprised at the gentleness in his voice. The story was not too complicated. He had been approached by a white man who had told him that some of the villagers might try to hurt Estelle since she was the wife of the man who had killed Mrs. Greaves' son. Most people believed Estelle and Mark were partners after the charge of money laundering had come out, so to ensure that nothing happened, he had been asked to go and stand guard in her gardens. He was to let her see him since this would reassure her. The man had gone with the Rasta boy last night but had not wanted to show himself. Aurelius asked for a description of the white man, although he really had no doubt about who it was. He soon hung up and walked back to where the prime minister still sat. He told him what the Rasta boy had said.

"Andy, pull this guy in. We can't have him running loose in St. Euribius."

"Pull him in on what charge, Aury? Telling a boy to protect Estelle? Pretending to be a researcher? I could just as easily charge him with screwing Marjorie."

Aurelius knew the prime minister was right, but he wanted to do something to assuage the deep, burning anger inside him.

"And what about sovereignty, Andy? What about that?" he asked, his voice rising. "Are you going to give up that as well?"

The prime minister was silent for a while, then he said, "Sovereignty is all well and good, Aury, but I'd rather we survived."

Aurelius looked at his watch, something foul reflected in his face. It was after eight o'clock. He had wanted to go by and see Mark to let him know the charges against Estelle would be dropped. That still left Mark in a bind, but something told him that Mark would be relieved. The more he had heard about the white man who claimed to be a researcher from Oxford, the more he had become convinced Mark was as much a pawn as they were.

The prime minister stood abruptly and walked into the house. Aurelius sipped his drink and thought about how their order was constantly threatened. The prime minister soon returned.

"He's gone."

Aurelius did not need to be told whom he meant, nor was it a surprise.

"He left today on a private jet."

"Where did the flight plan say he was going?"

"Cali, Columbia."

"Think he'll be back?"

"Doubt it."

Aurelius was quiet for a moment, then said, almost to himself, "I wonder what changed."

"What do you mean?"

"Well, something must have. If he is responsible for what happened to Estelle, then she must have been used to threaten Mark in some way, don't you think? If she's been cleared, then Mark must have agreed to something."

"Like what?"

"I have no idea. Maybe I'll ask him tomorrow."

Aurelius stood, stretching.

"I've got to go. I was up most of last night with Estelle, and I am still wasted from the last four days of flying around."

The prime minister walked him out, and soon he was heading down the driveway.

Behind him, Anderson St. Clair watched the red lights grow brighter at the automatic gate, and then, they were gone.

CHAPTER THIRTY-TWO

The quiet lay on St. Euribius. At least it did on the plantation, where, unlike the nearby village, there was no blaze of light from the Christmas decorations and no buzz of activity. The great house was as silent as it always was. Christmas had come, and it was almost gone, but it had done little to disturb the steady flow of life in this relic of history. Estelle had come to her mother's house after leaving Marjorie, still not sure that she could face a night alone. Deighton had called, but the images her mind retained from the night before were not quite at rest yet, and something still sat heavy upon her spirit. She did not want to be alone, and Marjorie, with the others gone, had slipped into a pensive mood that carried the edge of hysteria. She had been laying on the patio, intermittently sipping rum and coke, when Estelle had left. She had felt guilty about that, but she had wanted to deliver her mother's Christmas gift.

They had exchanged their gifts with the formality of strangers, the intent of goodwill entirely lost. Now, they sat on the circular verandah watching the night. It was a beautiful night. High above, the silvery twinkles pulled the eyes upwards, and the spaces between the stars seemed not so much like emptiness but a reality connecting those lights. Estelle smiled, remembering her first year in university taking the physics course. She had struggled with the idea of space being a real thing, not simply an emptiness separating the material of the universe, but a thing in and of itself. Her romantic soul had fought against this idea, though the professor's experiment with the swinging bucket had been meant to be persuasive. She had finally given in to the rationalism of Newtonian physics, but in her heart, she had never accepted the idea.

Something in the isolation of the planets that the spaces created appealed to her soul too deeply. Now, she looked up, seeing the hunter and the bear, and, low in the western sky, the hot, passionate light of Venus. Venus moved quickly in relation to the other stars, as if inpatient to get somewhere, to a new lover, perhaps.

Estelle sighed, hoping Marjorie would be all right. She would call her later, before she went to sleep. In the silky night, the wind moved the short blades of the sugarcane, and Estelle wondered how many women had sat on this porch in the last two hundred years. None of the original great house was left, except one cornerstone that had been kept. It said, "Built in Freedom, 1801." Her ancestor, who had bought his way out of slavery in 1799, against all odds had built a fortune. Was it this that had led her to history as an academic discipline? Or was it simply her confusion about the past? For that same ex-slave who bought his freedom soon became an owner of slaves himself, and from what little she knew, not a particularly kind one.

How do I now view the past? she wondered silently. *As a slave or a mistress?* The violence in the atmosphere during the last three weeks had shocked her, bringing into sharp relief the tensions that still stood like a potential hurricane upon this land. She had planned to take a gift for Mrs. Greaves in the village, but everything had been thrown into confusion when that boy had appeared outside her window with the long cutlass in his hand. The gift now lay in the room upstairs. She would ask her mother to take it. She did not think she would be visiting Mrs. Greaves again. On her left, her mother moved in her chair.

"Mother, how come you know Mrs. Greaves so well? She even calls you by your first name."

The old woman did not answer immediately, and Estelle could almost hear her ordering her thoughts.

"She and I come from the same village in the north."

"But did you come together?"

Again, the old woman hesitated.

"Yes. Your father brought us both from the village."

"Brought?" Estelle asked, a flare of alertness going off in her mind.

"Yes. Brought. I came as his wife, and she came as his maid, although it was difficult to tell the difference."

There was a bitterness in her mother's voice that she had never heard before, and she wondered what had brought it on. Her lips teetered on a question, but fear held her tongue. Her mother was angry, and such anger did not care about the past. Estelle stayed silent. Then, her mother said, "Estelle, I am getting old. I'll be seventy-seven in a few months. That is time to think of dying, to think of settling accounts."

The pinprick of alertness had become a maelstrom in her mind. At first, she thought it was the introduction of death, but then she realized that it was the hint of intimacy that now frightened her. Her mother was, it seemed, in a confessional mood, and suddenly, Estelle realized she did not want to know this past, did not want to add its pain to hers, for it made her too much like her mother. She stood up and walked to the rail, staring at the canes that waved like friendly creatures in the distance. Behind her, she could sense her mother's eyes on her back.

"Still running away, I see," the sharp, strangely resigned voice said.

Estelle turned, and in that moment, in the weak light of the low-wattage bulb that threw a false sense of reality on the verandah, Estelle did see her mother's age. The face still had the strength she imagined she remembered, but the arms had lost their potency, the flesh hanging loosely on the bone, and the dark freckles glared out of the pale, yellow skin. Estelle also noticed something else. The event of the night before had frightened her mother, had somehow brought the grave closer.

"I never ran away, Mother."

"Don't lie, Estelle. I have been a terrible mother, and so have you. Only in recognizing that can we be better. I have only one question. Why could you not see me?"

"What do you mean, Mother?"

"You could see your father. When you were a little girl, you would look at him as if he brought the sun up in the morning, but when you looked at me, your eyes would cloud over. You never saw me."

"Maybe that is because you never saw any good in me."

Estelle's voice, which she had meant to be angry, was petulant. Her mother did not reply for a while. Then she said softly, "I couldn't, Estelle. You were too much like me."

Something sat in the pit of Estelle's stomach. It was hard and almost immovable. She said nothing.

"He was not the great man you saw, that you wanted to see, and I resented you because you refused to see my bed of nails. Your eyes would slide over the bruises on my arms and face and look at him with a love I had never felt."

Estelle thought she saw a shininess to her mother's face, and something shifted in her heart.

"And do you know who was my friend during that time? The woman you call Mrs. Greaves. I had hated her at first, but she was kind and, in the end, I realized she was as much a victim as I was. Power can be terrible, and he used both of us."

High above, the stars seemed to have lost their rhythm, spinning about wildly. Then, Estelle realized she was seeing them reflected through her tears. In the darkness, in those waving canes, something looked out, its eyes full of malevolence. She thought of her history class and wondered if the truth of this land could ever be told. She wiped her eyes, thinking that her mother's story would always be lost.

"Why are you telling me now, Mother?"

The old woman fixed her dress, ordering the folds.

"Heather is coming home. I don't want her to end up like you."

"Am I so bad? Why do you hate me?"

Estelle could hear the insistence, the pleading in her voice, but she could not stop herself.

"Hate? Hate, you say? Look at yourself, Estelle. There you will find the hate. I simply defended myself. I have always defended myself. I have always had to."

Her mother's voice had gone soft, almost as if the last words had been said to herself. Suddenly, she cried out, "Why can't we love our daughters?"

Immediately, though, she straightened up, saying, "Sorry. All I can say is, when Heather comes, find a way to show her you care. I know you feel the world has hurt you, but maybe you ought to start your investigations with yourself. Don't hold back, waiting for your daughter to come to you. She's like you. She won't come. You will have to go to her."

The woman's voice broke on the last words, and Estelle stood confused, not sure what to do. In the end, she continued to lean against the rail, her confusion palpable. She did not know the woman whose face was streaked with tears and who was advising her about love. She wanted to respond, but respect and her own uncertainty held her in check. She felt split, seeing in her mind's eye the habitual picture of rejection that was her birthright, but juxtaposed with that, the images handed to her by Marjorie, who did not see Gweneth Prescod as Estelle saw her. A part of her wondered idly if history could ever be "true" since perspectives could be so divergent. Who was the woman before her? Obviously, it was her mother, but was she the ogre of her fantasy, or the benefactress of Marjorie's? Estelle could not bring herself to accept Marjorie's view, for too much of her way of looking at the world was tied to her perceived relationship with her mother, and so she stood, arms folded, feeling the gnawing at her heart but unable to move. She could sense in the stillness of the older woman's watchfulness that she was waiting. Estelle felt the pull but did not move, and the moment stretched beyond comfort. Then, it was too late.

"Heather is going to be here the day after tomorrow. She was quite distraught when I told her about Mark," Estelle said.

"Yes. She would be. Heather feels things deeply, though she shows little. I think Mr. St. Auburn may actually have loved her. At least, she was the only one he seemed to have had a consistent interest in. It is remarkable, though, that she should be so attached to him. Although, on second thought, maybe not so strange."

"Why 'not so strange'?"

"Your resentment created a vacuum. She must have sensed that even as a baby. Mr. St. Auburn must have filled that vacuum. That impression would be very powerful."

"That's the nicest thing you have ever said about Mark," Estelle responded, aware that the statement had been made at her expense.

"I did not like Mr. St. Auburn because I thought he would make you cynical, and I could see no good coming of that. Cynicism is not a quality useful to a mother."

Estelle did not immediately respond. Had Mark made her a cynic? No. She did not think so, unless cynicism could co-exist with the need for affection. History had given her perspective, had allowed her to step back, but, ultimately, it was protection against the past, a shield against the pain that the past brought and the future promised. *Do cynics cry?* she wondered. Once, she remembered, she had screamed at Mark that she did not know why she had allowed herself to become so tied to him since she got no pleasure from their being in bed. She could not remember what had prompted her to get into that argument, but then, there had been so many. She had meant to hurt him, to hit him where she knew every man was vulnerable. She remembered how he had looked at her that day, with something like pain in his sensitive eyes. The pain, however, had been for her tortured soul. He had not moved, except to turn those luminous eyes with the feminine lashes on her, and he had answered her question.

"Sex is your gift," he had said, "but you give it with resentment. It is all you think you have, so it is not so much a gift as a sacrifice, and who finds pleasure in sacrifice? You are worth so much more than you think. I wish somehow I could convince you of that."

The memory brought the tears to her eyes once again, and she sensed Gweneth Prescod tense as she realized her daughter was crying.

"No, Mother. Mark didn't turn me into a cynic, but his honesty helped me to see the world as it really is."

"That is as good a definition of a cynic as any. A person has to do serious violence to their innate sense of the world's innocence to see the world as it really is," the old woman said with a short laugh.

"I do think he gave me quite a lot, Mother. He taught me how to see."

"Yes. To see everything except himself. That is every man's gift."

Estelle was aware of a dark anger rising in her again.

"Can't you let me have anything? Not even this? Why must you make my experience ordinary? I have little enough as it is."

The old woman did not rise to the bait but responded quietly.

"Even as a girl you longed for the extraordinary, Estelle. Unfortunately, the world is not extraordinary, so we impose our own patterns on it, seeing what is not there."

"Are you saying I made Mark up?"

"No," the woman chuckled. "He was, is, real enough. If I could have made him less real, I would have. I could see you both had the same interest: him. I felt he would destroy you."

"I am not that weak, Mother."

They were silent for a while. Then Gweneth Prescod said, "He will not survive this. You know that, don't you?"

Estelle felt the fear rise like magma. She did not know that, had not considered it. In the darkness, her mother's outline looked primordial, without full form, a potentiality, and Estelle wondered if she was one of the Fates. The thought surprised her. She tried to hold in her mind the tone of her mother's voice. It had had an unusual gentleness, and she realized how much she needed that now.

"You should see him, Estelle. Not so much for his sake, but your own."

"What do you mean?"

"What were you when you and Mark noticed each other? Eleven? Twelve? You have had him in your consciousness for practically all of your life. What stops you from seeing him now?"

Estelle's first instinct was to say "you," but she held her tongue. Why had she not seen Mark? Could it really have been her mother's sense of propriety, drilled into her from childhood, that had kept her away from the prison? Was it simply another way of her separating the great house and the village? It was a separation she had learned from her mother. Or had she? Estelle thought of the day she had encountered her mother at Mrs. Greaves' home in the village. She had appeared to be much more comfortable there than Estelle had. She had not reacted to her mother's earlier comment about her father's abuse and infidelity. She could not, feeling a deep shame that had stolen her words, but she now wondered about the bond that had evolved between those two women, both slaves to something she did not understand. Estelle found herself wondering about her memory because she remembered nothing of Mrs. Greaves being at the great house. She certainly did not remember the bruises of which her mother spoke. Whose memory should she trust? She saw, in her imagination, her father, a tall, dark-skinned man of great dignity. She could remember no violence in him, only a sternness that held the house, like the plantation itself, in check. That sternness had imposed order on her life, had provided structure. What did it mean if she was wrong about that? Now, her mother was sending her into the heart of the village, for Dathorn Prison saw none of her kind. It was the village in its purest form, and it had been this as much as Mark that she had avoided.

Estelle glanced at the woman who sat quietly across from where she stood. Could she have been wrong about her all these years? No. It was not that she had been wrong, but maybe she had seen only one slice of her mother. She had categorized her as the harsh disciplinarian, and once the category had crystallized, she had been fixed in place, a known quantity. It bothered her now that her perceptions may have been wrong. But were they? What she had seen, still saw, was not so much wrong as it was incomplete, and this bothered her, for she could not decide if seeing an incomplete past was to create an entire falsehood.

"What did you say?"

Gweneth Prescod's voice had regained its customary distance. *Almost,* Estelle thought, *as if the allotted time for this engagement were up.* Still, she knew that was not fair, so she took the risk.

"I was thinking of you, Mother. About what you said. That I never saw you. I am sorry you feel that way. All I can remember is that you never seemed to be able to see me. You say I had eyes only for my father, but that's not true. It was more like he stood so high that you had to look up at him."

Her mother grunted in the darkness.

"Yes. He did block out the sun. Nothing grew to be healthy in that shadow."

When Estelle spoke, her voice was small, like a child's.

"Did you want me, Mother? Or did you hate me because of him?"

The older woman was silent for a moment.

"Love, hate, want. Why do you insist on making them distinct? Don't you understand that they all are interwoven, can't be separated? I know you must have heard the stories about my poisoning my brother. They are true. I didn't hate him. I only wanted him to stop. But they all turned against me after that. I was not wrong. I was not wrong."

She stopped, and Estelle heard the pathos in her voice, the uncertainty about her act, the fear that there might be something wrong with her, and Estelle wondered if that fear could have been passed on to her in her genes.

"Sex is your guard against your fear," Mark had said to her, and she had scoffed at the idea.

Off to her left, Estelle saw a firefly suddenly dart downward toward the ground, and she wondered about the cause. The wind moved across her back, bringing a chill, for although the days were hot, the evening breeze slid down the central hills like a cat rubbing against a table's leg, bringing the coolness from the eastern sea.

She did not want to feel sympathy. It was too confusing. Yet, her mother's voice asked a question she could not answer, indeed, did not want to answer. That voice challenged her foundation of the past, shattered her images of the life she had constructed, denied the truth of her history. Love and hate were two sides of the same coin, she knew, both with the same capacity to motivate action, but they were not mutually exclusive, and the presence of one did not mean the absence of the other. Now, she wondered about her feelings towards this woman who had ruled her for so long. What had it taken for her to have fought off her brother, the uncle who had disappeared into the English mists so many years ago? This was the first time her mother had mentioned him, and Estelle now looked at her, asking herself what lay beneath the secrets created by her mother's hard exterior. What had prompted this act of confession? It was so unlike her to provide the world even the slightest opening to her soul. Why had she opened up? And why now?

"Did he ever love you, Mother?"

The question hung like a dead animal tied to a tree, its rotting body attracting flies, and even before the woman answered, Estelle realized the words were just a disturbance, a way of ordering experience, of tearing from the body of history its face and searching beneath for motive.

"He saved me," the older woman replied simply.

"But you could not love him for that?"

"Estelle, you can't love your possessor."

Oddly enough, at that moment, Estelle thought of a line from a Bob Marley song,

"Never let a politician grant you a favor/He will always want to possess you for ever."

She understood immediately what her mother meant, as her mind jumped to Mark, her unwilling possessor. Mark did not fill space up the way her father had, did not dominate through force, but something in the way he had taught her to see the world possessed her as fully. She thought now of the hard, desperate acts of fear that had driven her relationship with him. It had been like trying to love a cloud, to possess a dream. He had always been there, yet never quite, for she had created him as much as he had created her, but he had always known that she was not quite real. Still, as she stood listening to her mother's disembodied voice in the soft St. Euribian night, Estelle knew she was different now, that somehow the twenty-plus years of absence had made Mark more real, more human. He was flawed in ways she could not have seen before. She could see that now because the flaws made him who he was. Like a color splashed on a painting simply for contrast, Mark had no independent existence. He was created by her, the very image in her mind, a prison. Had he fought to escape, to run away from this thing she had created, this god she insisted had created her? What was the truth? She could no longer tell. Their history was too interwoven, too indistinguishable, for her to judge.

You can't love your possessor, her mother had said, but who possessed whom? Did she still love the man who sat halfway across the island in a cell? If she did, it was different from those many years ago, for now she saw him as he was. No longer did his words create the world for her, for she now saw in those words of so long ago the same uncertainty as she did in any reflection on the past. Mark had used words to structure the reality he had not understood any more than she had. Language had given him power, for the words had the magic to impose order, to give structure to the chaos around him. She, without words, had accepted his vision, seen the order he created, and had given herself over to him, believing him fully capable of creation. It had been a magician's trick. In fact, it had not even been that, for that suggested he was in charge, that he understood the cause and the effect. Now, she knew that Mark had not understood anything. It had just been that he had words to express his confusion, and those words had blinded her. "You can't love your possessor." Estelle winced in the darkness, thinking she had possessed Mark, too.

She wanted desperately to touch some other body, to feel its reassuring reality pressed against hers, not sexually, but just in a simple act of connection. She felt alone in this world, as if this great house, with its connection to the darkness, had been whirled out into space, a single, spinning mote in the great cosmos, and she was its single passenger. Still, she was not alone, and Estelle drew back from the edges. In the darkness, her mother's voice reached out.

"Estelle, go and see him. No one should be alone."

The older woman stood, the brittle rigidity in her body evident even in the uncertainty of the dark, and as she walked into the soft light of the foyer, Estelle was not sure if her mother had referred to Mark, herself, or her. High above, the stars stared impartially down, and Estelle wondered what they saw.

CHAPTER THIRTY-THREE

Mark placed his foot on the rope he had made from the sheet and tugged. The knots held, and he slid over to the door of the cell, pressing his face against the bars and peering down the long corridor. The guard sat, head thrown back, his huge chest rising and falling gently. Mark could not hear his breathing but was sure he was asleep. He tested the rope again and then looked across the room. She had not come, but it did not matter. The letter he had sent would have to be enough. He had hoped she would have gotten Deighton to see him, so he could explain his decision, but neither had come, so either the guard had not done as he had requested, or she had ignored him. He sighed, walking back to the bed and sitting.

The angel was behind him, but tonight, she felt different, as if she were angry that he had kept her outside so long. She had scratched at the window all day, but he had ignored her, wanting to finish his writing. On the single, wooden shelf, he had placed the letter to Aurelius and the second one to Estelle. He placed his head in his hands, trying to think of anything else he needed to do. There was nothing. The darkness that the angel brought lay upon his soul, soft, encouraging, teasing him, just as it had done in the jungle. There was something he wanted to think about, but the darkness obscured it, leaving a hole in his vision. The tic at the side of his right eye pulsed in counterpoint to the throbbing in his head, and he brushed at it, feeling the angel's hand. It was warm and held his for a moment. That hand brought many memories back, the most prominent of which was of his body in full flight, lithe, muscles starkly outlined against the background of the sky. Mark smiled, thinking of the times those legs had carried him with such swiftness away from the certainty of his death, and he sighed again, standing up.

Estelle would be safe now, and Aurelius would understand. Mark searched inside himself, wondering what he really felt about these two who were almost two parts of himself. For a second, the darkness clouded his mind, and Ray and Aurelius became one, bringing the confusion of emotions.

"Ray is dead," he whispered to himself, seeing again the hard, black man who had fought with such assurance. He had killed him, and the death had been hard, almost as if he had sliced out a part of himself. Ray would have killed him had he had the chance because there was no possibility of any other death for their kind. Yet, even Ray had bullied and frightened those around him into competence, into machines that had the skill and the will to survive. *How many had he saved in doing so?* Mark now wondered. He could not answer that question, but Ray had fought with the instinct of a killer, just as he had. Mark looked at the envelopes on the wooden stand. They would understand, not what he had been, of course, but how he had felt. Why it was important that they know, he could not tell. He stared at the lock, seeing, in his imagination, the tumblers. It would be so simple.

In his befuddled mind, the pictures rapidly changed, creating a kaleidoscope of images. He tried to control them, to force them into some logical channel, but they had been taken over by the angel who was touching him on the side of his head. He brushed vigorously at her hand, but she was no longer gentle and was much stronger than he. Finally, the pictures slowed and coalesced around a clearing in the jungle and a small girl running toward him. The M-16 was jumping in his hand, and the little black dots were appearing, one by one, across her torso. Then, her hair was flying in a slow-motion arc, blocking out the sun as she fell. She looked like an angel with a black halo. He watched her face, eyes wide open in surprise and pain as she fell, the gun continuing to buck in his hands. As her body slid sideways and started to fall toward the ground, the face changed, metamorphosing into that of the Rasta boy whose dreadlocks made the same black circle around his head. Mark blinked as the faces crowded his mind, blinding him, bringing the angel close. When they landed, he had stood up, staring down at the cell floor, where the open eyes, like gray scales on the body, stared back at him. Slowly, he turned away, catching a glimpse of the angel among the bars at the window. Then, he climbed up to the top bunk and tied the knotted rope made from the sheet to the bars in the window.

CHAPTER THIRTY-FOUR

The wind was up, and the sea was running. The women sat, occasionally hunched against the buffeting of the gusts that came from the ocean. Four of them were on lounge chairs on Marjorie's verandah, not talking much, each caught in the vacuum of the other's thoughts.

"I still think we should go to Trinidad for Carnival."

Anis' voice was gay, and she, unlike the others, seemed energetic, alive, her thin body giving off a kind of vibration. No one responded, and she continued.

"Easter coming early dis year, and de Trinis start Carnival already. I talk to Diane – wunna know my friend from Arima – and she says dat t'ings getting hot down dere already. Parties every night practically."

The other women remained silent, staring down toward the sea where, in a small, isolated copse of stunted trees, they could see three women. Estelle, her mother, and Heather had come together to Marjorie's New Year's Day get-together. Marjorie looked at Anis, who had stood up as if the energy in her body would not let her rest. Her eyes were sympathetic, but there was, too, a kind of malice behind them. She looked away, her eyes going to the three women who sat in the trees on the cliff overlooking the roiling sea. The booming sound of the waves pounding into the rock sent a shiver through her. It sounded like a call from hell. She was glad to see the three of them together, though, and thought again of the effect of Mark's death. She, Heather, Aurelius, and Estelle were the only ones who had attended the funeral, which had had that awkward feeling of looking into someone's life unbidden. St. Euribius, with its combination of Catholic and Anglican history, was not sure what to do with suicides, but the prime minister, though he had not attended, had made sure that Mark had a good funeral. Estelle had been dry-eyed through the service, but Heather had fallen apart, and she wondered how this could be since the girl had known Mark for only two years, and the first two years of her life at that.

"It strange how t'ings does work out," she said to no one in particular.

"What strange?" Maylene asked, opening her eyes.

"I did t'inking 'bout how attach Heather was to Mark, even though she didn't really know he."

"True, girl. It almost like she pick up where Estelle left off."

"What do you mean?"

Sandra leaned now on her elbow, watching Anis, who had turned away, staring at the dark water in the distance.

"I ain't know fuh sure, but it look sometimes like she might just pick up Estelle feelings. Even though they can't get along, de two uh dem really alike," Maylene responded.

"The same could be said for Estelle and her mother. It is amazing they think they are so different, one from the other," Sandra said.

Marjorie looked down toward the copse. It was too far away to see if the women were talking, but the three of them sitting there together did fill her with a sense of peace. It was a peace she needed. She knew she would never see Bryan Edwards again. Aurelius had made that clear. But Bryan had made it even more clear two nights ago. He had called late in the night, just as she had been falling asleep, and the call had saved her, for the pain of losing him was different from the pain of abandonment, and whether he had lied or not, it did not matter. He had not stayed on the phone long. He had said he loved her, but he could not see her again. She had cried, but it was not so much the loss as it had been the relief from the fear that she had been worth nothing. The call had validated her and had made the loss bearable. Oddly enough, she had felt less anger toward John, too, in the last day or so and had made up her mind to call him. She was not sure why, but she felt that chapter in her life needed resolution.

Marjorie looked at Maylene, whose face had become more beautiful in the last few days, and she could not help but think that her home life must have improved. She caught Maylene's eye, and something passed between them, something subtle, feminine, and enigmatic. Yes, she was feeling better, and Marjorie felt sure that Mark's death had freed Deighton in a way he did not understand. Mark had written to Maylene, she knew, although it was probably more true to say he had written to Deighton. The letter had made sure Deighton understood that death was Mark's choice, and there was no need to fight on his behalf. He wanted it all to end. Deighton had complied with the dead man's wish, and so the country had slid back into its usual tensile comfort. Still, Marjorie knew something had changed, though she could not quite say what. The prime minister had been in the village twice in the last week, and someone had told her he had gone to see Mrs. Greaves. Marjorie's eyes again found the three women in the small grove of trees, and she wondered about Estelle's actions. Though the money Mark had left her still was not available, she had taken over the care of the old village woman, visiting every day. The twenty million she would transfer to Heather as soon as it was free of the investigation. Mark had probably intended it for her anyway, she felt. *Would she find happiness now?* Marjorie wondered. She was not confident of this, for Estelle was a rarity. She truly loved. Marjorie thought of Mark's letter to Estelle and wondered whether the love was not worth the pain. He had written seven pages, but it had not been a letter in any proper sense, for on the pages had been the words: "I ALWAYS LOVED YOU" in block letters. The words had been repeated two sentences to a line, for seven pages. Toward the end, the rigid geometry of the block letters had faltered and then collapsed all together, as if Mark's mind had been locked in a duel with his madness. Marjorie knew Aurelius' letter had shown the same tight control and then, collapse. To Aurelius, Mark had attempted a real letter, but it had been largely incoherent, with words thrown haphazardly together. One thought had been repeated, though. He had written "THIS MAKES YOU AND ESTELLE SAFE." She was not sure what he meant by that, but Aurelius seemed to understand. The writing had disintegrated towards the end, and Mark had repeatedly written a word that looked like Racugu. A nonsense word from the mind of a madman.

"So nobody want to go to Trinidad?"

Anis' voice had a bounciness to it, and Sandra said, "You could try to contain yourself, Anis."

Anis' face clouded for a second, then she smiled, her hand involuntarily straying to her tiny bud of a left breast. It had grown slightly in the last few days, and she could feel the tiny lump under the more natural feeling flesh. Then, she smiled and replied, "I'll show you how I contain myself."

The skinny woman walked briskly to the blue van that stood so incongruously in Marjorie's driveway among the more stylish cars. She opened the back doors and pulled a large painting out. The others had stood up, watching her manhandle the easel from the van and place it away from the cars. She then tacked the canvas painting on to the easel. The other three women came down, staring at the horrible destruction of the male body. Anis had completed the face, and they all recognized it in part. It was part skeleton and part physical perfection. She had captured the tension perfectly, an athlete in flight with half its body in the grave, and the obscenely huge and cancerous penis hanging like a flaccid rope, containing no threat except the possibility of contamination.

Maylene, Sandra, and Marjorie watched as Anis returned to the van and came back with a red can. It smelled of gasoline. Each woman felt something tremble inside of her at this act of destructive sacrilege, for the painting, though horrible, had its own intrinsic beauty, its own undeniable perfection. Still, no one stopped Anis as she splashed the acrid liquid on the canvas. Finally, she looked at them, and there was a brittle, shiny quality to her eyes. Tears were running down her face, and the three women moved to hold her. She shook them off and, reaching inside her dress pocket, took out a box of matches. In a second, the painting was dying, and Anis stood, a little apart from the other three who had stepped back from the fierce heat, hugging herself tightly.

In the distance, Estelle saw the blaze and stood up. Her four friends were standing in front of something that was burning, but they were not showing any sign of panic, so she assured herself that they were all right. Still, it was odd for Marjorie to burn trash so close to her home, her pride and joy. Satisfied that all was well, she sat again, watching the precise way in which her mother ate the sandwich. It felt good to be here. The breeze picked up an edge of the blanket on which they sat, and she moved to smooth it down. Heather had moved at the identical moment, and their hands met at the corner of the rug. For a second, they both froze, uncertain, and then Heather closed her hand over her mother's, giving it a small squeeze. Estelle smiled broadly, looking at the other two and wondering at the way of the world. Her mother had slept at Estelle's house every night since Mark's death, not saying much, but always around when Estelle felt the sharp, stabbing pain that occasionally came. "I always loved you," he had written. Had he meant it? Why had he said those words now, the words he had avoided all his life? Dying, he had given her the thing she had waited for all her life, and, in the end, it was simply emptiness he had left. Was it his insanity that had guided his hand or had he seen clearly at that moment?

Estelle pushed the questions away from her, trying to accept what he had offered. *Confusing to the end,* she thought, the memory of the closed casket dominating her imagination. Mark could never bring peace, neither to himself nor anyone else. She hoped he would find some peace now. Estelle was not aware of her tears until she felt the soft hand brushing them away. It was Heather's hand, and she looked into her daughter's face, seeing there, reflected, herself. Estelle leaned across to hug the girl, who threw her arm around her grandmother, completing the circle. She noticed, over her daughter's shoulder, that the fire had gone out, and the thin, blue tendrils of smoke rose in suggestive indolence to the sky. The small figures of her four friends stood around the ascending smoke, and she wondered what could have held their attention so closely. Marjorie's figure, a little bigger even in the distance, held her eyes. *She seems to have adjusted well to Bryan's leaving,* Estelle thought, once again breathing a silent sigh of relief. She was actually more worried about Aurelius. He had taken his half-brother's death hard, for though he had said nothing to her, she suspected he had seen the dead man in his cell, and that had brought the grave close. She had not seen Aurelius since the funeral, though he had spoken to her on the phone. He felt certain the money would be cleared soon, but she did not want it. It was not that she was rejecting Mark's gift, but its possession brought the pain too close. Heather would have it, and Aurelius would manage it for her. She looked back to the house again, and the women had disappeared. So had the smoke. *An offering to some ancient god,* she thought, squeezing her daughter closer. Her mother seemed so comfortable in Heather's embrace that Estelle reached across and placed her free hand around her shoulder. The older woman's face did not change, but her body seemed to melt, becoming more liquid and accepting. Estelle listened to the voice of the wind, and though she still felt sadness, for the first time in a while, a deep contentment filled her soul.

THE END